'Fantasy addicts will enjoy every page'   *Total Sci Fi*

'The strength of *Wolfsangel* lies in Lachlan's superlative storytelling skill. He evokes the frozen wastes of the Viking kings. We feel the biting cold, see the bleak wilderness, hear the myths of the Gods. Despite the oftentimes dark aspect of the novel, it is anchored by a warm heart and it is this that kept me reading long into the night. I can't wait for the next in this series. M.D. Lachlan has penned a winner' *Fantasyliterature.com*

Also by M.D. Lachlan from Gollancz

Wolfsangel

Fenrir

FENRIR

M.D. LACHLAN

The right of M.D. Lachlan to be identified as the author
of this work has been asserted by him in accordance with the
Copyright, Designs and Patents Act 1988.

First published in Great Britain in 2011 by
Gollancz
An imprint of the Orion Publishing Group
Orion House, 5 Upper St Martin's Lane,
London WC2H 9EA
An Hachette UK Company

This edition published in Great Britain in 2012
by Gollancz

1 3 5 7 9 10 8 6 4 2

A CIP catalogue record for this book
is available from the British Library

ISBN 978 0 575 08965 5

Typeset by Deltatype Ltd, Birkenhead, Merseyside

Printed in Great Britain by Clays Ltd, St Ives plc

The Orion Publishing Group's policy is to use papers
that are natural, renewable and recyclable products and
made from wood grown in sustainable forests. The logging
and manufacturing processes are expected to conform to
the environmental regulations of the country of origin.

www.orionbooks.co.uk

To Claire, my wife

And he caught the dragon, the old serpent, that is the Devil and Satan; and he bound him by a thousand years. And he sent him into deepness, and closed, and marked on him, that he deceive no more the people, till a thousand years be filled. And he sent him into deepness, and closed, and signed, *or sealed*, upon him, that he deceive no more people, till a thousand years be fulfilled. After these things it behooveth him to be unbound a little time.

THE KING JAMES BIBLE, REVELATION 20: 1–3

When the Æsir saw that the Wolf was fully bound, they took the chain that was fast to the fetter, and which is called Thin, and passed it through a great rock – it is called Scream – and fixed the rock deep down into the earth. Then they took a great black boulder and drove it yet deeper into the earth and used the stone for a fastening-pin. The wolf gaped terribly, and thrashed about and strove to bite them; they thrust into his mouth a certain sword: the guards caught in his lower jaw, and the point in the upper; that is his gag. He howls hideously, and slaver runs out of his mouth: that is the river called Ván; there he lies till the Weird of the Gods.

THE PROSE EDDA

PART ONE
Sword Age

1 Wolf Night

He had never seen a sight so beautiful as Paris under flame. It was dusk and the smoke lay across the low sun in a long stripe of black like the tail of a dragon, its head dipping to a mouth of fire on the river island town. He looked down from the hill and saw that the towers on the bridges had held: the Franks had repulsed the northern enemy. Though part of one bridge and an abandoned longboat beneath it were on fire, the saffron banners of Count Eudes still flew all around the walls above the water, like little flames themselves answering the dying sun.

Leshii inhaled. There, beneath the smell of the burning wood and the pitch the defenders had hurled down on the invaders was another smell he recognised well. Cremation.

He associated it with the Northmen, with the burning of their dead in their ships. He'd watched them in the aftermath of the battle to take Kiev, pushing the dead rulers Askold and Dir out of the town out onto the lake in a blazing longboat. They'd given them a fine send-off, considering they'd butchered them.

The smell seemed to suck all of the moisture out of his nose and mouth. People had burned down there. He shook his head and made the lightning bolt symbol of his god Perun across his chest with his finger. Warriors, he thought, had too much of the world. If it was ruled by merchants there wouldn't be half the killing.

He looked at the city. It wasn't big by his eastern standards but it was wonderfully placed on the Seine to stop the Viking raids getting any further upstream.

The dusk was cold and his breath clouded the air. He would have loved to have gone down to the city and sat by a fire with a mug of Frankish wine.. He found the Franks very relaxed and peaceful – at least when at ease in their own towns – and they were great lovers of silk. He'd always enjoyed Paris with its fascinating houses, square and pale, with arches for entrances and steep pitched roofs of checked tiles. No point letting that thought grow. The idea of warmth only made the cold seem deeper. There would be no shelter that night, beyond his tent. The hillside would be his bed, not an inn in the merchants' quarters.

He watched as, on the bridge, the defenders beat down the flames. The bridges had been put there primarily to prevent ships coming up the river. They had done their job, along with the other defences the count had built. It was difficult to estimate the size of the Northmen's army. If they controlled both banks of the river, he put it as massive, at least four thousand men. However, yellow banners spread themselves among the sprawl of meaner houses outside the city too. So perhaps the Danish force was smaller. Big enough, though, easily big enough to overrun any dwellings unprotected by the city walls.

Yet they hadn't bothered to take them. Clearly, the northerners did not regard those buildings as important. They were moving through to richer and bigger towns along the river. Paris was just an obstacle to overcome and they weren't going to lose good men fighting over a few huts. Leshii was impressed. Most commanders he knew had very little control over what their troops did once they got in sight of the enemy. This was a disciplined army, not a rabble.

Could he get down to one of those outlying houses, hire a bed there? No. The whole country would be in a terror and he'd be lucky not to be strung up by either side if they saw him.

There were Vikings on both sides of the river, he could tell. Their longships were moored on both banks and their black banners drooped in the still spring air for a fair slice of land about. Leshii gave a shiver when he thought of those banners.

He had seen them enough times in the east – ravens and wolves. Such creatures prospered in the Norsemen's wake. The city would fall, he thought, but it would take a while doing so.

'She is in there?' Leshii spoke in Latin, as it was the only language he shared with his companion.

'It was foreseen.'

'Good luck getting her out. They won't welcome a Northman in there.'

'I won't ask for their welcome.'

'Better declare yourself to your people and enter when they enter. They surely will, their army is huge.'

'They are not my people.'

'You are a Northman, a Varangian as you are called.'

'But I am not a Dane.'

'All Varangians are the same, Chakhlyk. Dane, Norseman, Viking, Norman, Varangian: these are only words for the same thing.'

'My name is not Chakhlyk.'

'But your nature is – it means "dry one" in my language. What is a name but what men call you? My mother called me Leshii, but at home they call me Mule. It's not a name I like but one that fits because I'm always carrying things here and there for one person or another – princes, kings, myself. They call me Mule: my name is Mule. I call you Chakhlyk: your name is Chakhlyk. Names are like destinies, we do not choose them.'

The Northman snorted. It was the first time since they had travelled from the east that Leshii had seen him smile.

Leshii looked at his travel companion, who was more than a mystery to him. He found his presence deeply disquieting and, if the instruction to show him to Paris had not come from Prince Helgi the Prophet himself, he would have found some way of avoiding the trip. Helgi was a Varangian too, the ruler of Ladoga, Novgorod, Kiev and the surrounding lands of the Rus. He had warred as far as Byzantium, nailing his shield to the gates the city closed against him. He was a mighty ruler, and when he commanded his subjects did well to obey.

Leshii had asked the name of this strange man, but Helgi had told him he didn't have one so he was at liberty to make one up. Chakhlyk then, which was more polite than what he might have chosen. Chakhlyk was tall, even for his race, but unlike many of his kinsmen was dark and thin and wiry, reminding Leshii more of something grown from the earth, a twisted tree perhaps, rather than a human.

Leshii knew everyone who had been to Ladoga, most people in the neighbouring city of Novgorod and a fair few even further down in Kiev, but he had never seen this fellow before. At first he had tried conversation with him. 'My business is silk, brother; what is your trade?' The man had said nothing, just looked at him with those intense dark eyes. Leshii had understood when the prince had sent them out without any escort what the man's trade was. He had understood it when other traders on their route had sat away from them at the fire, when curious farmers had gone creeping back to their homes rather than talk to them, when bandits had watched from the hills but not summoned the courage to come down. His trade was fear. It seeped from him like the musk of an animal.

Leshii guessed that the wolfman must be one of the northerners' wild priests, though he had never seen one like him before. The Varangians' kings were their main holy men but a variety of odd individuals sacrificed to their strange gods at their temples in the woods outside Lagoda. They wore symbols of hammers and swords and, he had heard it rumoured, even real nooses for their very secret ceremonies. This man, though, just wore a strange pebble at his neck on a leather thong. Something was scratched on it, but Leshii had never quite got close enough to see what.

The Northman took off the bag he carried on his back and unrolled something from it.

Leshii, to whom the contents of bags were always an irresistible spark to curiosity, came to see what it was. He recognised it immediately – it was a complete wolfskin, though rather unusual. The fur was coal-black and, even in the dusk, its

6

gloss seemed almost unnatural. It was huge, quite the biggest wolf pelt Leshii had ever seen, and as a trader he had seen a few.

'It's a fine skin,' he said, 'but I don't think the townsmen of Paris will be in the mood for business. If you are planning to sleep in it then in such cold as this I, your guide, should be allowed a share.'

The Northman didn't reply, just walked back into the trees taking the pelt with him.

Now Leshii had nothing to do. He began to feel sorry for himself. He had hoped the rumours of the siege of Paris had been untrue. If Paris was under attack it was likely that other bigger and more important trading centres, such as Rouen, had taken a hit too.

Had he struggled on with his cargo for nothing? He supposed there might be the possibility of finding some takers for his goods in the Viking camp. He went to see to the mules, in two minds whether to take off their burdens there and then or to keep them on in case any stray northerners came up the hill after dark and he had to get away quickly. Perhaps he could sell to the invaders. He had lived under the rule of the Varangians most of his life and understood them. He could do a deal, he thought, if he could persuade them not to hang him in sacrifice to one of their odd gods.

He looked down at the river plain. The longships to the north were withdrawing to the south bank. Something was happening there. The Danes were running away from the bank as if pursued. From the east, casting long shadows behind them, he saw two riders moving across the plain – one leading the other's horse. The Danes were rushing to greet them. Perhaps they were merchants, he thought, perhaps there was a proper market for his goods after all.

He was cold and he was old, too old for this. He might even have found a way to refuse Helgi and stay in Ladoga had his business been better. Five rough years with cargoes lost to bandits and a silkworm disease in the east had eaten into his savings. Helgi's offer to buy him a cargo had been too good to refuse. If he could get a decent price for it he would leave the travelling to younger men in future. Too tired to think any more, he untied the bags from the mules. Could he sit down to a fire and some wine? *Why not?* One more plume of smoke wouldn't matter in the darkness and, behind the hill, the fire wouldn't be seen by anyone.

He saw to the animals, laid out his rug, made a fire, drank his wine and ate some dried figs along with a little flat bread and some cheese. Before he knew it he was asleep, and then, under the light of a full and heavy moon, he was awake again. What had woken him? Chanting, an understated mumble of words like the sound of a distant river.

He shivered and stood to find his coat. His head cleared. Never mind the coat, where was his knife? He took it out and looked down at it in the moonlight. It was the one he used to cut silk – sharp, broad-bladed, single-edged and comforting.

The chanting went on in no language of the many he understood. He was faced with a choice: go towards it, ignore it or go away. With a train of six mules there wouldn't be much sneaking off. The noise was too disquieting to let him sleep and he knew that there was the possibility it was some strange enemy. Better to surprise than be surprised, he thought, and made his way towards the sound.

The trees cut sharp shadows into the moonlit ground, dark lines of ink on a page of silver. Leshii gripped his knife. There was a pale shape sitting thirty paces from him through the trees. He made his way towards it. The chanting stopped. A cloud blew across the moon. Leshii could see nothing. He went forward sightless, groping from tree to tree. And then, at his shoulder, he heard a breath.

He took a pace back and stumbled on a root, falling onto his backside. He looked up and, as the moon turned the edge of a cloud to crystal, it was as if the shadows seemed to coalesce into something approaching a human form. But it wasn't human because its head was that of a huge wolf.

Leshii shouted out and pushed forward his knife to interpose it between him and the thing that seemed to be drawing in the shadows, taking its substance from them.

'Do not fear me.'

It was the Chakhlyk, the Northman, his voice hoarse with stress. Leshii squinted into the darkness and saw that it was him, with that huge pelt draped over his shoulders, the head of the wolf above his head, as if it was his own. He had become a wolf, a wolf made of shadows, skin, fear and imagination.

The wind blew the clouds aside for a moment and the tall figure was caught in the stark light of the moon. The pebble at his neck was gone and his face was smeared with something, his hands too, something black and slick. Instinctively Leshii put his hand forward and touched the wolfman's head. The merchant felt wetness on his fingers. He put them to his lips. Blood.

'Chakhlyk?'

'I am a wolf,' said the Northman. The clouds returned, and it was as if he was a pool of darkness into which all the shadows of the forest poured as streams. Then Leshii was alone in the night.

2 The Confessor

Jehan could smell the plague setting in, the deep note of putrefaction beneath that of the filthy streets, beneath the sour starvation on the people's breath.

They carried him down from Saint-Germain-des-Prés at night, the smoke of the burned abbey still in his clothes. He felt the cool of the water approaching, the stumble of the monks as they put his pallet onto the boat, the sick rocking that accompanied the journey across. He sensed the tension in the men in the tight silence that they kept, heard the careful movement of the muffled oars, the strokes gentle and few, and then the harsh whisper of a password.

'Who?'

'Confessor Jehan. Blind Jehan.'

The gate opened and the perilous part began – the transfer from the little boat onto the narrow step. The brothers tried to keep him on the pallet at first but it was quickly obvious that would be impossible. He solved the problem himself.

'Carry me,' he said. 'Come on, hurry up. I am light enough.'

'Can you climb on my back, Confessor?'

'No. I am a cripple, not a monkey – can you not see?'

'Then how shall I carry you?'

'In your arms, like a child.'

The men escorting him were new to the monastery – warriors sent from a brotherhood to the south to help Saint-Germain defend against the Northmen, much good that the two of them had done. They were unused to Confessor Jehan and he could feel their uncertainty in the way he was taken from the boat. The warriors had never touched a living saint before.

It was a tight squeeze through the Pilgrims' Gate. The walls of the city had been built by the Romans nine feet thick. The passage through them on the city's north side had been cut later, to spare royalty the crush of the market-day crowds. It was not a weakness in the wall but a strength. Any invader breaking in would have to turn his body and sidle into the city, no chance to use a weapon. The passage from the gate was known as Dead Man's Alley for good reason.

So, though the monk who carried him went carefully, Jehan found himself bumped and scraped into the city.

He was carried up the steps. He heard the gate close behind him, footsteps and murmured questions to his companions. The wet scent of the spring river was replaced by the damp and piss of the tight alley and the astringent, strangely pleasant note of boiling pitch and hot sand as they reached the top. Clearly, if the Vikings were to try their luck at night by that gate then the defenders were ready for them.

The monk lowered Jehan to his pallet again and he felt himself lifted up. The pallet moved through the narrow lanes. They had come at the dead of night to hide from their enemies but also from their friends. With so many sick in the city, so many desperate souls, the confessor's progress would have been impossible by day – too many seeking his healing touch.

They came to a halt and Jehan felt himself lowered. A light breeze brought the stench of rot. He had heard that there was nowhere to bury the dead now and that corpses lay out in the streets awaiting a time they could be properly buried. If that was the case, he thought, it would do the people good. It was spiritually useful to confront the reality of death, to see the inevitable end and to think on your sins. He felt sorry for them, nevertheless. It must be hard to lose a loved one and to pass their mortal remains as you went about your business every day.

The confessor knew there was a chance he could be marooned on the island. A section of both banks of the river had held against the Danes, making resupply of the walled city, and expeditions like his own, risky but possible. However, the people were weak and dispirited from nearly four months of struggle. If the Norsemen attacked the city outside the walls, instead of concentrating on the bridges barring their progress upstream, the banks would fall and there would be no re-supply, no coming and going even for a small unlit boat in the middle of the night.

'Father?'

He recognised the voice.

'Abbot Ebolus.'

'Thank you for coming.' The voice was near his ear – the abbot had bent to Jehan's level. The confessor could smell the sweat of battle on him, the smoke and the blood. Up close, the warrior-monk reeked like a butcher's shelf. 'Do you think you can help her?'

'Surely it is we, not she, I am here to help.'

Ebolus shifted on his haunches. Jehan heard the jingle of mail. The abbot was still in his armour.

'You know why you are here?'

'Count Eudes sent for me so I came. His sister Aelis is af-flicted.'

'Just so. She is at the father's house at Saint-Etienne. She claims sanctuary there.'

'From what, an ague?'

'It is not an affliction of the body, rather one of the mind or spirit. She has taken to the great church and will not come out. Eudes feels it's bad for the sentiment of the people. They need to see the nobility confident and healthy.'

'Take her out and tell her to smile. There's no sanctuary for a woman from her relations who wish her to come to table.'

'She claims to be pursued, and as such my men will not force her from the house of God.'

'Pursued by what?'

'She will not say. She says something is coming for her and that she can only be safe from it in the church.'

The confessor thought for a moment.

'Is she a woman of the court?'

'No, she was raised half wild down at Loches on the Indre.'

'Then it's likely some country fancy has come into her head. There are plenty in that area who dance naked before bonfires in the night, only to go to church when the sun rises.'

'Aelis is a Christian.'

'But she's a woman. She has believed some peasant stupidity, that is all. It's troubling, I grant you, but is it really worth bringing me over here in the middle of a siege?'

The abbot lowered his voice. 'There is more,' he said. 'Count Eudes has received an offer.'

'The pagans want money to leave?'

'No. They want the girl. If she can be persuaded to go to them they've sworn that they will leave us alone.'

Jehan rocked back and forth – in contemplation or under the influence of his disease Ebolus could not be sure.

'A girl, a marriage, brings peace and security, even the possibility of conversion of the pagan. Silver is only like giving a lamb to a wolf – he will be back for more. You are certain the northerners will leave if they have her?' said the confessor.

'They have given their oaths, and it is my experience that, when they swear, they swear in earnest.'

'They gave their oaths when our fat emperor paid them off rather than facing them as Christ's enemies in the field, but they are back.'

'I think this is different. We may be wrong about why they are here. There is talk that they came just for her. They have no designs upstream, and if Aelis goes to them then they will retire.'

'A count's sister seems a poor prize for a Viking king,' said Jehan.

'She is high-born and a famous beauty. A Frankish farmer's daughter is too good for their highest king.'

'And yet,' said Jehan.

Ebolus shifted on his feet. 'And yet.'

The confessor thought out loud. 'So the girl can lift the siege, free her people from plague and send their enemies from the land if only she will marry this barbarian, and yet she will not. Is she so full of pride?'

'There is a problem in that—'

Ebolus was cut short by a stir in the street. Someone was coming. Heavy footsteps approached, ten men at least, thought Jehan, marching in step. Soldiers. The footsteps stopped near to him. Jehan became aware of a presence at his side, someone looking at him, someone for whom every nearby conversation halted, for whom even the animals seemed to stop braying.

'Monk.'

'Count Eudes,' said Jehan.

'Good of you to come.' The count's voice was as Jehan remembered it — curt, brusque, implying that time was short and he had pressing business to attend to.

'When the count commands, the brothers of Saint-Germain obey.'

There was a short laugh.

'Not so, or your monks would be here defending my walls instead of cowering in the countryside with their treasures buried more deeply than their sins.'

'The confessor is still at the abbey,' said Ebolus.

'You were there when the Normans plundered it?'

'No. But I returned after they had. Even Sigfrid can't burn somewhere twice.'

'I wish your fellow monks had your courage.'

'It seems courage would not be required if your sister were made to do her duty and marry this heathen. I would gladly go with her to help bring him to God.'

The count said nothing, and the streets around him seemed to empty of noise in respect to his silence. When he spoke again there was an edge of anger in his voice.

'They have not said they want her in marriage.'

'I did not get the chance to elaborate, Confessor,' said Ebolus. 'The pagans . . .'

He seemed to have difficulty continuing.

'Yes?' said Jehan.

Ebolus went on: 'Our spies tell us it's something to do with their gods.' The abbot's voice was almost ashamed.

Jehan fell silent. Somewhere far off a child was crying.

Eventually, the confessor spoke. 'That,' he said, 'changes the complexion of things. A sacrifice? We won't give up Christian daughters to heathen murder no matter what the cost.'

'We have no thought of that,' said Eudes.

Ebolus spoke: 'Why not? What choice do we have? If the people discover this offer has been made – and discover it they will – then they'll tear her from the church and throw her to the barbarians, sacrifice or no. You have not seen the streets, Confessor. The plague takes so many that we cannot bury our dead. We have no silver to offer, the king has given it to the Norsemen for twenty years now. We need to buy time and then strike at these heathens.'

'I will not send my sister to the slaughter,' said Eudes.

'How many warriors do we put in the way of death? I have lost one brother and expect to lose more. It will be a noble end for her,' said Ebolus.

'And what will they say of Eudes?' said the count. 'That he is so weak he gives up his only sister to rape and murder. I will stand alone against them with this city a field of ash about me before I let that happen.'

The confessor felt irritation building in him. He felt the need to move, to pace around, to slap the walls, to express the passion God had put within him in a physical way. His body, though, would not allow that.

'Turn me.' He spoke to his attendant monk.

'Father?'

'My hip is chafing. Turn me.'

The monk did as he was asked, rolling Jehan onto his other side and arranging the cushion beneath him.

Jehan paused for a moment, offering a prayer against wrath, and then spoke: 'There can be no concession in this way to pagans. It is one thing to marry the girl to a godless king, per-haps even a good thing. That way, through prayer, through devotion and humility, we may hope she will bring the unbeliever to Christ. It is quite another to imperil her immortal soul, to imperil all our immortal souls by knowingly handing her over to the worshippers of idols. *Et tulisti filios tuos et filias tuas quas generasti mihi et immolasti eis ad devorandum numquid parva est fornicatio tua immolantis filios meos et dedisti illos consecrans eis.'*

He said the words so quickly that Ebolus, though well educated in Latin, strained forward to hear them. 'What?'

The confessor twisted his head in frustration and said, 'In plain Roman, moreover thou hast taken thy sons and thy daughters, whom thou hast borne unto me, and these hast thou sacrificed unto them to be devoured. Is this of thy whoredoms a small matter, that thou hast slain my children and—'

Ebolus interrupted. 'My Latin is as good as yours, Father; if anything it is my ears that fail me.'

'Then hear this,' said the confessor, feeling heat come to his cheeks. 'Give that girl to the Northmen and you will imperil not only her soul but your own. Better a thousand righteous deaths than one that the Lord abhors. You are right to protect her, Eudes. The piety of kings is the protection of their people.'

'It is a hard god you follow, Confessor,' said the abbot.

'It is God, plain and simple.'

'Then go to her and make her show her face in the streets,' said Eudes. 'That's all I ask.'

'There might be a way that would satisfy us all,' said Ebolus.

'If fat Emperor Charles got off his backside and sent some men down here,' said Eudes.

Ebolus breathed out heavily. 'That would take a miracle and the Lord is sparing with those. No. Look, we cannot send the girl to the northerners against her will. That would make us as the Sanhedrin, who brought Christ to Pilate. But she can volunteer. That would make her a martyr. There are plenty of examples of saints who have willingly given up their lives to pagans to defend the faith. And you, Eudes, would not appear weak. You would have a martyr in your family. Will you not allow her the bravery that you show on our ramparts every day?'

'She is my sister,' said Eudes.

'And this is your city. If Paris falls, what will they say of Eudes then? If ever you have ambitions to be king of the Franks, then they will lie in its ashes,' said Ebolus. The abbot's eyes met Eudes's, searching to see the count's reaction to his words. He saw nothing, which he took for encouragement, so he went on: 'And there is a precedent. Saint Perpetua was torn to pieces by wild animals in the amphitheatre in Rome for refusing to renounce the Lord. It might be argued that was a pagan ritual, of a kind.'

Jehan felt his body twitch and convulse.

'This is sophistry,' he said, 'and I am not happy that we are using our philosophies to murder this girl.'

'What would you do, Confessor, if it was your blood they wanted?' said Ebolus.

'I would go to them,' he said.

'Exactly. Then can you say the lady should not even have the virtues of martyrdom and an eternal reward explained to her?'

The confessor thought for a second.

'I cannot.'

'So you will talk to her?' said Ebolus.

'Just get her to smile and face the people,' said Eudes. 'That will be enough.'

'But you have no objection to the confessor reminding her of her duties to the city? You will not allow a selfish pride to cloud your judgement of the necessary?' said Ebolus.

'I will not have her forced. '

'No one is talking of forcing her,' said Ebolus; 'we are simply seeking to remind her of her Christian duty to put her fellow men before herself. Confessor, can you do this?'

Again, silence from the confessor. After a time, he spoke: 'I will speak but I will not persuade her. Any decision must be her own.'

'Then let us not delay,' said Ebolus.

Jehan felt a strong hand on his arm.

'Concentrate on getting her to show herself to the people. If I find that you have coerced her in any way, monk, then do not expect to leave this city alive.'

Jehan smiled. 'I never expect to leave anywhere alive, Count. To do so is to presume too much knowledge of God's will. But I am an honest man and I will treat your sister honestly.'

'Then go.'

Jehan was lifted and carried forward on the pallet. They passed through the city. He heard the cries of starving children, the coughs of plague victims, weeping and even some drunken singing. It was, he thought, the music of despair. He longed to silence it but he knew that his powers of healing were very limited. Sometimes he doubted that he did anything at all when he laid on his hands for the cure of pain, made the mad sane or even, in some terminal cases, told the person their time was up and they should depart for heaven. They believed him to be a saint, so they got better for him, came back to themselves or they died, sometimes. The faithful benefited the most. Was God working through him? *Of course He was*, he thought, *what else could it be?*

He felt himself ascending a hill, the men carrying him slipping on the straw that had been laid on the cobbles. There was a lot of straw, some fresh-smelling, some stinking of rot. Either variety was no good sign – it was put down as a kindness to the inhabitants of nearby houses, to keep the sound of hooves and wheels to a minimum. This was a courtesy extended only to those on their deathbeds. He prayed for them – yes, that their lives should be spared but mostly that they should come to know God. Death held no dominion over the righteous man.

He had work here, he thought, administering the viaticum blessing, the preparation for the journey after death, absolving sins and getting people ready for heaven. Eudes had said the girl could save the city. No. The city could save itself, kneel down before God, ask his forgiveness and welcome him into its heart. Then physical death could hold no fear for those who lived there, as it held no fear for him.

Straw for silence. It was a symbol, he thought, of man's useless attachment to earthly things, a wafer-thin reality. Christ would come one day, Christ the wrecker, Christ the downthrower, Christ who sees all sins and holds us accountable for them. Where would be our pretences and our excuses then, our comforts and our indulgences? They would be as straw before the wind.

And yet the girl could stop the slaughter. He saw the point Ebolus was making. One girl's life against those of the whole city. It would be better for everyone if she could be persuaded. The confessor's view was different. One girl's life and eternal damnation against death with the possibility of salvation. It wasn't even a choice.

'Saint-Etienne, Father.'

They were at the great church of Paris. Jehan could almost sense its bulk before him, as if it did something to the air around it, or rather to the dark – intensifying and deepening it, turning it into something Jehan could feel on his skin like the presence of deep water. Since he had been blind, Jehan had come to almost feel the pressures that buildings and even people exerted on the air. He might have been tempted to say he had evolved an extra sense but he was a practical man. So long in the darkness, he thought, his mind simply looked for stimulation in other ways. And of course he remembered the church from before he had been afflicted. It was almost the first thing he'd seen when he came to Paris, brought by monks from the great forest of the Rhine. Perhaps that accounted for the resonance he still felt.

Jehan could recall little of his early life. He'd been a foundling. That building was almost his first memory. He remembered the huge octagonal dome rising above him out of the many-sided base. He had never seen anything like it. The monk who had brought him from the east had gone inside to discuss the boy's future, leaving Jehan standing in the overwhelming bustle of the Parisian street. He remembered how he'd run his hands all the way around the building and counted its sides – twelve, each bearing a fresco of a man he now knew to be an apostle. He recalled the deep dark windows, the sheer bulk of the stone and, when you went inside, the vaulted ceiling, the marble on the floor so shiny that he had feared to tread on it, thinking it was the surface of a pool. Then, as he'd waited for the brothers of Saint-Germain to collect him, he remembered the sun through the windows in the evening that cast shadows that seemed as deep as pits.

'Is she alone in there?'

'Yes, it is very late.'

'Carry me in and set me beside her.'

The monk was lifted from the pallet and carried into the church. He felt the warrior stumble as he went through the porch.

'Be careful,' said the confessor.

'I am sorry, Father. We are all blind men in here, there is scarcely a light.'

The confessor grunted. Since the siege the church would have given up its candles, and besides, why would it be lit at night?

'Can you see her?'

'No.'

'I am here, whoever it is who looks for me.' The voice was clear and strong, with that mild note of irritation that royals often employed when speaking to their inferiors. He recognised the tone. The nobility were occasional visitors to his monastery, though the men came more often than the women. Noble ladies, though, were interested to meet saints, and he had received her there when she was around twelve. He had been eighteen. Now she was eighteen and her voice had changed and deepened, but he still knew it. The girl had asked him why he was so ugly. He had replied that it was the will of God and he thanked Him for it.

The confessor breathed in, using the smell of incense and beeswax to calm himself and order his thoughts. What would he say? He had no idea now; he only knew what he would not say, that she must go, it was her duty. No, he would put the alternatives before her and the decision would be up to her.

'It is Confessor Jehan, lady.'

'They sent me a saint,' she said. The voice was not that of a frightened country girl with a head full of devils. It was absolutely that of a lady of the court, one of those educated women who liked to tease the priests with their knowledge of the Bible, to argue even – however demurely – about its interpretation.

'I am not dead yet, lady, nor would I presume to know the creator's view of me.'

'You are a healer, Confessor. Have you come to cure me of my resolve?'

Jehan, used to listening where he could not see, detected a note of fear in her voice. *And no wonder*, he thought. Her options in life were very unattractive.

'I have come to speak to you, lady, that is all.'

There was a noise from outside, shouting and screaming, the ringing of bells and the blowing of horns. It was the sound, Jehan knew, of battle.

'The Norsemen are attacking?' said the confessor.

'It would sound as if that were so, Father,' said the monk carrying him.

There was a great crash quite near the church. The monk gave a cry of surprise.

Jehan said, 'God smiles on those who fall defending his name, brother. It's unlikely to be a serious raid; I think they're just trying to prevent Eudes from repairing his tower. Carry me on, as I said.'

The monk walked on through the vast space of the great building. Jehan heard the scrape of a flint, smelled tinder and the burning beeswax that followed it. He heard too the lady's intake of breath as she saw him.

'I'm afraid the years have not improved my looks, Lady Aelis.'

'I hope they have improved my manners,' she said. The girl sounded genuinely shocked, and the confessor could hear she was struggling to control her voice.

'May I sit a while with you, then?'

'Yes.'

There were more screams from outside. The defenders would be fighting, thought the confessor, largely without armour. There would have been no time to put it on. His whole conversation, he thought, could very quickly become an almost grotesque irrelevance if the northerners got into the city. How many of them were there? Thousands. How many men-at-arms in Paris? Two hundred and fifty? While the towers held they were safe. If they fell then the city would be swamped. There was nothing for it but to proceed and to trust to the will of God, as he had always done.

'Set me down,' he said to the monk, 'then draw your sword and go to the ramparts to perform the office of a faithful man.'

The monk put him down then left, clumping his way from pillar to pillar as he walked out of the candle glow.

'You are . . .' She hesitated.

'Worse than I was? There is no need to hide from it, lady; it is a plain fact.'

'I am sorry.'

'Do not be. It is a gift from God, and I welcome it.'

'I will pray for you.'

'Do not. Or rather, pray as I pray. Thank God for visiting this condition upon me and the opportunity it has given me to prove my faith.'

Aelis caught the implication of his words. He felt blessed to have been tested in his faith. She should feel the same. She did not, however.

She looked at the figure in front of her in the candlelight. When she had seen him before he had been blind and confined to a chair. Then, she had been struck by his eyes, which didn't focus at all but ceaselessly scanned the room, as if he was trying to follow the flight of an annoying fly. His face too had been twisted into a permanent grimace. Though she had thought him ugly, she had seen worse deformity on any market day in Paris. Now, she thought, he could be the king of beggars, if he chose. His body seemed to have shrivelled, his arms to have withered and twisted; his head was cast back as if permanently looking upwards. She knew the joke was that he always looked to heaven, but, faced with the reality, she could not find it funny. The monk swayed back and forth as he spoke, like someone in deep contemplation. Aelis found the whole effect very unsettling.

Ever since she had been a little girl, and more since she had become a woman, she had been able to perceive people in a way that went beyond the normal understanding of the five senses. It was almost as if she could hear people's personalities like music, sense them as colours or symbols. She had grown up around warriors, seen their scars and heard their stories of battle and fortitude against the northerners. When they had spoken, the colour of iron had come into her mind, of swords and armour, and the dark skies of war. Her brother had a presence like a mailed fist, hard, uncompromising, but nevertheless insubstantial compared to that of Confessor Jehan. The monk's body may have been broken, but his soul, his will, seemed to sit like a great mountain in the dark, solid and immovable.

She took up the candle and went to the altar. The gold of the candlesticks and communion cups caught its flame and glittered as she moved. The abbot would not have them removed – that would be to admit that the Norsemen might get in. There had been hope that the monks at Saint-Germain would send over some of their relics. They could hardly expect the bones of Saint Germain himself, but there had been talk that the stole of Saint Vincent might be sent across. However, the abbot of Saint-Germain had pointed out that the monastery had been sacked by Norsemen three times already and the stole had provided no protection then.

Aelis kneeled beneath the altar.

'God has tested me too in a smaller way. Should I be thankful?'

Jehan measured his words carefully.

'We should be grateful for anything that comes from God.'

The confessor was just a voice in the darkness to her.

'I am not afraid of the Norsemen,' she said.

'Then what are you afraid of?'

Aelis crossed herself. Jehan heard her mutter a prayer. Her voice trembled, though she fought to suppress it, not to appear weak in front of a low-born man.

'Something is coming for me, and I know that if I consent to go with the Norsemen, or even if I leave this church, it will find me and take me. It brings peril for us all.'

'You can't stay inside a church all your life,' said the confessor. 'What is coming for you?'

She said nothing for a moment. Then: 'When your blindness came upon you, Confessor, you had a vision?'

'Yes.'

'Of the Virgin Mary.'

'Yes.'

'Did she speak to you?'

'No.'

'So how did you know it was her?'

'I knew. And from the gift she awoke within me.'

'The prophecies?'

'Yes.'

Jehan remembered the day that had changed his life. He had been found by hunters in the woods at the age of around five or six, and then deposited at a monastery in the East Frankish lands of Austrasia. He had been delirious. All that was certain was that someone had taught him to speak Roman and he had suffered a great shock that had left him with few memories. He had been taken west to Paris by a travelling monk, where he had been given a place at Saint-Germain by the mercy of the Church. His recovery had been as remarkable as it was quick. By the age of nine he was helping the monks, studying, playing and laughing. In many ways he outshone his peers. His facility for writing would have been surprising in a child who had been raised to it from his earliest years. Languages too came easily to him: the common tongue of Roman, Francique, as spoken at court, Latin for official business, Greek, even the Norse and Saxon that the missionaries taught him. More amazing was his ability at chess. He had watched two monks play the game and then sat to try for himself. In his first game he beat one of the abbey's strongest players. The boy, it was said, was blessed.

Then the Virgin had appeared to him. It was high summer, the hungry month of July, and he had nothing to do but walk the fields of unripe crops. The sun was over the corn and the sky was a burning blue. When the monks spoke of visions he had always imagined that an angel or the Virgin would appear on a cloud or in a haze. But she had stood beside him so real he felt he could touch her. She had spoken to him, or rather he had heard her voice in his mind, though he had never admitted it to anyone, too unsure of what she had meant. He had pondered her words for years, and he had never revealed them.

'Do not seek me.'

He had taken it for a warning against the sin of pride, of trying to be too holy and putting himself above other men in piety. Seeking heaven, he felt, was the surest way to lose it.

She had walked away from him and he had run after her, but the blindness fell upon him and he had been discovered wandering by the hives, lucky not to blunder into one and be stung.

His prophecies had been correct – raids along the coast, Rouen in flames, Bayeux, Laon and Beauvais ruined, the sons of the Church executed. The abbot had declared him a saint on earth – a confessor – and God had blessed him with further afflictions and further visions.

'They made you a saint because you saw her?'

'Yes. That and the monastery's desire to have a confessor among its monks. It was just and it was politic,' he said.

'What would they make you if you had seen ...' She couldn't finish.

Jehan was quiet, allowing her to compose herself.

'Do you need to ask for penance?'

Aelis gave a short laugh. 'I have nothing to confess, Father, no sin to be forgiven, but if I was to stand in front of the congregation, call what I have experienced a sin and ask a priest for forgiveness, my life might be over before I left this church. Can I ask you privately? Will you swear never to reveal what I have to say?'

'The sacrament of penance must be conducted publicly,' said Jehan.

'I have nothing to be sorry for. Will you swear?'

'This path is strewn with briars,' said the confessor under his breath. What if the woman told him she was an adulteress or, worse, a murderer? He could not, in conscience, hold on to a secret like that.

The noise of the fighting was getting closer. Had the Norsemen taken a tower? That was impossible, he thought, without mining. The enemy had already tried that, and to no success.

The cries and the curses focused the confessor on his task.

'I will swear,' he said.

'They made you a saint because you saw the Virgin,' said Aelis; 'what would they call you if you had seen the devil?'

'The common people might cry witch,' said the confessor, 'though belief in witchcraft is heresy. Someone might be held a heretic if they declared themselves a witch, but a vision is a vision. Of itself it means nothing.'

'So what would you call me?'

'You have seen the devil?'

'Yes. Am I a witch, unknown to myself?'

'Christ saw the devil in the wilderness – was he a witch?'

She bowed her head.

Jehan swallowed and began to rock more rapidly.

'There are many explanations for this sort of thing. An illness, perhaps, a passing brain fever. A dream is often just that, lady, a fancy without any connection to the day-to-day.'

'I dream him while waking. He is always there.'

More screams. Jehan heard a shouted word in the Norse tongue: 'Die.'

He didn't pause. 'And how do you know him for the devil?'

'He is a wolf. A man and a wolf at the same time. He comes from the shadows and the side of my sight. He is beside me as I fall to sleep and there in the instant of my waking. He is a wolf and he speaks to me.'

'What does he say?'

Aelis crossed herself again. 'He says that he loves me.'

There was a clamour right outside the cathedral. The fighting was close now. Aelis looked up. The darkness around the weak candle glow seemed to swim and to seethe, a liquid black. There was a thump against the door, so hard that it seemed it would splinter.

'Are we to die, Confessor?' said Aelis.

'If it is God's will,' said Jehan.

'Then pray for us.'

'No,' said the confessor. 'Pray for our enemies, that they might find the light of Christ in their hearts before our soldiers kill them and so have a chance of heaven. We are believers and so can be more hopeful we will go to God.'

She stood and Jehan heard her draw in breath. To Aelis the dark had now taken on a different quality. It seemed to bristle, to move and even to shine, like the fur on a hog's back. Then the shadow at the edge of the candle glow took form, moved and stepped forward into the light.

The lady gasped. There, like a creature of wrapped shadows,

stood the figure of the wolfman, his savage head leering down at her from the darkness, his pale skin taut and smeared with blood.

'He is here,' she said. 'He is here!'

'Who?'

'The wolf, the wolf! The devil is come!'

Jehan cast his head around. There was a dark, animal scent away to his left. He could hear the breathing of a third person now, hear the girl trying to catch her breath in her panic.

'We are clothed in the armour of God, Satan; you cannot harm us,' said the monk. His voice was steady and calm, almost bored, like a teacher speaking to a naughty child.

'*Domina*,' said the wolfman. He hacked out the word as if it was stuck in his throat, his accent guttural and strange. '*Domina*.' Aelis tried to make herself think. She had been taught Latin since her earliest years but she couldn't even make her mind translate this simple word. The monk, however, was unafraid.

'Do not call for the lady, devil; your business is with me.' The confessor spoke in Latin too.

The wolfman ignored him.

'*Domina*. My name is Sindre that is called Myrkyrulf, and I am here to protect you.'

Finally Aelis found her Latin. 'Against what?'

'Against this,' he said, and the doors of the church flew in.

3   Death and the Raven

Aelis would later recall only impressions of the first moments of the attack. There had been the flash of something, like a curve of flame, like a sliver of a blood moon glinting from the dark. It was the sword, she realised later, the sword that belonged to that hideous thing. It had caught the fire of the buildings that were burning behind the church, the blade sparking to life in an instant before turning from the light and vanishing from the sight but not the mind.

She had never seen a weapon that was curved like that. Its shape seemed like a symbol for murder, a shallow crescent of malice. And then that word that sounded like a talon tearing through the darkness.

'Hrafn!' It was the wolfman who spoke and though she did not understand what he meant it seemed to wake something in her, to bring images with it, smells and sounds. She saw a wide plain of the battle dead, saw ragged banners streaming in the breeze. The air was thick with what she at first thought was smoke but, when she identified the sound that accompanied it, she knew was not smoke. It was the buzzing of numberless flies. He was there on that plain, the wolf. She couldn't see him but she could sense his presence, a hot snuffling and grunting thing creeping at the side of her eye that she could not turn to see with her full sight.

She stood up, blinked and shook her head, forced reality to return. She put her hand to a pillar for support. The vision had been so sharp and had come on her so quickly that she feared she was going mad.

The church was suddenly crazy with battle. Men hacked, kicked, bit and punched at each other in the dark. In the fire-light she saw her brother, Eudes, his shield strapped on his back, slashing with his long and short swords into the enemy. The Danes had come, for sure.

Axe heads glinted in the dark, faces loomed and fell, spears were thrust and hacked down, friend became indistinguishable from foe.

The wolfman grabbed her by the arm and pushed her forward. 'Walk towards the door,' he said. 'You will not fall.'

'Aelis, Aelis!' her brother was screaming but he couldn't get to her, he was hemmed in by two opponents. The flickering light of the flames outside fought the darkness of the church; things flashed from the shadows, metal, wood, blade and spear tip, shields, faces, arms and feet. Three times men came at her, trying to grab her and pull her away, but three times the snarling shadows seemed to engulf them before they could touch her and they fell with terrible cries. She kept walking towards the door. Ten pillars from it, eight, now five, now two. She was nearly free. Then the arc of the crescent was sweeping down on her, the curve of flame that was that terrible sword.

'Aelis, Aelis!' Her brother's face was contorted in anguish, as though melting in the heat of the burning buildings. Fire seared her skin; the taste of ashes and blood was in her mouth. The sword was a tongue of lightning stretching towards her. There was a blur of movement, a sound like a sack falling off a cart as the shadows reached out to smash the swordsman to the floor. Then she was running, bundled through the narrow streets by an unseen hand. She glanced behind her, tried to see who was driving her on. It was the wolfman. Even though she was running as fast as she could, he was just sidestepping down the alleyways, watching for pursuers as he drove her forward.

'Hrafn!' he screamed back towards the church, then he said something unintelligible, though she could tell it was in the Norse tongue. The words meant nothing to her but she caught their intent clearly. The wolfman was warning away his enemy, telling him that he would die.

She stumbled but the wolfman held her up. Where was he

taking her? The moon was a lantern, casting the streets in a bright and empty light but leaving deep shadows beneath the eaves of the buildings.

Then they were out into the square and she saw where they were going – down the alley to the Pilgrims' Gate. There it was, but locked and guarded. Two men-at-arms came forwards with spears.

'Lady, we are here for you.'

The wolfman pulled her to a halt, ignoring the advancing warriors, still looking behind him.

'Up into the house,' he said. 'Jump into the water and swim. He will not follow you that way. Fall prisoner to any but him. Do not let him see your face. Do not let him see your face!'

'Who?'

There were two soft thumps, followed by a sound like the fall of a thousand coins. Both the men-at-arms had collapsed, hauberks crashing to the cobbles. Black-plumed arrows had caught one in an eye, the other through the neck.

'Go!' The wolfman leaped to shield her. Another soft thump and a heavy exhalation. The wolfman had taken an arrow to the back. He still had the strength to push her towards a door. She pulled it then pushed it. It opened and she fell into a small house.

Moonlight split the darkness inside and she saw the huddled faces of women and children looking at her in terror. She pushed through them to a ladder to the next floor. The room erupted in screams and clatter, as the crowd tried to avoid her, to get out, to do anything but sit in frozen fear. She went up one level, where sleeping mats were strewn around, and then to another above it, a lightless place. She felt around the walls, trying to locate a window. She bumped into something – a loom. It was a weaver's house; there had to be a window for light to work by. She tripped and hit the floor heavily, stood up and pressed on, her hands frantic on the walls.

Then she found it. Cloth had been nailed across the window in a poor attempt to keep out the cold. She tore it back and looked out. She was not on the river side but looking into the street. Something down there slipped from shadow to shadow. Was it the wolfman? There was movement beneath the arch of a doorway. Then it stopped. A figure walked forward from the direction of the great church. He went to the arch and knelt at the edge of the dark. She shivered to look at him. He was a lean dark man, his hair thick with tar so it stood up in a shock. Something had been put into it − feathers, black feathers standing up in a horrid crown. He was completely naked, his body smeared in white clay and ashes so it shone under the moonlight, pale as a corpse. In his hand he carried a bow and on his back was an empty quiver and that cruel curved sword she had seen in the church, now housed in a dull black scabbard. There was something wrong with his skin too, she realised. It had a rough quality to it. She squinted forward through the dark. It didn't look like smallpox, but she was too far away to tell.

The inhabitants of the house were streaming across the square, the women herding the children away. Eight of the Danish invaders came into the square − big men covered in tattoos, the one at the front carrying a large shield with the design of a hammer on it. His sword was drawn and he was pointing it at the naked man, warning him in some way. Not friendly.

The man was oblivious to him; he was tugging at something in the shadows. It was an arrow. It would not come free and, as he pulled it, the body of the wolfman came with it into the light.

'No!' said Aelis, and the man turned to her. She threw her hands across her face and peeked out from behind her fingers like a frightened child. He gave a rasping cry of exultation as he saw her and leaped towards the house. The big man with the shield cursed and Aelis scrambled across the room. She lost all composure, knocking over looms, falling over bales, crawling towards the opposite window. She pulled off the vellum covering it and crouched to look down into the river. It was three times her height beneath her.

She couldn't jump, couldn't bring herself to do it. She heard the creature make the floor below, his footsteps light and quick. She put a leg out of the window but brought it back again. The drop was too great. She stepped back inside the room and glanced around her. There was the hatch where the ladder emerged. She tried to kick the ladder away but it had been tied tight to the beams and she had nothing to cut it free with. She looked down, remembering the wolfman's warning to cover her face. There, just visible in the weak light of the floor below, was a face looking back at her, its eyes sharp and pitiless as a bird's. At first glance she thought that he was wearing a mask of some sort, but as he put his foot on the ladder she could see his face was a network of tiny scars, as were his neck and upper body. It was nothing like leprosy – in places the scars were neat and defined, more like a large pin had dug into him than like the ravages of disease.

He looked up and spoke to her in Latin: 'Thing of darkness, death bringer, you will not escape me.'

'Who are you?'

'A man of honour,' he said and leaped at the ladder.

And then Aelis was falling. She had done what she thought she could not and gone feet first through the window. The water hit her hard, forcing her wimple over her eyes, blinding her. She struggled for the surface, her skirts heavy and tight about her legs. She pulled off the wimple and cast it aside. The water was so cold, ice meltwater from the hills, crushing the breath from her body, but the current was not strong. The upstream bridge on the south side had partially collapsed. The Norsemen had made an abortive attempt to pile debris, bodies and whatever they could get their hands on onto the ruin to make a causeway to the city. They'd been beaten back but had succeeded in somewhat stemming the considerable force of the river. The downside was that the water was foul. Aelis clamped shut her mouth to avoid swallowing it and struck for the shore. Her country childhood served her well — she was used to swimming in rivers and lakes — though her skirts were terribly restrictive and she had to hold them above her waist and kick with her legs to make progress. Things were smashing into the water about her. A table leg went over her head, then something heavy splashed behind her. She coughed and shook, turned and saw a stream of cloth from a bale flying through the night. Her pursuer had no more arrows and was throwing all he could find. She hammered forward across the river, went under, panicked, her legs pumping wildly. Then she hit something. Solid ground was under her feet. She made one last effort and got to the bank.

She didn't turn, just kept scrambling up, her flesh shaking on her bones with the terrible cold. She heard the voice of the thing behind her.

'*I dag deyr thú!*' he shouted, and then in Latin, 'This is your death day, monster!'

4   A Necessary Sacrifice

Aelis clawed her way up the bank. She was on the south side of the river, though she couldn't tell exactly where. That is, she knew where she was in relation to the city but not to the Norse camps. The invaders were on both sides, though she had no idea how far their control extended.

There was still a clamour at the tower on the bridge. To her alarm, she heard the invaders were retreating; the bells had changed their pattern to tell the people the Norsemen had been beaten back. The screams of the fighting were dying and the men-at-arms on the tower were shouting cat calls and insults after their enemies, goading them for running, asking where their famous Viking fury was now.

The enemy would be returning to his camp and Aelis realised that she might well be right in the middle of their retreat. Men were moving through the houses and huts. She saw the outline of someone with an axe across his shoulder, another man with a spear. They could be Danes or they could be her people, she couldn't be sure. As soon as the bulk of the Norsemen moved to the main attack at the bridge, the Franks would come in from the forest to worry their camp. The number of invaders was so great that no victory could be gained, but they could injure a guard, steal a pig and, most of all, keep a few of the Danes from attacking the city. It was too risky to approach the dark figures, though. Who knew who they were?

Some of the houses were even still inhabited by Franks. It had been a mystery to Aelis why the Northmen had not taken the whole south bank, but her brother had explained it. The houses outside the city wall were very poor and the people many and strong from labour on the land. The Norsemen's numbers were great, but not so great they could be profligate.

They would take the houses, he said, but on their way back. They wanted slaves but had no intention of carrying them upriver if they ever got past the bridges of Paris. They'd be an encumbrance to further looting. They'd allow the Franks to feed and care for themselves until they returned, then they'd take them captive. The Vikings treated the Franks like a cook treats his hens, her brother had said.

She looked up to the weaver's house, her body still convulsing with cold. The feathered man had gone, but then she saw another face at the window. It was the warrior with the hammer on his shield. He threw the shield into the water and, in an instant, leaped to follow it. Then another man came to the window and jumped too. They were chasing her, and there were a lot of them.

She blundered forward into the darkness of the houses, running as fast as she could. There was another splash behind her, and a shout of complaint as one of the Norsemen hit the river too close to a comrade. She had to find somewhere to hide for the night, to spy out the land and try to find some way back into Paris — or out into the friendly country beyond — before the next day. Even that wouldn't be easy. She had lost her wimple in the river and her hair was uncovered. The Franks were tolerant people and women could even travel unchaperoned throughout their lands, but with her modesty so badly compromised, there was a chance she'd be taken for a whore for any man to use as he saw fit.

She could not approach anyone male, particularly at night, but if she could find a woman of her own people then she could explain her state of undress, borrow some sort of head covering and stay with her until morning. Then, with luck, she could get back to the city across what remained of the southern bridge. There was enough debris there to make it serviceable to anyone willing to wade and climb their way across. The few provisions the city managed to get came in that way.

A cloud took the moon and the night became very dark. She

made her way left, as she knew the Norsemen were camped nearer to the westernmost bridge. She kept low and moved from shadow to shadow, knowing that she could as easily be killed by her own side as by the enemy. But she still couldn't see who had possession of the houses and couldn't risk going in.

Then the cloud slipped away from the moon, the river turned to a shining silver path and she saw them – four men with shields in conference, two more heaving themselves up the bank out of the river. She knew that if she stayed she would be discovered, so she ran. She heard a halloo behind her. They'd seen her.

She plunged through the dark as she had plunged through the water, legs thrashing at the ground in an effort to go faster, falling, rising, driving on. The men were fanning out, moving through the houses. She came to the edge of a wood, which she knew stretched up to the top of the hill. She stumbled in, unable to find a track in the dark. Again, the cloud was her friend, blotting out the moon and casting the forest into blackness. She went on anyway, trying to keep silent, to keep her balance, to locate a path, to move quickly – so many contradictory things to do that she achieved none of her goals. She fell for a last time and gave up any attempt to stand. She crawled on through the tearing brambles, the nettles that stung and the stones that cut her knees. The men were crashing about in the woods behind her. She heard a shouted word she recognised. '*Hundr!*' They were calling for a dog. She was exhausted but had to go on. The moon crept from behind the cloud to reveal a trail, a slick path of flattened grass. She got up and ran to the top of the hill, and over the crest, shouting out in surprise as she saw the little fire.

A man stood up from beside it. He was small, squat and dark with a broad-bladed knife in his hands.

'*Chakhlyk? Volkodlak. Lycos? Lupus?*' She recognised the last two words. Wolf. He came forward, the big knife raised.

She thought of that terrible dream, and of the man who had

tried to protect her, who had been a wolf, and also of the thing in her visions, that had said that it loved her. The thoughts never settled to make any sense, but perhaps it was her sensitivity that let her see the connection between the stout little man in front of her and the tall wolfman who had fallen fighting for her. Whatever, she was at his mercy.

She said in Latin, 'I am Lady Aelis of the Franks, line of Robert the Strong, sister to Count Eudes. I am pursued by Normans and will offer great reward for any that help me.'

The man gave a smile big as a tear in a sheet.

'You?' he said. 'Lady, I was sent on a delegation to meet you here.'

'By whom?' She put her hand to her hair, trying to cover it.

There were noises from back down the hill – barking and the cries of men.

'Prince Helgi of the Rus.'

'Then, in honour of your prince, can you preserve me? I can't outrun them. Can you hide me?' said Aelis.

He stepped towards her and put the knife up to her throat.

'I am not afraid to die,' she said.

'Well, I hope there won't be any need for that,' he said. 'With your permission, lady?' And then he cut off a huge hank of her hair.

5 Voices in the Dark

The battle in the church had ended. The Vikings had driven the Franks outside and slammed shut the door but now they were trapped. From within, the confessor could hear the Franks assembling in the street, hear their excited cries.

'They're inside! They're inside! We have them.'

The words of the psalm came into his head unbidden, but he would not say them out loud.

'Arise, O Lord; save me, O my God: for thou hast smitten all mine enemies upon the cheek bone; thou hast broken the teeth of the ungodly.'

That was in him, to call up the god of the Old Testament, the powerful, protecting, avenging god. Instead, he thanked the Lord for his trial and prayed that the heathens might come to Christ's peace before they died. God's will, he thought, was all-encompassing and to complain or show weakness before life's trials was to rail against Him. If things were so, it was because He wished them to be so.

Around him the Vikings were talking. He knew enough of their language from previous sieges and from more peaceful meetings to understand them. The confessor's ability with languages was remarkable. Norse had come to him as easily as if he had been raised speaking it.

'We're stuck in here.'

The confessor could hear the Norsemen pacing around.

'How many dead?'

'Of us, none, I think. No one here anyway that I can see. Has anyone got a candle or some reeds?'

'Sigfrid's men? How did they do in the fight?'

'Four. Well, I think it's four, it's difficult to tell in here.'

'It can't be four. Only four followed us in.'

'I know. Doesn't say much for the skills of the king's warriors, does it?'

'One of them had a decent sword, though.'

'You can't have that, Ofaeti. If his kin see you with it there'll be trouble.'

'You're right. For them.'

Ofaeti. The confessor recognised it as a nickname. 'Fatty' was the nearest translation.

'You'll have to give it back. I can hardly see in here. Are you not wearing any trousers or shoes?'

'I'm not, no.'

'Thank Thor it's dark, then. Why not?'

'I was just about to treat one of the camp ladies to the benefit of my expertise when Crow-Arse went up the wall. I didn't think you'd appreciate it if I stopped to get my finery on before I followed you.'

'She stole your trousers as soon as you took your eye off her, didn't she?'

'You can't trust whores nowadays,' said Ofaeti.

Another voice spoke. 'No wonder the Franks ran away with that dangling at them.'

Laughter.

'I can't believe we let ourselves end up in this mess.' The voice had something of a chuckle in it.

'Following that shapeshifter was bad luck, for sure.'

'He would have taken her if we hadn't. And look on the bright side. We're surrounded by so many that even you will be able to hit at least one of them, Holmgeirr.'

'I blame you for this, Ofaeti, this is your god's doing – Tyr's blessing, many enemies.'

The voices were light and the men laughed as they spoke. The confessor recognised it for what it was – warrior bravado, but if it was an act, he had to admit it was a convincing one.

'Let's face it,' said the voice belonging to the one who had been called Holmgeirr. 'The one to blame is that Odin-blind crow-man we followed in here. Where is he now?'

'He followed the wolfman and the girl.'

'Oh, terrific. Kiss goodbye to the reward then. Helgi'll be as likely to nail us up by our nuts as give us anything now.'

'We might still be in luck. Fastarr and the others went after him.'

'Let's hope they skin the bastard if they find him.'

'Let's hope he doesn't skin them.'

The confessor had not heard the next voice before. It was quieter and more serious.

'It's too late. The Raven will have her. He said he would.'

'Don't say that, Astarth. That girl's worth seventy pounds of silver to us alive. What's he want her for? Sacrifice?'

'Nothing so fancy; he just wants her dead.'

'Why?'

'What do you mean, why? When did the servants of Odin ever need a why to want someone dead? Perhaps he's hungry.'

'Oh, don't. No, don't.'

'Fair point, though, isn't it?'

'I can't give Sigfrid a pile of gnawed bones, can I?'

'Why not?'

'Well. It could be anyone, couldn't it?'

'Now there's a plan,' said Ofaeti.

The men seemed to find this truly hilarious.

Jehan heard the church door creak open, a shout and then the door was slammed again.

'Try it, you Frankish bastard, just try it,' shouted a Norse voice. 'Come on, see what you get!'

The voice he had heard called Holmgeirr said, ' Look, it's as black as Garm's arse in here. Get a light, will you?'

The confessor continued to pray for the life of the Norsemen's souls and the death of their bodies.

'Never mind that. What are we going to do about this lot outside? I tell you, they'll burn us out. We'll have light enough then.'

'They'll never burn their own holy place, that's our job.

Relax. It's built like a mountain anyway, I doubt you could burn it. The worst that can happen is that you'll die by the sword.'

'Looked on like that, what am I worried about?'

'Actually, the worst that can happen is we get caught.'

'I ain't getting caught.' It was a fourth voice, low and rough.

He heard the sound of a flint being struck, some blowing and puffing and then: 'Hang on a minute, who's this?'

A sword was drawn.

'A beggar.'

'No, look at his hair – he's a monk. I'll tell you who this is, boys: it's our passage out of here. It's their crippled god. It's the god Jehan they're always on about.'

'Not God,' said Jehan in deliberately bad Norse. He decided that the less the Norsemen thought he understood of their tongue, the better for him. However, the suggestion that he was a god had forced him to deny it.

'He's a healer, they reckon.'

'Doesn't seem to have done a very good job on himself, does he?'

'Here, god, do my arm. Your boys gave it one hell of a whack.' The confessor guessed the arm must be broken. The Norsemen liked to make light of their wounds whenever possible. The man wouldn't have asked unless he was in dire pain.

'Need to set it,' said the confessor.

'Can you do that? Do you have the skill?'

'My hands bad but can tell you,' said the confessor, 'if you come to Christ.'

He felt his heart pumping and scolded himself for it. These northerners were not afraid to die, whatever lies they believed. Why should he be so?

'I'll come to any god who'll fix this bastard arm,' said the Dane. 'What do I have to do?'

'Baptism, water.'

'Careful, Holmgeirr,' said one of them. 'They eat human flesh that lot, it's well known.'

'Don't the Ravens do that too, and they follow our gods?'

'Odin ain't my god. A god of the living beats one of the dead.'

'I've made plenty of corpses following Lord Thor, but I've never eaten one, nor has the god ever asked me to.'

'Odin doesn't demand that; it's the Ravens who offer it.'

Confessor Jehan felt a jab in his side. 'You, Christ God, I'll suffer a broken arm for a year rather than eat anyone.'

'Never mind that,' said another voice. 'Open that door and tell them we want a chat. Tell them we've got their god in here and if they want to ever see him alive again they better let us out.'

'You go out and tell them. They'll stick an arrow in whoever opens that door.'

'I'll do it,' said the one who Jehan had heard called Ofaeti. 'Ask for Tyr's protection in this one. Stick close behind me.'

'Not you, you fat bastard. If they've got bowmen out there they'll never miss someone of your size.'

'You want to do it?'

'Second thoughts, you're the ideal man for the job. Keep your shield low, mate. After you.'

Jehan felt a strong arm around him and he was lifted into the air. Someone had picked him up as if he was a child. He felt the man draw out a knife and knew what was going to happen.

The door was opened and he heard Eudes shout, 'Hold!'

The Norseman screamed at the top of his voice, so loud it made the confessor wince, 'We're taking your god out of here. Stay your hand if you want him to live.' Then he spoke to Jehan: 'You, tell them to give us free passage back to our camp if you want to live.'

The confessor's voice was calm. He spoke in the high language of Francique so people would know his words were intended for the Frankish leaders. The time for praying for his enemies' souls was over. They had refused to convert and set themselves outside God's mercy.

'These men are enemies of God and I have hope of heaven. Strike, and if I die, know that it was with the Lord's name on my lips.'

Jehan heard the Franks step forward. A knife pricked the skin at his neck, but then Eudes was shouting, 'No, no, stand back. Stand back, put down your weapons.'

Jehan heard a voice, close at his ear. 'Thanks for that, god. I guessed what you said and you can be sure you'll pay for it when we get you back.'

'Give them passage,' shouted Eudes. 'Set your ransom and we'll want him back intact, northerners. Come on, let these men past.'

'Cut them down!' shouted the confessor. He couldn't work out why Eudes wouldn't attack. He would have thought the count would have been glad to get rid of a troublesome churchman, particularly one who was not amenable to bribes or threats.

'My name is Ofaeti. Bargain with none but me!' shouted the Norseman and carried him out into the night.

As Jehan was carried towards the bridge, he realised that the count was a more subtle politician than he had given him credit for. The king and the dukes of the Carolingian empire might refuse to come to the aid of little provincial Paris, but could they refuse to come to the aid of a saint?

6   Captives

Leshii had almost hated to cut the girl's hair. She was very
beautiful and her hair was an almost white blonde. However,
there were two advantages to slicing it off. The first was that it
would help disguise her from the Danes who were looking for
her, enabling him to claim a good ransom from the wolfman
– or rather via the wolfman from the rather richer Prince Helgi.
The second was that he could sell the hair to a wig maker. A
crop like that was a rare capture; it was even clean. *How much?*
he wondered. Ten dinars? Two good swords' worth at least.

She had understood what he wanted to do but instinctively
objected. 'The Bible says it is a disgrace for a woman to cut
her hair.'

'And for a woman to be raped and murdered by Norsemen?
Surely your god would prefer a lesser evil.'

Aelis saw his reason and held still while he worked. The
cutting was notable for speed rather than finesse, and her
remaining hair was reduced to clumps. The merchant had
the severed tresses inside his pack in an instant – along with
the lady's rings – and, just as quickly, produced some wide
trousers, gathered at the knee, and a long kaftan.

From down the slope they heard a dog barking and the calls
of the men following it.

Aelis kicked off her soaking dress and stuffed it into a bush.
Down to her hose and undershirt, she went to put the kaftan
on but the merchant stopped her and passed her a rough shirt,
no more than a tube with holes in.

'Better not to wear the wet one,' he said, 'it might provoke
questions.'

Aelis was deeply reluctant to undress in front of this man,

so she went a few paces into the woods. She stripped off her hose and tunic and put on the new clothes. They stank of horse and, worse, of man. Suddenly his hands were on her.

'I will die before you take me.'

'You have a taste for drama,' said the merchant. 'You are to be a boy; best cover the things that announce you, very much, as a woman.' His eyes bulged as he said this in a self-mocking acknowledgement of his sauciness. 'I know you Franks and Neustrians have no conception of real buttons.'

One by one, he pushed the twelve buttons at the front of the kaftan through their loops. Aelis was glad he did, as she would have had no idea how to put on such a strange garment herself. Then he put a rough cap on her head and smeared dirt all over her face. She looked like she was meant to, a young male slave, his hair cut short as a sign of his subjugation.

'You are a mute,' he said, 'and my servant. Your breasts are flat enough in that but it might be well to keep your arms crossed when in company. It's a good job you're a skinny thing — if you had big tits we'd have no chance.'

Aelis was unused to having commoners talk to her like that. Had he spoken that way at court he would have found himself doing very hard penance indeed. However, she realised she was in no position to argue.

'And one more thing. Stay here; pretend to be sleeping. Let me handle this.'

'Can you persuade them?'

He looked at her. He knew Helgi coveted this woman above all others, that prophecy had told him their destinies were linked. However, Helgi's was a new realm and the Franks held him in contempt. He would not be allowed to marry their lady. Hence, he had decided to take her. The reward for bringing her to the prince, thought Leshii, would allow him to retire into idleness and safety for the rest of his life.

'I've spent my life persuading people,' he said. 'Now lie down and wait.'

Aelis did as she was bid while Leshii went back to his fire.

He heard the men approaching up the hill, calling to each other and to her.

'Come on, darling. Best we get you than the Ravens, believe me.'

'You're worth too much for us to harm you. Come on, you can be in front of a fire in short order if you show yourself.'

The dog was barking with the hollow bay of the hunt. It came first, bounding into the camp and quartering the ground with its eager nose.

Leshii breathed out. He was used to making audacious deals, used to taking his life in his hands as he crossed the vast plains of the east, out to Serkland, where the desert people sold him silks and swords, west to the great markets of Denmark and Sweden and even south to Byzantium, the empress of cities. This, though, was going to be difficult. Six men at least, all fevered with the hunt and the day's battle; him with only his knife to protect all his wares and the most precious commodity of all – the lady who was going to make him a rich man. He got hold of his nerves and spoke in the Norse tongue, high and clear, allowing his accent to colour it more than was strictly necessary in order to sound exotic.

'Greetings to the sons of my good friend Ongendus, who is also called Angantyr. How fares the noble king of the Danes?'

'You're a bit late, foreigner – he's been dead these twenty years.' The men were all soaking wet, gleaming in the moonlight – as were the points of their spears. The dog, a large, smooth-haired beast, was briefly taken with the remains of Leshii's meal and was gnawing on a mutton bone. Leshii thought of his mother. She'd have taken it from the dog and boiled it for soup, small as it was. He preferred to discard such things, not because he was rich but because he had aspirations to be rich. Act wealthy and you will be wealthy, an Arab had once told him. It seemed good advice, but up to that point it had met with only limited success. Perhaps the saying had less truth than he had supposed. It wasn't the acting that had let him down, for sure – Leshii was good at that

'Then tell me his noble son Sigfrid has grown to rule you Danes. He was always the strongest and most noble lad. I played with him when he was a child. Does he still speak of me? Say that he does.'

'Our lord is Sigfrid, true. Are you a friend of his?'

'I was like a second father to the boy when he was young. I am Leshii, merchant of Ladoga known to you as Aldeigjuborg, ambassador of Prince Helgi the Dane, called Rus, ruler of the Eastern Lake, the lands of Novgorod and Kiev. Come and share my fire. We are kinsmen. I have wine here if you would like it.'

'My name is Fastarr, son of Hringr. No time for wine, brother,' said one of the men. 'We are hunting a girl who has been on this shore. Have you seen her?'

The merchant swallowed. He liked the sound of 'brother'.

'No one but me,' said Leshii. He watched as the two men at the front whispered to each other, one shooting him a sidelong glance.

'Can't we stop for a bit of wine, boss?' The one who asked was small and thin but had a cold impassive killer's face.

'We could be all night and not find her. Let's give it a bit longer with the dog and if he doesn't turn anything up, call it quits and drink this merchant's stash,' said another.

Leshii glanced nervously towards the packs with his bottles in them. It was good stuff, meant for trading, not quaffing by a bunch of hairy-arsed warriors.

'Plenty of time tomorrow, then,' said Leshii. 'My brother is coming with enough to drown us all. I will ensure you are the first to sample it. How Sigfrid will rejoice to have us both by his side again.'

'You have no bodyguard, merchant.' Fastarr spoke.

'I travel with a magician, a shapeshifter. He looks over me whenever I am in need. Incredible. A man only needs to raise his sword against me and it is as if the shadows themselves strike at him. Splat! He is dead.'

The men murmured to each other again. Leshii caught a word. *Hrafn* – raven.

'You arrived today?'

'Indeed.'

'We saw your welcome at the camp.'

Leshii realised his whole story was about to fall to bits. He had said he had known Sigfrid but not realised he had been made king of the Danes. Now the men thought he had been into the camp, so why hadn't he made himself known to the king? But he knew very well that the present has a way of shaping the past and thought that he might get away with it, once enough wine had gone into the Norsemen's mouths. So he did what he always did when he thought he was winning in a transaction. He said nothing, smiled and shrugged.

'Where is the Raven now?' asked the one with the hammer on his shield, who had been called Fastarr.

Again, Leshii smiled and shrugged.

'He can't have made it over that quickly, can he? Didn't he go back over the bridge?' said one of the younger men, looking about him. 'That Odin lot give me the creeps. Especially the woman. She's not here, is she?'

'That witch isn't bothered about the likes of you,' said Fastarr. He addressed Leshii: 'We're looking for a Frankish woman – a noblewoman – we saw her jumping from a house above the walls. She'll fetch a good ransom.'

Leshii didn't blink.

'I have no one,' said Leshii. 'I brought the Raven here and he was grateful and promised always to guard me. I have no idea what else he wanted.' He wondered who this Raven was. He had come with a man he was convinced was a shapeshifter but he had been a wolf. Still, if the Varangians were scared of ravens, he was quite willing to make Chakhlyk a raven.

'Why didn't you take the Ravens to the king?'

So there were more than one.

'I was waiting to gauge the reception they got,' he said.

'Good move. I'd have cut them into slices as soon as they

got there if I'd been Sigfrid, starting with the woman.' The one who spoke was thin and wiry and had most of the fingers on his left hand missing.

The dog finished its bone, sat up and coughed.

'A fine animal, brothers. How much would you want for it?'

Leshii knelt down and gestured for the dog to come to him, but it just looked at him and moved away. He stopped himself from sighing. He'd wanted to hold it so that it couldn't go into the woods and discover the lady.

'A good hunting dog like that would cost twenty deniers,' said the Dane.

'Bring him here and let me examine him,' said Leshii.

'Saurr, get here,' said the little one with the spiteful face. Leshii winced at the name. It meant 'Shit'. 'Saurr, do I have to beat your arse? Get here right now.' But the dog was gone, snuffling around in the trees. Leshii remained calm and concentrated on how he would explain if Aelis was discovered. The dog gave a bark and then there was the sound of it tugging at something, and of something else tearing. It barked again and again in a regular, high note. The noise meant one thing to the Norsemen. It had found something.

They went diving into the trees, spears held high as if to stab a boar.

'Honoured Danes,' said Leshii, 'your dog has simply discovered my servant.'

The Danes came out of the wood, pulling Aelis with them. In the dark, with her cap and short hair, she really did look like a boy.

'I thought you said you had no one else with you.'

'No man. This is not a man, it is a slave.'

'You lied to us.'

'Not so. To us a slave is less than a dog. Would you count your dog as a man?'

The big Viking grunted and looked Aelis up and down.

'What's your name, kid?'

'He is a mute and a eunuch,' said Leshii, 'taken from Byzantium, or Miklagard as you call it, when Helgi the Prophet attacked that town.'

'Why's he skulking in the woods?'

'He stinks,' said Leshii, 'so he sleeps where his smell can't bother me or the mules.'

Fastarr laughed. 'Smells all right to me, but I've been fighting a siege for six months and probably couldn't smell a bear if it got into bed with me.'

'Bears have better taste than that, Fastarr,' said one of the warriors.

'You'd know, you married one.'

More laughter. Then Fastarr spoke again: 'Wait here,' he said to Leshii. 'In fact, Svan, can you stay with him and make sure he goes nowhere?'

Svan was a huge man with forearms as big as Leshii's thighs, two heads higher than the merchant with a great axe slung across his shoulder. He smiled pleasantly, thought Leshii.

'I'm glad to stay,' he said. 'I'll get dry by the fire and this merchant can tell me tales of the east.'

'You'll do well under Svan's protection,' said Fastarr, 'but you'll find his nice manners disappear quick enough in a scrap.'

Leshii gave a thin smile at the threat. He was a captive and knew it.

The men fanned out into the forest, calling to the lady, calling to the dog. Leshii heard their voices fading down the hillside.

He sat staring into the fire, making conversation with the hulk at his side and wondering how best to survive the night with his body, his goods and his grip over the lady intact. He needed to make this man his ally. Svan wasn't keen to talk about himself, so Leshii told him stories of the east, of the towns of Ladoga and Novgorod, where the Norsemen ruled over the native population, partly by strength of arms, partly by consent. The tribes had been unable to agree on how to govern themselves, so they had called in the Norsemen, the Varangians as they were known, and asked them to rule in their place. Prince Helgi, the Varangian ruler, was said to be descended from Odin himself and to have powers of prophecy and who knew what other magic.

'So how did you come by the protection of the Ravens?' asked Svan. 'You seem like a sociable fellow. Why are you consorting with cannibals and lunatics?'

Leshii, who missed very little when it came to human weakness, noted the little glance Svan took behind him as he spoke. He was scared of these Ravens, whoever they were.

'Sometimes one doesn't choose: one is chosen,' said Leshii.

'Well spoken,' said Svan. 'So they forced their company upon you?'

'They frightened me half to death.' If Svan was afraid, he thought, he would be afraid too. Similarity and agreement, he knew, were the keys to getting this man to like him and perhaps ultimately to survival.

'As they should,' said Svan. 'He's a hard bastard that Hugin and you have to respect him for that, whatever else he is, but his sister's as mad as the moon. What's her name, friend? Remind me.'

Svan, thought the merchant, wasn't as stupid as he looked. He'd detected some uncertainty in Leshii regarding the Ravens and wanted to probe further. Luckily the merchant had a healthy appetite for stories and was well travelled. Odin's ravens, he recalled were Hugin and ...

'Munin,' he said.

'Ah, that's it, though you couldn't have got much chat out of them.'

'Less than from the boy here.' Leshii glanced towards the lady.

'Does he always sit with his arms folded?'

'It is the habit of his people.'

'They'd be better keeping their hands on their swords, that way they wouldn't end up as slaves,' said Svan.

Leshii grinned and pointed at the berserker as if to say 'you're a wise one there!' and Svan looked well pleased with his response.

There was a stirring in the trees. Leshii thought of the wolf-man. He didn't know whether his return would be his salvation or damnation. Could Chakhlyk take on so many warriors? But it was just the dog, which had lost interest in the chase and returned to the spot where it had obtained its last meal.

'You are Danes?' said Leshii.

'So you call us, but we are Horda men, from the land to the north and west of the Danish kingdoms,' said Svan. 'We're mates from a raiding longship. There are twelve of us in all.'

'Isn't twelve a magic number for a berserker clan?'

'I believe so.'

'Are you berserkers?' Leshii was wary of berserkers and had found them a very unsettling presence whenever they had turned up in Ladoga. They went into battle crazy with mushrooms and herbs, impervious to wounds that would kill normal men. It was said that they didn't leave the fight in the fight. That is, they treated their whole lives as a fight. It was one thing, thought Leshii, to have a bad temper, quite another to cultivate one.

'We are known as the Hammer God's Berserks, which is another way of saying that we're not. Nowadays "berserker" is used for any fierce warrior, and in that way we are berserkers. In my grandfather's time it meant only the cult of Odin lot, real madmen. We're not those, though it doesn't hurt to let people think we are.'

'Who do you follow?'

'God or king?'

'Both.'

'We follow Sigfrid because he pays us for our service – he has offered a bounty on the lady. For a god, we follow many, but my favourite is Thor, god of thunder. A more straightforward god than your raven lord, Odin. No madness, no magic, no stringing people up to sacrifice, just "Do as I say or get a hammer in the head."'

'That's your philosophy?'

'Not at all. I use an axe, not a hammer. Ah, here comes Fastarr now.'

The warriors were back, sweating and dirty from their exertions.

'Have you found her?' said Leshii.

'She's gone,' said Fastarr. 'Here, crack open the wine. Tell your boy, merchant, to bring me wine.'

Leshii knew the lady would not know which pack contained the wine so he stood instead.

'Don't let the boy see which pack the wine's in, honoured Dane. Brother, your slaves must be trustworthy indeed that you allow them such knowledge. I'll serve you myself.'

Fastarr laughed. 'In Hordaland there are two types of slaves. The first are the trustworthy ones. They can be allowed to know the whereabouts of valuable things.'

'And the second?'

'The dead ones,' said Fastarr.

The men burst out laughing and Leshii gave a deep smile. In the east it was said that laughter was a family house – you needed an invitation to get in. Laughing too enthusiastically would have been an intimacy too far, he thought. Better share the joke quietly and not cause resentment.

'If we killed all the bad slaves in the east we'd have none left,' he said.

He made a big show of making Aelis turn her back to him as he opened the pack with the worst wine in it. He took out two bottles and came back to the fire with them. He sat and took out the wood stoppers and removed the oily hemp padding that had kept them in place.

'Here, friends,' he said, 'drink your fill.'

'Two bottles is not our fill, merchant,' said the rat-faced berserker, taking one from him and swigging it back.

'You must leave me something for the king,' said Leshii. A

silence fell and he felt the mood darken. Fastarr looked at the merchant.

'You're a friend of our lord?' he said.

'A second father,' said Leshii.

'Very good. I think it's the least we could do to take you to him.'

'I have to wait here for my protector,' said Leshii.

'That Raven'll be back in camp soon enough, I should think, provided he hasn't found anyone dead to eat,' said Fastarr. 'Come on, Hastein. Svan, grab hold of those mules and packs and let's get back down to the camp. I want to be the man who brings such a dear friend to the king's sight.'

'I must wait here,' said Leshii.

But it was no good. Fastarr took his arm, pulled him to his feet and led him down the hill while the other men loaded up his mules. He'd be lucky, he knew, to ever see those packs again.

'I have gifts for the king in there. Don't open them,' said Leshii.

'We won't,' said Fastarr, 'until you've met him.'

Leshii looked back towards Aelis.

'Well don't just stand there, you idiot boy,' he said. 'Roll up my carpet and make sure it's stowed fast. If it hits the mud again you'll follow it.' Aelis stood looking at him in incomprehension and Leshii realised he had spoken in Norse. Still, it would benefit the girl's disguise if he treated her badly.

'I said get the carpet!' he screamed at her. He grabbed the edge of the carpet, mimed rolling it up and pointed at the mule. Aelis still hadn't understood a word he said.

'That is a bad slave who makes twice the work for his master!' said the rat-faced one.

'Are you sure it's the boy who's the slave here, merchant?' laughed Svan.

'Put the carpet on the mule,' said Leshii in a low voice to Aelis. Then, more loudly and in Norse, 'I ought to beat you, but bruises would make you even more useless. Do it, put the carpet on the mule.'

Aelis hurried to roll the carpet and Leshii mocked her, miming her inexpert actions, pulling faces at her. The Norsemen thought this high entertainment but Leshii had achieved what he wanted. By placing the lady beneath their contempt he had made her true nature invisible to them. They were looking at a simple boy, they thought, and had enjoyed Leshii's ridicule. He had placed the idea of a stupid slave in their minds and made it difficult for them to see anything that didn't fit that conception. It was a kind of everyday magic, but one he normally used in reverse, to make someone see the rarity and value of commodities that were neither rare nor valuable.

Leshii turned to Fastarr. 'I look forward to your hospitality.'

The Dane smiled at him. 'And we to yours,' he said, gesturing down to the twinkling lights of the Norse camp that lay in the deep dark of the valley like a mirror to the stars.

7   An Awakening

Aelis felt sure she would not survive until the dawn. Everything was going badly for her, right down to the smallest detail. The mules refused to move, the packs slipped on their backs, she stumbled and fell on the slippery mud of the slope into the camp, her toes were numb with cold and she feared discovery at any second.

All that she could have borne. She had been raised on a country estate and spent many nights roaming the forests near her home, sleeping out with her friends under the stars, drinking from streams and going hunting with the daughters of the count. Her aunt had taught her how to use a bow and said that Aelis might not be good but was certainly lucky when it came to shooting deer. She held the bow wrong, nocked the arrow wrong, drew it wrong, moved when she shot and, like as not, hit what she was aiming at. So she was used to the discomforts of the outdoors. She was unused, however, to the ridicule.

Her fear brought on clumsiness, and every time she slipped or a mule wouldn't move, Leshii led the chorus of derision. The little Norseman with the mean mouth had been particularly cruel, walking behind her and tripping her with his spear, laughing all the time. No one had ever treated her like that and she found it very hard to bear. Tears started to come down her face but that only made the men mock her more. In the end Leshii had come to her rescue, telling the spiteful little elf who was tormenting her that if his slave came to damage, he would ask for compensation from the prince.

The camp was a vision of hell. Hard faces, scarred and filthy, loomed from the firelight; women and men copulated like animals in the open air while, not three paces away, someone else sat eating from a bowl or sharpened an axe. This army had been ravaging the countryside for years and was more like a travelling town. The children were goblins, pulling at the packs, jabbering at her in their strange language, touching her even. The Vikings had taken over many of the mean houses, though their numbers were too great for all of them to be accommodated that way. So there were tents and shelters built from branches and foliage, but many were content to sleep huddled together beneath blankets and furs in the open air. *What do they do if it rains?* thought Aelis. There were so many of them, so many spears stuck upright in the mud, so many shields and axes. It really seemed as if this camp stretched as far as the night itself.

The mules pressed on, the warriors swatting away the children, calling to friends. They approached the river and Fastarr talked to a man on the bank. He gestured them towards a small beached longship. It was lying at an angle and the man put a plank up to its side.

The Viking turned from his negotiation and spoke directly to her but she didn't understand what he said.

'Come on,' said Leshii. 'Get the mules on the boat.'

Aelis wanted to speak, to tell the merchant that would be impossible. She loved horses and had grown up around enough mules to know they only worked for people they trusted. Mules were more intelligent than horses and needed to be coaxed rather than bullied. The animals were not going to walk up a plank onto a precarious boat for her.

She felt an intense shame building within her, an anger and a deep resentment. Her legs hurt and she had bruises down her back where she had been prodded. That feeling she had had since she was a girl returned, the ability to sense people's emotions, to hear their character almost as a musical note, to see it as a colour. When she was a small girl and given to sentimental descriptions she had told her nurse that she could hear the 'strings of the heart-harp'. The sickly sweet description made her blush now that she was a grown woman. But it really did feel like that, and the feeling was intensifying.

The Norsemen were a mixture: toughness, cruelty, generosity, bravery, humour; she experienced their minds as a thin band of sound, bright colours, a feeling both hard and cold. The merchant was more complex. When she thought of him she had a taste in her mouth sweet like honeyed almonds, but underneath was something else bitter and astringent: cloves and smoke, vinegar and tar.

One of the Vikings was screamng at her in Norse, gesturing to the mules and then to the boat. It was the little one again, the nasty imp with his pinched face and thin, strong limbs. Aelis understood nothing of what he said, but his presence was dull and heavy, baleful and narrow. He kicked her and her legs went from under her. She hit the ground hard, driving the wind from herself and banging her head. He was screaming at her, gesturing for her to get up with one hand and prodding her with the butt of his spear with the other. His voice was shrill and high like a pipe blown by a child, almost hysterical.

Fastarr grabbed him by the shoulder and spoke to Leshii: 'I am sorry for my kinsman, merchant; he has been unlucky in battle these two years.' His voice was softer, like a flute, she thought. What was happening to her? Her senses were jumbled by the fall but something else was taking over and the world was not as it had been. All her sensitivities seemed amplified, people and personalities understandable to her in new and confusing ways. It was as if the uncommon stress had unlocked something in her.

'Wounded?' Again Leshii spoke in Norse. She heard the word as two thudding syllables, like the beat of a drum and, though its exact meaning was obscure to her, she understood well enough what was meant. It was as if all the feelings and emotions of those around her were an open book. She understood what the Norsemen were saying but in a way that went beyond the comprehension of a straightforward translation.

'No kills,' said Fastarr. 'A case of bad luck, not cowardice as his enemies maintain.'

'What use is a slave that will not work?' It was the shrill pipe again.

'About the same as a warrior who does not kill,' said Fastarr. 'Now let the boy put the mules on the boat, Saerda, and try picking your next fight with a Frankish man-at-arms, not a mute idiot.'

Though the words were not quite clear to Aelis, she understood that the Viking with the hammer shield was defending her and that he was mocking the thin little one, who he felt obliged to have in his company out of some debt of duty. Aelis realised that Saerda – she recognised the word as a name – was in as much danger as she was from his fellows and, more than that, he knew it.

She stood up and the night seemed to teem about her, the thoughts and emotions of the people in the camp buzzing like insects over a swamp. An image came to her. She saw herself on a tall mountaintop overlooking a vast valley. Something was living inside her – it seemed to glow and pulse. It was one of many things, a note, a vibration, that she carried in her bones. She could not name it but she envisaged it as a shape, like a shallow Roman one thousand, M, shining in the darkness of her mind. It had a living lustre to it, deep like the flow of light on a bay mare's back. She smelled horse too, and the shape seemed to steam and stamp and sweat. It was like a living thing, something that expressed itself through her and that she, in living, expressed. She tried to give the shape a name in her mind but the only word that came to her was 'horse'. The shape, she knew, was associated with horses – more than that, it was linked in a fundamental way to the creatures.

'Get the mules on the boat.' It was Leshii who spoke. She looked at the animal nearest her. As she moved towards it, it turned away, but she persisted and put her hands up to its head. She envisaged that glowing, rippling shape floating before her and the sound of its breathing emanating from her. She could feel the mule's fear and mistrust, but the shape gave her a calmness that seemed to pass to the animal. The mule became quiet and nuzzled into her hand. Then she led it up the plank into the boat.

When all the animals were on board, the warriors climbed in, along with Leshii, and they pushed off for the far shore. The Vikings all sat down but there was no space for her, so she leaned her backside on the rail. She had never felt so strange in her life. It was as if her mind was no longer her own but had things growing in it, living there, shapes like the horse symbol that danced and spun at the very edge of her sight. She had sensed them before, she thought, when ill with scarlatina as a child. It was as if extraordinary fear and uncertainty called them forth, that the raw panic she felt under the eyes of the berserks had shut down her conscious mind and allowed them to appear.

She trembled. What was happening to her? It was as if the strangeness she had always had was now more present in her mind than her everyday self, as if she had been fundamentally wrong in her understanding of herself. She had been a count's daughter, a girl in a meadow, a child to be married for the benefit of her family, a wild thing under the stars. Now it seemed that the things inside her, the musical senses, her sensitivity to attitudes and moods, had grown to be giants, shadowing all that she had formerly been. How had she controlled the mules? Witchcraft? Was it possible to be a witch and not know it?

She looked up at the bridge that ran from the city to the opposite shore. They were giving it a wide berth, making sure they were out of range of bowmen. Even now its tower was being repaired and fortified, and men swarmed over it. She wanted to cry out or to plunge into the water and swim for it, but she knew the Vikings would spear her before she got ten strokes from the boat.

The city was still smouldering and she watched the smoke rising up against the moon like a fracture in the sky. Something dropped from the tower onto the bridge – the figure of a man. She looked around her. No one else on the boat had noticed it, and it seemed no one on the tower had seen it either. She had only glimpsed an instant of movement but she knew what it was. She felt something emanating from the figure like a chill across the water – a carnivorous presence, something sharp-minded and aggressive, with glittering little eyes. She could not put it into words, but the presence manifested itself in her mind like the sound of the sky cracking. It was a raven's cry

The merchant came and sat next to her and said softly in Latin, 'I am sorry for my disrespect. It is for your safety.'

She felt the tears in her eyes again.

'Don't worry; it will be all right,' he said.

She gave him a questioning look.

He smiled and nodded to the Norsemen, some of whom – unbelievably – had gone to sleep virtually as soon as the boat had pushed off. 'All these bastards will have their heads on your brother's gates one day, you'll see.' He put his hand on her back. 'Rest assured, I will help you. Your interests are my first concern.'

Aelis, who could hear emotions like music and see them like colours, looked at him and mouthed the word: 'Liar.'

8   A Meeting

The monk said nothing, though he was sure that the Norseman was about to break his ribs. He was being carried over the shoulder of what he could tell was a huge man who was running hard. The Viking's shoulder hammered into the confessor, driving the air from him, but the monk would not give in to complaint. The confessor sensed when they were outside the city – the temperature dropped when they were through the gate, the heat of the burning buildings shielded by the walls.

'Coming through, coming through!' shouted the man.

Jehan could hear other footsteps behind him, the warriors who had been in the church, he guessed. The man carrying him had been called Fatty by the others, but he didn't seem slow or to have any difficulty sustaining a good pace, despite his burden, although he panted heavily and cursed as he ran.

'How are we going to get him over this rampart?'

Jehan knew the bridge had been blockaded at both ends to deny the raiders access. The Franks shouted insults at them as they ran through their ranks but no one lifted a weapon against them. They honoured Eudes' command.

'Shove him over. Heave him up.'

The rampart was not a wall, just a collection of broken carts, rubbish and rubble.

The confessor felt himself hurled up into the air, to land with a thump. It was agonising but he had no time to recover. Rough hands were on him again and he was swung up further, coming down hard on the rubble again with a bigger crash. He cried out, his twisted and useless joints forced into movement by the repeated battering.

'Throw him down. I'll catch him.'

'No!' The word escaped Jehan's lips, but he was falling to

land with a fearful jolt in someone's arms. He thought he would pass out with the pain but his will kept him conscious.

'Safe!' said a voice.

'Thank Thor for that!'

The confessor felt himself simply dropped to the ground. He tried not to groan but couldn't restrain himself.

'Shut up, you. You're lucky I didn't chuck you over at one go.'

'Where to now?'

'Drag this god or whatever he is up to Sigfrid and see what reward he offers for him. He's a giver of rings, that king, and I don't think we'll be disappointed.'

'Best wait for the others, though, so we all get something.'

'Come on, let's get into the main camp. That work's given me a thirst.'

Jehan gagged with the pain and cursed his body for its weakness. He was ready for whatever fate the Norsemen planned for him but he was behaving like a quivering child.

He was picked up again, this time between two of them, grabbing an arm each. He could almost hear his joints squealing as they lifted him, but he was master of himself again and made no complaint. He sensed that he was carried up a hill, and gradually he came into noise – rough singing, the crackling of fires, the braying of animals, conversation and shouts.

He was dumped on the ground once more. He heard the Norsemen making a fire, collecting pots, pissing and laughing. One of the berserkers said he was going in search of a 'proper' healer to tend his arm. Again, Jehan thanked God for his trials. Other men, more able men, had the illusion of taking a hand in their fate. He could have run, if his legs would have carried him, fought, if his arms had held a weapon. The outcome would have been the same – whatever God willed. In his condition there was no lying to himself or misreading his place in the cosmos. He was a cork bobbing on the tides of God's mind, as all men were. God had just granted him the affliction that let him see it more clearly.

Then there were voices nearby.

'Ofaeti, why are you so fat?'

'Because every time I fuck your wife she gives me a hazel-nut.'

'That's as good as a password!'

'It's good to see you alive, my friend!'

There was laughter, backslapping and questions about what had happened to who; who had died and who lived.

'We walked in there with twelve of us and came out with twelve. We should tell the rest of this army to go home; we can take this city ourselves, I reckon.'

'Did you get the girl?'

'Oh yes, I just didn't mention it.'

'That's a no, then.'

'It's a no.'

'But we did get this kind merchant and his stack of wine. Merchant, introduce yourself.'

'Leshii, servant of your kinsman Helgi the Prophet, friend to King Sigfrid and to all who serve him.'

'Very nice, where's the wine?'

'Boy, a couple of bottles for our friends,' said Leshii with a note of forced jollity in his voice. 'I will take the advice of these fine warriors and allow you to see where I keep them but know that, should any go missing I will give you the best justice – the Viking kind!'

'Just two? Seems a bit skinny. Boy, get more.' That was a Norseman.

'He doesn't understand your tongue, friend.' The exotic voice again. An easterner, Jehan thought.

'Then translate.'

'Lady, the bag on the rear mule contains the best wine for these fellows. Take out a skin of that, would you?'

Had Jehan heard right? 'Lady'? The merchant hadn't said *domina*, which even non-Latin speakers would recognise. He'd said *era*, which was mildly less respectful but probably wouldn't be known to the Norsemen. So there was a woman there, a disguised woman.

The merchant spoke in Norse: 'Serve the wine, boy; don't stand there staring at the monk. Haven't you ever seen a god before? You'll be seeing another soon enough if you don't hurry up.' More laughter. Then the exotic voice in Latin: 'Take heart, lady. This is the easiest way to make them see what we want them to see.'

'The lad's crying again!'

'The monk's a cripple, boy, like you can see on any roadside. By Thor's bulging bollocks they don't breed 'em very tough in Miklagard, do they? Maybe we should try our luck there. If they don't like deformity we could just show 'em Ofaeti's bollocks and they'd open the gates to us. That's more like it, get another. Let's drink this lot dry and think about seeing the king later. We deserve a little reward after our labours, don't we, lads?'

It couldn't be her, could it?

'Give me that.' It was a cold, hard Norse voice, close by.

Under his breath, more felt than spoken, he said the word: '*Domina.*'

The confessor felt fingers brush his face, a gesture of tenderness. He had the strangest sensation, the only way he could have described it was to say that it felt like her, but he had never touched her, nor any woman that he could remember. Still, the touch seemed to carry her signature, the note of her, like a distinctive perfume, almost. The pain and the indignities had not daunted him. This did. No one had touched him but to lift or bathe him since he had been seven years old. A chill went through him, a delicious cold tingle from his forehead to his knees. He had warned people about the pleasures of the flesh since he had been old enough to speak in church but to him such pleasures had been only dry things, spectres raised from the Bible by the readings of his brother monks. He had despised them without knowing them. One touch, though, and he had understood. Who had done that? Was it her? For the first time in years he hated his blindness. He needed to see, to know.

The men settled down to drinking and the confessor felt the cold of night deepen.

He calmed himself by focusing on preparing to face Sigfrid. He would not beg or bargain for his life, he was determined. The monk knew that the longer he stayed in the camp, the more likely the Emperor Charles was to come and rescue him. A living saint could not be allowed in the hands of heathens. Jehan made himself forget the strange feelings that the touch had raised in him and tried to reason. What would he do if he was Sigfrid? The Viking was no fool and he must see that holding the monk was dangerous for him. Would he ransom him? Jehan doubted it. Why bother? The city would fall soon enough and then he'd have whatever was in it for free. No, while he lived, the confessor realised he was only a unifying force for Sigfrid's enemies. The Viking king would kill him, he felt sure.

He turned his mind to prayer but could only think of the touch that had set his skin singing. Jehan was in some ways a humorous man, and it did strike him as ironic that he had discovered the sin of carnal pleasure just in time for it to admit him to hell. He made himself pray: 'Heart of Jesus, once in agony, receive my sinner's soul.' In the morning, thought Jehan, he would see Christ's face and, he hoped, be taken into his peace. He knew his fate among the Normans was God's way of chastising him for his pride. It was Lucifer's sin, and Jehan's old weakness, to think yourself better than others. He had let them call him a saint, a living saint. Well saints suffered and died, so God had granted that he would do the same. The Norsemen had crushed three churchmen at Reims with great stones. He put it from his mind. He was going on a journey. The conveyance did not matter.

There was the sound of shouting and the men all around him got to their feet.

'Who are you?'

'King's man Arnulf. Sigfrid wants to see you straight away. You have something of his.'

'That will be me,' said the eastern voice.

'The Christian holy man, the flesh eater, he wants him.'

Perhaps, thought Jehan, he would be seeing the face of Jesus sooner than he had anticipated.

9 Alone

Confessor Jehan had been taken. In the rush of her flight and the fear of her capture Aelis had forgotten he had been at her side when the Norsemen attacked. And her brother, what of him? Eudes was a peerless warrior, a prodigy at arms according to his tutors. It had never even occurred to her that he could be hurt, let alone killed. But the Norsemen had walked away with the confessor. Eudes would never have allowed that while he had breath in his body. She went cold. Did her brother still live?

She had touched the confessor on impulse, to reassure him, or rather just to let him know he was not alone. She could imagine what he would say to that. 'I am never alone; I am with God.' And yet it had felt right to reach out to him.

Now her mind began to clear and she was terrified. Inside the church she had been unable to bring home to the confessor just how real her dreams had been. And then the wolf had appeared, a wolfman rather, who had given his life for her. The simmering sense of danger she had in her dreams of the wolf now spilled over into her waking life. What of that thing that had come from within her to speak to the mules – what was that? She tried to force her attention back to the present. The immediate danger from the Norsemen should be her concern, she thought, not the threat of devils.

The Norsemen were all very drunk and stumbled to find their weapons. She couldn't tell what they were saying but they seemed worried. She kept away from the imp, fearing him. The others had become louder and more friendly with the drink; he had become withdrawn, more sullen, sitting at the side of the fire with a weak smile of contempt for his guffawing companions.

They all went down a slight slope to the biggest house in the area. It was a mean dwelling, as all those outside the city walls were, timber-framed with unfinished mud for its walls. It had been decorated in a hideous pastiche of the Roman style, its steep pitched roof timbered but daubed in painted checks to try to give the impression of tiles, leaving it more unpleasant-looking than if it had been built as a simple peasant's dwelling in unadorned wood. Scraps of vellum hung at the windows. Aelis guessed the Norsemen had cut them through when they moved in, unused to anything to keep the draught out. It was a small thing, a very small thing, but it seemed to bring home their barbarity to her. How could the Franks lose to such a rabble? Because, as her brother said, the emperor was fat and lazy and preferred to fritter away his people's fortune in bribes to the Normans rather than face them in the field as a man. Eudes himself had shown they could be beaten, and more cheaply than they could be bought, but Charles insisted on paying them to go away. Her brother had maintained that payments in gold guaranteed the Norsemen would come back. Payments in steel meant they would not.

They arrived at the house and she stopped the mules. Warriors were all around, some standing in full armour, some sitting down playing at dice, eating or sleeping. Then she remembered one of the packs contained her hair. What would the king make of that if he saw it? The Norseman called Fastarr put up his hand and addressed the warriors. She couldn't understand what he said but Leshii, seeing her fear, whispered a translation.

'This is the king, boys. Remember, for once, that I'm the one you elected speaker so let me do the talking. It's me he struck the deal with and me he'll want to hear from. I don't want one word out of any of you, is that understood?'

'What if he questions us directly about what went on?'

'Say you just followed me. Any more questions, just say you don't know and that I had a better view of it than you.'

'What if he asks me about my cock?' said Ofaeti, scratching

himself. Leshii translated, seeming to find any mention of sex or the seats of corruption of the body vastly amusing.

'Well, I could definitely get a better view of that than you. You can't have seen it these fifteen years, you fat bastard.'

There was laughter but Fastarr quietened it.

'Seriously, no jokes. Don't speak unless you're spoken to. Let's get in and out of here as quick as we can. Get the monk.'

Aelis stood and watched as Confessor Jehan was dragged inside and Leshii busied himself with the mules. The Norseman had forgotten about him, too worried by the king's summons and he wasn't about to remind them. She felt cold and in her mind heard that voice again, the crack of a raven's call.

She looked down the slope towards the river, towards the formidable but battered tower on the bridge. She'd be shot by her own people before she even got within shouting range if she tried to swim for it. The only way was north, into Neustria, much of which was under Norman control. She would have to bide her time to escape; besides, it was her Christian duty to do her best to protect the saint.

She was too much in demand, she thought. Wolfmen, ravens, the Danes, all seemed to want her. For the moment it was safer to be a mute idiot boy.

She touched the leading mule's ears and it nuzzled into her. At least, she thought, she had won an ally there.

10 Bargains and Threats

Jehan smelled roast meat and a fire scented with pine needles. Fresh reeds had been scattered on the floor. There was a hum of conversation in the house which stopped as he was brought in.

'Lord Sigfrid,' said Fastarr, 'we have captured this man, one of their gods, and we bring him before you to await your pleasure.'

'Did you get the girl?'

'No, sir.'

'Why not?'

'She escaped us in the darkness of the south bank.'

'So why are you not there? It will soon be light.'

'We had lost her, sir, and this man is such a valuable commodity we thought you would want him straight away.'

'Or did you get bored, want to return to your drink and your women, and thought you might throw me a scrap to keep me sweet?'

No one said anything and Jehan heard the king snort. There was a noise like metal on wood. A cup or a bowl on a table? A sword?

'Did the Raven get her?'

'Not as far I know, sir. He shot another shapeshifter but didn't get her, I think.'

'Doesn't like getting his feathers wet,' said Ofaeti.

Fastarr breathed out. The monk could sense he was irritated that his request for silence was going unheeded.

'Another shapeshifter?'

'Yes, sir. A wolfman.'

'Where did he come from? Could he be the wolf that was prophesied?'

'I don't know, sir. Anyway, he's dead.'

'Unlikely to be that wolf then. Has anyone seen the Raven since?'

'I expect he'll be back in the woods with his sister, provided she hasn't died.'

'In which case he'll be cooking her,' said Ofaeti.

'Shut up, Ofaeti,' said Fastarr.

The king gave a dry laugh. 'You don't fancy cutting the crow's throat, do you, Fastarr?'

'I would have done it in the city if he didn't move so quick, sir.'

'Really? I wasn't being serious. He's useful to me and an ally. We just have a disagreement on the correct path forward, that's all.'

'Above my head all that, my lord.'

'Good.'

The confessor heard footsteps approaching. Sigfrid's voice said, 'This is the god?'

'Yes, sir.'

'The crippled saint. That's not a god, Fastarr; you should get your terminology right. But you act for God, don't you, priest?'

Jehan said nothing.

'You're renowned, do you know that? Your men-at-arms shout your name as they pour fire and stones down on my ships. Is he a mute? Is his tongue as twisted as his body? Does he speak our language?'

'He can talk, I reckon,' said Ofaeti. 'He said something in their temple.'

'What did he say?'

'He wasn't a god.'

'Well, we're agreed on something then. How did you come by him, Fastarr?'

'He was with the girl in the temple.'

'So you had her and you let her go?'

'The wolfman got her out, sir. He's a sorcerer; there was

nothing I could do. I broke a good sword hitting him with it and the lads here snapped a few spears on his hide.'

Jehan doubted that. The Norsemen hadn't mentioned it, and something so remarkable would have been bound to excite comment.

'And yet the Raven did for him.'

'Enchanted arrows, sir. They can only be harmed by magic, and the Raven is a well-known magician.'

'I wonder. So what happened to the girl?'

'She jumped out of a window on the south bank. Ran up into the woods, and that's where we lost her.'

Jehan heard someone breathe out and pace the floor.

'The reason I allow you Horda in my camp at all is that you are supposed to be great heroes. Mighty men! And yet a girl loses you in the dark.'

There was much shuffling of feet.

'Where would this girl have gone, priest? Is there anywhere on the south bank she would have run to?'

The confessor remained silent.

'We're not the only ones looking for her, you know. If I take her then she'll live. If others get hold of her she'll need all your god's help and more. '

He felt breath on his face. The man had bent to address him.

'Our Raven wants her, and he is not a tender man. She'll be eaten by him, most likely alive. If you want her to avoid that fate, help us find her.'

For the first time Jehan spoke: 'Why do you want her?'

'So he does talk. Answer my question: where is she?'

'I did not know she had been taken. My knowledge of the back country is poor. As you see by my condition, I am not used to wandering the fields.'

The voice came closer to his ear.

'You don't seem scared, monk.'

Jehan said nothing again.

'You're a prophet, aren't you?' said the king.

Silence.

'Come on. I know it. Don't think your Eudes is the only one with spies. We're not quite as backward as you think, you know. You're a prophet, I've heard it said.'

Jehan could smell something underneath the pine needles, underneath the reeds and the roasting meat. What was it? The same smell he'd experienced in Paris. Dead flesh. Rot. Human putrefaction.

'Let's do this the easy way. I want you to work for me. You tell me what you need and I'll give you what you want. What do you want?'

Jehan knew only one response to such a question. 'Your soul for God.'

'No. I am a king and Odin's man – it is well known. But let me make you comfortable. Would you like wine? Food?'

'Yes. But I cannot feed myself.'

'Well, I'm not going to feed you. I draw the line at touching cripples.'

'Use the boy.' It was Ofaeti's voice.

'Silence, fat bellows,' said Fastarr.

'What boy?'

'A merchant outside has a boy slave, a mute and an idiot. He's from Miklagard and simple anyway, so it's not going to matter if he catches anything off the cripple.'

'Mute I like,' said Sigfrid. 'Send him in. You, berserkers, get out of here. And the rest of you. Go. I'll speak with the monk alone.'

'Out!' It was Fastarr's voice. Jehan heard the men leave.

It was quiet for a moment and the confessor listened to the fire crackling, the sound of the king pacing the reeds. There was that smell again. Death.

The confessor heard footsteps.

'Feed this monk. Meat and wine.'

Silence.

'What's wrong with you, boy? Feed the monk.'

'He doesn't speak your language.'

'Do you speak his language?'

'Yes.'

'Speak to him then.'

'You are to feed me and give me drink. If it is you, lady, then spill a little wine as you do,' the monk said in Greek, which he knew the lady spoke and was almost certain Sigfrid did not.

Jehan heard a plate lifted, the glug of wine into a cup. When the cup was pressed to his lips, it was too high and the wine spilled down his front.

'Careful, lad. That stuff's too hard to come by to waste,' said Sigfrid.

The confessor was fed bread and meat in quantity. He hadn't realised how hungry he was until he started to eat.

'Have faith, lady,' said Jehan. 'We will prevail here.'

Again, that hand on his shoulder, the cold tingle that shivered through his body.

'Let me tell you my problem, priest.' It was Sigfrid's voice. 'Your lot on the walls are holding out rather longer than I had anticipated. It's not easy to keep my army together. Many of them will go home if we don't break in soon, or even offer themselves to my enemies. There are enough warlords here who are only loyal as long as I keep the plunder rolling in. Do you understand?'

'Yes.'

'Now, my people are a superstitious lot. Me, I'd convert to your religion tomorrow and take advantage of all the alliances and marriage possibilities that would bring. Your god talks of peace but he's mighty in war – we saw in our grandfathers' time the power of the old King Charles. So I like your god: he makes his kings rich and powerful.'

'Christ doesn't want men who come to him for such reasons.'

'I didn't ask him what he wanted, did I? It was more me telling him what he was going to have. Anyway, there is a prophecy. Our seers have seen it, the thing that pursued your lady has seen it, half the holy idiots of the north have seen it. Our god, Odin, will come to earth in the form of a man.'

'That is a lie.'

'Maybe. Maybe not. Doesn't matter. The people, the vast majority of the northern men, will follow the one who they believe to be this god on earth. If this god happens to be me, then they will follow me.'

'So why do you not claim to be him? If you believe it all to be no more than a lie, then why not make it a useful lie?'

'I do claim to be him. And I didn't say I thought it a lie. However, the prophecy is widely known and it comes with certain conditions. "How ye shall know him" – you know the form. The person, or the thing, that will identify the king of gods in earthly shape is our friend Hugin, known as Hrafn, he who staged a single-handed assault on your city not five hours ago, obliging a good number of my men to follow him to prevent him performing the darker aspects of his desires. He is of the cult of Odin the hanged, the mad, the wise, deep in magic, lord of poetry, blah blah blah. He himself is said to be the incarnation of one of the mad god's ravens, his intelligencers, who spy on all the world for the god and return to whisper their news in his ear. So much bunk you may think but no more ludicrous than what you're peddling. What's a living saint if not a bit of god on earth, eh? Anyway, he needs to give the nod to Odin made flesh, announce him and proclaim him.'

'Why don't you just make him do that for you?'

'You can't make that thing do anything. Believe me, if I put him to torture it will be sweet rest compared to what he's put himself through. I would love to but it isn't practical. Also, the people wouldn't stand for it.'

Jehan felt the wine cup raised to his lips again. Aelis, he was sure it was her, was trembling.

'So I'm left with fulfilling the prophecy. Which is where it gets interesting. Our people believe that, on the final day of the gods, Odin will fight a creature called the Fenris Wolf.

That creature will kill the god. The appearance of this wolf here in middle earth will indicate who Odin is. It will come to kill him.'

'So you prove yourself king of kings by dying?'

'Just as your Christ did, eh?'

'That is sacrilege.'

'Calm yourself. The way I see it is this. If we can fulfil this prophecy, get this wolf to turn up, then I can rewrite destiny.'

'How?'

'I'll kill it. I'm good at killing things, it's been my only profession. That way we make our own myths. I will be Odin in triumph. If it kills me, I have a hero's death and renown down the ages. I really don't see how I can lose.'

'And if it doesn't appear?'

'It will. If we can get hold of your lady.'

'What has she got to do with this?'

'Our Raven has a sister. She is a prophet of a sort and she has identified your lady as the key to the appearance of the wolf. Odin has come to earth before, fought the wolf before, and in some way this girl, who has lived before, was caught up in all that. Where she goes, the wolf will follow. That's why we want her.'

Jehan swallowed. He thought of what Aelis had told him in the church. It was becoming clear to him what had happened now. She had heard the rumours of what the Norsemen intended for her and it had given her nightmares. As it would anyone.

'And why does the heathen sorcerer try to kill her?'

'He doesn't agree that I'm Odin. He thinks the wolf has not come yet. If he can kill this girl before the wolf catches her scent, so to speak, then he can weaken it or even avoid his master's death. It's like your seers who read the future in the night sky. Could they shape the future if they could reach to the heavens and snuff out a star? The Raven believes that is possible and your lady is the star he wants to snuff out.'

'You don't think that is necessary?'

'I believe the god – me – can cheat his destiny too. We just want to go about it in different ways. I want the girl to live, to snare this wolf. Then I beat it in combat, as I've beaten everything that has stood before me. He wants her to die sooner. It's a difference of theological opinion.'

'This is poisonous nonsense,' said the confessor.

'Maybe and maybe not,' said Sigfrid. 'I have seen enough of prophecy to know that it can be true. Why not then the gods? I am supposed to be of the line of Odin. Maybe I'm the god; maybe I'm not. All I know is that if I can get this wolf to turn up and then kill it, our friend Raven will declare me a god.'

'There is one god, one almighty power, Jesus, who is Christ, risen and glorious.'

'Well,' said Sigfrid, 'why don't we put that to the test? You prophesy where the girl is and I'll convert to your god. I'll have to do it on the quiet of course, but I'll convert openly once all the armies and the warlords have rallied to me and sworn allegiance. Really, I will.'

'Prophecy is a gift from God: he will not send it under such circumstances.'

'He must.'

'I will not do this thing. Use your heathen Raven woman if you must, for all the good it will do you.'

'I'm afraid she's not really up to that at the moment. The methods for obtaining prophecy are rather' – Jehan heard the king tap on something in thought – 'draining, I think it fair to say.'

'Do not look to Christ for your answers. He has only one answer for the likes of you, and it is eternal damnation.'

'You refuse me help at your peril.'

'I am not afraid of death.'

'Well good, because I think you're about to meet him.'

The smell of putrefaction became overpowering and Sigfrid heard the lady draw in breath. There was a light step upon the reeds.

'Saint,' said Sigfrid, 'this is the Raven Hugin. He has already half killed his sister pulling prophecies from her; he can quite easily do the same to you.'

11 Hrafn

The thing's eyes seemed to bore straight through Aelis, the same glittering black gems that had looked at her in the attic. She felt herself trembling and backed into the shadows. Had it recognised her? It looked down at the priest. Perhaps it hadn't.

It came forward into the candlelight and she could see it properly. It was bone-thin and wrapped in a cloak of black feathers, its black hair stuck into a shock with an oily tar, feathers within it sweeping up into a sort of black crown. Its face, now she could see it more clearly, was a terrible mess of scars, deep but tiny wounds, some festering and swollen, some healed and some still seeping blood. The creature reeked of corpses.

Aelis watched as it approached. The monk flinched as it bent close to his ear and spoke in Latin. 'The prophet,' it said. 'Are you Jehan, who they call Confessor?'

'I will have no dealings with devils.'

'I am not a devil. You will work for us, prophet. If you have the gift I can show you how.'

'How do you speak our tongue, monster?' said the confessor.

Jehan felt himself shaking, as he often did when he was angry and cursed himself knowing that his enemies might mistake it for fear.

'I was raised as a monk, for a while.'

'So you turned your back on Christ.'

'At Saint-Maurice he found me—' the man clasped his fist, fingers up, '—and then at Saint-Maurice he threw me away.' He cast his hand down to the floor. 'Conversions can go both ways, Confessor.'

Jehan swallowed. He recognised the name of the monastery. Saint-Maurice was an Augustinian house to the east, in the mountains of Valais. It was one of the great centres of Christendom, known for its treasures and relics and the song of ages, the *laus perennis* – the monks had begun to sing the psalms nearly four hundred years before and, working in shifts, had never stopped since. How had this monster come out of such a place?

'How do you know me?'

'I have heard of you. I should fear you, I have been told.'

'Fear God,' said Jehan, 'for he reserves special torments for the likes of you.'

The creature smiled. 'And for you, it would seem.'

Aelis tried to place the thing's accent. Northern certainly, but not a Dane's. It was nearer to the merchant's.

'Can you make this monk find the girl?' said Sigfrid. Aelis didn't understand him but she guessed what he said from his urgency and his gestures.

The Raven nodded, though it replied in Latin. 'In a short time perhaps, perhaps not. Given longer, yes.'

The king became angry, waved his arm to indicate the whole camp and, Aelis could tell, asked the Raven to be as quick as possible.

'Then we will try. The method will be quick. It will kill him but we will have our revelation.' Again the Raven spoke in Latin. Aelis knew that by speaking in a tongue the king understood poorly the creature was in a weird way expressing its superiority, its power even, over the king. And he was threatening the monk.

The king said something in Norse.

'He thinks you are a risk to him alive, Confessor. Doesn't he know they will come after your bones, your relics? Should I grind them to dust?'

'No one will seek me,' said the confessor.

'Not so. Even dead you are a rallying point, but let's not run ahead of ourselves.'

'How long?' said Sigfrid.

There was another conversation in Norse. Aelis sensed the king didn't trust the Raven. The king raised his voice.

The Raven shrugged and bent to where the confessor sat on the floor. In the firelight the confessor's twisted body reminded Aelis of a melted candle stub, the long form bending over it like a shadow it had thrown.

'Will you work with us, Confessor? Will you use your abilities to help us? It will cost you little.' He spoke in Latin.

Silence gave the Raven its answer.

'Do you know how magic works?' said the creature.

The monk said nothing but Aelis felt a coldness coming from the Raven, a sense of high and desolate places and of something else she couldn't quite identify. She was tempted to say it was loneliness, though she couldn't imagine the creature having any tender feelings at all.

The Raven continued: 'I do. Through shock. Your thoughts are intertwined, like the weft on a loom. If there is magic in you it is a single thread obscured by many others, the illusions of the everyday, of hungers, lusts, the babble of your priests, the senses and smells of the world. Those illusions must be removed. Something that scars or revolts, or throws the thoughts into chaos is required. Something that cuts the duller threads and leaves the scarlet of the truer, magical self shining through. Your hermits do it in their isolation, so that the thoughts fall in on themselves to reveal the magical self beneath. Your Christ did it on his cross, calling down lightning and causing the dead to walk while those next to him only spluttered and died. Not everyone can achieve this, or, rather, exactly what we can achieve is different. Some people can prophesy. Some can see far in distance but not in time, put their mind into a raven's body and fly with it on the upper airs. Some can slow time and see everything at half its speed, become mighty warriors. Most can just scream.'

The thing walked around the confessor, looking at him as a man might inspect a market-day pig.

'Believe what lies you like.' The comparison of Jesus to a magician had incensed the monk and he was unable to stop himself speaking.

'Tell me, Confessor, when you first saw, when the visions first came to you, your body was struck as it is?'

'God blessed me twice that day.'

'Did the vision produce the affliction or did the affliction produce the vision? And when you see, the affliction gets worse, does it not? I ask my question again. Are the visions the cause or the symptom of your frailties?'

'It is all from God.'

'From the fates,' said the creature. 'Even the gods must follow the skein that is woven for them.'

'Then your Odin will die and be replaced by a kinder god, isn't that what your prophecies say?'

'We will defy the prophecy. In my time on this middle earth the dead god will rule. He will escape the teeth of the wolf and will live to start a battle that will consume the world and stock the halls of the dead with many heroes. I will see him king over all the world. What happens in eternal time I cannot influence. The wolf will take him eventually but not until I am drinking with the slain in Valhalla.'

The confessor, who was a good reader of men's voices, sensed something behind the Raven's words. There was the faintest tinge of deceit, like the quiver in a novice's voice when he asks to be allowed to go into town with a healer when really he is intending to meet some girl in the market square. Had Christ completely let this man go? The confessor could not believe it. He decided to test him on his faith.

'You control nothing while you worship idols.'

'Wrong,' said the creature. 'I control you. You will prophesy, monk. You will reveal the girl to us. She is the wolf hook, the thing that draws him on. Do you think the wolf gladdens when he thinks of his death in the final battle? No. Only she spurs him forward to his destiny. She is the fates' instrument. It has been foreseen.'

'I will do nothing for you.'

'You will, one way or another.'

Aelis felt cold. The grey light of the predawn was coming into the house, banishing the shadows of the fire. In a short time she would be visible to the thing again. She moved to the furthest corner of the room, like a new and timid slave hoping to escape notice.

Hugin stood up and turned to Sigfrid. There was a conversation in Norse between them and the Raven pointed north.

Sigfrid looked pale. The creature smiled and said to Jehan, 'The king is of a tender stomach for a warrior. But he must realise there are no easy ways to magic.' He gestured at his scarred and torn face. 'And I should know. Now, if you'll excuse me, Confessor, the people are calling for me. I have a sick child to cure.' He went out past the monk into the growing light.

12 A Matter of Will

The berserkers were sleeping at the feet of the mules, lying on Leshii's bags, when Aelis came outside.

Leshii had paid them to guard his goods. The merchant had vowed to himself to have the money back off them in some way before he left, particularly as their services hadn't been necessary beyond some initial scuffling. When the people of the camp discovered the wine had gone and there was no food on the mules, interest quickly waned. You couldn't eat or drink silk and the only trade anyone was interested in doing was for a square meal, so when Leshii showed them a length of yellow silk, they had gone back to what they had been doing before – starving, complaining and preparing their weapons.

Leshii was tired but he'd been unable to sleep. He felt old and cold in the morning mist. He'd seen the creature leave the house and had recognised him for what he was – a shaman, a magician and very likely a madman. The strange figure made the merchant shiver. Never mind, he told himself, he'd seen more terrifying men. At that instant, though, he couldn't recall where.

The king came out of the house. He bowed deeply, wondering how he would explain it when the king didn't realise it. He too hadn't slept, Leshii could see.

'On your feet, warriors!' he shouted.

The berserkers creaked up slowly, shaking the dew from their hair and then wishing they hadn't as the reality of their hangovers dawned on them.

'Get the monk up into the woods, to the Raven's camp.'

'I'd prefer not to go up there, sir,' said Fastarr.

'And I'd prefer you did.'

Aelis went to the merchant. He was red-eyed and yawning.

'I had to watch all night,' he said. 'That should have been your job.'

Aelis gave him a look to tell him that though she was disguised as a slave he shouldn't make the mistake of treating her like one. He smiled. She wasn't a slave, for sure; more like a precious possession now.

Ofaeti brought the monk from the house, carrying him over his shoulder. Leshii could see the confessor's pain and his efforts to hide it.

'I'm not traipsing all the way up there with him, merchant; lend us a mule,' said Ofaeti.

'The one that had the wine will be considerably lighter, practically unburdened,' said Leshii. 'Put him on that. I'll take my animals to a safe place in the woods.'

'No,' said Sigfrid. 'You are to do me a service, merchant, and can accompany these men.'

Leshii forced his face into a smile. 'As ever for you. I only aim to please, lord,' he said.

'Follow the monk. Be with him for the coming day. Do not leave his side and report to me what he says.'

'Always your servant, great lord.'

Sigfrid looked at Leshii oddly and the merchant thought he might question his familiarity, but the king just said 'You can leave the bags and the mules you don't need here.'

'My lord, I prefer to guard them.'

'It was an instruction, not a request. The packs will not be stolen from, nor your animals eaten – you have my word. You can have them back if I find your report satisfactory.'

Again Leshii smiled. This place, he was sure, would be the death of him. There was no trade to be had one way or the other, no entertainment and not even any food. The best he could hope to come away with was a case of scurf. The worst, well, that would be not coming away at all. Still, Leshii was a practical man and knew the northerners stood by their oaths. The bags might be safer with the king than at his own side.

And at least the Vikings had not mentioned that he had claimed to have known the king since he was a boy.

They went out past the smouldering fires of the camp, through the bands of mist and up the incline for a very long way. Leshii looked behind him as they climbed. The mist sat in the shallow valley of the river like broth in a bowl. And what a broth, a brew of trouble, plague, suspicion and death. They reached the edge of the forest, where already people were chopping logs, and went under the trees. There was a narrow track, just a depression in the grass really, and they followed that. The woods were wet and lovely: the dew sparkled in the pale sun and bluebells flashed like jewels in the web of the low mist. Leshii could not enjoy the morning, though. He was a captive. He glanced at Aelis. What was she? The captive of a captive. Quite a fall for a noblewoman in just one night, he thought.

They were no more than a spring hour into the woods when they came to a clearing. The trees were high here, huge oaks budding into leaf.

'It's here,' said Fastarr.

Leshii could see nothing to indicate a camp. They went into the clearing.

'Hrafn!' shouted Fastarr. 'Hrafn!'

From up in the trees a raven stirred from its nest.

'Wrong one,' said Ofaeti. No one laughed.

The bird sat looking at them from a high branch.

'They're strange things, those,' said Ofaeti. 'They won't nest together, but as soon as one of them gets a sniff of food they're cawing their heads off calling for the others to come and join in.'

'Let's hope there's no more like Hrafn around,' said Fastarr.

'You should let me gut that corpse-muncher,' said Ofaeti.

Fastarr smiled. 'If we ever meet him out of the protection of Sigfrid's people then I'll race you to cut his throat.'

'You shouldn't say that,' said Svan. 'He's a priest of Odin.

He cures people, and he's worth ten men in battle, I've seen it.'

Fastarr grunted, clearly unwilling to debate the subject. 'Hrafn!'

There was a stirring down in the wood.

'Oh, on Freyr's fat cock, it's her,' said Ofaeti.

'Let's leave the prisoners and get it over with then,' said Fastarr. 'I don't want to be around to watch this.'

'Are you so soft, Fastarr?'

Leshii looked around. It was Saerda, the hard little man who had delighted in tormenting Aelis.

'I have killed a score of men,' said Fastarr, 'but they have been the honest deaths of sword, axe and spear. This offends me.'

'You don't like to see your enemies suffer?' said Saerda.

'I like 'em dead and quick,' said Fastarr, 'the quicker to return to my ale and my women.'

'Each to his own,' said Saerda with a shrug, 'I can stay with them if you like.'

'Do as you want,' said Fastarr. 'Just the sooner ...'

His voice trailed away. Leshii's mouth fell open. Aelis actually screamed, but no one seemed to notice, they were too busy holding on to their own stomachs. Leshii had encountered a leper on his travels, though he had run from him quick enough. This, though, was another kind of deformity entirely.

A woman had appeared at the edge of the clearing. Her hair was black and disordered, she wore a dirty white shift stained red with blood at the front from two raw wounds at her neck, and she swayed as if almost too weak to stand. It was her eyes, though, that caught Leshii's attention. She didn't have any. Her face was marked with cuts, like her brother's, but much more numerous and severe, and her head was swollen, almost spongy in appearance, like a monstrous oak gall. There was no discernible nose, just a ragged slit for a mouth, and where her eyes should have been were torn and vacant sockets, the shape of them hardly distinguishable. *What had done that to her?* Leshii wondered. Disease? It looked like no disease he had ever seen, though her face was bruised black and red with infection, puffed out unevenly on one side, almost shrunken away on the other. Her, eyes, though, her eyes were truly terrible. He remembered fetching bread from his grandmother to his mother when he had been young. The old woman had given him half a loaf, and on his way home he'd thought he'd just take a nibble, so he'd pinched a little off as he walked. It had been delicious and he couldn't resist taking another pinch, then another, until the inside of the loaf was nearly hollow. That was how the woman's eyes appeared, like the inside of that loaf, ruined by tiny degrees.

The woman swayed forward across the clearing and then tripped and fell, groping blindly on her hands and knees, sniffing and feeling her way towards them.

'What do we do?' said Fastarr.

'Don't look at me,' said Ofaeti.

'This is their camp. She wants the monk; give her the monk,' said Saerda.

'How, in the name of the Norns' icy tits, do you know what it wants? Are you a bastard mind-reader now?' said Ofaeti.

The woman heard their voices and craned her head. Leshii watched as she got to her feet and stood facing them, arms by her side, about twenty paces away. This was becoming rather too weird for the merchant's tastes. He was, he thought, only a morning's hard walk away from the area the Norsemen controlled. If he could, he would take the lady and just strike out for Ladoga. He'd have to leave his silks and his mules, but the prince would provide him with ample compensation for those if he delivered him the girl. For the first time since he'd left the east, Leshii wished the wolfman was back by his side. He at least would give him a chance of escape.

'This is meant to be where we leave the monk. Let's just leave him and get out of here,' said another berserker.

Fastarr shook his head. 'We need to find out where this girl is. If that's what the Hrafn's after, we need to get to her before him. We have to hear the prophecy and react before he gets his claws into her.'

'Well, shall I get the monk down or not?' said Ofaeti.

'Yes.'

Leshii looked around. The tall figure of Hugin had appeared from the other side of the clearing. He was carrying three small bags across his shoulders and wearing a pair of ragged trousers and a torn smock of dirty grey wool, still greasy as if it had just come from the animal and had not been soaked in hot piss to get the grit and the grease out of it. At his side was that cruelly curved sword. Leshii had heard of such swords, of course – they were a legend among the Moors and the blue men of Africa – but even when he had travelled down the camel roads to Serkland, he had never seen one and wondered what smith had the skill to make such a weapon.

'Leave the monk,' said the Raven. 'Set him down here, at the edge, under the branch of this oak.'

Leshii watched as the confessor was taken from the back of the mule. It almost broke his heart to see. The value of a saint had to be huge, he thought. Even the man's bones would be worth a fortune to the right monastery. Perhaps, thought the merchant, he might get a chance to steal the corpse – as he was certain the confessor was about to become – once Hugin had finished with him.

The confessor didn't complain as he was taken down. The Raven kneeled beside him and put his hands on his brow and on his chest. Leshii thought he almost looked as if he was tending to him. It was when he saw the noose, with its tricky, sticky knot, that he knew for certain he was not.

The Raven cast the rope up over the branch of the tree and then slipped the loop over the head of the monk. He took up the slack, pulling the confessor up into a seated position. The rope was not strangling the monk, Leshii could see, but it was forcing him to work for his breath. The merchant was meant to stay to find out for the king what the confessor said. As far as Leshii could see, the confessor would do very well to keep breathing, let alone issue any prophecies.

'You can discover where the girl has gone like this?' said Ofaeti.

'Perhaps,' said Hugin.

The monk groaned and then was quiet. Leshii admired him. He could tell that he wouldn't give in to pain, to argument or to pleas. The confessor was the stuff martyrs were made of. Leshii's mind was ever on profit and he thought that he might be able to get a few hot meals out of monasteries in return for an account of how the man had died.

Hugin opened his first bag. It contained a white powder. He took a handful and smeared it on the confessor's face and hands. The sorcerer wasn't rough, Leshii noticed; in fact he was very careful, patting at the powder, wiping it smooth with his thumb like a mother taking dirt from her son's face in preparation to meet guests. Then he opened the second bag and removed a very curious item indeed – a carved wooden shape, like a short double-headed spoon with ties of leather coming from each end. Hrafn held it up to the monk's eyes. Leshii could now see what it was – some sort of eyeguard, like the metal ones the Norsemen occasionally put on their funeral helmets. These were impractical for fighting use – the metal would like as not direct the tip of any thrust into the eye as much as away from it – but they looked impressive. This one, though, was not attached to a helmet and had no holes in it. Anyone wearing it would be able to see nothing. Hrafn did not tie it on; he seemed to think better of it and put it to one side. Then he opened the third bag. In it was a human hand, one finger tied to a looped cord. The shaman put this around the monk's neck.

Leshii glanced at the berserkers. They were muttering to each other. The merchant could see the ritual – as it appeared to be – made them very uncomfortable.

Hugin walked to the ruined figure of his sister in the middle of the glade. He took her gently by the hand, guided her across to the monk and sat her down beside him. She put her arms around the confessor and sang.

Her voice was beautiful. It was a song in no language Leshii understood but it seemed almost to chime and ring as she sang. It was dizzying too. He felt himself drifting off, as you might doing dull work while the sun shines outside. The song carried him away and he forgot where he was. Presently he noted that it had become darker. The light had begun to fall. At first he thought it must have gone cloudy, but then he realised that it was dusk. There was a smell of fires from down the valley and the sun was low through the trees. The berserkers were quiet, laid out on the grass, as if asleep. The woman thing, the faceless horror, still cuddled and crooned at the monk; the Raven still sat on his knees nearby, staring into the middle distance. There was a noise Leshii couldn't place. At first he thought it was the wind in the trees. It had that quality to it, rising and falling, but was not quite like the wind. More like the breath of a great crowd, a babble of voices.

The woman's song went on. Leshii looked into the trees. All around them, silhouetted against the falling light, ravens were assembling, scraps of black dropping onto branches. They were beneath a ravens' roost, where the birds gathered from their nests at night to seek the protection of numbers until the dawn.

Now one fell like a dark leaf from a tree and alighted on the woman's shoulder, its head turning this way and that in apparent curiosity. Leshii watched as she held up her finger. It pecked at it, drawing a gout of blood. The woman seemed not to notice but slid the finger under the bird's foot. It took hold and she felt with her free hand for the monk's shoulder. Then she blew on the bird and it hopped forward onto the confessor. Leshii watched as the monk sensed its presence. He tried to draw his head away but it was held firmly in place by the noose. A normal man may have been able to writhe away, to frighten the bird, but the confessor could not. A tiny turn of his head was all he managed. The raven pecked, but not at the monk. It stripped off a tiny piece of meat from the hand hanging around Jehan's neck and gave a loud caw. Leshii thought that if the night had a voice, that was what it would sound like. Now other birds tumbled from the trees with cackles of delight. The merchant watched as the birds tore into the hand at the monk's neck.

There was another sound, an exhalation, a deep sigh, more like one of despair than of pain. The monk, noticed the merchant, had blood running from his cheek, then from his forehead, then from his neck and his ears and his lips.

Hugin went back to the confessor and crouched at his ear.

> 'Odin, lord, in this offering of pain,
> Odin, lord, your servants beseech you,
> Odin, lord, who in agony won lore,
> Odin, lord, direct us to your enemy.'

The words were a mumble, repeated and repeated.

The monk's body convulsed, and one or two of the birds took flight, but four remained to tear at his flesh. They seemed almost leisurely in their feeding: pecking, swallowing, turning around, cawing and calling and pecking again.

The berserkers were standing up, some shaking their heads, some turning away and feigning indifference, one watching in fascination. Saerda seemed to be enjoying the spectacle. The merchant saw that Aelis couldn't look away and was trying to speak, her voice reduced to an appalled stammer by what was happening. In a few seconds, thought Leshii, she was going to betray herself. He put his arm around her as a token of comfort but also as a means of restraint. He knew it must look odd to treat a slave that way but no one was looking at him; all eyes were on the confessor's suffering. The red sun cast long shadows through the trees like welcoming arms to greet the incoming night. Leshii realised they had been there for hours.

The monk could hardly move but his voice was strong, passionate even. 'I have come back for her. She is near me.'

The merchant pulled at Aelis. 'Come away,' he said. 'Come away.'

'She is here!' screamed the monk. 'She is here.'

'Where? Where is she?' Raven was at his ear, speaking low like a parent coaxing a fretful child to sleep.

'Here, she is here.'

'Can you see her? Where is she?'

'Near me, she was always near me. Lord Jesus, let me resist this. I will not reveal her.'

A raven hopped up onto the monk's face and took a tentative, inquisitive peck at an eye. Hugin held the monk's hand and intoned again.

'Odin, lord, take this agony for your agonies,
Nine days and nights on the storm-racked tree,
Odin, lord, who gave your eye for lore,
Lead us to your enemies.'

'Aelis! Aelis!' the monk was screaming. 'Come to me, come to me. I have looked for you for so long. Aelis. Adisla, do not go from me – it will be my death!'

Adisla? Who was that? wondered Aelis. It sounded like a Norse name. And yet it seemed strangely familiar to her. She was overwhelmed by the urge to help the confessor. She started towards the monk but Leshii stopped her. His solemn faith that this magic would not work had been replaced by an equally solid conviction that it would. In a second, he thought, the monk would identify the lady.

Now the birds fell from the trees like leaves in a black autumn, mobbing the confessor's body, shrieking and cawing.

Leshii had made up his mind. The silks didn't matter, nor did the mules. His life and whatever reward he could get for the lady were all he had.

'Come on,' he said. 'We're going.'

He couldn't move her. She was rooted where she stood, trembling, her eyes fixed on the confessor.

That terrible woman was singing again over the coaxings of Hugin.

Then the monk gave a scream unlike any other, a sound of torment, a high note in the music of hell. There was confusion and shouting. The Raven was up, shooing the birds away from the monk's body. He hacked at the rope with his knife and the confessor collapsed like a bag of wet sand. Aelis, unable to stop herself, ran to him, pushing past the berserkers, rushing past Hugin, who had turned away from the confessor with his head in his hands.

Leshii dashed after Aelis and then bent to try to control the weeping girl. 'Remember,' he whispered, 'you are a mute, a mute. Say nothing or join this man in his torments.'

He had been trying not to look at the monk, but as he pulled Aelis away caught sight of him. The confessor's tongue was lolling from his head. It reminded Leshii of a piece of liver, slick and shiny with blood, and ragged at one edge. The merchant could only marvel at the sort of mind capable of doing what the confessor had done. Jehan would not give them a prophecy, no matter how they enchanted and tormented him, and had done the only thing he could to spite his captors and stop himself from revealing Aelis. He had opened his mouth to let the birds tear out his tongue.

13 The Reward of Honour

A silence fell on the clearing when the Raven cut down the monk.

Ofaeti walked over and looked down at the merchant's boy, who was cradling the confessor in his arms. 'Of your religion, I guess, son,' he said. 'Well, if that's the measure of these men then we can all pack up and go home now. That is a man of iron, I'll give him that. Eh, Raven? He did for you, didn't he? Crippled, trussed, tied and enchanted, but he beat you at your own game.' Aelis didn't understand a word he said but caught the sentiment in his voice.

She looked down at the monk. His blood was black and shiny in the moonlight, one eye swollen and raw. The bird had virtually removed the eyelid, though the eye itself looked intact. His face and ears were a mass of cuts, the white nub of a cheek bone showing through and a hole in his cheek exposing a tooth. She removed the remains of the horrible hand at his neck and threw it away. No one tried to stop her.

'He won't recover from this,' said Leshii. 'The wounds won't kill him but they'll turn bad. I've seen it before.'

'How much are god bones, by weight?' It was the voice of Saerda. He gave a short laugh and prodded his boot at the monk's side.

Aelis was on her feet in a second. Without thinking what she was doing, she had pushed Saerda in the middle of the chest. He was taken by surprise and fell back over a tree root. He didn't take long to recover, though, drawing his knife even as he tripped, regaining his balance before he hit the ground and springing to stab at Aelis. It was four strides between Saerda and the lady. He took two before Ofaeti, with surprising quickness, stepped across and dropped his shoulder into the thin man's side, battering him into a tree. All the wind went out of him as he hit the trunk. He slumped to the floor and lay there panting.

Ofaeti pointed at the monk and spoke: 'This man has earned my respect for tonight. Let the boy care for him, if it suits his temper. If it's a fight you're after, Saerda, you needn't be disappointed. I stand ready to oblige.' Again, Aelis couldn't grasp exactly what he was saying but the meaning of his words was clear enough to anyone.

Saerda stood and dusted himself down, still trying to recover his breath. Then he gave Aelis a look that needed no interpretation at all, smiled and backed off towards the camp.

It was night now and the big moon turned the clearing into a silver circle. Hugin said something in Norse to the merchant.

Leshii shook his head. 'I don't think he knows we are here.'

For the first time, the Raven fixed his eyes on Aelis. 'Keep him warm for the night and give him water if he calls for it. He won't die before tomorrow.' He turned to Leshii again and said, 'Tell the king what he said and that, one way or another, the monk will have given us all he has to give us by this time tomorrow. Now I need to think.'

He walked back across the clearing, taking his sister by the arm and escorting her into the trees

It was quickly obvious that Jehan was going to die. He was very cold and he shook. His wounds were awful, oozing stab marks across every inch of exposed flesh. Strangely, the birds had not pecked through his clothes. The habit and undershirt had put them off and they had gone only for the skin they could see.

Jehan was delirious, clinging to Aelis's hand, gargling and babbling. His tongue was terribly swollen like a fat blood sausage and he could hardly close his mouth. Aelis tended to him, dabbing his mouth with a damp cloth to keep it moist, squeezing in a little water. From away in the trees, from the direction of the Raven's shelter, chanting came, low and indistinct, a smoke of words, just a tinge of them on the breeze.

Leshii sat with her. He was a hard man who saw the world in terms of profit and loss, but even he had been shaken by the monk's ordeal, she could see. A boy came running into the clearing and spoke to the Vikings. She saw the one called Fastarr nod and point towards her. The big fat Norseman came up and said something to the merchant. Leshii replied and the man went away.

Leshii said, 'I have to go to report to the king. He has sent for me.'

'On what?' She spoke low, careful to see if she was observed.

'What the monk said under torture.' Leshii did not dignify what he had seen with the name of magic. The man had been half killed and had nearly revealed what he had guessed – that the lady was near him. No prophecy to that, he thought. 'You have to come as well. They were insistent. Seems like you might have more slave work to do down there.'

She touched him on the arm. 'The confessor is dying,' she said.

'Yes.'

'I need to stay here with him. Let me stay here.'

Leshii shrugged and turned to the Norsemen and shouted something at them that Aelis didn't understand. The fat one replied, shaking his head.

'No, you have to come,' said Leshii.

'I will not leave him,' said Aelis, averting her face.

The merchant spoke to the berserkers again. There was a brief discussion between them. Then the fat one shook his head and made an odd gesture. She heard the king's name mentioned.

Leshii turned to Aelis. 'Ofaeti says Sigfrid can fetch and carry for himself for one night. The priest has earned some comfort. The berserker will do your work for you if the king demands it. You look after the monk. If you can move him then go down the river to the woods by the ford. I will meet you there and I swear I will reunite you with your people.' Leshii made to stand. 'You have a friend there in the fat Viking, it seems, but I must be gone.'

Aelis stood and nodded to Ofaeti. She was afraid, but inside her a certainty was growing. God had put her together with the confessor. And God, she thought, knew well his friends from his enemies. If anyone should be scared, it was the sorcerer and his horrible servants.

14 A Discovery

Leshii and the berserks made their way back down into the camp, towards the house Sigfrid was using as his head-quarters. The assault had been a substantial one that day and the Norsemen had taken many casualties. Fires blazed in the night, and the sound of rough music, pipe and drum, was cut through with groans and screams. Faces, pale and thin, loomed from the darkness. *This*, thought, Leshii, *was what the land of the dead would be like*.

The house was visible from a way away under the bright moon, its checked roof gleaming in the silver light. Leshii was tired and looking forward to the hospitality of the king. The advantage of dealing with monarchs was that – even in times of hardship – there was good wine to drink and good food to eat. He went in to find the king sitting on a chair in the centre of the room. It was no throne but had been put in such a position that it was clear it was intended to stand in for one. Leshii wondered if some formal court was taking place. In all his other dealings with the Norsemen they had rarely stood on ceremony, particularly in times of war.

The king gave Leshii a curt smile and held out his cup to be filled. Leshii noted that the man who did so was not Sigfrid's normal servant but the skinny berserk Saerda. So this was where he'd gone when he left the camp.

'You haven't brought your boy with you, merchant.'

'He is tending to the monk. The Frank has had a rough time of it today,' said Ofaeti.

'I said he was to be brought here.' Sigfrid was pale and clamped his jaw tight, as if trying to bite down the anger that was rising inside him.

'One servant's like another,' said Ofaeti. 'I'll stand the boy's place, if I have to.'

'I said the boy was to be brought, now bring the boy, fat man.'

'It's an hour up the hill,' said Ofaeti. Then he looked at the simmering king and said, 'I'll go, I'll go.'

'Good. Bring him and make no fuss about it. Do not alert the Raven.'

'You're the boss,' said Ofaeti. He turned and went out of the hall, gesturing at Fastarr to come with him.

The king took up his wine and swallowed down his temper. Then he spoke to Leshii in a more even voice. 'So what did he say, the saint? What revelations did he bring forth?'

Leshii glanced about him. The warriors in the king's house seemed almost to crackle with excitement. All eyes were on him and Leshii had been in enough losing deals to know when it was time to call it quits and get out. This was one of those moments. However, while the king was there, there was no question of that.

'Come on, merchant, what did he say?'

Leshii wondered if he should lie but thought better of it. Latin was spoken widely enough for the king to have heard from elsewhere. The truth was the only safe course.

'He said she was here,' he said.

'Really?' Leshii could see that behind the king's light manner was a boiling rage. 'Why do you think that was?'

'I am not a magician, lord.'

The king stood, so quickly that Leshii almost leaped backwards. Sigfrid was clearly only just managing to keep a hold on his fury.

'Oh, but you are, merchant, you are. I have heard that I knew you as a child – my men here tell me. But I have no memory of you. Have you wiped it away?'

Leshii was relieved. If that was all this was, he could talk his way out of it.

'I merely said that your renown was so great that I knew of

you and your father as a child, even in my home beyond the Eastern Lake. They sing of your deeds there. Perhaps your warriors misunderstood me. My command of your language is not so sure.'

'It is good enough to lie in,' said Sigfrid.

Leshii said nothing, as he guessed whatever he said would not do him much good.

The king clapped his hands together. 'Good Saerda,' he said, 'show our esteemed guest what you found in his packs.'

'You gave your oath not to touch them!'

'Nor did I. Saerda caught a boy trying to steal from them,' said Sigfrid. 'A thief opened your packs, merchant, not one of my warriors. And why are you so keen that no one should see your wares? It's an unusual merchant who doesn't display his goods.'

'I prefer to be there when they are displayed, my lord, or I find I get a rather poor price for them, nothing being the poorest price I know.'

'There are worse payments than nothing at all,' said Sigfrid, tapping at the hilt of the sword on his belt.

Saerda shot a brief smile towards Leshii and dragged one of the packs forward. It had been opened. Leshii felt his heart beginning to race as the berserk reached within and pulled something out. There was a flash of pale gold in the candle-light. Aelis's hair.

'What's this, merchant?' The king's voice cracked in his anger.

Leshii breathed out slowly and spread his arms wide. He needed to calm himself.

'I bought it from a peasant woman on the way here. It will make a fine wig; any of your warriors would be proud to take it to their wives.'

The king set his jaw. Then he took something else from the bag, something small enough to fit into his fist. He held out his clenched hand.

'What do you think I have in here?'

'I am a low man and would not like to guess the minds of kings,' said Leshii.

'A good answer. Mine is better. Would you like to hear it?'

'If it pleases you.'

'I have your death, merchant.'

Leshii swallowed. He had thought, in the safety of the clearing with the lady, that he had lived a long life and would not mind leaving it for the chance of riches. Now his life seemed very short indeed. Strange thoughts came into his head. *I haven't done anything*, he thought. *I haven't lived.* He had walked the silk trails with a camel, gone to the frozen shores of the north, seen the Holy Roman Empire and the southern olive groves, but, facing his own death, he saw the reality of his life. He had done all these things alone. He thought of his mother. She was the last person he had really loved, been willing to die for. That, he realised, was what he meant when he told himself, *I haven't done anything*. He had never replaced that love – with that of a friend, a woman, a child. Trade had been everything to him, and now here he was in his last deal, trying to bargain for his life.

The king came over to where Leshii was standing and opened his hand. In it were two fine lady's finger rings, one with the single lily of the Margrave of Neustria on it, the sign that would announce the wearer as a high-born woman, a descendant of Robert the Strong. The Vikings had suffered at his hands and eventually killed him, so they knew his crest very well.

'Taken in payment for silk, my lord. Who has made a story from some tresses and a few baubles here?' He glanced at Saerda.

The king seemed to think for a second.

'Where was this trade made?'

'Just the other night, lord. A strange fellow brought these things, tall and clad in a wolfskin. I did not like him much but he seemed willing to pay a good price for—'

The king held up his hand. 'We will see,' he said. 'Your boy will be back before the night is out and we'll see what tales he has to tell.'

'He is not a talkative fellow, sir,' said Leshii.

'He'll say enough, whether he speaks or not. If he is, as I suspect, the lady I'm looking for, then I'll gut you here on the floor myself.'

There was a commotion outside and a man entered the hall, short of breath. It was one of the berserkers who had met him on the hill on the first night – a tall, wiry man with a scar that ran across his cheek and sliced off the top of his ear. He was carrying something over his arm. It was a bundle of wet cloth.

'What do you have for us?'

The berserker threw the cloth down. It hit the reeds with a squelch. It was stained but anyone could see it was the fine silk and brocade of an expensive dress.

'Found where the merchant had his camp,' said the man. 'It's Frankish, my lord, and no mistake.'

'Exactly as worn by the lady we pursued,' said Saerda.

Sigfrid drew his sword and strode forward as Leshii threw up his arms to try to fend him away.

15 The Agonies of Confessor Jehan

Voices, and pressures in his head. Dizziness, confusion and pain. The confessor had known the Raven was trying to enchant him but he had struggled against it.

They had come at him, knowingly or not, through his weakness for human touch. He had felt the woman holding him, the brush of her hair against his face, heard the beauty of her singing and, against himself, had drawn comfort from her embrace.

It was a woman – he could tell from the shape of her, the softness of her thin arms, even the sound of her breath. He had tried to get away from her at first, to move as best he could, but he was so cruelly tied it was impossible. The pain at his throat from the rope was awful, the Raven's chant hypnotic, the woman's voice entangling his thoughts like a coil of smoke from an incense burner entangles a sunbeam. He could have resisted them all, remained as himself fully present in the agony of the rope, had it not been for her touch.

He began to lose track of time. He would drift away from the pain, and her embrace would seem like the warmth of a fire after a long cold journey in the wind and rain. Then the constriction at his throat would begin to dominate his thoughts, his whole consciousness condensing to that tight band around his neck. After a while he couldn't tell who was asking him the questions, or if he was replying. He seemed to be somewhere else, not in the clearing at dusk but somewhere much darker. He was underground, he could sense it. The air felt close on his skin, damp and cold. Was this hell? Voices were around him. He recognised one as his own but, bizarrely, he couldn't tell which one it was.

'Where will we find her?'

'Who?'

'The girl who was with you in the church at Paris.'

'She has always been with me.'

'Where is she?'

'I know.'

'Where is she?'

'She has come to me.'

'Where is she?'

'I must fortify myself for the struggle ahead.'

And then he moved, the rope dug into his neck and he choked. He felt hands adjusting his position, alleviating the tightness slightly. The odour of putrefaction was in his nostrils, the horrid voice of the Raven in his ear, resuming that blasphemous chant.

> 'Odin, who gave his eye for lore,
> Odin, who hung for nine days on the storm-racked tree,
> Odin the bold, the furious and the mad,
> Odin accept our gift of pain.'

Jehan forced the words from his strangled throat: 'Jesus, who died for our sins on the cross, who suffered so we may be free, forgive my sins and welcome me to your heaven, Lord.' The confessor was certain he was to die there and offered a prayer against pride that God had selected him as a martyr.

He heard the Raven snort in frustration. Then the woman's voice changed, took on a different quality, more cracked, urgent, imploring. That was when the first bird came to him.

It had been more of an irritation than anything when it had first dropped onto his chest. He hadn't known what it was, its touch as light as a spider's until he heard it call. Of course he had heard the birds gathering in the trees, but in his pain and his anguish he hadn't registered the noise above any of the other sounds of the evening. When the second bird descended, dread set in. He had heard them pecking but couldn't feel them on his own skin; they were tearing at something about his neck. Then the first wound had come, just an exploratory nip at his cheek. He gasped but then there was another stab at his cheek, harder, and the rasp of the bird, hoarse and exultant. He tried to writhe away but the rope bit deeper into his neck. The birds were on him then, shredding his flesh and his willpower in a torrent of pecks like the fall of an agonising rain. He managed to turn; the rope tightened and he blacked out for a second.

When he came back to consciousness he heard voices.

'Adisla, come back to me!'

'No, Vali, no. You are trapped in the schemes of the gods and I want no part of that.'

'I love you.'

'And I you. But it is not enough.' He recognised neither of the names, but they seemed to resonate within him, like the shadow of a memory, known and then slipping away, leaving no more trace of itself than the feeling that something of huge importance lay lurking at the limit of the mind, ungraspable.

Then the memory sparked in his mind, as real as if it was happening right there. The Virgin Mary was in front of him gathering to herself the light of the cornfields and the blue of the sky. She was beautiful and she touched him on the shoulder.

'Do not seek me,' she said; 'let me go.'

He was crying out, screaming and moaning as the birds tore his flesh to a bloody lace.

'Where is she?'

The voice brought him back. He had betrayed himself, not known himself. Who knew what he had said, who knew what he would say, under such torture? They wanted the lady. He knew where she was; he needed no divine presence to tell him. She was with the merchant. He could stop the pain and the sharp *tac tac tac* of the bites, the stabbing and the tugging at his skin, in an instant. The confessor knew he could not hold out much longer. As a bird tore a red string of meat from his lips, he recited the words in his head: *I put my faith in Christ.*

Then he opened his mouth to the savage beak. After that a blackness seemed to come up from inside him and his senses failed.

16   Running

Aelis went to the mule and led it to where the confessor lay. It came quietly and without complaint. She didn't know how to get the monk to stay on its back – it was a pack animal and had no saddle. She glanced across the clearing. The low drone of chanting from the shelter in the woods went on. The torturers were still in their den. Aelis looked at the smouldering fire the Vikings had left. She had a powerful urge to take up its embers and use them to burn the horrible pair in the middle of their sorceries.

She knew that she could not succeed, though. All she would do was get them to come out.

The monk's eyes were glassy and he was scarcely conscious. She spoke to the mule in a low voice, telling it to be quiet and hold still, summoning that shape in her thoughts, the one that said *horse* to her. *There it was* – she felt it, shivering and stamping in her head. For a moment the strangeness of that struck her, but she was too scared of the Raven and his awful sister to dwell on it for long. She picked up the confessor. He exhaled heavily as she lifted him. He was not heavy, his body wasted by his paralysis, but still she struggled to get him up. She spoke again to the mule, wedging the confessor against the animal's flank. Her kaftan was wet with Jehan's blood as she slumped him over the mule's back. He gave a short cry, more like someone dreaming than in pain, as he fell into position.

The chanting in the shelter stopped and Aelis froze. The chanting did not start again but she heard no other noise from that direction, just the sounds of the Viking camp drifting up through the night. She led the mule forward but the confessor started to slide off its back. She caught him beneath the armpits just before he fell and shoved him back up.

The monk would not remain on the mule by himself. She put one hand out to steady him and took the halter with the other. She was having to escape by edging sideways, nearly backwards. There was no immediately obvious track through the woods, other than the one that had been beaten down by the Raven to get to his den.

Which way to go? Should she follow the merchant's instructions? She didn't trust him but she had no other protector. She would go to the ford. Where was it? Over the hill. In her panic she couldn't even remember if the woods thinned on the top of the hill to allow her a view of the river. Never mind. The grass was long and there were many brambles but she chose what looked like the easiest way and pulled the animal on. It responded to her, stepping forward into the darkness beneath the trees. She hadn't gone five paces when the monk slipped again. This time he let out a loud cry.

She heaved the monk back up and went on. Beneath the trees the dark was shot with a web of moonbeams that sparkled and teemed with insects. Fireflies flashed green against the blackness and the moon frosted the trunks of the great oaks. It was like a trap though, the whole wood. She couldn't move forward without snaring her feet, without the mule blowing and snorting enough to wake a thousand Vikings, without the monk falling.

From down towards the Viking camp she heard voices. Someone was coming up the hill. She breathed in. She could not continue as she was. Almost without thinking, she shoved the confessor forward and jumped up behind him onto the mule's back. The animal gave a sigh of complaint but didn't buck or shy. She gently kicked it in the ribs to encourage it forward. It didn't move. Then she realised: the mule hadn't been trained for riding. It was a good pack animal but it had spent all its life in a train.

Again, that shape came into her head, the one that steamed and whickered. She thought of it and the animal moved, finding its feet easily in the dark.

They went through the wood, the mule more confident than she was. To her, every shadow was the Raven, every tree at the limit of her vision a Dane. Aelis thought she heard something and stopped. There *was* something coming after her. She could hear its tread behind her, fast and light, moving quickly where she was forced to plod. She knew that any further movement would give her away, so she drew the mule into the shadow of a big tree. She could not make it be quiet, so she tied it to a branch and hauled the confessor fifty paces to a brook and lay flat against its bank.

Aelis was quiet for some time. She heard nothing but the breeze in the trees. She returned to the mule and untied it. Then they were on her, two of them, taking her to the ground at the leap. She saw their knives gleam and heard words.

'Where is he?' It was her own Roman tongue. 'Where is the confessor?'

'I am Lady Aelis of the line of Robert the Strong,' she gasped out the words as quickly as she could speak.

'Lady?' A man was squinting at her through the dark. He was wearing a stiff leather jerkin. She didn't recognise him. His companion was more lightly dressed, though he had two small axes in his belt. There were noises from her left. She looked around. Other faces were looking at her from the trees. Her mind took a few moments to adjust. The men were warrior-monks, she realised, their hair cut short and shaved on the crown. There were ten of them. The two nearest her were clearly puzzled, so Aelis spoke quickly to explain herself, to tell them what had happened.

'We are from Saint-Germain,' said the monk who had attacked her. 'We're trying to capture a Dane and find out what has happened to the confessor.'

Aelis bowed her head. 'He's here,' she said, and led them, along with the mule, back to the little brook. There was a gasp as the monks looked down at the saint.

'What have they done to him?'

'A foul abuse,' said Aelis.

'Lady, we need to get him around the back of the hill and across the ford to the monastery.'

'Then secure him on the mule.'

The monks worked quickly. They had rope with them, brought for the purposes of tying a captive. Now they used it for the confessor. He was in a bad way, his skin cold, his breath no more than a flutter. Aelis prayed for him and the monks led the mule across the brook.

'We will stay inside the trees as far as we can,' said the monk, 'then we drop down to the river and away from our goal to the crossing. From there, the way is easier and less fraught with danger as we double back to the monastery. There are northerners everywhere, lady; we must be careful.'

There was more noise through the trees. Horses. One of the monks crouched. The others went for their weapons. There was a skittering movement to Aelis's left. *What was that?* She had assumed it was the monks when she had heard it before. No. Now it seemed to be to her right.

Then it was as if the air fell apart. A scream cut through the shadows. She saw her, the terrible woman in the bloody robes, fifty paces away, her white shift almost glowing in the moonlight, her hands down by her sides, her body rigid but her ruined face emotionless. Aelis realised that the scream was not one of pain, or of anguish, but one of summoning.

There was a stutter of hooves from deep in the trees. Then there was quiet. Whoever had heard the scream was listening to see if it was repeated. It was, so loud it was almost unbearable to hear. From much further off came an answering call splitting the night. The hooves turned towards Aelis, the horses moving slowly through the trees.

'We need to go before they see us,' said Aelis. 'Kill her.'

'I will not strike down an unarmed woman,' said the monk.

'Then give me that,' said Aelis, pulling a knife from his belt.

She ran towards the woman but it was as if a shadow had gone over the moon. The witch, and Aelis was sure she was a witch, was nowhere. She peered through the columns of trees, looking for her. She saw something glint. A sword. Every Frankish sword was in Paris, defending the city. It was the Norsemen, she knew.

Aelis ran back to the monks. 'We need to go, now, before we're found.'

'No.' The monk shook his head and spoke in a low whisper. 'Our movements must either be quick or quiet, and either way we will be discovered. Brother Abram, Brother Marellus, take the lady and the confessor back to the monastery. We still might surprise whoever is here if we act now. Brothers, we are Christ's men, we are pagan-killers; let's take the fight to them.'

The monks nodded and crept away through the trees, crouching low and saying nothing. One of the remaining monks took her by the arm while the other led the mule.

'Lady, the river crossing. We must be quick,' he said.

They moved away up the hill and she followed them through the dark of the trees.

17 A Deal

Leshii had never spoken faster: 'I have sent her away with the monk. You kill me and you will never find out where she has gone.'

The king didn't pause in his advance but didn't raise his sword; he just smacked a brutal headbutt into Leshii's nose.

A white light split the merchant's sight and he realised he was sitting on the reeds.

'Do you think, merchant, that you can separate a god from his destiny?' said Sigfrid, standing above the little man with the sword point pressing into his belly.

'My lord, I was in a situation where I had to choose my deaths. I was being loyal to my own king by concealing the girl. If I had given her to you I would have had to break my oath and face Prince Helgi's wrath. What choice did I have?'

This time Sigfrid drove his boot into Leshii's chest, knocking him flat.

'Where is she?'

'I will show you, my lord.' Leshii put his hand to his face. His nose was broken, he was sure.

'You will tell me.'

'My lord, I am a merchant. This knowledge is all I have to bargain with. Give it up and I am dead.'

'You'll die anyway. What's a day to you?'

'Before I reveal her whereabouts I would require an oath that you would let me live.'

Another kick, harder. Leshii curled up in a ball on the floor.

'Impossible. You have concealed her from me, lied to my face. I would rather lose a thousand women than accept such an indignity. I offer you a quick death, no more. Decide now or I'll give you to the Raven.' The king raised his foot again.

'A deal,' said Leshii through teeth clamped together with pain. 'Nice doing business with you.'

'Don't provoke me, merchant,' said Sigfrid.

Leshii lay where he was. He had given up on his life and accepted he would die. An attempt to remain cheerful was all that he had.

'We'll go now,' said Sigfrid.

A bodyguard pulled Leshii to his feet. Sigfrid put out his arms. Another bodyguard put the king's hauberk on him and passed him his shield with its terrifying wolf's head design.

'Do we need our byrnies, lord?' said a warrior. 'We're only going to fetch a girl.'

Leshii knew he was referring to the mail coat – the Varangians at Ladoga called them that too.

'If the Raven finds out where she is, then we'll need them,' the king said. 'That is a mighty man. He's supposed to be on our side but imagine what might happen if he turns against us.'

The warriors dressed and armed themselves, went outside and mounted horses. There were eight of them, in full byrnies and helmets, their shields across their backs and spears in their hands. *Escape?* thought Leshii. *No chance.* He looked around for a horse.

The king caught his eye. 'You go on foot.'

'But won't that slow you down?' said Leshii.

'No.'

'Why?'

'Because,' said the king, 'you are going to run. Saerda, drive him.'

'My lord.' The skinny berserk turned his horse and rode it at the merchant. Leshii tried to dodge but was too slow, and the berserk fetched him a whack about the ear with the flat of his sword, sending him stumbling forward.

It had been in the back of Leshii's mind to lead the warriors to the trees and then give them the slip when he got the chance. At the pace Saerda was slapping him on he wondered whether he could even make the wood.

They raced up through the camp, Leshii's boots slipping on the mud, children shouting and trying to trip him. Some even threw shit and stones until some hit the king and they all ran for it like rats down a riverbank. Leshii was a tough old man who'd lived his life walking beside caravans, perched on a mule or a camel, but the pace Sigfrid demanded would have tested someone half his age. He panted and heaved. The king brought the flank of his horse alongside him and barged him to the ground.

'Get up, merchant. Your meeting with death is pressing and you wouldn't want to be late.'

Leshii couldn't reply. It was as if the air was too thick for his lungs, like he was trying to breathe soup. He lay face down and waited for the inevitable – the stamp of Sigfrid's horse, the stab of a spear.

'My lord, the merchant will be in no fit state to lead us anywhere if we continue like this.' It was one of the king's bodyguard, a hard-looking bald man with the tip of his nose missing.

'Get him to his feet,' said Sigfrid. The bodyguard got down off his horse and helped Leshii up. 'Now cut his throat unless he tells us where the girl is in his next breath.'

Leshii bent over panting, shaking his head. The bodyguard unsheathed his knife and Leshii just sank to his knees, looking up at him.

'No, no, no,' said Sigfrid, tapping aside the blade with his spear. 'Just get him on your horse and bring him on. Is it up here, merchant?'

Leshii nodded and coughed out a 'Yes.'

The bodyguard mounted then helped the old man onto his horse behind him. They went forward at a slower pace, Leshii's mount unwilling to go at anything faster than a walk with the extra weight of the merchant on its back.

They climbed the hill under a small, sharp moon, and went into the dark of the wood. Leshii was clinging now to desperate hopes. First he hoped they would encounter the Raven. He had no idea how that would help; he just knew it would be a difficulty for Sigfrid. Leshii had decided that he would lead the king to the lady but he thought she might see them coming and try to run, which might create a diversion. Leshii counted the 'mights'. Three. He remembered his mother's saying 'two "mights" are as good as a "won't"'. After that, what? Hope the confessor could call on the help of his god.

It was very dark beneath the trees and progress was slow. A scream, not a natural sound at all, more like a long scrape of steel on stone, came from their right.

'What was that?' Sigfrid turned to a bodyguard.

'Could be anything, lord. One of our men with an unwilling woman, I should guess.'

'I didn't like the sound of it,' said Sigfrid. 'Let's take a look.' He turned his horse in the direction of the noise.

Another scream, equally as unnatural but from deeper in the woods, came from behind them. Then another, in front.

'Is the lady in that direction, merchant?' Sigfrid pointed straight ahead.

'Yes, lord.'

All Leshii knew was that there lay a possible delay. Of course the lady was in that direction.

'Come on. That sound has the mark of the Raven about it. We can't let him get her,' said Sigfrid, and spurred his horse off the track into the long grass and brambles.

The light beneath the trees had almost an underwater quality to it, the leaves mottling the moonlight and turning the ground to a shimmering seabed. A dull thump and the first throwing axe hit the horseman to Leshii's right in the shoulder, bouncing off his byrnie and catching him in the face to smash his teeth. Five more followed. A horse caught one in the side of the neck and went into a crazy, screaming, spinning dance, crashing into the other animals. Leshii saw Saerda fall from his horse, his animal bolting into the trees.

'Franks! Franks!' It was Sigfrid's voice.

The bodyguard sitting in front of Leshii on their shared

horse drove the beast forward and his elbows back to rid himself of his passenger. Leshii fell heavily. He saw Sigfrid leap from his horse and go howling into the undergrowth with his sword; three of his men did likewise, ditching their horses to plough into the battle. Another, beset by two attackers, was trying to stab them with his spear. He was unused to fighting on horseback and in the end just threw the weapon and leaped off to fight on foot with his axe.

Something glinted on the ground in the moonlight. It was a throwing axe, a *francisca*, as the enemies of the Franks called them. Leshii picked it up and just ran, not even looking where he was going. He was exhausted but fear drove him on, up the wooded slope away from Paris, over a little brook and into the darkness. He willed himself forward. He knew he didn't have long. He had glimpsed the Franks and there weren't many of them. The one he had seen close was lightly armoured and his weapon no more than a big knife. Against Sigfrid's men, he knew they wouldn't stand a chance. They'd had their opportunity in the ambush and it had passed them by. So the king would be after him soon.

What to do? No new plan occurred to him, so his old one would have to suffice. At least if he found the lady he could use her to his advantage.

He felt himself laughing as he pushed through the woods. Hadn't he taken this mission for the comfort it had promised him? And hadn't he cheated death, at least so far? He muttered a word of thanks to Perun, the thunder god of his people, and pressed on.

From somewhere behind him, far but not so far, came another terrible scream. The voice before, thought Leshii, had been a woman's. This was definitely a man's.

He came to the edge of the woods at the top of the hill and looked down at the Seine, a metal ribbon under the moon. It was a long drop to the flood plain and he would be visible all the way. Still, once he had gone a few hundred paces he would be indistinguishable from any other drunken Norseman or vengeful Frank stalking the dark. *Well, cling to that hope anyway.* He looked up at the moon, for the first time in his life wanting to see cloud.

Then he saw them, down below. There were two figures carrying spears or staffs, another smaller person and, following behind, a bandy-legged mule carrying a large pack. He recognised the animal's gait. It was his and so there was a good chance that the lady was with it.

There was a noise to his right. Sigfrid had regained his horse and had come out of the trees, the animal shaking and stamping away the underbrush from its coat. Leshii went flat to the ground as the king drove the horse up and down the edge of the wood. Another rider emerged further up the hill but halted, apparently watching Sigfrid, unnoticed by the king. Then Sigfrid gave a whoop and galloped down the hill. Leshii got to his feet, a tree trunk between him and the watching horseman. *Who was it?* Leshii saw the people with the mule turn and look towards Sigfrid. The two larger figures levelled their spears and stood against the king while the third ran with the mule down the hill.

Then he heard the scream again. This time it seemed close.

18   Royal Blood

Aelis heard the clash behind her but didn't dare to turn to see how the monks were faring against Sigfrid. She knew it would be badly. The Viking king seemed cut from the same cloth as her brother Eudes, a man raised to arms from his earliest years. She knew the two monks were no more than armed scribes, more at home with ink than spears, and would not do well against him.

She hurried down the hill. It was a broad grassy expanse, eaten short by sheep, and there was no hiding anywhere. Her only hope was a collection of little farmsteads below her. The sound of the fighting stopped but still she rushed on, leading the mule. The confessor, she thought, might be dead. He hadn't moved or made a noise since they had tied him to the mule, and although she had checked him regularly, it had been difficult to tell if he was breathing or not.

Down, down, down the slope towards the group of houses and tiny fields. She heard the horse behind her, coming on at the trot. Sigfrid had no need to exhaust his mount by galloping, she thought; he had seen her and had all the time in the world. She gripped the knife she had taken from the monk. She was determined that Sigfrid wouldn't take her without a fight but her hand was trembling. The king had just done for two young men, both armed with spears. What chance did she have? Next to none, but not none, she thought.

The sound of the horse came closer but still she didn't turn, tugging the mule on through the moonlight.

Sigfrid shouted something in his own language and his words were harsh. She guessed he had lost men in the fight. That would have been her brother's first thought.

'Stop,' he said in grating Roman. 'Stop or die.' She kept

going, holding the knife by her side. The hoofbeats followed right behind and the horse drew alongside, the rider nudging its flank into her.

'The saint is dead,' said Sigfrid. 'Stop and I might persuade my men to spare some of your monks. Come on.'

He leaned down from the saddle and slapped her fingers away from the mule's reins with the flat of his sword.

'I said stop.'

For the first time she turned to face him. 'I am the daughter of Robert the Strong, scourge of the Norsemen and defender of the faith,' she said. 'My father was a second Maccabaeus to your heathen hordes. If you want me to stop, then stop me.'

'You can walk back or I can punch you into unconsciousness and put you over the back of the mule with the saint. Your choice.'

It seemed as if Sigfrid's physical self was not big enough to contain the strength of his soul. But there was something else too. He seemed to have a force emanating from him, which pushed others down, bullied and belittled them. Here was a man, she thought, who had only ever considered his own needs, his own glory, a man of violence and risk who was prepared to do anything to make the world see him as he saw himself. Aelis was used to such men and was not intimidated by them.

She brought up the knife. 'I choose the second. It will be difficult to subdue me without taking a little damage yourself, I think.'

Sigfrid snorted and brought the flat of his sword against the back of her knife hand with a stinging rap. The weapon went spinning to the ground.

'I've lost enough men today to darken my humour to pitch,' he said. 'I think I've given you enough chances. You are a virgin, lady, aren't you?'

Aelis just spat at him.

'Well, I think I'll put you on your back and show you what you've been missing. If I have to break your jaw to do it, that suits me fine. After that I think you'll come quietly enough.'

He began to swing himself out of the saddle. Aelis felt a great rage. She saw her brother's city burning, her friends and subjects beset by Norsemen, the confessor tied and tortured, her father tricked by the Norse King Hastein into taking off his armour and then cruelly butchered. She was a woman and had never been able to take arms against the enemies of her people. She hated the Norsemen but she had never had an outlet for her hate. Now something gave it expression.

Again the shape came to her, the one that shone and stamped, breathed and sweated the idea *horse*. She had the shape in her mind and she saw it projected onto the form of Sigfrid's animal. The king had one foot in the stirrup as he dismounted. He gave a slight shake to free it, but as he did so Aelis imagined the shape bursting into gallop. She saw wide plains of grass, felt her heart full and strong, and a sensation of effortless power swept over her as the horse symbol manifested inside her. Something between a word and an emotion leaped from her towards Sigfrid's horse.

'Go!'

The horse surged forward as though a wolf was on its back with Sigfrid's foot still in the stirrup. His sword arm was flung back and he dropped the weapon, his body falling with a terrible twist. His head hit the ground hard, though he remained conscious, fighting to get his foot free. The horse pulled and bucked, dragging the king down the slope for ten paces before his foot came loose and he came to rest, lying panting on the ground.

Aelis wasn't idle while this was happening. She ran to the sword, picked it up and rushed to where Sigfrid lay writhing. He had sat up to clutch his leg but his instinct had proved wrong. Aelis guessed the limb was broken and the pain of touching it had doubled the king over. She saw the fingers of his sword hand were shattered too, pushed back up into his palm.

Sigfrid nodded when he saw the sword and tried to stand,

but it was impossible. He set his jaw and said, 'I am to die. In battle, good. Will you let me say some fine words before the Valkyries come to take me? You will tell them to your skalds, your masters of song? Kill me but let me be remembered.'

Aelis looked down at the man in front of her, everything she despised made flesh. It was Sigfrid and his kin who had burned Chartres and taken her father's lands in Neustria, they who controlled what should have been hers. It was Sigfrid who had put the sons of the Church to the sword and brought plague and starvation to her people.

'I'll tell them nothing and you will be forgotten,' she said.

She went to push the sword into him two-handed, but Sigfrid caught the blade in his one good hand.

Blood poured from his fingers as he tried to force it back. Sigfrid smiled. 'I regret having this sharpened, now,' he said. His hand was shaking, blood streaming down the white of his arm. Aelis shoved as hard as she could, driving her full weight into the pommel of the sword. But Sigfrid, facing death, was still terribly strong and he held the blade.

'Do you know what the prophecy says, Aelis, what the raven woman gave her eyes to discover? Do you know? You have a wolf on you, a wolf, and he hunts you eternally, through many lives. But the wolf knows only destruction, and when he finds you he will destroy you and all you care about. You are cursed, Aelis, for ever, tied to the destiny of the gods.'

The king could hold the sword no longer. He gave a great cry and threw the blade aside, but Aelis brought it back to his face and lunged again. He tried to turn away but was hampered by his injuries and the sword plunged into the side of his neck. Blood pulsed from the gaping wound. Sigfrid put his hand up to try to stop the flow but it was useless. He fell back, looked at Aelis and, with his last available strength, shook his head and smiled. 'A woman, some sort of wolf, then. Perhaps I was Odin after all,' he said, and died.

Aelis sat down, panting and shaking. She was covered in the king's blood. She looked around her, back up the hill. No time to recover, no time for delay. She ran to where the monks were. Marellus was dead, a scarlet bloom of blood visible on his pale skin where his habit was open at his chest, but Abram was alive, if unconscious. He bore no obvious signs of a wound other than a hugely swollen jaw. The king must have punched or clubbed him down, she thought.

She went back to the king's body. Quickly she stripped off his clothes and put them on. They buried her, as did his mail hauberk, but she wore it anyway. It felt very heavy on her shoulders, but once she had tied the king's big belt around her, the weight was spread and more bearable. There was a comfort in the heaviness too, a feeling the armour might do some good. She strapped on Sigfrid's sword and knife, threw on his swamping cloak and put the shield on her back as she had seen her brother do so many times. She almost hated to take it because it bore the loathed symbol of the wolf she had seen flying from the Vikings' banners. The helmet was so big it was useless, but she put his boots on, glad to get something on her bare feet. The king had money with him – two dinars and three tremisis. He also had a fine arm ring in silver, a serpent eating its tail. She pushed the purse into the front of the hauberk and the ring after it.

She checked the confessor. He was breathing, but faintly. She needed to get him somewhere he could rest, but what about the unconcious monk? Sigfrid's horse was too big for her to lift him on and the mule wouldn't carry two men. She peered at the farm buildings near the river. They were burned, she could now see. There was the ford just beyond the buildings and, past that, the edge of another big wood. The trees offered the best cover and a place to weigh her options, she thought. She'd have to make two trips, one with the confessor and the other with Abram.

She looked up again. Up on the hill she could see someone moving. She had to go. She called to Sigfrid's horse, almost too softly to be heard. The animal turned as if ridden and came to her. It was a big beast and she was encumbered by the cloak and her boots, but the horse was patient and eventually she got on, shaking her head in disgust at the saddle. It was made of turf, as many of the Viking saddles were. No seat for a king, she thought, nor even for a lady. Still, it was a saddle and it worked, so it would have to do.

Aelis turned the warhorse around and walked it to the mule, leaning down to gather up the pack animal's halter. She glanced behind her. The figure on the hill was now running down the slope waving at her crazily. From the big baggy kaftan tucked into his stockings at the knee, his lopsided cap and pointy little grey beard, she could see it was the merchant, puffing and blowing towards her, flapping his arms to attract her attention but not making a sound, like a court fool conducting a mad mime.

She guessed that he must be pursued, or rather that he feared attracting the attention of pursuers – that explained his silence. She knew that the merchant would try to ransom her but, then again, wasn't that what she wanted? She couldn't risk capture by the Norsemen. The merchant might get past whatever enemy forces stalked the riverbank, reach her brother and send help to get her home. He could help with Brother Abram too.

She brought the horse around to face him. Leshii bent over, resting his elbows on his knees, and wheezing like a clapped-out hunting dog.

'You kept your oath!' he said, as if each word was the weight of an anvil and had to be heaved out of his breathless body.

'Did you keep yours?'

'I had business with the king. As I see you had. Did the monks do for him? I can't believe that.'

'He died by the sword,' said Aelis, 'just his own, and wielded by a woman.'

'You killed him?' said Leshii. 'All the warriors in Francia haven't managed that. How did you do such a thing?' He was bent double, still trying to catch his breath.

Aelis ignored his question; they had to move. 'One of the monks is alive. You can carry him,' she said.

'Then you'll have another body on your hands,' said Leshii. 'Let me help put him on your horse.'

Aelis nodded. That was, she had to admit, the best plan.

'We'll go to the woods,' said Aelis. 'From there you can cross to the south bank. Go to Saint-Germain or, if the way is blocked, try to send word to the city. There are men who can get in and out for the right price.' She reached into the sagging byrnie and pulled out the arm ring. She threw it to Leshii.

'Tell my brothers' guards his sister sent you this, from the body of the king she killed.' Leshii examined the ring, nodding in appreciation of its workmanship.

Brother Abram was not as light as the confessor, and it took a good deal of heaving to get him across the horse's back. Aelis led the horse while Leshii steadied Abram and led the mule. Clouds scudded across the moon as they descended towards the black ribs of the charred buildings. In the gloom the ridge of the woods behind them vanished into shadow.

They didn't see the rider at the edge of the trees come down the hill, nor the figure in the feather cloak who stepped from the darkness to take the hand of the pale woman and watch him descend.

19 A Fight for Saerda

Leshii was hungry now and frozen. It was that moment in the predawn when the night seems coldest, perhaps because you know the warmth of day is so close.

The lady had refused him even part of her cloak, preferring instead to use it to cover the senseless monks. He did point out that the big monk wasn't going to notice if he was warm or not, and that it was better a man who was awake should take it, but the lady gave him a look that was not likely to warm him up. Still, he couldn't complain too much because she suffered herself. Underneath the mail coat, which she showed no signs of removing, all she had on was Sigfrid's light trousers and silk shirt. Not much for a chilly night.

As a man of lands of the Rus, he was used to the cold, but he was used to being adequately dressed too. The night had been chilly when the air was still, but there was now a breeze in the trees, blowing the cold of the river across their camp, if you could call it a camp. There was no question of having a fire, nor any flint or steel to start one with. Anyway, fires invite curiosity, the last thing they wanted.

The lady, against his better judgement, had released the mule and horse to forage in the wood. He thought they might as well kill one and eat it as lose it to whoever found it. The animals didn't run off, though; they even came back after they'd been to the river to drink. The river. There was another problem. The spring rains had been heavy, and it was deep and fast-flowing. The ford could be crossed by a skilled rider or by five or six people, all linking arms against the flow, thought Leshii. An old man, a girl and two injured monks? Never. Still, he thought, he might just about make it alone if he could take the mule.

What do with the lady? He could disarm her as she slept and tie her up. But he couldn't transport her bound and gagged all the way to Ladoga. An obvious captive was an incitement to robbery – bandits would try to ransom her themselves. And he couldn't trick her into going willingly.

He lay down and tried to sleep, his mind churning over his problems. The horse had wandered around behind him, he thought. He could hear it snorting in the trees. Then he came to himself. No, both animals were there, next to the lady, untied but content.

It was another horse. He stood.

'Lady, lady.'

Aelis was on her feet with the shield up and the sword in her hand.

Leshii could see nothing. He heard Aelis say a word under her breath in her native Roman. His command of that language was poor but it was a word any trader would know: 'horse'. She was staring into the trees. She said the word again and there was a voice, almost in reply.

'Stay there. Stay there. Hold it. Hold. Ahhh!'

There was a crash in the dark, the sound of someone falling. Aelis held up the sword. It gave Leshii no confidence at all. She looked exactly what she was – a fine lady dressed up as a warrior. She held the blade upright, the handle high at the side of her ear as if the weapon was a fan and the shield had its face to the ground, her entire chest and head exposed.

Movement in the trees, something coming at them fast, far too quick to be a man. A riderless horse. As it drew level with the lady, it slowed and went to join the other animals. Leshii watched in wonder as it did so. It was the strangest behaviour he had ever seen from a horse. One second it seemed in a terrible sweat; the next it was rubbing into the other beasts as if they'd shared the same field all their lives.

He didn't have time to think about that. He saw a blink of white in the dark and a slower movement, left to right. He had the impression of something creeping, almost crablike.

'That's a Viking horse,' said Aelis.

'How do you know?'

'The saddle, see. They're so badly made, they—'

He never knew what she was going to say. He saw a face through the trees and, with his merchant's ability to remember names, immediately knew who it was.

'Saerda, friend, have you taken a fall?'

The man came forward, snarling like a dog who'd had a bone snatched from him.

'You, lady, owe me weregild,' he said. 'You killed a king. What's the rate for that? More dinars than Paris can hold, I think.'

'She doesn't speak your language,' said Leshii, 'but nothing is beyond negotiation. Work with us to return her to her city and she will see you're rewarded.'

He guessed what Saerda had done – watched from afar until the trouble was over and then approached them when there was less chance of others taking his prize.

'I know the reward the Franks would give me,' said Saerda. 'Rollo is my king now. He doesn't want the people to kneel and call him a god. He's content just to see them kneel. He'll pay a good price for this girl and then he'll either marry or ransom her. She can come back with me.'

'Tell him if he takes a step closer I'll kill him,' said Aelis.

'The lady invites you to sit a while with us and talk things through,' said Leshii.

'Yes, it looks like it,' said Saerda, 'very much indeed. Do you want to fight, lady, is that what you want?'

He moved towards her across the glade. Aelis thrust forward the sword but her arm was straight and stiff, her body taut, like she was reaching with a pole for clothes drying high on a hedge. Saerda moved more fluidly. He put his sword up to hers and tapped it a couple of times. His arm was a whip, fast and accurate. Twice she thought he would shake the sword from her hand just with the force of his blow against it.

He withdrew slightly and she instinctively poked the sword

after him. He had been waiting for that, Leshii could see. Saerda caught her blade with his in an enveloping motion. He whirled it round and round in four quick circles before a sudden jerk of his arm sent it singing into the trees. He feinted a blow at her head, and Aelis took the bait, raising her shield to her face. There were two smart smacks on the shield but Saerda's sword had gone nowhere near it; he'd driven it straight down through the toe of Aelis's boot. Late and clumsily, Aelis brought the shield to the grass between them. Saerda's mouth fell open like a gargoyle's as he saw the two black-feathered arrows protruding from it. He turned to look behind him, and Aelis hammered into him, sending him sprawling. A noise, no more than twenty paces away, a war cry, thought Leshii, a strangled croak of aggression.

'No!' Aelis's eyes were wide with terror. She retreated a couple of steps, dropped the shield and then turned and fled through the trees, Sigfrid's big boot still pinned to the floor by Saerda's sword.

Saerda got to his feet and retrieved his weapon but went no further. Just visible through the shadows, twenty paces away, Leshii could see a terrible, lean, naked figure drawing a bow. It was the Raven. How could he aim in the dark? Leshii thought of the shield, stuck with arrows. It had been rare luck that Aelis had moved it in front of her face at the right moment. Leshii picked up a heavy stick and hurled it. He hit the bowman square on the arm, causing him to loose an arrow into the dirt.

'Oh dear,' said Leshii to himself as Hugin turned and lowered the bow. The merchant ran. Leshii couldn't see where he was going – the moon through the trees robbed the forest floor of all perspective, every shadow containing the possibility of an ankle-breaking depression, a root or stone. He fell and fell again. Then he rose and tripped once more. He was flat exhausted and could not run any further.

He sat up. The grim figure was coming towards him through the bars of moonlight, his cruel sword drawn. In a frozen instant of terror, Leshii saw his opponent, the thin limbs, the muscles wound onto his bones like creepers around a tree, the face eaten by the self-inflicted torture of the birds to who knew what purpose, that cold weapon, death made steel, which seemed to shimmer and flash in the moonlight.

The Raven was still twenty paces from him when Leshii fainted to the ground.

20 Caught

Aelis ran too, flat out and blind with terror through the wood. There was a thump, a blinding light and she was down. Witless with fear, she had blundered into a tree.

She could hear the monster behind her, his pace quick and light. She knew that to hide was suicide. Raven had sunk two arrows into her shield from thirty paces, through the deep darkness of the trees. He would find her, she knew. There was his call again – horrible, almost mocking.

She ran on, as quickly as before. She couldn't afford caution, though she stumbled and tripped on roots, sudden dips and unseen rises. She crashed into a thicket of ferns, sensing the river's cold before she saw its glitter, the moonlight turning the water to a road of sparkling ice. But it was no road you could walk on. The cry was near her now; she had no choice, and she leaped in.

In her haste she had forgotten the mail coat. It was heavy but not so heavy that she couldn't keep her head above water. Her brother and his men held races across the Seine in full war gear in times of peace, and she told herself she was of the same stock, though her limbs were tiring quickly.

Aelis hadn't expected the current to be so strong. It swept her downstream, and she had to pump her arms to keep her mouth above water. The cold was a serpent, crushing the breath from her body and dragging her down. She kicked for the opposite bank but she was exhausted and couldn't fight the pull of the freezing river. The black mass of a fallen tree loomed in front of her and she snatched at a branch. No good. Her numb hands couldn't grasp it. The water took her and spun her, but then the little breath she had in her body was driven from her. Her leg had caught on something submerged.

She gulped in an icy mouthful and was certain she was going down. She cried out and beat her hands against the current's pull.

Her foot was stuck fast but she managed another breath. As she did, her hand touched something rough, cold and hard. It was a tree trunk, beneath the water. She hugged it, turning her back to the stream, clinging on. She was pressed against the trunk of the tree, frozen but breathing.

She looked around. The tree emerged from the water and went under again, but it was attached to the bank. If she could free her foot she could pull herself to the shore. She tugged at her foot. It had become wedged at the ankle between a branch and the trunk. Every time she tried to free it, the bitter cold water threatened to shove her forward and down. There was nothing for it, though, she had to try. Aelis crossed her feet and used her left leg to hook back on her right. The ankle came free, the water tried to tear her from the trunk but she was ready and clung on. She felt her way along the tree to the shore.

The ravaged face of the sorcerer looked down at her from behind a drawn bow. Aelis looked up at him and realised that all hope was lost. She shook and shivered on the trunk.

'Go on then.'

The Raven put down the bow and crouched at the side of the river. His eyes were just blank spaces; his face under the moonlight was a moon itself, pitted, torn and unreadable.

She went to climb onto the bank; she had to get out of that icy water no matter what. Hugin moved his head to one side and looked down at her. Then he drew a long thin knife from his belt. He wasn't going to let her get out.

She knew she was going to die. How long would it take?

Longer than she had expected. It got lighter, and lighter still. She didn't die, though she shivered and her hands were blue. She knew it was impossible to get across the river, impossible to get past the Raven. How much time passed? The spring hours, the divisions of twelve between sun and dusk, seemed as long as those of high summer. How many had gone by since she entered the river? One? Two? Still he sat there, a great carrion bird, watching her like a crow watches a dying sheep. The sharp moon hung in a sky of duck-egg blue and the sun through the trees turned the air to crystal. It was day, she realised.

Her vision faded, the moon dancing and wheeling, blurring and finally fading from sight. A sharp crescent of light split the darkness and at first she thought it was the moon again. But it was not. It seemed she was standing inside a cave, and the crescent of light was its mouth. She walked to the mouth and saw that the cave was set in the wall of a dizzying cliff. The air seemed to rush beneath her; wisps of clouds hung like mountain spirits at her feet. She held something heavy in her arms – a man. He was dead and he had died for her. She looked behind her. Somewhere inside the cave was someone else she had loved, she could sense it.

A thumping, rhythmic song came into her head.

'Then fares Odin to fight with the wolf ...'

She had never heard it before, but she knew its meaning was bound up with her life. The cold sent pins and needles through her body, but it wasn't just a physical sensation; something seemed to fizz and spit in her mind.

She could see more now – a huge wolf, its head bloody and its jaws red, was tearing at a fallen warrior beneath a sky of ravens on a wide bleak plain. As it shook and ripped the man's flesh, shapes seemed to appear in her mind, and she knew them for what they were – magical symbols, expressions of the fundamental relations of the universe, living things that could plant themselves to shine and chime from the dark shadows of the mind.

She spoke the words in her head:

Runes I took from the dying god,
Where the wolf tore men on Vigrid plain.

She should be dying, she knew, but there were things inside

her that did not want to die, and would not let her do so until she had fulfilled a purpose.

She saw another symbol, a jagged tear in the fabric of the blue sky. It was one of the magical shapes, a rune, as the rhyme had said, but different from the others. What did it mean? A hook, a trap, a trap for a wolf. But it meant more to her than all the other shapes combined, more than the one that seemed to burst with flowers, wither and grow again, the symbol of rebirth, more than the symbol that seemed to her like a shield around her, more even than the one that gabbled and talked, to chuckle at the good fortune that it brought.

Again, that voice in her head. She seemed to recognise it. It was like a child's but worn and heavy with experience.

> *The fetters shall burst and the wolf run free*
> *Much do I know and more can see.*

A strange realisation swept over Aelis. She would not die because she was linked to something so much greater than herself through those strange shapes, the runes that had taken root in her in lifetimes she had lived before when she had watched a god die under the teeth of a wolf. One of the symbols emanated in her mind – the horse rune, which sweated and stamped and now careered and galloped. There were others too, growing within her, whispering to her, coming to bloom.

She came back to herself. She was still on the trunk in the river. The Raven was still crouching, his cruel knife in his hand.

When he saw her move he stood up and retreated a pace, but she remained within his reach and the knife was pointed towards her. She clawed herself up onto the bank and lay retching and convulsing on the ground. The Raven prodded her with his foot, examining her, almost as if he was trying to understand the woman he had made his enemy. There was a sound in Aelis's mind like the rushing of blood, like drums to call the wind.

She didn't know where the words came from, but she spoke to him: 'The thread of my fate is woven. It doesn't end today.'

The Raven didn't seem to notice that Aelis had spoken in Norse, a language she barely understood. He just shrugged and took her by the throat.

21 Last Rites

'Confessor. Confessor. God. Saint.'

The voice called him back to consciousness, though Jehan could sense that it would not be for long. He felt as though he was on the brink of an abyss, his thoughts teetering and threatening to fall into nothing.

Where had he been? In a dark, deep place where the rocks sweated moisture and his enemy waited.

'No, Vali, no. You are a different thing now, trapped by fate. You are the ending, the destruction.' It was a woman's voice, speaking in Norse. It was Aelis's voice. 'Vali.' He recognised the name. She had infected his mind with her touch, set a vibration in him that had shaken the mental structures he had built through denials, willing and unwilling. He wanted her and God was showing him a vision of the hell to which that love – no, Jehan, call it by its rightful name – that lust had condemned him. The lady had said she feared she was a witch and, like a witch, with a touch she had turned him into something else.

'Confessor. Priest.' The voice again. He was in agony, his skin felt too tight for his body. The wounds he had taken were beginning to swell and ache dreadfully. The worst was his eye, throbbing and raw. The pain filled him up; he could think of nearly nothing else. He forced himself to speak, though his jaw was bruised and swollen from where the hanging rope had pulled up under his chin, and he hardly had the strength to move his mouth. His tongue was thick and swollen but his will was strong and the confessor made himself talk.

'You are a Norseman – I know you by your speech. Are you of the faith? Are you a priest? Say mass so I might pass over.'

The confessor gave a cry as something brushed his torn nose.

The Norseman couldn't hear much of what he was saying and had pressed his ear to Jehan's mouth.

'What is mass?'

'The body and the blood of Christ. Anoint me in blessed oil and prepare the way.'

'You are dying.'

'Yes. Give me unction so that I may be more certain of heaven.'

'What is unction?'

'You are no man of God. I will die unshriven. Forgive me, God, for I have been a prideful and arrogant servant to you. What is your name, Norseman?'

'Saerda, priest. Your friends have left you.'

'Then be a friend to me. Allow me to bring you to Christ and then pray for me.'

Even at the last, Jehan wanted souls for Jesus.

'How shall I come to Christ?'

'Partake of his body and blood with me. Let me bless you as I bless myself.'

There was a snort from the Norseman. 'I will help you perform the ritual.'

'You have the bread?'

'That becomes the flesh? Is it true you drink the blood?'

'Yes, the wine that becomes the blood, the bread that becomes the flesh.'

'I have bread.'

Jehan thought. He didn't have the oil to anoint and purify the seats of corruption, his hands, forehead, feet and genitals, but he would have to do what he could while he had strength.

The confessor felt his whole body shaking as he repented his sins, the pride in his holiness, the pride in his strength in accepting his affliction as God's will, his presumptuous certainty that he was intended for heaven. He asked for pardon and recited the Apostles' Creed: *'Credo in Deum ...'*

Jehan could hardly get the words out. He said the Lord's Prayer and then he was ready for his final mass. Calling on

Agnus Dei, the Lamb of God and, amending the words to fit his terrible situation, he said, 'Bring me the bread to bless it.'

There was a short laugh, a wet sound and a low groan. Then a noise like the slapping of lips. Jehan, who had to use his ears where his eyes had failed, recognised the sound as the cutting of meat. Then the man came to Jehan and cradled him in his arms.

'Say your words.'

Jehan spoke: 'This is the Lamb of God, that takes away the sins of the world. Happy are they that are called to his supper. The body of Christ. Give me the bread so I can bless it and eat it. You must put it to my lips; I cannot raise my hands.'

Jehan felt something slip into his mouth. It wasn't bread. It tasted of blood. He choked and coughed.

'Animal flesh will not do!'

'That is not animal flesh,' said Saerda.

'What is it?'

'Your brother monk.'

Jehan tried to spit but he couldn't. His body twitched and convulsed; his lacerated tongue tried to push away the corruption that was in his mouth but the blood taste would not go. He called out, but his cry was nothing beyond a whisper.

'Your friends are gone. Our man Hrafn is seeing to your lady; your merchant has fled, and your monk is your supper. I will perform your dirty ritual, you flesh-eater, who cowers in the face of his enemies and calls it virtue.'

'Our father—' Jehan began the Lord's Prayer.

More of the filthy stuff was pushed into his mouth, fingers shoving it past his tongue. He tried to bite, but his mouth would not close and he realised his jaw must have been broken by the rope. The agony went right through him as Saerda forced open his mouth. There was something else in there, something slick and wet, which slid into his throat like a bloody oyster. Saerda had his hand on the confessor's nose, clamping shut his mouth.

'It's one of his eyes, holy man. Come on, priest. This is the body, this the blood. Here, drink and eat to go to your god.'

He threw the confessor back on the ground and for a second Jehan thought his ordeal was over. It had only just begun. Saerda called out the names of the parts as he forced them into Jehan's mouth – the liver, the kidney, the heart and the balls. Jehan vomited but the slick meat was only shovelled back in.

'Do you think you could eat all of him, priest? Think how holy you would be, think.'

Jehan's thoughts were scrambling under the horror he was enduring. In his mind he saw a plain with a hollow, dead light, a body in front of him, its armour torn, its spear broken.

Saerda was pacing around him, now, taking his time.

'Stop!'

'I won't stop. I lost my king and my horse tonight; the Raven's taken a lady who could have brought me riches, and all I have is whatever I can get for your useless bones. That has put me in a fearful bad temper. You'll eat until that temper's spent.'

He pushed something more into the confessor's mouth, wrenching back his head. He cursed as the monk convulsed and shook from his grasp. Saerda pulled him up by his habit but the monk wrenched back in a terrible spasm, tearing away from his fingers to lie trembling and jabbering on the floor. Jehan saw a cave, saw himself lying unable to move, not because of illness but because a rope, terribly thin and strong, wound about him, lashing him to a great rock. He saw the Virgin and heard her screaming at him that his destiny was to kill and to die.

'You broke my bastard finger!' said Saerda. 'Now you really are going to pay for that.'

The berserker took up the glittering rope of Abram's bowels, sat astride Jehan's chest, and thrust it into the confessor's face, forcing as much as he could past his teeth.

'You'll eat, you'll eat and you'll eat again,' said Saerda.

The monk's whole body twisted and writhed, and Saerda could not hold him. Jehan threw him off. The monk felt as though every muscle was trying to break free of the bone. His head turned and shook, his legs kicked, driving him around in a wild spin. His lips foamed blood. All he could think of was blood, Christ's blood, streaming in the sky. The sun was blood, the moon blood, the air blood, the water and the light blood. He heard the words of the Bible in his head:

> He hath led me, and brought me into darkness, but not into light.
> Surely against me is he turned; he turneth his hand against me all the day.

No, God had not turned against him; God had loved him and marked him out as special. But the words would not stop rattling through his head like a rat in an attic.

> My flesh and my skin hath he made old; he hath broken my bones.
> He hath set me in dark places, as they that be dead of old.
> He hath hedged me about, that I cannot get out: he hath made my chain heavy.
> Also when I cry and shout, he shutteth out my prayer.

The words seemed to speak to him, telling him something that was more bitter to him than any torture, any affliction or pain. God had deserted him. He could not believe it to be so. It was the work of a devil. Hell had set a worm in his mind.

> He hath filled me with bitterness, he hath made me drunken with wormwood.
> He hath also broken my teeth with gravel stones, he hath covered me with ashes.
> And thou hast removed my soul far off from peace: I forgot prosperity.
> And I said, 'My strength and my hope is perished from the lord.'

Jehan screamed, more in his mind than with his voice: *No! No! No! The Lord is my portion, saith my soul; therefore will I hope in him. The lord is good unto them that wait for him, to the soul that seeketh him.* The words were like a high and melodious music but underneath them something deeper beat out a dark poetry.

> *Much have I fared, much have I found,*
> *Much have I got of the gods,*
> *What shall bring the doom of death to Odin,*
> *When the gods to destruction ride?*

He had never heard that verse before but he knew the answer, it was on his lips.

Saerda drew his knife and leaped at the confessor's chest, pinning him down, shoving the point into the side of his cheek.

'Shut your rattle. You'll eat him or you'll eat yourself. I'll cut you up and stuff you down your own throat.'

Jehan saw himself. He was lashed to the rock, his fetters tourniquets, his mouth wedged open by something sharp and strong. He knew the answer, knew who it was who would bring death to the pagan god.

> *The wolf shall be the bane of Odin,*
> *When the gods to destruction ride.*

Jehan reached up his hands and found Saerda's head. He saw that cave in his mind, felt the sharp thin bindings cutting his flesh and pinioning him to the huge rock. The wolf, the wolf would bring death to the god. It was all he existed for, all that he did. There was a sensation of release and freedom. He was the wolf.

'The fetters have burst,' he said, and he broke the Viking's neck.

22 Helpless

Leshii had come round to find himself alone. The Raven, he thought, must have gone straight by him.

It was morning. He thought of the lady. At first he found it hard to orientate himself to determine which way she had run, but a gasp drew him to where she was. He was about to go to her but a glint of steel stopped him. It was the Raven, he knew, that naked figure, pale as a corpse, crouching in the grey dawn light by the river.

Leshii wanted to creep closer but he couldn't make his legs do it. Fear overcame his will and kept him from moving. He was in terror of that awful man.

For the first time since he had met the berserkers, he thought of Chakhlyk. Where was the wolfman? Dead, he didn't doubt it.

He thought of that skinny berserker too: where was he? His mind came back to what it always came back to – value. He'd seen enough of the berserkers who had drunk his wine to know they owed no blood loyalty to the king at the camp. They couldn't speak Latin, couldn't bargain with monks. His one way forward, which was not attractive at all, was to ally himself to those men. He turned the arm ring over in his hand. At least he had something of worth, as necessary to him as a weapon to a warrior. Now he could buy and sell again, now he could trade, now he was himself.

He outlined his position in his mind, the deal he was making with fate. The least he wanted was safe passage home. Helgi might have him killed if he came back empty-handed, but his mission had only been to lead the wolfman to Paris. However, it would be much better to return with the lady because there was no guarantee how the king might react and it was better

144

to be certain of a reward. Ideally he wanted the monk to sell and the lady too. The lady was about to die, he had no doubt, and there was nothing he could do to prevent it. So then, find the berserkers, employ them as bodyguards and get the monk, or his bones. He could promise to pay them once he was paid for the monk. He couldn't ransom him, alive or dead, without someone to defend him.

But no, he wasn't thinking straight.

Leshii fought to put his thoughts in order. He'd been Sigfrid's prisoner. As soon as the king's body was found the whole place was going to be crawling with Vikings looking for his killer and Leshii would be high on their list of suspects. The risk of going back to the Viking camp was just too great. He was faced with walking back to Ladoga with nothing to protect him but the coat he stood up in and his wits.

There was a movement in the trees. Horses, coming past at the trot, keening and fretful.

What was wrong with those animals? He'd heard that sound they were making recently, when the Viking horse had taken a throwing axe in the neck. It was the sound of terrible, mortal distress.

He looked through the trees, away from where the Raven crouched at the water's edge.

There was more movement. Yes, the king's big horse. A horse would make his journey much easier, if he could make it come to him. But it seemed to be having some sort of fit, stamping at the ground, sweating and frothing. It was looking towards where the Raven was crouching. It was Sigfrid's animal for sure, the one Aelis had been riding. Further off in the trees he heard another call, a bray. It was his mule! Now he could get that. If Leshii knew anything, he knew mules, after thirty years on the trade routes. He felt sure he could catch it and got to within about twenty paces, whistling softly. He could see the animal was scared but it was in nowhere near as bad a state as the horse. 'Come on, girl, come on.'

The mule took a few paces away.

Something came running through the trees to Leshii's left. There was a huge cry, another answering it. Against himself he ran to see what it was. It was the wolf.

23   Wolf's Blood

Death did not come to Aelis, but something like it did. The shadows unwrapped, reached forward and took the Raven to the ground before he could strike.

Hugin was standing again almost before he'd gone down, slashing up and around with the knife with a terrible speed. At first, as the two figures grappled in front of the sharp morning sun, Aelis thought it was a wolf. It sounded like a wolf and was as quick, but she saw, as an arm flashed out to block the knife, that it was a man, the same man who had come for her in the church.

'Run, run,' he was screaming. 'He will kill me soon and then he will come for you again. Run!'

She tried to stand but her legs wouldn't obey her; they were frozen dead. She got half to her feet but fell like a drunk, grabbing for a tree with an arm that was numb with cold. She fell, head smacking into the ground. Then she tried again, but she couldn't even feel her limbs, let alone use them.

'Run, run!'

Aelis heard that sound in her head – like a great rushing of water, the movement of wind in the mouth of a cave, the tide of the blood in the ears, but it was none of those things.

The Raven was on top of the wolfman. He had his knife in both his hands and was straining to get the point into his opponent's neck. The wolfman had caught the blade, the blood on his fingers bright in the dawn light. Hugin gave a great hoarse cry and drove the knife down, but the wolfman snapped it and used the Raven's downward momentum to drive his head into his opponent's nose. Then he was on him, screaming and biting and punching and tearing. The sorcerer went for his sword but the wolfman pinned his arm, making it impossible to draw. The men were on their feet now in a brawling embrace, staggering from tree to tree. They fell, broke, got up again, but the wolfman never let Hugin get far enough away to free his sword. But the Raven didn't need a weapon. With ferocious speed he smashed his knee upwards into the wolfman's midriff, driving him up into the air. The wolfman hit the ground like something wet.

Aelis thought her mind was going to split. That sound was within her and without her, coming from that pulsing, breathing, running rune. What was it?

The Raven reached for his sword; the wolfman lunged to stop him, and for a second they stood swaying together by the river's edge. Then the big horse smashed them both into the water. Aelis finally placed the sound. It wasn't water, blood, wind or drums. It was hooves.

Leshii came running. The Raven was gone, but the wolfman was clinging by one hand to the branch of the tree that had saved Aelis. Leshii could see he wouldn't last long. The horse had knocked him almost senseless and he was groaning. Leshii had never heard him acknowledge any hardship before. The wolfman was twenty paces out in the powerful current; Leshii was old, he couldn't save him. But he had to. It was not heroism or fellow feeling that drove him on but, as ever, practicality. He needed a protector and he needed someone to help complete his mission. Chakhlyk was his only hope.

'I am coming, dry one, I am coming.'

The king's horse had knelt down beside Aelis, lightly pressing its body into hers, offering her its warmth. The other animals had come in too – Saerda's horse and the mule. Leshii knew what he needed to do. The mule was a pack animal and wouldn't like to be ridden, but it would be led. He took its halter and walked it out into the rushing water, standing upstream so his weight pushed into its side. He knew there was no creature on earth as sure-footed as a mule, and the animal went out into the river with a slow confidence.

About ten paces in, the pressure of the water became too

much for Leshii and he draped himself over the mule's back, driving it on with a slap on the rump. The water was only up to the top of its legs when they reached the wolfman, but the flow was so strong that the merchant knew he wouldn't be able to stand unsupported. His plan was to wedge himself against the mule to resist the current. He dropped into the water and immediately realised he'd been too hopeful. The water caught his feet as the mule skipped free and back to the bank. Leshii slipped and grabbed for the wolfman on instinct, pulling him from the branch. The water took both of them, and drove them backwards but Leshii got some purchase on the riverbed and with a great heave shoved himself and the wolfman towards the bank.

The current pulled and turned them and then it had them, surging them on. For a few seconds they were lost, but then Leshii felt a great crack on his side, solid ground beneath his feet and grass in his hands. He'd been smashed into the bank fifty paces from the tree, where a bend narrowed the course of the river. He and the wolfman were alive. From across the river he heard something between a croak and scream. He peered across the bright water. On the opposite bank a naked figure with something tied to its back was pulling itself onto dry land.

Leshii coughed and stood, almost laughing.

'Well, he won't be coming back over here in a hurry. Chakhlyk, my dry one, you're wet enough now.'

The wolfman heaved himself up onto his bleeding hands. Now Leshii could see the wound in his side, a thumb's width of broken arrow shaft protruding from just below his last rib. No wonder people were scared of him, thought Leshii. He had fought the Raven with that in his guts. But the wolfman couldn't be long from death.

'He is calling to his sister,' said the wolfman. 'We need to go, and now. He has seen the lady and she is in great danger.'

There were sounds through the trees – shouting, lots of men.

'No time,' said the wolfman. 'Come on.'

Aelis was trembling as the blood returned to her limbs. 'What about the confessor and the monk?'

'Murderers! King-slayers! They have his clothes, they have his clothes!'

There was one Viking, a boy, fifty paces off, just visible between the trees and the river.

'Go,' said the wolfman. 'Now. I will find you. Merchant, get on that animal and take the lady to Helgi.'

'I am going to my people,' said Aelis.

'No. You have very little time. The wolf is coming into flesh – it is foreseen. You must get to Helgi; only he can save you from what stalks you.'

'What stalks me?'

'Death, destruction, again and again in many lives.'

He lifted the lady onto the horse and Leshii got up behind.

Aelis looked down at the wolfman and stammered, 'W-why are you doing this?'

'For love,' he said. 'I will find you. Aelis, Adisla, I will find you. Now go!'

A shadow sang across the light. The wolfman stepped forward and took it from the air. It was a spear.

'Go. They are near.'

He slapped the animal's rump, and it took off through the trees with the Norsemen at its back.

24 At Ladoga

Paris was still unscorched, Sigfrid living and the confessor still a lost child grubbing in the great forest of the Rhine when Helgi went up to the roof of the loading tower to survey his new lands at Aldeigjuborg, or Ladoga as he was learning to call it to please his subjects. He had something else to celebrate beyond taking possession of the town – the birth of a daughter.

The Viking king looked out over his lands and waters. Stretching out in front of him in the clear day was the river leading to the trembling blue of Lake Ladoga, its green islands just specks in the distance. Spread out around it like stars around the moon were the turquoise flashes of other lakes, so many he had never managed to count them. He looked at the winding rivers that connected them – some like threads, others more like blue roots, all reaching out from the great shimmering boss of the lake, stretching east to Miklagard and the steppes, west to the Eastern Lake, and north to home.

His men, the northerners, were lords of the water, kings of ships. No wonder the native tribes of Slavs and the Finns had asked him to rule over them. He had been surprised when he received their ambassadors asking him to be their king, but when he came to think about it, it was only a just reward. Who had warred more than he had? Who had stocked the All Father's halls with so many dead warriors that his armies would stretch from horizon to horizon? Who had sacrificed slaves and cattle at summer *blöt* and winter feast? Helgi. Odin was his god, the god of kings, and he had rewarded him handsomely.

Years before, his people had come in conquest, ruled for a while and been overthrown. But the chaos that followed was so bad and the memory of their easy and liberal rule so good that within twenty years a tribal faction, too weak to make a bid for power on its own, had invited them back.

It felt good to be king – *khagan* – of such a fertile land. Helgi climbed down the tower to take in the celebrations going on below. The Slavs might have some funny customs but they liked a *blöt* – a celebration and feast – as well as any man of the north. Helgi took to the streets, his bodyguard closing in behind him. He stood for a while watching some sacrificed slaves, naked and painted, swinging from a gallows under the wide blue sky. The sight of this proof of his power and riches was pleasing to him. The smell of the piss and shit that had fallen from the dead men as they choked mingled with the temple incense, the stink of the animals, the perfume of the garlands that the young girls wore, the herbs of the beer in the horn he drank from. He found the sensation rich and intoxicating.

Summer in the lands of the Rus was a beautiful thing – you could almost smell the heat, although there was a freshness to it that blew in off the river and made even the midday sun bearable. This was an abundant land: wheat in the fields, the nets of the fishermen on the lake heavy with fish, furs and honey in great supply and fine forests for hunting and firewood.

The nine dead men dangled from the scaffold in the temple to Svarog, master of wolves, who was Odin by another name, as far as Helgi could see. The ruler's concessions to Slav culture stopped at changing the names of his own gods, who had brought him such fortune, and he had actually sacrificed the dead men to Odin, lord of the hanged. By that stage the locals were so drunk they assumed the sacrifice was to Svarog. But Helgi had been careful to honour the native gods too. The temple of Perun had even been given a new statue of the god, with his great hammer raised, ready to strike the blows that split the sky with thunder and lightning.

Their creeds were very similar, thought Helgi, especially the belief in a world tree on which sat the various realms of existence. The Slavs were wrong to believe it was as oak because Helgi knew very well that it was an ash called Yggdrasil, but the difference in detail was so small that the *khagan* had taken it for confirmation of the compatibility of the northern and Slavic peoples and evidence of the truth of their beliefs. Even the *blöt* was a Slav tradition. They called it a *bratchina* – a brothering – but they were talking about the same thing. Drink, women, sacrifice and a good scrap to round it off in all likelihood.

Ladoga was thronging that day. The harvest was shaping up to be a good one; the *khagan* had donated ten prize cows to be slaughtered, and the army was in fine shape. Helgi's own men from Skania had accepted the name the Slavs had given them as the ruler's bodyguard – *druzhina* – and a good fleet was moored on the river and out on Lake Ladoga. Khazars had joined the force too, and the farmers and fishermen of the wider countryside were behind him, keen to move south and east for a taste of plunder. They were all in town, happy to throw flowers upon the river by day and drink and fuck their way into their gods' favour by night.

Helgi paraded the streets, handing out small gifts of money and loaves to the people, conspicuously directing his heir Ingvar to assist him. He needed to be seen to direct Ingvar because the boy was not his son, only his nephew. Part of the bargain that had seen him gain the loyalty of his *druzhina* – four hundred men – was that his own sons would be overlooked.

The arrangement was not unusual, and the Norsemen had no tradition that the first son, or any son, should immediately take the throne when a king died, but Helgi was a modern man. He saw the virtue of a clear heir and of that heir being beyond dispute. However, Ingvar was not subject to the special curses the gods held in reserve for those who killed their fathers. A blood heir might be more patient than a named successor in waiting for the current king to die. Ingvar was now six. In ten years, maybe as little as six, he would seek his inheritance. And Helgi was only *khagan* thanks to the Slavs. They remembered his father Rurik and had backed him for the throne. Ingvar, his dead uncle's child, had as many warriors from Skania as Helgi, and the boy's own uncles had forced oaths from Helgi that he would be his heir.

Helgi touched his sword and remembered the words he had spoken to his sons on the days of their birth as he placed it between their infant hands: 'I shall bequeath you no wealth and you will have nothing except what you gain for yourself by this sword.' It was supposed to be a formality, an encouragement to be self-reliant. But Helgi had started with nothing himself and had hoped to give more than that to his boys.

The king, though, had schemes. The cities to the south and the east, Novgorod and Kiev, were tiny and barbarous. He intended to take them and to give Ingvar the task of ruling them. He'd call Novgorod his capital first, and when he was ready to strike at Kiev would say it was time to move on there. Ingvar could spend his time fending off the mad Pechenegs and the incursions of the Greeks from Miklagard. When the boy failed, as he would, his authority would be fatally undermined and Helgi could step in to take over with the support of Ingvar's own kinsmen. Perhaps Ingvar would even be killed fighting the maniac southerners.

Helgi would not have broken his oath to protect and nourish the child; he would have fulfilled it by putting him to work as a ruler before he was even eight.

'*Khagan.*'

It was one of the *druzhina*, a small wiry man who on ceremonial occasions wore full war gear including a coif of mail that covered his entire face apart from the eyes. Over it he wore a gold-inlaid round helmet and he carried a fine sword by his side.

'Yes, friend.' This was the traditional way the Slav *khagans* addressed their bodyguards, and the Norsemen had quickly picked up the habit.

'The priestess begs your presence.'

'For what?'

'You have sacrificed mightily. You are a great friend to the wolves, so much a feast do you prepare. The priestess of Svarog, of the sky and the blue of the sky, would entertain you now.'

Helgi grimaced. The idea of sex with the woman didn't appeal to him, though he knew it might be required. The Slavs had all sorts of traditional rituals for their kings, which could be pleasant when it came to deflowering virgins to bless the land but asked a little too much when it came to lying with one of the ancient, unwashed and crazy priestesses of Svarog.

'She would grant you a prophecy.'

Helgi laughed. 'I hope I can keep my trousers on for it.'

'I understand you can, lord. You just have to go down to see their oracle.'

'Good, good. I should think our sacrifice should have ensured a fine prediction.The witch should be happy with what I gave her.'

He would remember that place for the rest of his life, the darkness of the hut, the closeness of the fire and the cloying smoke of the herbs the priestess had thrown onto it, foul things that burned with the smell of pitch. He never knew whether he had only dreamed that they had brought the corpses in to sit beside him in the tiny room.

The priestess had said only that Svarog was a complicated god, lord of the bright air and of the sun but also guardian of the sun in the underworld when it disappeared at night. Svarog knew the dark places of the earth and the realms of the dark gods, and it was to that side of his nature that the rite of prophecy appealed.

She had cast her herbs into the fire, murmured her rituals and uncovered the oracle, a carved tree of wood, a face daubed on it in a childish way.

His mind lost focus and wandered. When he came back to himself, his limbs were stiff and he felt far too hot. The dead men were around him, their ripe berry heads dark and swollen in the light of the witch's baking fire. The place was an oven, and Helgi wanted to get up and leave, but it was up to him to bless his kingship by emerging with a favourable prophecy.

He had had no idea that the ritual would be so arduous. He had thought he would go in, receive good words from the priestess and come out again. Not so. He was to prophesy; he was to be the gate through which the magic would pass, so said the witch. And for that he needed to suffer.

More logs were put on the fire, more herbs, and he tried to tell her he had endured enough, that kings were to be obeyed not tortured, but the herb smoke seemed to rob him of speech. Were the corpses there? It seemed so one moment, not the next. Helgi was a warrior, a man of cold certainties. It bothered him greatly that these dead men were neither quite there nor quite absent. They seemed to blame him for something, their eyes bulging and bloody. And, strangely, he seemed to care. He seemed sorry, although he had no idea why. He had paid for them: their lives were his. No man could say he had done wrong by killing them.

The daubed face looked at him, its expression seemed full of smirking knowledge. The oracle knew things, Helgi could tell. The oracle had inside information, he was a sly one, a secret titterer behind the backs of great kings, he was no woolly headed man that oracle, he was a smart fellow indeed. What was happening to Helgi's thoughts? He chewed at nothing, he stretched the muscles of his face and stuck out his tongue; his nose streamed with snot; he longed for water but could not move.

The priestess was alongside him, a woman in a wolfskin snuffling and scratching near his side. No, not a woman. A wolf.

'Where am I?'

'At the well.'

He looked around. The room was gone, the dead men too. Instead he stood on a wide plain of black ash under a bright steel sky. The plain was utterly featureless apart from a protrusion that seemed like something grown from the same stuff as the ground, like the stump of a tree but rootless, black and hollow.

He walked up to it and looked in. A sheen of silver water was inside it, coming right to the brim of what he realised was indeed a well.

Helgi looked to his side. Two figures were there. One was a terrible old man, his face contorted into the drooling fascination men show when watching dog fights or duels. Around his neck was a strange noose tied in a complicated knot, and he stood frozen, his hands out wide. He carried something in one of them, something that dripped blood to the floor. It was an eye, his own. Helgi realised the man had torn it from his head. He stood by the well as if offering it to the heavens.

On the ground was another figure, headless. Next to it lay the crude head of the oracle, looking up at Helgi from the black floor.

'This is the well.' Helgi couldn't tell who was speaking.

'Whose well?'

'Of Mimir, the first man.'

Helgi knew the legend. This was the well of wisdom where Odin had given his eye for lore. Helgi plunged his hands into the water and drank deeply. Now he was no longer on a barren plain − a gigantic tree stretched up above him, a black ash tree spreading its branches across all of the sky. Snakes slithered and spat at its base, all around his feet, around the well, around the body on the ground, around the feet of the strange old man who had ravaged his eye.

Helgi saw visions. A rearing horse with eight legs was stamping him down, all his lands were burning and Ingvar was at the head of his army, taking his glory, stealing his plunder. He was being buried alive, a thick stream of earth dropping into his mouth, stopping his nostrils, denying him breath. He was in a pit, a pit that was being filled up, a grave in the Christian manner, sealed in and weighed down by soil.

He heard a voice in his ears: 'Odin is coming and will tear

you from your throne. Ingvar will be king. You will be killed by the creature of hoof and mane, and Ingvar will take your glory.'

'I shall kill him.'

'You will never kill him. The god is coming, and his manifestation is your death. Bar his way.'

Helgi choked on the soil, his vision gone, his breath denied.

And then he was in the light and the air of the market square, under a cool and smoky evening sky, his people around him, his *druzhina* offering him wet cloths, drink and food.

'A premonition, *khagan*?'

Helgi swallowed, spat and forced his voice to speak. 'Great fortune,' he said, 'great fortune.'

'This,' shouted a *druzhina* to the crowd, 'is the blessing of the gods, a prophecy sent to honour the birth of the *khagan*'s child!'

25 A Change of Identity

It was not the wind that awoke Jehan, nor the clear blue cold of the spring day. It was the voices of the Norsemen. He heard them shouting, one phrase heard many times: 'King-slayer, king-slayer, we will find you!'

He had an intense pain in his eyes, a searing ache. He put his hands up to his face and blinked. The agony of his torn eyelid was gone. This was another sort of pain. He blinked again and again.

He had a sensation of light, swimming brown and green and gold. There was a broad vertical line in front of him. What was it? A tree, a big oak. Jehan coughed and tasted blood. He turned to his left. There was a flash of bright gold. The river.

He breathed out, leaned back on his hands and realised it wasn't a dream. He could move. He could see.

He got up and staggered against a tree, unused for so long to standing. At his feet was the body of Saerda, his head twisted almost to face the opposite way nature intended. Jehan sank to his knees in prayer.

'Dear Lord God almighty and father everlasting, who hast safely brought me to the beginning of this day, by thy holy power, grant that this day I fall into no sin but that by thy restraining care my thoughts be set to keep thy holy laws and do thy holy will.'

Jehan had never cried, not as long as he had lived, but he cried then. God had granted him release from the bondage of his body, and Jehan had used it immediately to kill. The commandment was clear: 'Thou shalt not kill.' But the Viking had been a devil, an enemy of Christ.

Jehan put his hands to his head. He felt in such confusion. What was happening to him?

'A Frank!'

Three men were dashing towards him, two with spears, one with an axe. He wanted to wait for them, wanted to accept the punishment of God's will, but he couldn't. His legs began to move, haltingly at first but with increasing fluidity. He was running, for the first time since he was very young, he was running.

The sensations were nearly overwhelming – the feel of the forest floor digging into his tender and uncalloused bare feet, the dazzle of the light through the trees, the rush of greens and browns as he fled from his pursuers – and he just wasn't used to it all. He fell, stood and tripped again. Finally, a tree root took his leg and they were on him. It was then that he gave up. He had surrendered all right to try to preserve his life. He had partaken of unclean meat. He would accept death and, inevitably, damnation. A man must accept the will of God no matter what it might be.

Others were around him now, faces pink and angry. He was unused to seeing, to focusing, and the faces seemed to whirl and smear, a circle of flesh hemming him in. He had to get back to what he knew. Jehan closed his eyes.

'Is this the king-slayer?'

'It's a monk by his clothes, though a rough one.'

'He's not a monk; they cut their hair funny.'

'Well, whatever he is, he's a Frank. Shall I kill him?'

'Best.'

'Hang about, son.'

Jehan opened his eyes again to see a fat Viking with a big blond beard shoving through the crowd of faces.

'Before you go killing anyone, why not ask who might have a use for him?'

Jehan recognised the voice. It was Ofaeti, the one who had carried him from the church.

'Can you speak our tongue?'

Jehan tried to remain still but found himself nodding.

'How did you get here? Are you one of that party that ambushed the king last night?'

'He couldn't ambush a tree with a piss. Look at him – he's as frail as an old woman.' It was another voice.

Ofaeti crouched beside him. 'What happened to your confessor? He's a mess. Did the Raven get him? Hang on, that shield looks like the king's. And I recognise those arrows.'

'The king was robbed after he'd been killed. Maybe one of the thieves paid the price,' said someone else.

'Maybe the king was felled with arrows and the thieves dropped it here in their flight,' said another.

'Those are the Raven's arrows.'

'Did he kill the king?'

'More like whoever stole the king's stuff.'

'Perhaps this is the killer.'

'Are you saying our king could have been killed by an unarmed slave like this?'

'Of course not.'

'Well don't open your mouth if you can't speak sense.'

'Watch who you're talking to.'

The men fell to arguing. Ofaeti ignored the rising hullabaloo and spoke to Jehan.

'There's one of our men with his head facing the wrong way down there. I guess you'd have noticed if someone had done that in front of you.'

Two of the Norsemen picked Jehan up and dragged him back to where the bodies of Abram and Saerda lay.

'Are these the god's bones?' said one, poking at the bloody remains of the monk with his foot.

'Last time I noticed the Raven was mutilating monks. That's a mutilated monk. Raven's arrows are in the king's shield down there. Leaving aside how that got here, that makes the man down there that confessor, I reckon,' said Ofaeti.

'Are we in the god bones trade now, Ofaeti?'

'Well after two nights making the lady who we'd been sent to kidnap fetch us drinks, and then the man who was going to pay us for her being killed, I'd say we should move out of the noblewoman abduction line of work and into something else, wouldn't you? We can't be any worse at it.'

'I can't believe we had her there and didn't know.'

'I'm going to pretend it never happened. I thought she was too good-looking for a slave.' Ofaeti shook his head and looked at Jehan again. 'You, Frank, we've got your saint's bones. If you want them back, you'll have to pay for them.'

Jehan hadn't thought of that. Abram would need a proper Christian burial. He couldn't allow him to be taken by wild animals.

'We will pay,' he said.

'What did I tell you. Speaks Norse like a Haithabu whore – that is to say, well enough for what we want him for. Frank, you are going to help me sell his bones.'

'To Saint-Germain?'

'No chance. You'd like that, I bet. We're going east, son.'

Men were streaming past the confessor into the trees.

'You don't know me?'

'No, should I?'

'I'm the confessor. I'm the one you took from the church.'

'Of course you are. You're blind, you're crippled and you've had half your face eaten by ravens. On top of that you were shaved bald on top yesterday and today you've got a fine thatch. For someone who's been tortured to death, I must say, you look pretty well. Now get that mess over there into a sack. Once you have, we're going on a little journey.'

The confessor touched his head. His tonsure had grown out. It was only a small detail but it left him mildly panicked. It was if part of his identity had been removed. He looked down at his body. It was wasted and thin still and yet it moved. He could walk. God had released him. It was all too much to take in. The implications of his cure were so huge. Jehan breathed in and tried to focus on what he needed to *do* rather than what had happened to him. If Aelis was with the merchant, she would be on her way to Ladoga by now – he had heard the easterner pressing the case of Prince Helgi.

Jehan knew he had no way to get back to the city, or even to Saint-Germain. Could he rescue Aelis if he followed her? That morning, standing upright, the sunlight through the trees dappling the forest floor and turning it to a shimmering stream, he felt anything was possible. Everything was so beautiful. But it was more than that. He felt bound to the girl, almost compelled to follow her. God, he felt, had picked him out for the task and cured him so he might accomplish it.

And there was one further advantage of travelling east. The sea way would be impossible, thick with Norse pirates, so they would go by land and he would learn what stood between him and the lands of the Rus. It was a chance to gain information about the enemies of God, even to seek out evil and uproot it.

He looked at the fat Viking, the one who seemed to be the leader, if not in name then in the respect the men gave him.

'I am a monk and I can help you. There is a monastery I know that is in need of some relics and would pay well for them,' he said.

'Where's that?' said Ofaeti.

'In Agaune, to the south and east in the Pass of Songs,' said the confessor. 'The abbey of Saint-Maurice.'

'Why so far?'

'You need to step out from the shadow of war to a land where you will be seen as merchants, not pillagers. If you approach an abbey in this land then you will be cut down. Not all monks are men of God, as you know, and some grew up with a sword rather than a Bible in their hands.'

Ofaeti looked the confessor up and down. 'A word spell,' he said. 'Magic or sense? There's no way back to our boats, for sure.' He snorted. 'Yes, Fastarr? What do you think?'

'Yes.'

'Then follow,' said Jehan.

Saint-Maurice, thought the confessor, was where the Raven had said he was found and lost by God. The Raven had been described by Sigfrid as an intelligencer, so someone had sent him. Jehan had no idea who but he thought the abbey of the black saint was as good a place as any to try to find out.

26 Shelter

'Melun,' said Aelis as the horse slowed in the trees. 'We'll go to Melun. The town is loyal to my brother and the Northmen have not come so far down this time.'

Leshii nodded. He didn't like the sound of that. In Melun the lady would go back to her people. Yes, they might reward him for looking after her, but then again they might not. He knew very well how capricious and unpleasant rulers could be. What if her brother decided that cutting her hair had been dishonourable or that no foreign man could have stayed on the road for so long with a young woman without taking advantage of her? He didn't even know who was in charge in Melun – some local noble or bishop who would want the glory of finding the lady for himself? Helgi and his promised reward remained the best bet.

The trouble was that the lady had got her bearings and knew exactly where she was going. He had thought he might fool her, take her on his path and call it her path, so to speak. But he could think of no other option, so if the lady wanted to go to Melun, then he had to go there too. Her horse pressed forward through the trees, heading south down the river and Leshii followed, leading the mule.

'Lady, following the river's too obvious; they will think of searching for you there.'

Aelis said nothing, just kicked her horse forward. They travelled all day, passing the burned remains of three monasteries. The Vikings wouldn't make a full push without their ships but were willing to make the occasional incursion on foot.

Eventually the trees thinned and gave way to a conglomeration of little fields and houses. It was dusk and a big red sun dipped behind them as they approached. Peasants came out to look at them, at first shouting and hissing and fetching staves, but Aelis spoke to them in Roman, calming them and telling them she was the cousin of Robert the Strong with a message from Count Eudes to the bishop on his island monastery. She had killed the Viking king and was here to encourage the men of the countryside to take heart and rally to Paris's defence. She did not reveal herself as the count's sister because she knew her people. It would have been too much for them to take in that she was dressed as a man, let alone travelling unchaperoned with a strange foreigner and her hair exposed for all to see. They would kill the merchant and brand her a whore. The disguise would have to remain intact for now.

The news of Sigfrid's death soon spread through the farms and quickly there was such a throng that Aelis and Leshii could go no further. The farmers called out questions – 'Did he die well?' 'Is his head on the city walls?' 'Do his men withdraw?' – and offered ale and bread, praising the lad who had done such a fabulous deed. 'Stay with us tonight and tell us your stories,' someone called. 'Please, lord, favour your people.' Aelis was tired and suddenly the cold she had felt in the river came flooding back to her. It would be good to take a bed among these people. She looked to Leshii and he smiled. The merchant reflected that it was bad luck to lose the chance to take the lady east but consoled himself with the thought that at least he was used to it. The way the fates had treated him in the last few days would have been too much of a shock for a man accustomed to good fortune.

Leshii and Aelis were taken to the biggest house in the village. It was a mean place, low-roofed with walls of wood, straw, mud and dung, but the fire inside was warm and there were chairs to sit on and a bed to lie down on. Aelis did not dare remove her war gear for fear of exposing herself as a woman, but was so tired she fell asleep on the reeds of the floor and was covered with a blanket by the farmer's wife. Leshii fared less well. Foreigners were always suspect and he was left to sleep as best he could. These were not the cosmopolitan people of Paris but peasants, some of whom had never even been to the town of Melun, whose walls they could see from their own fields.

Aelis slept dreamless and deeply with the farmer's family around her, some on the floor, most in the bed they had been glad not to have to give up to the young lord. The fire was low and the night was dark by the time the first raven alighted near the smoke vent, its landing as soft as a raindrop's. Then a second bird joined it, and a third.

27 Munin

A shape emerged from the shadows to stand by the seated figure of the woman with the ruined face in the firelight. The man himself had a face that was ravaged and torn and in his hand he carried a cruel curved sword in a scabbard.

'Not yet,' he said, 'though it will be death by water, I know.'

The woman did not turn from the fire. The voices were few and distant in the empty spaces of the evening but the woman knew they were not alone. Men were camped around them among the trees. She could sense their breath, sense the heat of their animals and the sour note of fear on their skin, fear of what was behind them in the camp and what was in front of them in the half dark. They were scared of her, she could tell, but they were not there to kill her. Murmurs stirred in the trees like the rustle of leaves. 'What next?' 'She will know.' 'She is a Norn and weaves the skein of our fate now.' 'What does she want?' 'What they always want.' 'What?' 'Death.'

Hugin ignored the whispers behind him and took his sister's hand. She squeezed gently on his fingers. He uttered a single word: 'Success.'

The woman turned to him on instinct, though her eyes did not see him. As she moved, the whispers fell silent.

'I saw her face,' said Hugin. 'We will catch the monster now; it is only a matter of time. Don't be scared, my sister. Our struggles and sufferings will bring their reward.'

Munin squeezed her brother's fingers again. 'You're troubled,' she said.

'It's nothing.'

'You're troubled.'

'The wolfman found us again.'

'He has the stone and I cannot see him. But that is not what is troubling you.'

'I have seen her before,' he said.

The woman now put her other hand over his. 'Here?'

'Not here. Before.'

'This has happened before. It's a powerful magic that she carries with her. You have had a glimpse of something, that is all.'

'Of what?'

'She and you. In another lifetime. It has been revealed to you already. She was the god's death before, and unless she is stopped she will be once more.'

Hugin nodded. 'Then she will be stopped.'

A horse somewhere breathed out and a man said a word to calm it.

'Who are these?' said Munin.

'Grettir's war band. Hated by Rollo. Their ships have been seized and they have put the thread of their fate in my hands. They are here if we need them. They are two hundred and fifty men. Will we need them?'

The woman bowed her head in thought. Beside the fire was a tangle of branches bearing the long-leafed fingers of the ash tree. Hugin took one up and cast it onto the fire. Then he sat back by his sister, gave her his hand again and listened as she chanted.

'Blood, by blood begot,
Flame, by flame begot,
Death, by death begot.'

Over and over again she intoned the words until they were no more than an numbing haze of noise. There was restlessness around them. The war band now depended on the guidance of the sorcerers but were very uncomfortable in their presence. Some men paced back and forth. Some went and sat deeper in the trees. Only a few stayed to watch the chanting woman spin a web of sound through the forest.

Hugin felt something move in his head, as if his brain had acquired a terrible asymmetric weight and was far heavier on one side than the other.

Images rose in his mind and he knew his sister was taking his thoughts to use for her magic. Hugin had his own magical abilities, gained through privation, ritual and contact with the gods, but he was a man and he could never have what Munin had – runes, the symbols that express and shape the energies of creation. Her strength was so much greater than his. She concentrated on the symbol that grew within her, feeding off her and feeding her, sustained and sustaining. Hagalaz, the hail rune, symbol of destruction and crisis. Hugin felt its presence as his sister touched his mind – the driving wind, the sting on his face, the vision dying under the needles of ice.

As the coldness entered him, he knew that he and his sister were becoming one person, the division of their flesh an unimportant detail, nothing beside the unity of their minds. He saw a boy in the water, helpless, his lips blue and his flesh pale with cold. No, it wasn't a boy; it was the woman, the one they had been following. They had known she would be in the church, so their visions had suggested, but they had been unable to see what she looked like. All they saw when they tried to summon her image was the jagged rune, the Wolfsangel, with its three meanings, storm, wolf trap and werewolf. Now Hugin had seen her and Munin could see her too. In her mind Munin was not blind, and Aelis was as clear to her as if she had been standing in the firelight in person. The sorceress looked into the lady's pale blue eyes. Then she breathed in the scent of the ash fire.

The ash was the world tree on which all creation sat, gnawed at by the serpents that writhed in the earth beneath it. She said their names in her head. Nidhogg, the malice striker, Iormungand, Goin, Moin, Graftnitvir and Graback. But one was missing, the one she was looking for. She saw the world tree towering above her, and her mind seemed caught like the moon in its branches, a shining thing that spread its silver light over the trunk as it searched for what it needed. She let herself sink, falling through the leaves and the loam and the roots to the unstill earth beneath. She seemed to drop through writhing bodies, feel coils around her, things that crawled and crept over her skin. Then she had it, the one she was looking for.

'Svafnir,' she said. 'The masked one.'

Hugin and Munin felt the serpent writhing in the cavern of their shared consciousness, squirming through their thoughts like a worm in the soil, curling around the thin bars of the hail rune that enchanted it. Then it was as if something had gone wild inside them, thrashing and turning. Images of hate and death sprang up, Danes and Franks with twisted faces dying under Hugin's sword, a body found cold in the morning, a woman weeping with only the mocking call of a crow for an answer.

A raven descended from the tree.

Blood, by blood begot. Hugin could not tell if the words were in his head or were spoken aloud.

The bird hopped up onto Munin's shoulder and pecked at her ear, drawing blood.

Hugin heard his sister's voice in his head, addressing the bird: *You shall find her.*

A second bird dropped onto her other shoulder and drove its beak into her neck.

Fire by fire begot.

A gout of blood ran down her breast.

You shall mark her. Munin to the other bird.

Now a third, a black leaf dropping from a branch. It too drew blood on her neck.

Death by death begot.

The bird sat looking at her, as if waiting for instructions.

And you shall carry the blood of the serpent to where she rests.

The first raven gave out its cracking cry and flew up into

the night, the other two calling after it as they chased it into the dark.

Hugin felt the heaviness in his head shift. He was cold, tired and vulnerable, though he still got to his feet. 'The birds will do for her?'

The woman said nothing but Hugin nodded anyway. 'Then I will go to make sure. Grettir's men will burn the earth to find her.'

'Take forty men to the farms to the south, and if you cannot find her there, she will no longer be your concern. You have business elsewhere. The girl has been seen. If she can be killed then I will kill her.'

'And if she can't?'

'Then a hard road opens to us. We must find the wolf and contain him.'

'So where for me?'

'The road east to the dead lord's well. The wolf will seek the god's trail there. We must see him at least, to know how to act.'

'How shall I summon him? I am a man, not a woman. My magic is a weak thing.'

'Yes.'

'So?'

Munin's head bowed for a second. 'You know who is in the hills and streams of Aguanum. You know what he wants. Give it to him until he reveals the wolf to you. The waters of the temple are hungry. It is up to you to feed them.'

'How many?'

'How many what?'

'How many deaths?'

'All of them,' said Munin.

Hugin breathed out and glanced towards the men in the trees. 'You will not come with me?'

'I will stay here and try to kill the girl.'

'What of the rest of the war band?'

'They will travel with me to track the girl. If I cannot kill her by magic they can do it by more usual methods.'

The Raven bent down and squeezed his sister's hand. 'It'll be all right,' he said. 'We will survive this.'

'That doesn't matter,' she said.

'It does to me.'

'The god must live.'

'And you too, my sister, and you too.'

The woman said nothing, just felt for a bundle of yellow rags at her side and pushed it into Hrafn's hands.

He could feel something solid beneath the cloth. He shook it and heard liquid. He touched his tongue to his lips.

'All of them?' he said.

'All of them.'

Hugin kissed his sister on the forehead. He went to the men waiting among the trees and told them they were to split into two groups. The two hundred-odd who were to stay with Munin gave a cheer and tall Grettir himself shouted that they had a powerful witch on their side and that their fortunes were now secure.

'We will have our boats back!' he shouted.

Hugin nodded. 'She will help you get into the camp,' he said. 'If you take twenty men you can get your boats. Then head down the Seine and meet your main force there.'

'When will we be reunited?' said Grettir. 'I am lending my men, not throwing them away.'

'You will be reunited,' said Hugin, 'before the year is out. You have my word. My sister can find me through her art.'

Grettir smiled, though Hugin noticed some concern in his eyes as he glanced towards his sister.

'She is a good woman,' Hugin said, 'and you will prosper by her side.'

He raised his arm as a signal to his chosen men to follow him. The forty hurried to shoulder their shields, to be out of the presence of the torn and tattered thing that sat by the fire in the woods relaying messages from their gods. Then they followed Hugin as he walked into the forest night.

28 Ravens

The young man had at first thought to kill the bird that dropped from the smoke vent. Boiled raven was barely edible but meat was scarce enough to make anything welcome. But then it had looked so funny, perched on the shoulder of the sleeping lord. The bird then hopped up onto his head, and the young farmer had wondered, half hoped, that it would make its mess on the nobleman's hair. He bore no ill will to the lord at all, in fact he rather respected him, but his sense of humour was such that birds messing on the hair of sleeping men was extremely amusing to him.

But then there had been a flutter and a tumble of wings, and he felt a sharp sting on his cheek. It was another raven, flapping to the smoke vent. He put a hand to his cheek then his fingers to his lips. Blood. The thing had cut him, pecked him or slashed at him with its feet as it flew past.

He said nothing but just looked down at the blood on his fingers. The bird on the nobleman's shoulder was looking at the young farmer, its eyes two little gleaming coals. He felt no inclination to move, though the heat of the embers seemed oppressive. The bird kept looking at him. Was it his imagination or did it seem to be standing in a sort of questioning posture, its head cocked as if evaluating him?

His hands went back to his cheek. The wound was painful, not like a normal cut, more like a bee sting. He felt his heart begin to race. Nothing seemed clear to him. It was as if something was writhing in his head, as if he wanted to stand up, sit down, be still and run all at the same time.

The breathing of the young lord seemed abnormally loud, irritatingly loud. The man might have killed the enemy king but did he have to hem and haw so? Had the lord really killed the king? He knew those noblemen were full of lies, despite their airs and graces. The heat was becoming unbearable. He took off his smock and sat bare-chested. He was sweating heavily now. The pain on his cheek was spreading a numbness all the way down his right side.

The bird's eyes never left him.

The young farmer stretched out his arms. 'What answer would you have me give?' he said. He realised he was talking to the raven. The stupidity of that struck him and he fell to giggling. The bird watched him still. The young man had never been so hot nor found anything so funny. He was shivering despite the heat. The giggling subsided and he felt another emotion growing inside him. Anger. He knew, of course, what the noble intended. To rape his sister, take his crops and kill anyone who stood in his way. *They did that sort of thing, those high men; it was well known.*

The nobleman wasn't really sleeping; he was lying there like a fox, biding his time until everyone dropped off. Then he would get up to begin his foul acts. The nobility took its portion by right, but the people expected defending in return. What had they done, these fine fellows? Allowed the country to be overrun by Norsemen, Neustria pillaged and Paris besieged. If a common man did not pay them his dues what could he expect?

The heat in his head was unbearable. He felt something biting and writhing within him, tearing at his reason, shredding his thoughts. The bird's eyes were on him, glittering black stones. He stood up. He picked up a knife from the bench at the table. They had had meat as an honour to the lord. The blade was a good one, used for fine boning. He looked down at the fat foreigner who was the nobleman's servant. *Him first?*

The nobleman stirred.

No, better to take the warrior in his sleep and deal with the servant afterwards.

The raven cawed as the young man stepped forward and plunged the knife into Aelis's belly.

29   Strange Companions

Jehan wondered why the Norsemen had agreed so quickly to his suggestion that they head for the mountains. There was no return to camp, no leave-taking of companions; in fact, there seemed to be some urgency about their departure. Ofaeti had four men with him, and they hurried north to meet up with six more.

They found each other at the beginning of the wood where the Raven had tried to work his magic on Jehan. Down the hill they could see the Viking camp. There was activity, noted Jehan, men gathering, tiny but visible under the big moon. The six brought four mules with them and one riding horse, though they were lightly provisioned. The animals bore mail hauberks, spears, axes and a couple of bows, bedding and not much else. The men had clearly left in a hurry.

With his restored sight he could not help but stare at them, stare at everything. The night was cloudy but the moon was visible, crisping the edges of the clouds with silver. The air seemed charged, the land to glow. *Did Eden know a light so lovely?* he thought

These men were different from the other Vikings he had seen in the wood. They were blonder, taller and for the most part more strongly built. Ofaeti was a sight to behold, fat but powerful, using a spear for a staff. Svan too was a giant, with a great red beard that seemed to burn like copper in the day's strange light. He carried a large single-headed axe. Fastarr, the one with the hammer on his shield, was a lean and nimble-looking man who wore a sword at his belt. He had a large and ugly scar on his cheek – clearly he had taken a spear point or sword tip there at some point. Then there was Astarth, the youngest with his wispy beard, and the rough and coarse Egil, whose profanity stood out even in that company of battle-bitten warriors. The rest of the eleven had not yet been addressed by their names and the confessor had no urge to ask them. One was older than the rest. He was grey-haired and two fingers on his right hand were missing. Another carried two swords at his belt, though the rest of his dress was poor.

The men were having a debate as to whether they should put on their war gear. Ofaeti ended it. 'The sooner we're out of here the better. No time for all that,' he said.

'You know the way?' said Fastarr to the confessor.

'I know of it,' said Jehan, 'it is south-east by the trading route to Lombardy.'

Ofaeti nodded. 'Get us there and emerge with our gold and you'll never hear from us again. On the courage of Tyr, I swear you will come to no harm. Betray us and I will kill a monk for every day of my anger, and my anger does not cool slow,' he said. 'I want your word, on your god, that you will treat us as fairly as we treat you. That is to say, well. You'll have no trouble from us if you give us none. Do you swear?'

Jehan looked at the men. He was in their power and had little choice. He needed to get to Saint-Maurice and these men looked capable of getting him there. How much money would he get for the monk's bones? None. So his oath would be discharged the moment he told the berserkers they had earned no pay for their booty. Then the monks would be free to kill them. Was that the most satisfactory outcome? It was certainly the one that most churchmen would favour. But surely it would be better to bring these men to Christ. He would try, he thought, he would try.

'You have my oath,' he said. 'I will serve you in this task.'

'Good,' said Ofaeti. He went to a mule and took out a pair of sandals.

'It's a long walk so you'll be needing these. Don't think it a kindness. I don't want you slowing us with blisters or taking up space on a mule. Where do we go from here?'

'There is a ford. I think it's down this hill.'

Jehan strapped on the sandals, his fingers fumbling at the knots. He was unused to tying on shoes, unused to doing anything at all for himself.

'Hurry it up,' said Fastarr. 'Lord Rollo is about to express his gratitude for what Ofaeti did to his son. A ford where?'

Jehan pointed to where the memory of his childhood told him the ford was but the berserkers were staring back down the hill. He turned to see what they were looking at. A group of warriors was assembling. How many? Forty or so, more joining from down in the camp, some on horseback.

Ofaeti shrugged. 'He was a grown man and it was he who issued the challenge.'

'After you'd punched him in the face and knocked the teeth out of his head.'

'After he'd called me unmanly. The law's plain. I could have killed him for that on the spot. I was willing to leave it at a broken nose. He was the one who wanted to take it further.'

'They are massing,' said Holmgeirr.

'We could stand and fight,' said Astarth.

Fastarr shook his head. 'If few are to succeed against many then the many need to flee. They are Rollo's men and will fight with a grudge. We can't kill enough to rout them. We'd never run so many.'

'We could just roll you down the hill to flatten them, you fat bastard,' said Egil.

'If you like,' said Ofaeti. 'The walk back up will do me good.'

'It's Hvitkarr, one of Rollo's chieftains. At the mead bench I heard him confess he couldn't understand a word the skald was saying. I think a man who cannot understand poetry must be a poor warrior,' said Astarth.

'True enough,' said Ofaeti. 'I once heard him telling the tale of a victory, and a dog could have made better verse. The spirit of Odin is not in him, so why would it be in his men?'

'They are too many. Come on,' said Fastarr. 'If we make the woods to the south we'll lose them. We'll make for the ford.'

'And then what? Steal a boat? Does the river go to this monastery, monk?'

'It goes part of the way,' said the confessor. 'There is a short cross-country part where you can take the old Roman road, the Transversale, until you meet the Saône going south, and then you follow the Rhône to the door.'

Jehan was speaking from what he had heard from pilgrims; he had never travelled the route himself. The pass Saint-Maurice stood in was the quickest way through the mountains to Lombardy, Turin and ultimately Rome.

'We'll walk,' said Ofaeti. 'The rivers will be alive with spies looking for northerners. Come on. We don't want to get caught by Rollo's men while we're crossing. The river's high and it'll be hard enough without those bastards coming after us.' He took the halter of the mule and descended the back of the hill at a trot.

Jehan glanced back. Riders were joining the men at the edge of the camp. The confessor knew he and the berserkers would be caught. That did not frighten him much. However, a different anxiety was gnawing at him. The taste of that human meat in his mouth would not leave him. He felt sick but strangely elated, as if part of him had enjoyed his grisly meal. He also realised, with surprise and horror, that he was anticipating the fight to come. Saliva had risen to his mouth and his limbs felt light and quick. As he moved through the trees following the warriors, he offered a prayer that, should he kill, he should kill justly and take no joy in it. The Church was clear – it was good to kill heathens but not to revel in slaughter.

Everything felt so strange: there were so many changes for him to come to terms with. He had been blessed, he was sure. God had looked down on him in his torment and released him from the bonds of his disease. Whatever came after could only be God's will. All he had to do was to pray and accept whatever happened, react as he felt God wished him to do.

Jehan also noticed he felt stronger. The pace was fine, though the warriors were running. He tried to pray and the words of the Creed, the statement of belief on the nature of Christ, came into his head: *God from God, light from light, true God from true God, begotten, not made.*

They reached the edge of the wood and looked at the long drop towards the ford.

By the power of the holy spirit incarnate, through the Virgin Mary made a man.

The Vikings trotted down the hill with Jehan beside them. He kept glancing back but he could see nothing behind him. He felt joyful and full of life, and ashamed at that joy when he considered what had passed his lips not a day before. He felt a hand on his arm. It was the fat one, panting at his side.

'Not so fast, monk,' he said. 'You wouldn't want to leave us behind.'

Jehan came to himself and checked his pace. He didn't feel like slowing, though; he felt like tearing through the night to give vent to the boiling energy rising inside him.

30 A Question of Fear

Aelis felt the thump in her ribs. She awoke to see the half-naked man standing over her. He was sweating heavily, his eyes rolling in his head. She tried to stand but he kicked her legs from under her, driving the knife down between her shoulder blades. This time, as it hit the mail hauberk she wore beneath the cloak, the knife snapped. The blow was a heavy one, though, and she fell face first to the reeds.

People were on their feet, the whole house in uproar. The young man seemed nonplussed by the fact that his weapon had broken and sat down on the floor.

Aelis stood and a terrible pain shot through her. Her ribs were broken, she thought, front and back, but the mail coat had saved her life.

She bent for her sword but she was in agony and her movement was slow. The young man looked up at her, almost as if seeing her for the first time. Then he lunged from his sitting position, driving himself forwards to slam into Aelis, sending her sprawling. His hands were at her throat, but she had Sigfrid's sword free from its scabbard. Her vision constricted to a tunnel, her head thumped, her ribs were on fire, but she shoved the blade into the man's belly and kept pushing until the crosspiece hit his navel.

Her sight faded, the voices of the room were distant and echoing. The hands at her throat were unyielding. Then there was a thump and she could breathe again. The merchant was standing over the young man, who tried to get up but the handle of the sword dug into the floor and he gave a terrible cry. He pulled at the weapon, struggling to get to his feet as if drunk, one leg gaining purchase on the floor, the other flailing, refusing to obey his commands. For a second he was upright but then lurched forward and dropped to his knees, his shaking hands still tugging at the unmoving handle of the sword.

Aelis was doubled up on the floor, gasping for breath, coughing and choking, still uncertain as to whether she had been stabbed, so great was the pain in her ribs.

'You'll die for what you've done, nobleman!'

The boy's father was striding towards her, an axe in his hand, but Leshii leaped between him and the spluttering figure of Aelis. The merchant had drawn an axe and held it above his head, ready to strike. An angry crowd of around twenty people faced them. The farmer's wife, a big woman with raw cheeks, ran weeping to her son.

'No one does anything until we find out what's gone on,' Leshii said. 'Look to your boy rather than a fight you won't win. The lord did for Sigfrid; he'll do for you.'

The farmer looked at Aelis, clearly wondering what his chances were in a fight against the young nobleman. Not good, he seemed to decide. He went to where his wife was cradling her son's head. The young man was still sitting upright, his eyes staring into nothing.

'What happened?' The farmer's wife's voice was gentle.

The youth's mouth fell open.

'My thoughts were a snake,' he said. 'He had been hiding inside me and he came forward to strike. The raven called him out. The bird bit at me and my thoughts went wild.'

'This is sorcery,' said Leshii. 'The boy was bewitched. The Raven is a noted necromancer, an unholy priest of the Viking invader. Look, there is his instrument, the bird, that is what drove your son to this.'

The raven was in the open doorway. As if it heard its name, it took wing and flapped into the night.

'He came at me while I was sleeping,' said Aelis, each word forced out with what little breath she had. 'If I had attacked him first with my sword he would have had no chance to strike at me. Look, he broke the knife on my mail.'

The farmer looked up to where the boning knife was snapped to its handle.

'Get out,' said the farmer. 'Go from this place. You are not welcome to come here bringing devils to our door. Get out!'

Aelis stood and limped towards the door, the eyes of the crowd on her. Leshii, though, stayed.

'What are you waiting for, foreigner? Leave!' said the farmer.

Leshii stepped forward. 'I'm afraid,' he said, 'I can't leave you with my lord's sword. It is too valuable a weapon. It's worth three of your farms.'

'I will kill you before you take it.'

'Let him take it, father. I can abide it no more.' The boy's voice was faint.

Leshii looked into the farmer's eyes. The man looked away and then at his son. He kissed the boy on the forehead and his wife squeezed her son's hand.

Leshii stepped forward and took the handle of the weapon gently. Then he put his foot into the youth's chest and with a wrench pulled it from his body. The boy gave a yelp but then was quiet.

Leshii stood above him holding the bloody sword.

'I'm sorry,' he said. 'Apply to the count for compensation. Tell him the one he thought lost did the work. Ask in the name of Lady Aelis.'

'Get out!'

Leshii left the house and went to Aelis. She was lying in the mud and shit next to one of the flimsy animal shelters.

'Well, lady,' he said in a low voice, 'we have the clothes we stand up in, weapons, two horses and a mule. You are followed by enchanters who have shown their skill. Will you put your trust in me now?'

She said nothing.

'Now will you believe me? There are sorcerers hunting you. You must get to Ladoga and Helgi. He is a great magician and will drive these evil things from your back.'

He put his arm around her to lift her, but as he did became aware of a presence in the shadows. It was the wolfman.

'Chakhlyk?'

'Ladoga,' said Sindre. 'You must get her to Ladoga. I can help you as long as the arrow lets me live.'

Leshii nodded. 'Then let's get the animals,' he said.

Aelis looked up from the mud. Her mind felt dislocated, knocked sideways. She thought of the horses at the river, of how she had killed Sigfrid and she shuddered. What explained that? Supernatural forces seemed all around her and within her. She stood. She was in no condition to ride but she had seen the look on the young farmer's face, and, more than that, had sensed what was within him. There had been an acid feeling to his presence. A sensation like heartburn sprang up inside her when she thought of him. Something more than human, venomous, had hissed and coiled within him. She felt certain Leshii was right: it was sorcery and she knew it was unlikely that this attack would not be the last.

She glanced at the two men with her. Would one of them come for her in the night, his eyes wild, his body burning? She couldn't think too much on that. She had to get away from this thing that was following her, and to quell the odd sensations that afflicted her.

The wolfman, she could sense, was a good man acting for good, his presence complicated and odd, wild yet not hostile. When she looked at him she saw great spaces, valleys, rivers and woods, felt a longing, but a solidity too. He would not let her down, she knew.

'Come on,' said Leshii. 'Let's at least get away from here. Who knows what'll happen if these countrymen suddenly decide they want revenge for the death of their kinsman.'

Aelis allowed Leshii to help her up onto her horse, her ribs were agony. The wolfman mounted the other animal and the merchant led the mule out of the village, heading north by the Pole Star. Aelis could not decide what to do. The forces against her seemed overwhelming. She wanted to go to Melun but couldn't be sure she wouldn't be making things easier for her enemies by going there – surrounding herself with men who could be enchanted. They made slow progress over wet fields and finally came out into common land and woods. Passing through a clearing, she heard distant screams, sounds of anguish and terror from back the way they had come. She turned to look behind her.

'Don't think about it,' said the wolfman. He drew his horse alongside her. He was not used to riding, she could see, and was lucky Sindre's horse was a well-trained gelding. He flopped on the animal as a passenger, not a rider. She wondered if it was the effect of his wound or if, like the northerners, he had never been taught to ride properly. 'We must press on, and quickly,' he said.

'What is it?' said Aelis.

'The Raven is not easy to kill,' said Sindre, 'but he will not know where we have gone and neither will the farmers. If we can make the River Oise then we can take a boat. We must not sleep until then.'

'He will kill all the farmers?'

'He will spare some of them for a while to try to gain the information he needs but then he will kill them too. He can't risk them running to their lord, and a party of warriors searching the countryside for him and whoever is with him.'

'He seems a match for any warrior.'

'Perhaps. But what if your kinsmen find us? He means to kill you and doesn't want anything delaying that. If your people rescue you it will make things difficult for him.'

'Then I should go to my people.'

'You will only delay your death. You were with your people when he came for you before. Helgi is your only hope in this.'

'Why does that thing want to kill me?'

'Just press on. We have no time to talk.'

'Why does he want to kill me? I have a right to know.'

The wolfman swallowed and went to put his hand on her

hair in a gesture of affection. Then he withdrew it. 'He is afraid of you. Now let's be gone.'

'We go nowhere until you tell me more. Why am I pursued? Why am I harried? How can something like *that* be afraid of me?'

Sindre looked across at her. He leaned heavily on the pommel of his saddle.

'Because something else follows you too. It always has and always will.'

'What follows me?'

'You dream of a wolf?'

Aelis nodded. 'How did you know that?'

'I dream of him too.'

'Does he say that he loves you?'

The wolfman was silent but Aelis could see the fear in his eyes. He looked very old, she thought, or rather he had an air of great age about him. He had, she thought, travelled a long way to be with her, and not just in distance. When she looked at him she felt the wheel of the seasons turning – rain, sun and rain again. But she sensed something else too. His life was passing. It would not be the arrow that killed him, nor the Raven. His death would come quickly and unforeseen.

When she was a child she had taken her meals in the kitchen at Loches. She was a girl and so was not invited to the high table, but she had not wanted to go. In the great hall there was an iron stand as tall as a man. It held a brazier at the top of it which lit the room on feast days. She had hated it and not known why. It seemed to her like an evil presence simmering by the table, a tall, pendulous thing full of harm. Her cousin Godalbertus was hardly more than a baby, just able to walk. The stand had fallen, caught by a drunken nobleman, and had struck the child and killed him. Count Albertus had had the stand taken outside. Someone had filled the brazier with earth and grown flowers in it. All her youth it had stood in the garden, flowers spilling from its basket, like death in his victory garland. When Aelis looked at Sindre it was as if the stand – or rather the evil feeling the stand seemed to generate – was behind him, ready to fall.

'What will happen to me?' she said.

'You will go to Helgi and you will be saved.'

Aelis sensed the uncertainty in his voice.

'Will the Raven kill me?'

'He will try. I cannot tell. No one can tell. It will not profit you to know more until you are with Helgi. I promise you, he will give you a better explanation than I can.'

'And you do all this for the love of your prince?'

'Lady?'

'You said you were acting for love.'

The wolfman looked into her eyes. Aelis had that feeling of great age again, but this time seemed to share it. She went back in her mind to her childhood and then beyond that. She had the sensation of a weight in her arms, of falling and of a terror at her back that she could not shake.

The wolfman winced and grasped his side.

'We must move quickly. I am in no condition to fight the Raven if he finds us.'

'If he is scared of me then shouldn't we wait for him?'

'The Raven expresses his fear in sword cuts and tortures,' said Sindre. 'He does not hide from the monsters of his dreams, he hacks them down.'

'Can we get on?' said Leshii. 'We can find the river. The current is too strong to take a boat, but if we can find a crossing we can cut north and lose our pursuers.'

Aelis looked at Sindre. In her mind she was standing on a ledge in a high cold place. She was holding something in her arms. It was a man. She could not see his face. Was it the wolfman? Someone like him, though she couldn't tell. She didn't know what to make of the vision, nor did she know if she saw the past or the future. Perhaps, she thought, she saw something that had never happened, nor never would be. But it told her she was linked to this man in a way that went far deeper than his rescue of her or their present conversation. But when she looked at him, she did not think of love. Another word came into her mind: *daudthi*. It meant nothing to her – that is, she couldn't translate it – but it too seemed to come in a rush of images and sensations: a warrior, his white hair gleaming from the dark and then gone like a fish in a pond, cries of anguish, her body aching and bruised, and a smell, a deep animal smell seeping from somewhere at her side, a smell that brought her around again to that word and a knowledge of its meaning. *Daudthi*. Death. And it was death she saw when she looked at Sindre, not love.

But still, better death for her than against her. The wolfman had tried to protect her and she felt compelled to act on her instinctive trust of him.

She looked up at the Pole Star and then east to the constellation of Cassiopeia. Its flat upright M-shape seemed to her like the symbol in her head, the one that called the horses, and she imagined the stars as a rearing horse pointing her way. There lay her destiny, she was sure, with Helgi and his magic in the lands of the Rus.

'Take me to the east,' she said, and squeezed her legs against the horse's flanks to urge it forward.

PART TWO
Wolf Age

31 Helgi's Sacrifice

Years before Aelis set off to seek Helgi's help, the child had been taken to the roof of the river loading tower – the highest structure in Ladoga, nearly five man heights tall. Logs had to be removed from the roof in order for her to be passed up through a gap.

Her father laid her down there himself.

'Nearer the apex, *khagan*.'

The healer chinked like coins in a purse as he spoke, his whole body adorned with charms and trinkets. Prince Helgi glanced at him and moved the girl nearer to the top of the roof.

'The surest cure is at the apex,' said the healer. 'That is where the cooling humours of the sky settle.'

'They'll be no cure for her if she rolls off to her death,' said Helgi.

'I will sit beside her and make sure she comes to no harm,' said the healer.

'Yes,' said Helgi, 'you will.'

He touched the girl's head. She was boiling in her own sweat. He cursed himself. It never did to love your children too much, least of all the girls.

Helgi was a troubled man and the little girl had been one of his comforts. She was bold and funny, even going as far as to ridicule his stern manner. He would have cut a warrior down for that but she just made him laugh, made him forget his tormented sleep and the nightmares that woke him ranting in the darkest hours of the night. In those awful dreams he always found himself back by that well, the vision of his own death, of the trampling hooves, waking him with a shout. When he returned to sleep there was worse. He saw a warrior on an eight-legged horse – Odin was coming to earth and would march at the head of Ingvar's armies. The god was treacherous, it was well known, but Helgi felt cheated. He had sacrificed so much, given so many slaves, so many cattle, so much gold. But the portents were clear – he was under divine threat.

So he had sent throughout his land for wild women and holy men, for priests and witches, wanting to hear that the prophecy had been wrong. The mystics came pouring in to Ladoga like a market-day crowd, rattling bones, casting runes, sweating and fasting for prophecy. So many came that Helgi earned his nicknames 'Helgi the Magician' and 'Helgi the Prophet'. All the troll-workers told him nothing, just that he would be a great king throughout all the known lands of the earth. He did not believe them and saw that they only sought to please him.

One mountain woman, though, had drawn a shape in the dust of the floor. 'This is your destiny,' she had said. The outline was that of a horse.

'I will be killed by my horse?' He glanced left and right. The hall was empty, the *druzhina* sent outside to prevent them hearing anything that might upset them and, through them, the people. 'Could the horse be a symbol? Might it mean something else? Might it be that a god is the only thing that can kill me? Could it be a sign of great fortune?'

'Anything can mean anything,' the wild woman had said and put out her hand for gold.

There had been a sound from beneath a bench at the side of the hall, and he'd turned to see what it was. It was his little girl, Sváva, poking her face from the shadows. He'd laughed when he'd seen her.

'You know I should beat you for sneaking, don't you, girl?'

The girl had just chuckled and come up to him.

'Can I have an apple?'

'This woman isn't a farmer, she's a witch. A troll-worker. Shall I get her to eat you?'

'I might eat her,' said Sváva.

'My girl,' he'd said to the wild woman, 'as bold as any boy and ten times as cheeky.'

But the wild woman had her gold and was heading to the door, plunging Helgi back into his thoughts of what Odin was about to take from him and give to Ingvar.

Helgi had tried to weaken the boy but Ingvar's faction was strong, the loyalty he commanded from kinsmen in the *druzhina* not far from Helgi's own. His uncles were hard and cunning men and watchful for any plot, so that way was not open to Helgi. He would have to let his original scheme stand: conquer the south and leave the boy to make his mistakes. He was at the mercy of the god and there was nothing he could do about it.

And then in January, the traveller had come, fighting through a terrible blizzard, hunched against the cold. The men had thought him a beggar in his rags and wolfskin, but had been shocked to see anyone emerge from that storm.

The guards had let him in to the town out of amazement and pity. He'd gone to one of the fires they kept going behind the gatehouse to warm himself. A man came to tell Helgi because lone travellers on foot were unheard of in that country at that time of year. No one could travel in such weather and live. Helgi told the *druzhina* to stay where they were in the mead hall. It would be a dark day when the prince of all the east needed a bodyguard to face a frozen and wandering beggar. He'd been bored, to tell the truth, by the men's boasts and the drinking games where a mistake in the rhythm of a complicated pattern of clapping forced the error-maker to take a swig. Helgi had played the games so many times that he found it impossible to fail at them and sometimes broke his rhythm deliberately just to wet his palate.

So he had gone alone, shielding his face with his cloak as he walked half blind through the storm.

The man had stood by the fire, the snowy wind turning the back of his body white, looking like a thing of ice himself, a statue topped by a shock of red hair. Helgi told the guard he was a poor host and to get the visitor some food, and the travel-ler had smiled at him. With his smile, the blizzard stopped and the wind died.

Helgi had looked up. It was night, just past dusk, and the sky was a dark and frozen purple, the stars shards of ice, the slim moon an icicle ready to drop. Without the shrieking wind the special silence of the snow fell upon the town and with it a sense of complete stillness. Helgi felt strange. 'I know you,' he had said.

'And I you, my burning prince, whose desires have melted away all the storm.'

'What do you know of my desires?'

'The only thing worth knowing about them.'

'And what is that?'

'They will never be fulfilled.'

Helgi felt his blood fall to his knees, though he maintained his composure. It occurred to him to strike the man down where he stood for his insolence, but he felt strangely vulner-able. The freakish change in the weather had unsettled him, but there was something else. What? This man, the firelight crawling over his body like so many snakes, had come half naked through weather that could kill a horse under its rider.

'Then I should make them greater,' said Helgi. 'That way, in falling short, I will have enough.'

The man smiled. *A grin of ancient hunger like a wolf's*, thought Helgi.

'You know what will kill you.'

'My horse. I am glad of it. It means I am immortal for Helgi owns no horses. All he rides, he borrows.'

'What a fate! To be master of nothing but a borrowed horse, your lands snatched away by the dead god's hand. Would you see him?'

'Show him to me.'

The man moved his hand and the snow in the gatehouse square rose from the ground. It swirled and eddied, turned tiny whirlwinds and finally took shape. It was a scene from the sagas. The dread lord Odin, one-eyed and fearsome, his face contorted into a scream, sat on his great eight-legged horse Slepnir, driving his spear down at a terrible wolf that tore and bit at his shield. The sound of the battle grated through the town and Helgi wondered why none of his *druzhina* came out to see what was happening.

The spear stabbed into the wolf, lodging in its flesh, and the animal gave a terrible keening howl but it didn't falter in its attack. The rider's shield shattered, and the wolf's front paws dug into the horse's flank, its teeth snapping at the man's throat, its body tossed around in a crazy spiral as the monstrous horse screamed and bucked to be free of it. But the wolf did not let go.

And then the snow spectres crashed to the earth and the night was quiet again. Helgi walked forward to where they had fought. All that lay on the snow was a twisted rope. Helgi recognised the triple knot of Odin.

He picked it up and took it to the beggar. It seemed the natural thing to do.

'When he died last time,' said the man, 'this happened.' From nowhere he produced a long knife and with skilful fingers cut the knot into three pieces.

'He is in the world, sundered,' said the man, holding the pieces of the rope out to Helgi. 'If he ever becomes whole again you and the armies of mankind will have never known such destruction. He will light a fire from the shores of the blue men to Thule, and from the green hills of Albion to the sands of Serkland.'

'I don't understand,' said Helgi.

'He is in the world, as three. If he becomes one again, you and all the kings of the world will run from him like rats from a fire in the corn. Only his favourite will remain. Ingvar will triumph. Ingvar will rule.'

The man's words seemed to fizzle and sizzle in Helgi's mind with the sound of a branding iron on an animal's back.

'And how does he become one?'

'How he does anything – by death. Three live with the runes within them. Fragments of the god. Eventually there will be just one, and your destiny will fall upon you and sweep you from the earth.'

'Who are they? What do I need to do?'

'Those who drink at Mimir's well pay a price so to do. Odin gave his eye for wisdom; the bright god Heimdall gave his ear. What did you give?'

'My peace.'

'It was not enough. More is required.'

'What?'

'A child.'

'Which child?'

'The one who sits beside you in your great hall.'

'For what?'

'For death.'

Helgi felt a delicious current of anticipation flow through him. Could the god really be asking for Ingvar?

'And if I do this, the god you have shown me does not come?'

'Your debt to the well will be paid. Your name will echo down the ages as the mightiest *khagan* of the earth. You will have a vision, and the way forward will be revealed to you.'

Helgi smiled. 'You are a god,' he said. Helgi could sense it. The air around the man seemed to have a pressure to it that rendered the prince's senses dull, as if he was underwater. Next to him, Helgi felt slow and fragile.

'I am.'

'What is your name?'

'I have many. Here I am Veles and in Rome I am Lucifer. To you I am Loki.'

Helgi felt fear stopping up his breath like a suffocating hand. He composed himself. The terror quietened. He had come to the attention of the gods. He was important, marked for greatness.

'They call you lie-smith,' said Helgi.

The god smiled. 'Those who do not listen make me a liar,' he said. 'Men hear what they want to hear, and when they curse me it is not for lying but for speaking the truth. Thank you for the warmth of your fire. I shall repay the gift when I return to take what you have promised me.'

He turned and walked out into the snow. Helgi watched him go, thinking how foolish the gods must be to demand as a sacrifice what he had been praying for them to take away.

That night he had dreamed of a lady who lived in the land of the Franks, blonde and beautiful, a lady who walked in gardens by a river.

'Who are you?' he asked.

'One of the three. You shall know me by these signs.' She held out her hand. In it were eight wooden counters, all marked with a rune.

'What is your name?'

'Aelis, of the line of Robert the Strong.'

'While you live, I prosper,' he had said to her.

He had sent a delegation to her brother at Paris the next day, asking for her hand in marriage. He didn't even receive a response. He had considered an attack but his army was tied up at Kiev, keeping the Pechenegs at bay. That's when he had decided to kidnap her.

On the roof by the healer Helgi looked down at Sváva. He had not thought the god would ask for her. The god had said, 'The one who sits beside you in your great hall.' Ingvar was there at all meetings, beside him at every judgement he made, every farmer's squabble he sorted out, every warrior's weregild claim, even when visiting kings were entertained. He had given his oath to raise the boy, but if fate struck him down, if the gods struck him down, then Helgi would be free of him without breaking his oath and free to name any heir he chose.

The prince hadn't even considered the girl – he was a warrior, how could he have thought her important or in any way interesting to the god? She was a scrap, a little thing not six years old. How could the god want her when he could take a boy now thirteen and already battle brave? But the god knew his weaknesses and Helgi had come to realise that you don't bargain with such as he and walk away without paying in meaningful coin, never mind smirking up your sleeve at your own cleverness.

Helgi looked down from the tower roof. The town was on an elbow of land that stuck out into the wide River Volkhov. Facing inland he could see clear green lands – the barrows of his dead countrymen nearest to him, the woods like a sea themselves beyond. They were digging a barrow for Gillingr now, his Viking brother, who had fought with him as far south as Miklagard, as far west as the Islands to the West. A gash of red soil had been cut behind the last complete barrow, ready for the construction of the burial chamber. There was a problem there, he had heard, but he was too taken with his daughter's illness to enquire much about it.

His daughter would not have a barrow. She was a thing of movement, bright and quick. He couldn't bear to think of her entombed under the earth. It would be fire for her, to match her spirit. He looked over the river. He felt like a bird, floating on light above the water, a bird that could turn in a moment and follow the river south to swoop on Miklagard, to plunder the treasures of the Byzantine emperor, to fly on to the Caliphate and return with all the jewels of Serkland. The girl moaned in her fever. He looked down at her and shook his head. He had allowed himself to love his daughter. Men, and kings in particular, should never love their girls, he thought. They were bargaining tokens, no more, to be traded with other kings for gold, land or peace. But he had loved her, for her fierce heart as much as anything.

Sváva and her sisters were banned from approaching the king without a lady or their mother to supervise their behaviour. She, though, recognised no bans. She'd come to see him, sneaking in to watch as he dealt with traders, princes and war chiefs in his grand hall. The little girl thought he couldn't see her, crawling beneath the benches with the dogs, but he saw her all right, catching his eye as he settled a dispute between farmers, robbing him of all sternness at the very moment he might have screamed at the complainers to get out of his sight. She made him chuckle, and although he should have beaten her until her legs were blue, he didn't. He winked at her and threw her one of the apples the peasant plaintiffs brought as gifts.

He could never turn her away, and eventually she'd just sit by his side on the floor with Ingvar his heir on the other side on a chair as he did his work. He was aware of how it made him look to his men and was careful to pick occasional fights in order to show that, though he might be tender-hearted to his daughter, warriors could expect less kindly treatment. 'There's no respect like corpse respect,' was a maxim his own father had drilled into him from an early age. However, he was pleased when he saw some of his chieftains had begun to allow their own girls to sit beside them at the mead bench.

'Aeringunnr.' He went to her and sat down, put his hand to her head and was sure she would die. He had called her by her full name only once before. To him she had always been Sváva, or Mouse for her habit of appearing where he least expected. But Mouse was too timid a name for her and he had dropped it and settled on Sváva, after a Valkyrie, one of Odin's battle maidens. 'Aeringunnr.' He had called her that when he'd gone to see her on the day of her birth and given her the name. Now, he knew, he was using it to say goodbye.

Tears came into his eyes so he turned his face away from the healer. He spoke to the girl, his eyes on the distance. 'See what you've done? I can't go down like this.' Below, warriors were gathering. It was one thing to be seen to have a soft enough heart to have the child on his knee, another to be seen nursing her like a servant.

The healer, who only understood the East Norse of his masters if he listened very carefully, said nothing.

Eventually Helgi composed himself and turned back to the healer. 'If she dies,' he said, 'so do you. She'll have a boat burned for her to take her to the afterlife. You'll be in it. It will be a privilege for you, so be happy.'

'She won't die, *khagan*, not on the roof and surrounded by charms.'

'Good,' said Helgi. 'If she lives I'll leave you to seek a less noble death. You can fuck yourself to death in a whorehouse at my expense.'

'You are generous, *khagan*,' said the healer.

The girl turned slightly and the healer grabbed at her to stop her slipping off the roof.

'*Ulfr*.'

'What did she say?'

'I can't tell, *khagan*.'

Helgi bent his head to the girl's ear. She moaned again, repeating the word.

'It's likely nothing, lord,' said the healer. 'In fever people say all sorts of things that—'

'*Ulfr*.'

Helgi fixed the healer with a stare. 'What are you talking about, man? She said "wolf" as plain as I can hear you. What does it mean?'

'There are many forms of spirit that can enter her. It may well be that a wolf spirit has come upon her and—'

The healer was stopped by Helgi's look of simmering, almost murderous appraisal. The prince was a good judge of men, the healer knew, and had seen through him. But the healer also knew he was the only hope Helgi had.

Helgi spoke slowly and the healer could tell he was struggling to keep his famous temper. 'Keep her cool up here. If it rains bring her in. Apart from that, make sure she doesn't fall off.'

'Yes, *khagan*. Yes, lord.'

Helgi took one last look at his daughter. She was wet with fever, scarlet patches covering her face, her hair sodden with sweat.

'And pray to our gods,' said Helgi, 'because tomorrow I think you are travelling to their lands as escort to a princess.'

32 Saved for Christ

The rain-swollen river was a sheet of crumpled lead under the moonlight. The air was beginning to spit with moisture and Jehan knew that the best he could hope for was a cold and wet night in sodden clothes, if they managed to make the ford and get away. They hurried down the hillside towards the water where it passed some ruined farmsteads. The river was flowing unusually fast. It had been a wet spring, the rain prolonged and heavy. But the ford should be passable, he thought. Then again, he had never had to consider such a thing in his life. He had spent most of it cloistered in Saint-Germain, never travelling anywhere.

The Vikings seemed less sure they could make the crossing. Up the slope horsemen had gathered. Jehan counted twenty. Beside them were more warriors on foot, maybe twice that number. They had seen the berserkers and the lead rider pointed his spear towards them and kicked his animal down the hill.

'Can we make it?' said Astarth. The young man seemed in a fever, undecided between attack and retreat, stepping one way and then the other, certain only that he didn't want to stand still.

'We have to,' said Ofaeti. 'Come on, get the mules in. Those not leading an animal link arms. The river's shallow here but it will be powerful. If we can cross before they arrive, we can disappear in the woods the other side. Let's make sure we don't get caught in the water.'

The men splashed in, pulling the mules after them. There was no order, no line. They all leaped in at the same time, straining towards the far shore – a distance of a hundred and fifty paces. Jehan had no choice. He followed them.

The river was thigh deep and very powerful, and Jehan staggered as he stepped into it. Then he steadied himself. The wonder of his transformation had not left him and he was amazed by how strong and stable he felt, despite the push of the water. The Vikings were not so sure-footed. They staggered, stopped, tottered forward and stopped again, all the time fighting for balance.

Down the hill the riders came at an uncertain trot. Vikings were no horsemen, it was well known, and they struggled to get the animals to go faster. Still, there was no need for great haste. They were four hundred paces away but the berserkers were only ten paces into the river and already they were grabbing on to each other, forced to link arms to make headway. Jehan saw that some of the horsemen carried bows across their backs. The rain was coming down now and if only the clouds would cover the moon there would be the protection of darkness. But the clouds did not cover the moon.

The horsemen were three hundred and fifty paces away, the berserkers only fifteen into the river. It would be slaughter, and Jehan needed these men to get him to Saint-Maurice. Astarth had the idea of mounting a mule and rode it to the other bank. Three followed his example, clambering up onto the animals over their packs before making for the far shore.

Jehan strode forward through the racing water, seven Vikings struggling in his wake.

'No good,' shouted Ofaeti. 'Best turn and face them.'

'No!' shouted Jehan. Astarth had collected the mules and was forcing his way back into the water with them, coming to the rescue of his comrades, riding one and leading three.

Jehan reached back to the first of the chain of seven. 'Take my hand!' he said to Egil, who grasped at him with a curse. Then Jehan pulled, dragging the men behind him.

The horsemen were two hundred paces away, Jehan could hear their catcalls now: 'Run, you cowards, too unmanly to fight!'

'Come in here and say that!' shouted Ofaeti, though he was having terrible trouble standing.

Jehan drove on. He felt strong and stable in the water. The berserkers made better progress with him pulling. Fifty paces, fifty-five. The horsemen were now on the bank. Sixty paces, seventy. Something splashed into the water. An arrow.

Astarth had the mules alongside his friends and the berserkers leaped for the animals. Three got on and another three managed to clasp the packs as the animals turned for the far shore. Only Ofaeti had run out of energy. He stood swaying in the stream like a drunk man trying to remember the way home.

More arrows. Three horses had entered the river and were wading towards them. Ofaeti fell in a slow tumble, waving his arms for balance. As he fell he managed to twist and grip the riverbed, crouching on all fours facing the surging current. More arrows, but this time coming from the opposite bank. The berserkers were now firing back at the approaching horsemen. Jehan stepped forward, but the horsemen were too near. He might get ten paces dragging Ofaeti but no more. The confessor faced the oncoming riders.

There were three of them, their horses moving on with high and careful feet. A ridiculous situation had occurred. Now the berserks on the far bank were trying to ride the mules back to their friend's aid, But the animals had made one return journey through the powerful current and were refusing to make another. The beserk called Vani was wading back but his progress was very slow.

The three horsemen had spears. Jehan didn't know what to do. He helped Ofaeti to stand and the big berserk drew his sword, but it was all he could do to keep his feet, let alone fight.

Jehan went to take the weapon from him. Ofaeti gripped it and wouldn't release it.

'Please,' said Jehan. 'You can't fight them without your legs.'

The Viking nodded and passed over the sword. The monk strode towards his attackers. The riders were unused to fighting from the saddle but had no choice. If they got down they'd be in exactly the same situation as Ofaeti, unable to balance, vulnerable to arrow or spear should their enemy allow his friends a clear shot.

Forward the horsemen came, stabbing down at Ofaeti and the monk. Jehan made sure he was the main target, leaping at the riders and slashing with the sword. A spear snicked past his chest but Jehan was quick, bringing the sword down hard on the rider's leg. The man cried out and his horse caught his fear, staggering sideways in the stream and throwing him into the water. In a breath he was gone in the darkness. Another spear was driven down at Ofaeti, but he managed to grab it, tugging hard at the weapon. His opponent, though, was no fool. He just let go of the spear, causing Ofaeti to overbalance and go sprawling back into the river. Jehan flung the sword towards the bank and dived after him, out of the shallows of the ford and into the deep water. Suddenly the remaining horsemen were isolated and five arrows sang across the river. Jehan heard screams, animal and human, as he plunged forward through the black water.

Almost the second that he dived in, Jehan regretted it. The man he was trying to save was a pagan and an enemy of his people, but he had acted on instinct, not even knowing whether he could swim. But he cut through the icy water with ease. He caught a glimpse of something a way in front of him – the Viking's big blond head bobbing on the surface.

Jehan didn't have time to think how strange it was that he, who had been so afflicted he couldn't even perform the most basic functions of life without help, was now shooting forwards through the bone-biting cold of the river to rescue a man who had been hailed a mighty hero by King Sigfrid.

Ofaeti had nothing to cling to, nothing to stop him being carried back towards Paris and the Viking camp; that, though, was the least of his worries. The water was numbing and the current strong. Jehan, though, was quick through the water, arrowing towards his target. The confessor seemed guided, the big man his clear objective, despite the dark, the rain and the swift-running waters.

In four breaths he was on Ofaeti, taking him in a powerful grip.

'No good,' said Ofaeti. 'I will pull you down. Let go of me.'

Jehan said nothing, just kicked for the shore. The current was strong but he was stronger, and he quickly made the bank, dragging Ofaeti out of the water. The big Norseman lay spluttering on the cold grass.

Upstream Jehan could see Rollo's forces hesitating on the opposite bank, peering through the darkness. On their side of the river the other berserkers were moving off.

'Your friends are making for the trees,' said Jehan. 'We had better join them. I need your protection on the way to Saint-Maurice.'

Ofaeti lay back, his arms above his head, trying to get his breath.

'How can you see so far? I can hardly see past my own boots in this darkness.'

'You're shocked from the cold,' said Jehan. 'You'll regain your eyes soon enough.'

Ofaeti got to his feet. Jehan looked at the Viking's face. The big man was staring at the confessor with something approaching fear.

'My eyes are good enough,' he said. 'Let's go before Rollo's men gain the courage to cross. I thank you for what you did for me.'

'Don't thank me, thank God. None is saved nor lost but by His will.'

Ofaeti nodded.

'Will you pray with me?' said Jehan.

Ofaeti gave a short laugh. 'When we are safe from our enemies, if it pleases you, I will. If it's your god that saved me, then Lord Tyr won't begrudge me giving him thanks.'

The confessor smiled. Was this what God had freed his limbs for – to convert the heathens? It had to be. He had thought none of the berserkers would ever return from Saint-Maurice. Now he saw a different way. These men would make formidable soldiers for Christ. They would welcome Jesus and his divine presence into their hearts, which would drive out the pagan lies they had been raised to. 'Lord Tyr' would be exposed for what he was, nothing more than a shade in a story that any child could see through.

'Come on then,' said Jehan. 'Follow close if you can't see your way.'

The two men scrambled up the bank and ran towards the line of trees.

33   One Gift Demands Another

In Ladoga, all those years before, the healer had sat and watched what he confidently expected to be his last dusk turning the river to a winding path of flame, like the road to hell. He was a Bulgar, a happy, dark little man dressed in bright yellow silks that did nothing for his pale complexion. Helgi had gone down to be with his warriors and the healer was alone on the roof apart from the little girl.

He shook his head and thought of the warning his father had given him: 'You have a talent, but use it sparingly. Cure too many and the gods will be jealous.'

He hadn't listened, of course, and had travelled from all the way beyond Kiev practising his trade. The charms and the potions were what he sold, but he knew that these, which his father had taught him, were only useful up to a point. The real secret of his success was that he had worked his first years for little or no pay, just taking a meal when he needed it. All he asked in return was that, if he was successful, people spread the word.

It had worked. The healed sang his praises and the dead never complained. By his third year he was sought all over the east. And then he had heard that Helgi was seeking a new physician. Like a fool, he had been pleased when the king had chosen him, not realising that a healer relies as much on his luck and reputation as on his skill.

He looked down at the child beside him. She was hot enough to set fire to the roof. She would burn him up too, for sure, if he didn't cure her. It occurred to him to simply jump from the tower to save himself the pain of the flames. He had nothing more to give. His last hope had been to take her to the roof, to show her to the eyes of Tengri the eternal sky, but it was failing.

But then he remembered he had been taught a charm by a stranger who had joined him on the road to Kiev. He'd been travelling with a party of Khazars who were heading west. They'd kept their fire going all night because there was a rumour that a wolf was stalking the road. The healer had no liking for wolves and had found it difficult to sleep. Of course there always were wolves – he heard their howling in the hills – but to be told one was nearby and had raided a camp, taking only a goat when it could have taken a child, unsettled him.

Eventually, in the blackest part of the night when the clouds ate the moon and the only light came from the campfire, he had drifted off, slumping to the ground from his sitting position. A low snarl tight by his ear had snapped him back to consciousness. The wolf was sitting close by his side. He had started to scream but suddenly a hand was across his mouth, silencing him.

A voice: 'You were about to cry wolf but which wolf is it that gives you alarm? The one that sits by the fire or the one who dwells in here?' He felt a sharp prod in his chest, and when the hand at his mouth was released he turned to see a very strange fellow indeed. The man was tall, pale and beardless, with a shock of red hair protruding from beneath the bloody pelt of a wolf, worn as he had seen some shamans wear them, its head over his head, as if the creature had crept up behind him and sunk its teeth into his skull. Apart from that, he was entirely naked, his pale skin writhing with snakes of firelight.

The healer looked around for the wolf. It was gone.

'There was a wolf here,' said the healer.

'Now it is here,' said the stranger and drove his finger into the healer's chest again.

'I do not take your meaning, sir,' said the healer.

'Ambition is a wolf, is it not, that chases us on to who knows what heights? So I say again, here is the wolf.' Once more the stranger's finger jabbed hard into the healer's chest.

'Do desist from poking me so, sir,' said the healer. 'I bruise easily.'

'Do you not have a salve for bruises?'

'I do not.'

'What can you cure? For I see you are a healer by your charms and philtres.'

'I—'

'Headache?'

'Yes.'

The man cuffed the healer hard about the head.

'Ow!'

'Vomiting?'

'Yes, I—'

The man thumped the healer hard in the stomach, so hard that his dinner came back up and he was sick on the ground.

'Broken limbs?'

'I have some skill—' The man raised his hand but the healer quickly added, '—though not in that area.'

'Ah, the gift of healing is so rare nowadays. It is hard to tell the honest man from the charlatan.'

'I am a truthful man.'

'All the best liars are. You are the king of charlatans because the first person you deceive is yourself. You are sincere in your insincerity, truthfully false. Liars have more truths in them than all the honest men of the world. You lie to yourself so much that you empty yourself of them. Then, when you tell the people you can heal them, that cannot be false, for all you have left in you are truths, so men must believe them. You eat lies and belch truth, such is the way of the self-deceiver. Sincere thieves are the best ones, I tell you most earnestly. The gold ring you wear on the chain about your neck, I need it. Pass it to me.'

'Need it for what?'

'It is a cure for the lying tongue.'

209

The healer had thought at the time that seemed a reasonable explanation and had taken off the chain to give it to the man who, if he recalled correctly, had dangled it above his lips before lowering it into his mouth and swallowing it whole.

'That was my ring,' said the healer.

The strange man leaned towards the healer and it seemed that his head became that of a gigantic wolf which opened its mouth improbably wide and said, 'It prettifies my bowels now. Reach in and tickle it out!' He spoke with such force that the healer flinched away from him.

'You will bite my arm,' said the healer. For some reason it didn't seem odd that this man had become half wolf.

'You see,' said the half-wolf. 'I have cured the liar in you, for now you speak the truth.'

'What shall I have for my ring?'

'Advice,' said the wolf-headed man, smacking his lips with his tongue as if savouring the taste of the fine gold ring.

'What advice?'

'Go north.'

'For what?'

'To wait upon the lord of deceit himself. He who lies lying in Ladoga. That priest of pretence, hierophant of hypocrisy, monarch of mendacity, the tricky sticky fellow, the fakir of fakement, the wolf in wool, oath-breaker, foreswearer and god. King Shit himself. I am his servant, you know, but like all servants I hold my master in cold contempt. I will better him one day, though it may take me a year or two. Today we give him what he wants; tomorrow he may not be so lucky.' The half-wolf's tongue slapped around his muzzle as he spoke, and the healer feared the creature might fly into a rage.

'You're talking about Helgi the Prophet?'

'Helgi? Do you know his physician has found all ailments' surest cure? You should hurry to that king's service.'

'I cannot compete with a man who holds such knowledge.'

'This is the cure!' said the half-wolf, and from somewhere he produced a hangman's noose tied with a tricky triple knot.

'Surely you can hang as well as he. There is no talent for hanging, my fine fibber, no skill to it – the most untutored farm boy takes to it as well as the highest king.'

'I do not wish to hang,' said the healer.

'Only he wishes to hang. Only he.'

'Who is he?'

'He is three.'

'Three what?'

'People!' He cuffed the healer across the back of the head. 'A triple knot like this, waiting to be tied. And what is a knot that is not tied? Not a knot? Not so. For if a rope is not a knot then all things are not knots that are not knots and that is not a useful distinction. However, a rope that has been a knot but is a knot no more is more not a knot that one that has never been tied, which nevertheless is still not a knot. So we have degrees of notness matching our degrees of knotness, former, present or future, the triple knot of time. When something has once been something else, can it ever be what it once was again? I think knots. And what is a knot unknotted? Not a knot. And if the knot is retied? It becomes not not a knot, that is a knot once more. This is not a knotty problem, though it does concern knots, does it not? Three of them.' The creature seemed exasperated, as if he had explained the obvious to the healer and found him simply too dim-witted to understand.

'You are a man of the Christian god. I have heard their tales of three in one but I prefer my own gods for the luck they have brought me,' said the healer.

'Who are your gods?'

'The sky and the blue of the sky.'

'How conveniently ungraspable,' said the wolf. 'They're all at it nowadays – mysteries and cant. What would you say to a god who gave you something actually useful? A solid god, a big pale, beautiful flame-haired immortal who occasionally likes to appear as a wolf?'

'I would follow him.'

'And if he didn't want scabby scratchy followers like you?'

'I would ... I would ...'

The half-wolf put his fingers to the healer's mouth and slapped him on the back with the other hand so that he coughed out air.

'I would say thank you,' said the healer as the creature manipulated his lips to form the words.

'I will offer you a charm.'

'And what must I do to get it?'

'Go to Helgi, take his gold. But let his little girl, the one fierce in heart, drink this.'

'Drink what?'

The wolf took a bottle from the healer's pack and poured its contents onto the floor. Then he bit deeply into his hand until blood dripped into the bottle.

'I offer rare bargains to those who please me.'

'I will take your charm.'

The creature put the bung of cloth back into the bottle.

'Here is the charm,' he said. 'Congratulations. You are an instrument of destruction. But be of good cheer. It is death that we destroy. We are its enemies.'

He scratched something onto a piece of birch bark and passed it to the healer.

'This one must the sons of men know, those who would heal and help. Carve it once when you need it most. It calls forth the fever.'

On the roof, under the stars, the healer didn't know how he had forgotten that night. How had he forgotten the fever charm? It had not seemed at all strange to him to sit talking to a man who was also a wolf. It had not seemed strange when he had given the girl the blood for a fainting fit she had suffered one day. And it had been alarming, but not strange, when the fever had fallen upon her shortly afterwards.

He stripped a piece of bark from the roof with his little knife and carved the sign the stranger had given him. He didn't know what to do with it so he just put it on the girl's chest.

*

The girl spoke – 'Liar. Where are you, liar?' – and sat upright, clutching the bark to her, staring wide-eyed over the town.

Then he was no longer alone on the roof. Beside him, squatting next to the girl, was the pale flame-haired man.

He smiled at the merchant and chanted,

'When I see up in a tree
A corpse swinging from a noose,
I can so carve and colour the runes
That he walks and talks with me.'

'Who are you?' said the healer.

'I am a fever,' said the pale man, 'a fire to light the bones within you.'

'You are a man. I have seen you before.'

'House-rider, troll-witch,' said the man to the healer, 'make your way back to your shape.'

The little girl did not understand the literal meaning of his words but understood the man was telling the healer to return to being something he had once been before.

The healer climbed down through the hole in the roof and the pale man sat holding the girl's hand. She stirred and looked up at him.

'I have dreamed of you,' she said.

'And I of you. What did I say in your dream?'

'My home is in the darkness,' she said.

'Yes.'

'I am of the dark.'

'Yes.'

'Is there a darkness near here?'

'They have found one under Gillingr's barrow,' said the pale man. 'Would you like to see it?'

'I would see it,' said Sváva. 'I know you. You are the wolf's father. The begetter of death.'

'Yes.'

'I have a fierce heart, everyone says it. I am not afraid of you.'

'No.'

'What am I?'

'A little broken thing,' said the man, hugging the girl to him.

'Will I ever be mended?'

'First you need a little darkness, where the lights inside you can shine,' said the pale man. 'Do you fear the dark?'

'No.'

'Then come with me.'

Sváva went down the ladder in the loading tower, past the winch that pulled up the goods, where the healer now hung from a rope like a forgotten sack, and out of the town, hand in hand with the pale man.

They went to the barrow, the naked grave, its black mouth open to the stars. The height of two men down was a deeper darkness, a hole.

'The Romans mined here,' said the man, 'but bad luck dogged them. Many men were sacrificed, by accident and design. Mercury was worshipped here. He lived here. Old man Odin, to you modern people. This is the place.'

'What place?'

'The appointed place. Here the things that need to be seen can be seen.'

'These tunnels are a city beneath the earth and its people are the dead,' said Sváva.

'You can see that already?' said the man.

'Yes.'

The pale figure trembled and let go of her hand. 'You are sure you are not afraid of the dark?'

'No,' she said. 'I think rather it is afraid of me. See how it shrinks from me. Even in there it dare not face me.'

'The dark is a wolf who runs from fire.'

'I am a fire.'

'You are a fire.'

214

'I would talk with these dead fellows,' she said. 'The ghosts must be merry now they have no lives to lose.'

'Then go in.'

The little girl walked forward and bent to the mouth of the hole. Then she crouched down and crawled inside. The god smiled his wolf smile and turned away.

In his great hall, Helgi was dreaming of the vast offerings he had given to Odin – the warriors he had taken in battle, the slaves and the cattle, the gold cast into mires. He saw himself piling them up – the bodies of animals and men, the treasures of silver and gold – but every time he looked away from the pile it seemed to shrink, requiring ever more corpses, ever more jewels to make it look right again. Dreams have their own sense of right and wrong, and to Helgi it seemed that a body hoard was only satisfactory when it challenged the mountains with the shadow it cast.

In his dream Sváva stood in front of him, a pale child in a dirt-stained shift.

She spoke: 'Better not to pray than to sacrifice too much. One gift always calls for another.'

Had he killed too many, been too keen in his wars, given too many slaves to the gods? What were they asking for now?

'My darling,' he said, 'I did not think he would ask for you. I did not think the god would take you.'

The girl moved her right hand from where it rested on her left hip, up across her body, a back-handed gesture almost of dismissal.

All around him strange symbols sang and hummed in the air. Runes. He counted them. There were eight. He was in his bed and wet with sweat. He could not get up. It was as if he was oppressed by a vast weight, and his chest could not rise.

Something was crawling across his skin like a snake – a rune, a single upright stave with two others sloping away from it. It creaked and groaned like a rope on a ship, like a rope taut with a dead man's weight. He knew its name. Ansuz. He lifted his hand to touch it where it writhed on his face. He saw gallows, black lines on a hill against an angry dusk. Phrases of poetry went screaming through his head like hurled spears. He saw a rider hurtling across a plain, a girl in a garden under a metal moon, a well and, next to it, the headless corpse of a man. Mimir's well, the well of prophecy. He knew that this was no ordinary dream; this was a communication from the gods.

The rhymes rattled through his mind like pebbles down a staircase, the runes singing around him, calling out to him to embrace them.

> *Know how to cut them, know how to read them,*
> *Know how to stain them, know how to prove them,*
> *Know how to call them, know how to score them,*
> *Know how to send them, know how to send them.*

He looked at the rune, the gallows rune, creaking and twisting on his skin and within his thoughts. The rune was wrapped around him, constricting him, crushing the breath from his body. He felt a tightness at his throat, all his weight, all his consciousness, suspended from his neck. He knew whose rune that was. Odin, Odin the treacherous, Odin the ruination, lord of the burned earth.

'This is the meaningful letter,' said Sváva, 'though it is not what it seems. This is the deceiver's rune. Your rune, for you deceived me.'

'Sváva, I did not know.'

He was reaching out for his girl but he could not touch her. He could not sit up no matter how hard he tried.

'I have your prophecy, father, the one the god promised you.'

'Sváva, Sváva!'

The pale child looked down at him. 'If three become one, then the ravener will come,' she said. 'Find her and give her the protection of the dark.'

Sváva turned back to the darkness and sleep pulled Helgi down.

216

34   A Haunting

As Jehan headed east, the rain was unceasing, turning the fields to mires and the trade tracks to swamps. The Seine was in flood, the current too strong to row against for long, even if the Vikings could have scouted out a decent boat. The stars were invisible under the cloud by night, so when they came to forks in the river they either guessed the way or waited for day and took direction from the sun. Jehan knew that the Vikings might be seen as raiders and told Fastarr to hide his splendid shield with its hammer motif and on the plainer shields chalked the sign of the cross. The berserkers agreed to this but would not cut their cloaks in the Frankish fashion. Ofaeti said he'd rather die of a spear than a frozen arse.

The Transversale to Lyon was a good old Roman road but fraught with danger. When they met travellers he told them the Norsemen were Christian converts, protecting him on a pilgrimage to Rome. The eleven proved their worth. Bandits lurked on the road, and about forty of them barred the way near Auxerre, too scared to attack but testing the northerners mettle. They found the mettle in good order and scattered when Ofaeti screamed for his men to charge. There were easier targets than a troop of well-armed and battle-bold northerners, and the thieves disappeared as quickly as they had come. But it was all Jehan could do to talk one group of merchants – a hundred or so strong – from attacking the Norsemen, so when they got to the Saône, which flowed in the right direction, they took the broad river south.

Huddled on a stolen river barge – hardly more than a glorified raft – wrapped in their cloaks and travelling by night when the moon allowed, the Norsemen were less conspicuous than they had been on the open highway. The abbeys they passed were poor and mean-looking and the Vikings took Jehan's word that there were no great bargains to be made there. They didn't even make use of the pilgrim hostelries the abbeys kept for travellers both religious and secular; they were too wary of the reception they might get. The human remains they carried with them were kept in a sack which was towed on an improvised raft of branches because of the smell. Jehan had to admire the Vikings' woodworking skills. The little raft took them next to no time to make and even he – who had spent most of his life inside a monastery – could see it was better built than the one they had stolen from the riverbank.

The Vikings fed him nothing, but he wasn't at all hungry. He drank from the river and felt he needed nothing more to sustain him. This was just part of God's blessing, the same one that had cured him of his affliction, he was sure. The words of Romans 14: 17 came to him: *For why the realm of God is not meat and drink but rightwiseness and joy in the Holy Spirit*. The Holy Spirit did really seem to be filling him. Sometimes the rain was so heavy it was almost painful, but he was not cold and he put back his head to drink it in, enjoy its taste and delight in the looseness and power of his limbs.

He had, he was sure, been blessed. The trials he had undergone, the tortures at the hands of the Raven and Saerda, had been a gateway of agony through which God had stepped. He had eaten of unclean meat, true, but even that did not seem so bad now. The taste of the blood haunted him but he did not find it unpleasant. That in itself, he thought, was a message from God telling him not to blame himself for what had been forced upon him and not to question what had happened to him. He had been freed from the bonds of his infirmity for a purpose. Every instinct he had told him to pray, to know God's mind.

When Jehan prayed it was not as the weavers, butchers, candlemakers and reeves of Paris prayed – requests for help, a word of thanks, something like a silent conversation. Jehan had spent years with God as his main companion, a presence by his side in the dark of his cell, the guiding principle of his every thought. Prayer was indivisible from his life. In some ways his life was a prayer, every action, every mouthful of food enabling him to serve God. So he sat in the dark and the chill on the raft as the Vikings steered it on under the black sky, sinking down into himself, surrendering will, surrendering personality, to God.

'Let me know your purpose, Lord.' The movement of the raft lulled him, the cold seemed to leave him. He fell through a thicket of his own thoughts, jolting awake as he relived the shock of the moment when he realised strength and freedom had returned to his limbs. Infirmity and constraint had been so familiar to him that the sensation of free movement was very disconcerting.

As he prayed, the feeling of Saerda's head in his hands came back to him, the quick snap with which he had broken the Viking's neck repeating itself over and over in his mind. He remembered something else from that moment: a presence – yes, a presence, and not one he had ever felt before. There was a sort of signature note to the way it felt. He was tempted to say that it was evil, but it wasn't quite that. No, this presence that watched him unseen did not have a moral nature at all. He tried to think of a word to sum up what he thought of it, 'hungry' seemed to fit best.

The movement of the raft seemed indistinguishable from the movement of his mind towards God. The words of Psalm 51 came into his head. He knew it well, the Miserere, and the memory of his brother monks singing its verses rose in his mind, a chant as rhythmic and restful as the lapping of water against a riverbank. The beauty of the Latin carried him away, though three lines came to him in plain Roman.

> Restore unto me the joy of thy salvation; and uphold me
>   with thy free spirit.
> Then will I teach transgressors thy ways; and sinners shall
>   be converted unto thee.

*Deliver me from the guilt of blood, O God, thou God of
my salvation: and my tongue shall sing aloud of thy
righteousness.*

The guilt of blood, the guilt of blood. That taste was in his
mouth now, the meat that had been forced through his lips.
He could smell it too, coming from the little raft behind, blood
and rot, putrefaction and something else. What was that smell?
It was the body of Brother Abram, he could tell, but it wasn't
a smell he'd noticed in the streets of Paris or on the countless
occasions when he had been brought to the sick, dying and
dead. It was deeply disturbing. The odour, strong and deep,
was almost pleasant. He was hungry, he realised, very hungry
indeed, but curiously the idea of food repulsed him. Only the
subtle flavours of decay that seeped from the little raft that
bore the monk's remains seemed appealing.

His mind wandered and the poetry he had heard in his
agonies before came back to him.

Brother will fight brother and be his killer,
Axe age, sword age, shields are split asunder,
Wind age, wolf age, before the world plunges down.
No man shall spare another ...

He forced his mind back to prayer. He needed to summon
his powers of concentration, to hear nothing but the words in
his head, but at the same time he had to surrender himself, to
let go of ordinary thought and let God come to him. *Why have
I been chosen, Lord? What is it you want from me?*

The budding trees beside the river stretched up their
branches as if in supplication to the sky, as if they too were
begging God for an answer.

There was a movement on the bank, something pale.

Jehan peered into the darkness. Someone was watching the
boat, not twenty paces away. At first Jehan thought it was a
child, but as the raft moved nearer he could see that it was a

very strange figure indeed. It was a girl, he thought, or, rather, it was female. She was a pauper and all she had was a rough blanket of dirty wool pulled around her. Her face, though, was what really took his attention. It was not that of a child, but not quite that of an adult. It seemed to hover between youth and age, terribly drawn, pale and shrunken, with eyes that burned and hated. Jehan guessed she must be starving, though there was no need to starve so close to a river and easy fishing.

'Do you see?' said Jehan, gesturing to the figure.

'What?' said Fastarr.

'The child, on the bank.'

'I see nothing,' said Fastarr. 'Beware of tricks, monk. You'll find we have a few of our own you might not like.'

Jehan could not believe the Viking couldn't see her, but when he looked back, the child was gone. He returned to his prayers and tried to think no more about it. But that face kept coming back to his mind, the face of a child who had seen too much suffering for her years, a face that looked at him with an unswerving stare into which he could only read animosity.

The boat was coming to a bend in the river, where a broad but shallow beach bore a couple of huts. A big wooden cross marked the beginning of the road towards Mont Joux, and then on into Italy and Rome

'Here, monk?' It was Ofaeti, the fat one.

'Here,' said Jehan. 'You will wait while I speak.'

'It's a bold slave who gives his masters orders,' said Ofaeti.

The confessor looked hard at the big Viking. 'You are in my country now,' said the monk, 'and everything you dream of, everything you are, depends on me. If you want to live you will do as I say.'

'You gave your oath that you would serve us.'

'And I am keeping it,' said Jehan. 'You need me now, do not let pride blind you to that. I serve you best by leading you. The first thing you will do is buy some blankets and, if you can, a tent or two here. The local farmers will have something.

If you don't have shelter in the mountains you will freeze to death.'

Ofaeti looked at the confessor and nodded. He turned to Fastarr. 'These monks have more nuts than a squirrel's larder,' he said, 'but they see the truth right enough. Let him be our voice for as long as he is useful.'

They were met with stares, but the fisherman at the beach was too mindful of the safety of his family to ask many questions of the Norsemen. Jehan again explained that they were his bodyguards, hired to take him on a pilgrimage to Rome. The fisherman nodded at the Vikings and said something about thanking God that such men could be bought, for if they couldn't the whole country would be in ruins. Then he took their money and sent his boy off to buy blankets and two small tents.

When he returned, the berserks set off, Jehan at the front, up into the icy mountains and the valley of the black saint.

35   The Valley of the Black Saint

The way up into the mountains was hard. Rain turned to sleet as they climbed and then to snow. The winter snow had gone and the fresh falls came down on a cold, green landscape. On the lower slopes it didn't settle. Further up, though, the mountains were shrouded in white.

They rounded a great lake with settlements all along it. They didn't stop but Jehan cut a staff and made a cross, holding it high before them. Pilgrims were common on that route, if unusual at that time of the year, and the locals seemed reassured. The Vikings sounded their horns and trusted to luck. No one attacked them and they were even able to buy a little bread. Jehan did the talking and the Norsemen kept silent. The mules were loaded with firewood on the advice of the locals. The way into the mountains would be cold and they would need all the warmth they could get when they camped.

The body of the dead brother was dragged on a roughly constructed sled. The smell of rot was becoming unbearable to the Norsemen, though Jehan did not find it unpleasant.

'We should boil his flesh off,' said Egil.

'And where's the pot big enough for that?' said Ofaeti.

'Then burn him,' said Egil. 'Hey, monk, is a cooked saint as good as a raw one?'

Jehan said nothing.

As they turned south into the pass the snow set in properly, and the river they were following up began to turn to ice. The berserkers were northern men and so well dressed for such weather, but they had to keep moving throughout the day to keep the cold at bay. The nights were made tolerable, though not pleasant, by a fire, but there was little to eat, save some fish the Vikings had caught in the river and the bread they had bought.

Luckily the dead monk's body soon froze and the smell abated. The mountains were closing in, dark walls rising up into grey cloud. It was as if they were trapped in a trough between gigantic waves that towered above them as though suspended in the moment before collapse. Five days in and the waves vanished, invisible in the snow. There was little shelter in the valley and the firewood was running low. The tents were a mercy, even though they bulged with the number of men they held. The cramped conditions at least meant they were warm.

They pressed on, faces cast down to the ground. Only the feel of the track beneath their feet, worn smooth by traders and pilgrims, kept them going, though often they stumbled and fell. None of the Vikings complained, though Jehan could see that they suffered. The confessor couldn't get the face of the child who had watched him from the riverbank out of his mind. He imagined her watching him still, just out of sight. When rocks or icefalls loomed out of the mist, for a second he thought it was her.

On the sixth day the weather relented. The cloud was still low but the snow was lighter and they could see their way forward. Jehan saw Ofaeti looking at him.

'You are a strong man, monk.'

Jehan kept going.

'When did you last eat?'

'I can't remember.'

'Two weeks at least. And yet you stride out like a man on a good breakfast. You don't even wrap your feet in rags. What is it that drives you on?'

'God.'

Ofaeti nodded. 'Tell me about this god.'

So Jehan told him the story of Jesus' birth, how he had been born among the animals, raised as a carpenter and died on the cross so mankind could live eternally.

The Norsemen loved stories and they all listened with great interest. Ofaeti in particular seemed intrigued. 'I will try this god of yours. He will sit alongside Tyr in my heart for a while and I will see the luck he brings.'

'Christ sits alongside no one. You must reject your idol.'

'That I will not do. Is your god so jealous that he cannot admit another?'

'Yes,' said Jehan. 'If you were baptised but did not reject your devil then God would punish your descendants to the third generation.'

'For what?' said Egil. 'I have a wife, but can't I lie with another woman if I choose? Will my wife curse me if she hears of it?'

'Your wife should curse you. You should be bound to one woman only.'

'I am bound but not so tightly I can't take a roll in the hay with another if I choose. What woman would begrudge her seafaring man that? Do such witches exist?'

'The Lord tells us, "Thou shalt not commit adultery." I will tell you a holy story and see if it can sway your pagan heart.' Jehan told the story of Moses and how he had brought down the Ten Commandments from Mount Sinai.

Ofaeti and the berserkers laughed.

'So you Franks believe, "Thou shalt not kill?" How many of us northerners would you slaughter if you went to it without a tender heart?'

'It is permissible to kill the enemies of God. There is just and unjust killing, the Hebrew makes that clear. The command is closer to "Thou shalt not murder."'

'How do you know an enemy of God?'

'Ordinary men need not worry about such things; the priests can point them out,' said Jehan.

The Vikings laughed again.

'A convenient set-up for all, I think. I like this God, he who knows the difference between noble fight and murder,' said Ofaeti.

'He is my strength and my light.'

'And for that reason I'll think him a good god. He has made you a mighty man.'

'He has,' said Jehan, 'though I would thank him more if he had made me the weakest.'

'Why?'

'Because God tests those that he favours. From his own son, he asked the sacrifice of life.'

'That is not such a great sacrifice,' said Ofaeti, 'not to us. You go on to dwell in the halls of the All Father to feast eternally and battle eternally. Death is like moving to another land, as so many of our people do.'

'In pain, crucified, nailed to a cross?'

'A funny end for a carpenter,' said Ofaeti.

'King Nesbjörn crucified a shoddy boatbuilder once – said he'd teach him how to drive in nails,' said Egil. 'Perhaps it was similar.'

Jehan swallowed his anger. 'He knew what his fate was and went willingly, for our sins.'

'To be fair,' said Ofaeti, 'I've got any number of uncles who knew the Valkyries were hovering above them. Heggr and his boys got trapped by a bunch of islanders out west. They could have surrendered and waited for ransom but a man called him a coward – only word the bastard knew in Norse – so they showed them they weren't. Two out of ten came out alive, but no one in those parts has ever called us cowards again, so it was worth it. A brave man, this Jesus, no doubt, but the world's full of brave men. Or rather the next world is!'

'When you are downtrodden, when you are at your lowest, when every one of your fellows has deserted you, my god lifts you up and walks beside you. Does yours?'

'Tyr likes powerful warriors. He leaves cowards to make their own way,' said Ofaeti.

Jehan turned to the big Viking and took him by the shoulder. 'Am I a coward?'

Ofaeti looked into his eyes. 'I believe you are not,' he said.

'No Christian is. Let me tell you the story of this place. Do you know who the black saint was?'

'No.'

'A saint is someone perfect in holiness, as Maurice was. He is known as the black saint because that was the colour of his skin.'

'Black skin!' said Egil. 'A dwarf then?'

'A man of the Roman Theban legion, a descendant of the ancient pharaohs.'

'The people of those lands are blue,' said Ofaeti. 'I know it because it is said that is why they are called *Blaumen*.'

'One man's blue is another's black,' said Jehan. 'The Theban legion was composed entirely of Christians, 6,666 men strong.'

'That's a mighty force,' said Ofaeti.

'Depending on the mettle of the men,' said Egil.

Jehan went on: 'They served the pagan king Maximium Caesar, who ordered them, for the pleasure of his god Mercury, to kill some Christian families who were living in this place. The legion refused.'

'They were wrong to do so if they had taken an oath to the king,' said Ofaeti.

'They had a stronger bond to their god,' said Jehan. 'When the news of their refusal came back to Caesar he ordered that one-tenth of their number be killed.'

'What is a tenth?' said Astarth

'A lot.'

'More than a dozen?' said Ofaeti.

'It is 666 of them,' said Jehan.

'And their fellows stood by and saw so many slaughtered?' said Egil.

'They welcomed martyrdom.'

'What's that mean?' said Egil. 'Your Latin means nothing to me, priest.'

'The chance to die for their god.'

'They'd have been better men if they'd killed for him. It'd

be a mighty king who came in and took so many from Rollo's army, I tell you that,' said Egil.

'When the first tenth had died, the emperor sent his orders again. They were refused. And he killed 666 men again, and again, until only six remained. Then he killed them and the whole legion was dead.'

'Would they not have been better defending these families of their god? The Roman king could now order his other soldiers to slaughter them,' said Ofaeti.

Jehan ignored the question in order to drive home his point. 'Six thousand, six hundred and sixty-six men stood and died in this place. Their bones may be beneath your feet. Do you call them cowards?'

'I don't know what to call them,' said Ofaeti. 'I know what to call a man who fights; I know what to call a man who runs. One who does neither I have no name for.'

'He said he was called a Saint Maurice,' said Egil.

Jehan spoke in a low voice: 'You are less than serious, Egil, and yet you should quake in fear before my god. I am not a warrior. Your idols would not be interested in me. I have been downtrodden, taken from my homeland by savage men, my companions killed, my future promising only death. Do I tremble? No, because my god is a god of love.' He grabbed the tip of Egil's spear and held it to his own breast, staring the Viking down. 'You are brave men, but it is the bravery of fools who do not know what is arrayed against them. You would shake to your boots if you knew his wrath. Yet God wants to love you. He offers you deliverance, asks you to dwell for ever in his house. If you refuse, damnation awaits. You will be tied and pinioned and thrown into the mouth of hell, where the eternal suffering of fire awaits.'

'Burned for eternity by the god of love?' said Ofaeti. He seemed puzzled.

'He offers you his mercy. If you refuse it, you condemn yourself,' said Jehan.

'I could do with something to warm me up,' said Egil. 'It's like Nifhelm up here.'

'Nifhelm?'

'The realm of the ice giants,' said Ofaeti. 'It's underground, so I'm fairly certain it's not around here.'

'It's a silly myth,' said Jehan.

Ofaeti shrugged. 'It is cold, though, isn't it? There could be white bears here, which wouldn't be a lot of fun. I'll tell you what,' he said: 'if your god sends us this monastery, a warm bed and a bowl of stew before the night's out, then I'll believe in him.'

'You worship God without conditions. You don't make bargains with him.'

Ofaeti looked genuinely nonplussed. 'So what do you do?'

'Praise him.'

'Flatter, you mean. Lord Tyr would strike such a man down. You offer him the death of fine warriors in battle, gold and cattle, not words to please a lady. If you can't bargain with a god then the god is no good to you.'

The mist in the valley was thinning. Jehan peered through the grey air. There was a cliff rising out of the main slope, and beneath it was a structure too regular to be natural. It was just a shape, a darker grey on a field of other greys, but the confessor knew it could only be one thing – the monastery. From along the valley he heard a sound. It was the wind, though it reminded him of what he would soon be hearing. Singing. The monastery was famous for its *acoemetae* – the sleepless ones. The monks sang in shifts, unceasing for nearly four hundred years now. He looked at the sky. It would be around mid-afternoon, the little hour of nones. They'd be singing the songs of ascents. He recited the words of one of them to himself.

> *He who goes out weeping,*
> *Carrying seed to sow,*
> *Will return with songs of joy,*
> *Carrying sheaves with him.*

The message of the psalm cleared his head and renewed his strength for the struggle to convert the northerners. He had to accept that he was dealing with a simple people. There are many ways to Christ, his abbot had told him. Perhaps he should let the northerners walk theirs. He looked up. The great cliff curved around to his left, the monastery tight to it. Could none of the Vikings see it?

'If God sends you the monastery, will you renounce your idol?'

'He'd have to chuck in a whore as well for that,' said Ofaeti. 'He's a god of love; he should have a few at his disposal. But I hear your god doesn't like whores, begging the question of what he does like.'

The confessor waved his hand. 'Honest men and good women. Whores are tolerated by some in the Church for they keep the good women of the town chaste. They are not tolerated by me. Pray properly and God will send you a wife.'

'All whores are thieves too,' said Ofaeti, 'but they're gone by the morning. It's one thing to get done by a pirate, it's another to invite him into your house and let him complain when you fart. I'll have no wife.'

'You don't want children, Ofaeti?'

'Don't you, monk?'

Jehan snorted and looked to the mountains, just gigantic shadows in the mist. He had often lectured people on the sins of the flesh. What had Eudes said to him when Jehan had warned him that his whoring would see him in hell? 'It is easy to be chaste when God has made it impossible for you to be anything else.' Had Jehan known lust? Of course, but he had prayed for it to go and it had, largely. Those feelings were not the hardest ones to control. God had stricken his body, rendered him blind, and Jehan had known why. God had wanted him for Himself. In darkness and constriction he had no closer companion than God, certainly no greater love. But with a touch in the dark of the Viking camp something else had stirred inside him – a longing greater than lust for true companionship, for touches that did more than lift him, wash him, cut his hair or trim his beard. For most of his life he had been alone in the darkness with God. He cursed the ingratitude that made him hungry for something more.

He knew, to his regret, that it was possible there were whores at the monastery. The abbot's position in recent years had been given to warrior nobles. While a core of monks kept the hours and attended to God's works, there were many at such places who preferred to eat, drink and satisfy their lusts. They weren't monks, just lesser sons whose families had nothing better to do with them.

The monastery seemed clearer to him now, and he was surprised none of the Vikings had yet seen it. There was a smell in the air – something sweet, the scent of cooking perhaps. No. Not cooking, but something like it. It was a note he'd never quite noticed before, an alluring aroma like ripe cheese, pungent and strong yet delicious.

'Hey! Look!' Varn was flapping his arm. 'Can you see that?'

'I can,' said Ofaeti. 'What is it?'

'It's Saint-Maurice,' said Jehan. 'If there's a whore in there, then your soul's Christ's.'

Ofaeti laughed. 'If she's a pretty one, then why not? Whatever's inside, let's hope it's a gift from your god and not from mine.'

'Why?'

'Because that would be fifty angry monks come to cut our throats,' said Ofaeti. Jehan recalled the big man's words in the chapel: 'Tyr's blessing, many enemies.'

Jehan glanced at the Vikings. They were not in a good state – hungry, frozen, ice in their beards, their cloaks and blankets tight about them. Were the monks of Saint-Maurice in a belligerent mood, he thought, the northerners would not last long.

It was better to be cautious.

'You stay here,' said Jehan.

Ofaeti shook his head. 'We're coming with you.'

'If you do, they'll think you are bandits and kill you. There are five hundred monks in there, and their house possesses some of the greatest treasures in Christendom.'

'Got what?' said Ofaeti.

Jehan realised too late what he had said, but the damage had been done. He was glad he'd exaggerated the number of brothers by at least five times.

'This place is in the mountains on one of the main routes between Francia and Rome. Do you think they have never seen a bandit before? Or a hundred bandits, or a thousand? You are eleven. If you let me speak, you'll be in the warmth of their guest house before nightfall. If you don't, you'll be spending another night in the cold.'

Jehan would fulfil his oath, he thought: he would put the Vikings' case to the abbot. But he would not lie. The bones were those of a brother, not a saint. And he knew that when he explained exactly who the Vikings were and that they were pagans, their lives would not be worth much. The abbot of Saint-Maurice was the second son of a powerful and warlike Burgundian noble. Such men were drawn to the Church for the power it offered rather than by piety and weren't slow to use their swords. He felt sure of the answer the Norsemen would receive. He didn't want them dead and would argue that they could be brought to Christ, but he knew the outcome of his visit to the monastery would not be good for them.

The Norsemen muttered but Ofaeti knew they had no choice but to accept what Jehan said. However, before the monk went, the big man took him by the arm.

'You are a hardy man and a brave one,' he said, 'but I remind you of your oath. We are offering no threat. If they come to kill us then they will be the Caesar and we the Theban legion saints.' He prodded Jehan firmly in the chest. '"Thou shalt not murder," so your god says.'

Jehan nodded.

'And one other thing. This warrior puts his head on a block for no man. If your brothers come, we will bless them.'

'Bless them?'

'They want to go to their god, don't they? We'll speed them to his side.'

Jehan smiled at him. 'We spend our entire lives preparing to die,' he said, 'but I will seek their protection for you – if you come to Christ.'

'Protection first, then we'll see.'

Jehan didn't move, just looked into the big Viking's eyes.

'You are very wonderful,' said Ofaeti.

'What?'

'You look blank when I bargain, so I thought I'd try praise, like you said. Your mother raised a mighty man. Is that not praise enough?'

'My mother didn't raise me,' said the monk, 'or anyone, as far as I know.'

36   Rescue

The riders caught them as they made the river on the third day. Aelis had not even been aware anyone was following her, but as they broke from the woods into an open meadow, they heard the horses behind them. The wolfman's wound had turned bad and there was no way to outrun them. There were no boats at the river and there was no prospect of escape.

Sindre had been riding with increasing difficulty and eventually Aelis had had to take his mount's reins. The wound seeped through his tunic, bloodying his fingers where he held his side. Each evening he would search the woods and return with a strip of bark on which he would scratch a symbol. He would sit staring at it until sleep took him and throughout the next day would hold it in his hand as he rode, glancing at it and mumbling into nothing,

> 'The meaningful rune that the dead god stained,
> That the rune lord of the Gods carved.
> Odin for the Aesir,
> Dvalin for the dwarves,
> Asvith for the giants and the sons of men,
> I myself carve here.'

As the river approached, Aelis had seen his skin turn pale. She knew that he was teetering on the edge of death. When the halloo of the riders sounded behind them, Sindre hardly looked up. When he did, he was shaking and his teeth were chattering. He could hardly sit on his horse, let alone fight.

There were twenty of the horsemen, and two levelled spears at them, but Aelis was not scared. The way they rode told her all she needed to know. The riders were confident, holding their spears with ease and poise, their movements as they directed their animals hardly noticeable.

'Northerners, you're going to get it, you bastards!'

The rider was speaking Roman and had a Parisian accent, nasal and reedy without the guttural crunches and rolls of the people with whom she'd been raised.

She shouted back to them in the same language, 'I am Lady Aelis, brother to Count Eudes, harried and pursued by Norsemen and monsters. Get off your horses and bend your knees to me.'

The lead rider lowered his spear and came forward to draw his horse alongside her. He looked at her war gear, the helmet stuck on the cantle of the saddle, the sword at her side. He put his hand to her head and touched it.

'Where's your hair?'

'Take your hands off me. If my brother was here you would be flogged on the spot for that impertinence. I was attacked by the Norsemen and had to disguise myself.'

'No lady would ever cut her hair,' said the horseman. 'What are you, a witch?'

Aelis was so pleased to see Frankish riders that she was willing to indulge the man's rough ways. 'I'm the lady who will be kind enough not to mention your behaviour to Sieur de Lanfranc, if it ceases now.'

Aelis had mentioned the name of her brother's master of horse. As a knight, the horseman would not be subordinate to Lanfranc, but the old cavalry commander – whose grandfather had won his rank under Charlemagne – made life very difficult for those who crossed him. Lanfranc was notoriously sweet on Aelis and not above calling a man out in a duel if he thought it would please her. Few people would relish testing their sword skills against his.

The horseman glanced back to where a second rider, a taller man, was trotting in.

'A little less rough if you would, Renier. I can't imagine the count will be happy if his sister reports your manners.' His accent was stronger – eastern, thought Aelis.

'I can't see why she'd cut her hair,' said the first man. 'It's a shame and an indignity.'

'Next to rape and murder?' said the taller horseman. 'You were raised in little Paris, Renier. Had you been brought up in one of the great cities you might be less easily shocked. A spell in Aachen would have done you good. Chevalier de Moselle. Madam, you are our mission, we have been sent to find you.'

'The siege is lifted then?'

'No, we broke out. But that means we can break back in again. The Norsemen are not as united as they were and are busy fighting among themselves at present.'

'You didn't come just for me?' Aelis was appalled that men had been taken from the defence of Paris just to look for her.

'No. We have delivered a message to the emperor. He will now move to help us, I am sure. Our task is over. We have you and all that remains is for us to dispatch these foreign dogs who have taken you prisoner and we will return you to Paris and your brother.'

'We are not foreign dogs,' said Leshii; 'we—'

'No,' said Moselle, 'you are not even that; you are the corpses of foreign dogs.'

He drew his sword but Aelis put up her hand. 'These men have rescued me.'

Moselle looked at Leshii and the wolfman. 'That one is a northerner,' he said, pointing to Sindre.

'Some of the northerners have worked for us in the past and still work for the emperor. This man has no allegiance to the Paris Danes.'

Moselle made a tight little nod.

'Tell them to get down from their horses. A merchant and a pagan should not be riding fine animals like that.'

'Fine animals?' said Leshii. 'This is a common pack mule!'

'Too good for you,' said Moselle.

Aelis gestured to Sindre. 'He killed the Viking king.' She

knew no Frankish warrior would accept that a woman had killed Sigfrid. In fact, to suggest it would be to mock them, to say that she had achieved what they could not.

Moselle nodded again. 'And Sigfrid gave him a blow for his pains, by the look of it.'

'He took an arrow. It's still in him. Can you draw it?'

'Fiebras!' Moselle turned in his saddle and shouted.

'He's a healer?' said Leshii.

Moselle snorted at him. 'He's a warrior. Just happens to be handier with the pliers than the rest of us.'

Leshii got down from his horse and helped the wolfman down. Aelis could see he was not best pleased to meet the Franks.

'Your ransom gone, merchant?' she said to him in Latin.

'I am sure your brother will reward me for my pains.'

'Let's hope he doesn't give you pains for your reward,' said Aelis, though her tone was light enough and she intended to see the merchant compensated for the loss of his wares at least. She pulled her cloak up to cover her shorn head but Moselle immediately took a silk scarf from around his neck and passed it to her. In a second she had regained her modesty. Then she went to the bushes and took off the big mail shirt. She rejoined the horsemen and gave the sword to Moselle.

'Give this to my brother from the wild man,' she said. 'It belonged to the Viking king.'

Moselle looked impressed. 'He was a strong man,' he said.

Sindre was on the ground, scarcely breathing. Fiebras, who had produced a big pair of long-nosed pliers from his saddle bag, knelt beside the wolfman.

'Not long for him, lady,' said the Frank. 'The kindest thing is to leave the arrow and let him die.'

'Might he live if it's drawn?'

'Might is a big word,' said Fiebras, 'but yes, he might.'

'Then draw it.'

Fiebras told his colleagues to make a fire, then went to the river and pulled out a reed, which he split with a knife. He put the pieces in his cap and returned to the wolfman. Sindre was secured with a length of rope, bound tight around his arms and legs. Two of the biggest Frankish knights pinned him, one lying across his legs, the other across his chest.

'Why are you doing all this?' said Aelis.

'I might have to reach down past the shaft of the arrow and crush the barbs on its head,' said Fiebras. 'He will not like it, though it's the right time. The wound has a lot of pus.'

'That's a good thing?' said Aelis.

'Our doctors say so. The Arabs disagree.'

'And you?'

'I do what I can.'

Fiebras approached the wolfman. Aelis could see Sindre's eyes were glazed and he was sweating heavily.

'Hold him,' said Fiebras.

He pushed one of the split reeds into the wound, wrapping it around the shaft of the arrow. The wolfman bucked but the men on top of him held him firm.

'What are you doing?'

Fiebras displayed only mild irritation. This was, after all, the sister of his lord who was asking the questions.

'I'm covering the arrowhead. If we can push aside the flesh it might come out. The reed stops the head from causing more damage.' He gave a gentle tug at the shaft and Sindre twisted. 'Keep him still,' said Fiebras, 'or it will be worse for him.'

He tried again. This time Aelis thought Sindre would lift off the ground and two more Franks knelt to hold him down.

'Strong,' said the fat one lying across his legs.

'Have you no wine for him?' said Leshii. 'In my country we give men wine before such procedures.'

'Wine is for Franks, not foreigners,' said Fiebras. He gave another tug on the arrow and Sindre cried out. 'No,' he said. 'It's stuck.' He withdrew the bloody reed and threw it to the ground. 'Are you sure you want him to go through this, lady?'

'If he can live, I want him to live.'

Fiebras picked up the pliers. They were long and at the tips splayed out like a duck's bill. 'My father bought these off an Arab twenty years before. They're the best tools for the job. Malger, heat some oil.'

From a flask a stout Frank poured oil into a pan and put it into the fire they had made.

'Now,' said Fiebras, 'hold him as firm as you can.'

The men bore down on Sindre as Fiebras worked the pliers into the wound. Sindre was delirious now. He was shouting in Norse, but his words were unintelligible even to Leshii.

Fiebras had the pliers about the arrowhead. Sindre fainted and the stout Frank got off his legs with, 'Thank the Lord for that.' The biggest man they had was a barrel of a country knight in a yellow tunic. He squeezed on the pliers as hard as he could. Fiebras called for the oil and took over again. As he worked the arrow free, the oil was poured into the wound.

Aelis could not watch this and turned away, offering a prayer of thanks that Sindre was unconscious. Finally he was bandaged and left to recover. She took him some water and used it to wet his lips. Her countrymen looked at her strangely but she did not care. She owed this man her life, she was sure.

Her euphoria at finding her own people receded and she began to think clearly. She remembered the wild-eyed boy in the peasant's house raving about the bird that had been sent to bewitch him and suddenly felt afraid. Leshii came to sit beside her.

'Not near the lady, old man, you understand?' said Moselle.

'Let him approach,' said Aelis.

The knight shook his head and turned away. Aelis adjusted the scarf on her head, emphasising her modesty. She had to regain the esteem she had lost by allowing her hair to be cut.

'You should tell them,' he said, 'about the ravens. These men are a danger to us if they become enchanted.'

'My people are apt to blame the person who is pursued by such things as much as the pursuer,' she said. 'They might wonder what devils I had conjured to spark the interest of hell.'

She thought for a second. 'It is heresy to believe in witchcraft, but there might be a way.'

She stood and approached Moselle, then drew him to one side. 'Knight,' she said, 'I am about to entrust you with information that may seem incredible to you but is true. Can you keep a secret and relay it to your men in a way they will find palatable?'

'I will try, lady.'

'You may know that Father Jehan from Saint-Germain came to see Count Eudes just before I was attacked and fled.'

'I do.'

'The confessor had one of his visions ...'

'God blesses him with many insights.'

'Indeed. Well, this is what was revealed to him. I am in grave danger of dying in a very unusual way. The birds of this country carry disease, and Confessor Jehan told me he had seen one peck at me in his vision and cause me to fall ill, die even.'

'Yes.' Moselle looked serious.

'For this reason no bird can be allowed to approach our camp.'

'No bird ever does, not unless it wants cooking.'

'Exactly so. But the confessor has proved correct many times before. So, if you could alert your men to be on their guard against birds. It is necessary to set a watch in the night too.'

'A bird will never come by night. I never heard of anyone getting attacked by an owl.'

'Nevertheless, this is what I want, and as my brother's sister what I command.'

Moselle shrugged. 'As you wish, lady. It will be an easy thing. No bird will come near.'

'Then the task should not trouble your men.'

Moselle gave his instructions without offering an explanation. However, the horsemen were not a military unit in the old Roman army style. Three or four – the ones Aelis recognised – were Eudes' *vassi dominici*, or at least that was the title they would adopt if he became king. They were his vassals, members of powerful families, and not accustomed to obeying orders blindly. But war had taught them the value of recognising a leader, at least in the field, so Moselle received polite enquiries, rather than an interrogation. However, the more noble riders would not demean themselves by watching for birds and Leshii was given the job. Aelis had to argue strongly that it was important someone else kept watch at night too and the merchant could not do it all himself, and in the end it was agreed that the lesser knights would take it in turns.

The sun was already setting, so they made camp. To Aelis's delight the Franks had tents with them, and she was given a whole one to herself. They carried no poles but cut them as required. She crept beneath the heavy hemp cloth, its musty smell reminding her of the garden at Loches where she and her cousins had slept the summer nights as children. Apart from privacy for Aelis, the tents also gave everyone some protection from the ravens. Only the sentries would be outside.

Sindre was a barbarian and lay beneath the stars. At least the night was dry and Aelis put a horse blanket over him. Leshii was not given shelter either, so would keep the fire going beside the wolfman. She also warned the merchant against taking the blanket.

Wrapped in the Viking king's cloak Aelis sank to sleep and to dreaming. She was back at Loches and the girls around her were in a state of high excitement. The little tent they played in had something inside it. She stood by its side and listened. An erratic flutter. Something was trapped in the tent. What was making that noise? She knew! The sound, she realised, was the panicked beating of a bird's wings.

37 What Happened at Saint-Maurice

Jehan held up his cross and walked towards the monastery below the great cliff, towards the walls and the buttresses of the church, which rose above him like a headland from the sea.

No one came to greet him. The squat villa outside the walls that served as a guest house was empty save for some chickens sheltering from the cold. This wasn't odd in such a season – pilgrimages wouldn't start until the threat of winter had subsided. Only the very, very holy or the very, very mad would try to cross before the snows melted. With the country at war – northerners to the west and the north, Bavarians and Slavs stirring in the east, and infighting between the emperor and his nephew all around – there would be few even when they came.

He went across to the doors in the monastery wall. They were strong and thick, though wide enough to drive a cart through. Cut into them at the bottom was a smaller door to admit pedestrians. Jehan knocked. There was no answer. He turned the handle and pushed at the door. It was open. Jehan felt a sense of disquiet, although he wouldn't have expected the door to have been barred. The monastery was far from the sea and access to it was through well-defended lands. The door would only be locked at times of threat.

He looked back at the Vikings. They were scarcely visible in the mist. They'd get restless soon enough and go into the guest house, he thought. They weren't the sort of men to freeze to death for fear of offending anyone. He stepped inside the doorway. The church was in front of him, the arches of the cloister stretching away to his left, but there was no one at the gate. More worryingly, he could hear no singing. The song of ages should have been coming from the church. It was a building of pale stone with towers at either end. Into the wall facing Jehan were cut four arched windows, glazed and patterned with rich blue glass. Jehan remembered how wealthy the monks of Saint-Maurice were said to be and barred the door behind him.

He walked to the church. The door to that was open too and he went inside. His eyes took a second to adjust to the dark of the interior. That smell was there again – deep, sour, appetising. Jehan couldn't place it at all. What was it? Some sort of dough? Incense? There was another smell too, slightly incongruous – a powerful scent of horse.

He passed through a vestibule, which was plain and unadorned. This was clearly the poor door. The main and nobles' doors would be on the other side of the church. He continued through into the church proper. The light from outside was weak and at first the arches of glass looked like doorways of light floating in a black void. To his left, an arched walkway curved around behind the altar; in front of him were the aisles where the monks stood before the splendid altar of gold and silver topped with an image of Christ on the cross. The light on the gold seemed to dance and swim like the shimmer of bright coins in a fountain.

Why had that image come to him? There was a fountain at his monastery, and visitors could never be dissuaded from throwing small coins into it. The monks tolerated the practice but Jehan disapproved. It was a tradition left over from the Romans, he knew, and therefore not far from the worship of idols. It was his last childhood memory before the Virgin had taken his sight away.

He became aware of a noise. Someone breathing. Or rather something. There was movement beneath the altar. He peered into the darkness. The light was fading further, the windows just dim blurs now. He could see very little of the interior of the church.

He went to a branched candlestick and took up the flint and tinder beside it. In a few moments he had a flame and lit a candle and then another, until all four candles on the holder were alight. He walked forward. At the altar he stopped and held up the light. There was movement and a snort, and then a different kind of lustre to the gold of the altar, a deep chestnut brown. Behind the altar, tied up next to a font, was a horse. It was calm but noisy as all horses are. Its blowing and stamping had been so incongruous and unexpected in the church that he'd failed to realise what it was. A saddle lay on the floor – it had a high cantle and pommel in the Frankish style – along with a healthy pile of shit. Jehan felt his anger rise that someone had chosen God's house as a stable. A Frankish knight would never do that.

He considered leading the animal outside but something was very amiss in this place. Should he get the Vikings? He looked at the gold on the altar. No, they'd have torn it off and be halfway to the coast with the rest of the monastery's treasures by morning if he did.

He went to the rear of the church, taking the candlestick with him, and the horse went back to staring into nothing. The door to the night stair leading to the monks' dormitory was in front of him. It too was open. He walked into the cold air outside. The dormitory was a large two-storey villa he could just make out in the light of his candles. There was no light leaking from it, though that was no surprise. He was going to look stupid and be very unpopular if he woke the monks. Perhaps keeping animals in the church was a Burgundian custom, though he doubted it.

He walked down the stairs, the candles guttering as he moved. He was cold and decided that the best chance of finding anyone awake was to go to the warming house, the only part of the monastery other than the kitchen that would be allowed a fire. Monks were supposed to live an austere life, but it would not be unusual to find half the monastery asleep by the fire in really cold weather like this. He guessed the warming house was on the ground floor of the dormitory building, so the heat would rise into the sleeping area.

To his right was a low building with a tiny door cut into it. He knew instinctively that this was the sacristy, where the holy vessels for celebrating mass would be kept. The snow by the doorway was a different colour, almost black in the weak candlelight. Someone had dragged something from the sacristy, and it had left a long dark trail on the white of the snow. It smelled of something deep and sour. Without thinking, he put his hand down and scooped some up. The snow melted in his fingers, leaving them strangely sticky. Jehan licked his fingers and felt a cold thrill go through him. The snow tasted delicious. Had someone spilled some food there? If it was food, it was none he had ever tasted. It seemed to carry a sensation of the frost inside it, and sent a tingle rippling over the skin of his arms and back.

He looked around him and breathed in. The taste of the snow filled him up, prickling the hairs on his neck, causing him to swallow, jolting his mind as if he had suddenly woken from dozing at the side of a fire.

Jehan walked on, following the trail. Away from the wall more snow had fallen to cover the stain but the smell didn't go away. He put his hand through a knuckle's depth of snow. The sticky stuff was beneath it. He put down the candlestick. Then he cast his arms about him, scrabbling at the ground. It was as if the whole surface of the inner courtyard was covered in the dark goo, just under the sheet of freshly fallen snow.

Jehan smeared the goo onto his face, scooped handfuls into his mouth, lay down in the snow and lapped at it like a dog. He had never been so hungry. It was as if all the days without food, the meals where he had watched uninterested as the Vikings cooked their fish and game, came back to him now and sent him into a wild hunger for whatever it was beneath the snow.

He didn't know how long he had lain and lapped like that but the sound brought him to himself. Again, it was horses. He stood, soaked and shaking though not cold, not cold at all. His mind seemed a thing of many parts, as if he couldn't quite get his reason to engage, as if his normal patterns of thought were there but unavailable to him, as useless as a book to a blind man. He picked up the candlestick. Only one candle remained alight and he used it to light the other three. Then he went through another open door into the large building to his right. It was the refectory, the large dining hall of the monastery, benches pushed to one wall, a long table overturned next to them. He shook his head to clear his thoughts, offered a prayer for guidance to help him think and slowly he regained his clarity. There were the horses, six of them. This time he noticed that, though the horses were good riding animals, the saddles stacked in the corner of the room were all pack saddles. Or rather, two of them had been fine Frankish riding saddles but they had been adapted to carry big baskets at either side. Jehan had seen enough horses before his affliction to know that animals as fine as these should not be used for hauling. You could buy five nags to carry your pack for the price of one of these animals. Norsemen, he knew, were neither great riders nor judges of horseflesh.

He went out of the refectory and back to the dormitory building. The warming house was a good one, complete with the Roman system of underfloor heating, the vents at his feet. He bent down. Someone had sealed them with earth. He opened the door and went in.

Jehan stepped back and gave an involuntary cry. There were forty or fifty Norsemen crammed into a room not ten paces by ten, huddled around the cold hearth of the warming house. The air was heavy with the smoke of the dead fire but he could make the bodies out through the murk by the light of the candles. They were sitting upright, leaning on each other or against the walls, rich plate and candlesticks strewn about them, one, a big man with a three scars across his bald head, seated on a glorious chair of gold and enamel – the reliquary of Saint

Maurice, which contained the saint's bones. No one moved and Jehan could see that not one of the Norsemen was alive.

A celebration had been interrupted here, thought Jehan, by the angel of death. He felt his heart racing. He was sweating despite the cold, salivating so heavily that drool ran down his chin. Was this the beginning of the condition that had claimed the Norsemen? He was so hungry. The Vikings had clearly raided the kitchen before retiring, and half-eaten fowl, bread and cheese were in their hands, in their laps and on the floor. It held no appeal for Jehan, though. He must, he thought, be ill. To be starving but unable to eat was surely a sign of the onset of some sort of malady.

He held up the candlestick and stepped into the room to examine one of the dead warriors. He was a young man of around fifteen, blond and beardless. His mouth smelled of pitch and at his lips was a black froth. The same with the next fellow and the next. In the lap of the man with the three scars was a big bowl of the monks' cloudy beer, still unspilled. Behind him was a barrel, a hole smashed in one end. Jehan sniffed at it. The smell of the pitch was there too. Poison. But why was the room so very smoky? Jehan looked down. Someone had broken a hole in the floor. The smoke from the warming fire would be able to go directly into the room. Someone had killed these men in the most deliberate way.

He was suddenly very cold. He took one of the Vikings' cloaks and, for good measure, the sword, scabbard and belt of the big man in the chair. It was a good Frankish blade. The people would trade with the invaders, no matter what penalty their nobles threatened.

Before he left, he put his hand on the chest that was built into the chair – the one that contained the remains of Saint Maurice. His reason was available to him only in glimpses but he used a moment of clarity to talk to God.

'Strengthen me,' he said. 'Let me know your will. Make me your right arm, God, that I may serve you.'

It was no good, though. He couldn't clear his head, couldn't work out what do. His reasoning powers were failing him. All he could think of was his hunger. Even the fate of the monks seemed to pale beside that. But what was he hungry for?

He went out of the warming house and over to the infirmary. There might be some sort of physic or purgative he could use to get this sensation out of his head. He opened the door and peered in. The iron smell of cut meat filled the room. There were five or so monks asleep in their beds, their bald heads reflecting the candlelight like a row of strange pink flowers shining from the dark. Jehan felt relief coursing through him, but then he realised what was missing. There was no snoring, no breathing. His heart was the loudest thing in his ears. It was only then that he really looked at what was in front of him. The two nearest him were lying normally, but the others were at odd angles, limbs half out of bed. They had been slaughtered.

Jehan desperately wanted help but there was nowhere to go to get any. He would need to send a messenger to the next monastery. Where was that?

He walked forward to the end of the infirmary. Was there no one alive here? And then he saw him. In the candlelight, watching him, was a figure. It gave him a start. A man was standing stock still at the far end of the room looking at him but saying nothing.

'What happened here, brother?' asked Jehan.

The man didn't reply. Jehan took a pace forward.

'Brother?'

As he drew nearer Jehan saw there was something wrong with the man. His weight was distributed incorrectly. That is, he seemed hunched forward, as if leaning over a high bar. Jehan moved the last few paces through the dark and drew level with him. He was a monk – he could tell by his tonsure – but that wasn't what took the confessor's attention.

The noose at his neck was suspended over a ceiling beam. Jehan put out his hand and touched the man's cheek. He was cold as a fish on a slab. There was no point cutting him down, clearly. Jehan looked at the knot that tied the noose. It was a strange affair, three knots in one, in tight interlocking triangles. Jehan swallowed. He had seen that somewhere before, he felt sure. He drew the sword, his hand brushing his tunic. It was wet at the front and a thin stream of drool dribbled down from his lips.

How many monks were there at Saint-Maurice? Five dead in this one room. That left maybe fifty or sixty others at a minimum. What had happened to them? Where were the boys, the scholars and the novices? Jehan could only think that, by God's mercy, they lived down the valley in the winter or had been away for some reason.

He felt powerfully intrigued by the dead men. His mouth ran with saliva. Jehan shook his head, overcome by horror, unable to acknowledge the thoughts that were growing in his mind. He had to get out of the infirmary and he blundered for the door, dropping the candlestick as he went.

The horse in the church neighed. Jehan heard a voice say a single word in Norse across the still air. He recognised it. 'Easy.' Someone was soothing the animal. He left the candles where they were and made no bid to relight them.

Jehan gripped the sword and crept across the courtyard then up the night stairs towards the door, just visible in the gloom. It was still ajar, as it had been when he'd gone out. As quietly as he could, he made his way into the church. He drew back the curtain covering the internal porch.

A single candle burned, a bud of light in the great soil of the church's dark. He could see no one in the darkness, only the lustre of the candlelight on the gold of the altar. Something caught the candlelight lower down, a flash of silver near the floor. At first he couldn't make out what it was. It was as if there was a crescent moon of light but a piece of blackness ran up and down its length.

'I am cleaning my sword, monk of Saint-Maurice. Do not make me dirty it again.'

Jehan couldn't see who it was but he replied in an even voice, 'I am not a monk of Saint-Maurice.'

There was a clatter and someone stood up. The horse, disturbed by the noise, blew and whinnied in the darkness.

'Then who are you?'

Jehan said nothing. An animosity and anger he had never felt before was buzzing through his bones. He had never seen the man's face but he recognised the voice. Hugin – Hrafn – the Raven, the man who had tortured him.

The Raven said in a faltering voice, 'You must have seen some things here that are difficult to understand. I—'

'Where are the monks?' Jehan cut across him.

The Raven tilted back his head as if in thought. 'Come, share my meal. The day has been hard for me, and I would welcome conversation and forgetfulness for a while.'

Jehan stepped towards the light. Hugin's eyes flicked to the sword the confessor held. 'There can be no calm talk while that is in your hand,' he said.

'You killed them?'

The Raven pursed his lips. 'Not all of them, not yet,' he said, 'though that may yet turn out to be necessary. Please. Sit. I am not the monster that I might appear.'

Jehan lowered the sword to the floor and sat down beside it, pulling the Viking cloak about him. He had the instinct to attack this abomination but needed to know what had happened, why such strange forces were arrayed against the Lady Aelis.

The sorcerer stank of something, a deep, enticing odour of iron and salt.

'Where are the monks?' Jehan watched his breath clouding the candlelight in the freezing air.

'Below.'

'Live or dead?'

'Both.'

'Below where?'

'I will show you soon enough.' The voice was not the one

that Jehan had heard in front of the king, or nursing him through the torture beneath the beaks of the birds. That voice had been calm and even. Now the Raven stammered and his words were faint and weak, scarcely audible.

Jehan felt dizzy. The hunger had not gone from him, that terrible hunger for the sticky sweet stuff beneath the snow. What was it? Raven was covered in it, he could tell. The confessor swallowed, offering a prayer for guidance.

'You killed all the Vikings.'

There was no reply. The Raven just sat staring into space.

'Why did you kill them? They were your kinsmen. Why?'

The Raven looked around him. His eyes betrayed fear. 'The will of God.'

'How can you know the will of God? It is given to us through prayer and the edict of the Pope.'

'It would seem to be his will that Vikings die. Do not your monks, your Ebolus and your Joscelin who died at Paris, fight to kill them?'

'For just reasons, according to Saint Augustine. In a war waged for good, sanctioned by holy authority and with peace the aim.' Jehan kept his voice calm.

'You are not a monk – I see by your hair – yet you speak like a monk,' said Hugin.

'I am a monk,' said Jehan, 'though I have travelled a hard road.'

Jehan looked around him. Something seemed to move in the shadows, there and gone in an instant. The Raven stroked his forehead and looked at the floor. He seemed to be struggling for the strength to continue.

'Then know that there was nothing to displease Augustine in the Vikings' deaths, nor that of your monks. They died, or will die, for good, sanctioned by the holiest authority there is, and, as you say, with peace the aim.'

'Did you eat them?'

'What?'

'They say you eat corpses.'

'They say that of your priests too. I have eaten no one. That is a route to madness. Men have misunderstood certain practices, that is all.'

'What practices?'

Raven swallowed. 'I am, whatever you might think, a man of compassion. The berserkers told you this, the ones you travel with?'

'How do you know who I travel with?'

'I watch the land, before and behind. The fat one is distinctive even at a distance, and I know they are not a people with a talent for deceit. The cross that went before them was carried by you, no?'

'Yes.'

'I was with your band in Sigfrid's camp. Some of the men there are Christians, there with their families. They heard that I could heal. I tried for their daughter and failed. I could do nothing. She had been hit by a horse and her body was broken. The priests of your land are cowards and fled when they heard Varangians were on their way. They would not come to tend to her. I said I'd do what I could. The girl was dying. She was a Christian; her family were distraught. I said the mass for them and administered the unction. Ofaeti and his men took it as true that I was eating flesh.'

'You are a heathen.'

'I am a man,' said the Raven, 'and my god is not jealous.'

'Nor is he compassionate.'

'His halls are full of the souls of warriors dead in battle. He doesn't seek the soul of a little girl. Where it goes is of no concern to him. Your god should be pleased that I would cast his magic for him.'

The Raven cupped his hands around the flame of the candle for warmth, reducing the light in the church to a ball in his hands. When he spoke again, his voice was stronger.

'Our gods are not so different. Mine wants blood. So does yours. Sometimes, as when the black saint marched through these passes, it seems their desires are as one. Odin is here, in the stones, in the mountains, in the pass. He is the god of the dead and he seeks deaths to please him. How lucky then that your god wanted the same from his Theban martyrs.'

'My god is not your god.'

'What do you know of my god?'

'Only that he is false.'

Raven nodded. 'He is that, he is that.' He seemed to ponder for a few moments. 'But isn't it just a matter of how you look at it? My god's treachery is well known. He kills his heroes to take them to his halls. Yours lets his martyrs die to test their faith and sends them to heaven.'

The confessor forced himself to think straight, willed his mind back to the favour he had asked of God with his hand on the saint's casket. There was the movement again at the side of his eye. Jehan remembered the conversation in Sigfrid's house, the Raven's revelation that he had been a Christian once and that this place had found him and lost him in the faith. *To know his purpose was to know his weakness.* Jehan said those words over and over in his head. Reason was now a candle in a storm, only kept alight by diligence and great attention.

'You are not a monk, yet you speak like a monk,' said Jehan.

'I once was,' said Hugin.

'So why did you desert Christ?'

'Because Christ deserted me.'

'He is always there for you.'

'He was not there for me when I asked him to be. Something else was.'

The Raven took his hands from around the flame. The sudden illumination caught the gold of the altar, the dancing light rendering it liquid in the darkness.

'What?'

'Another way.' The horse shifted from foot to foot and the candle guttered in a draught. The Raven had his face in his hands, almost as if grieving, his emaciated head like a golden skull in the candlelight. He spoke in a low voice: 'Christ abandoned me. I prayed and he abandoned me.'

In the shadows, like something half glimpsed through murky water, was a figure. It was the child Jehan had seen on the riverbank, the dreadfully starved waif with the lined and drawn face. The Raven had not seen her, and Jehan did not draw his attention to her, afraid of what the sorcerer might do. As the Raven stared at the floor, Jehan gestured, trying to shoo the girl away. She didn't move, just stood looking at him, her face a pale mask in the darkness.

'My family were poor people of this village, and they had many sons and daughters. I was not their own but a foundling who the monks had paid my mother – the woman I called my mother – to wet-nurse. I stayed with them until I was five and my father died. Then the monks took me in as an act of charity. They schooled me and fed me and were to make me one of them.'

'That was Christ's work indeed,' said Jehan.

'Indeed. The life here for boys was not so hard, and I still could get away down the valley to see my family. My sister, in particular, was dear to me.'

'Better to have looked forward to God than back to earthly ties,' said Jehan.

He was speaking almost by rote, doling out the wisdom that had been doled out to him, counselling as he had been counselled. It was as if the very ease of the words was a line to which he could cling as the rage inside him threatened to sweep away everything that he had been.

'I didn't think so,' said Hugin. 'She meant more to me than God did. My mother was busy with the flock and her children, my father was dead, my sister was the focus of any tender feelings I had. When I had been five years at the monastery, the fever took her.'

'She died?'

'She would have died, had I not acted.'

'Did you pray?'

'Yes. And I petitioned the abbot to send for a healer. He said that the valleys were overrun with little girls and one less wouldn't displease the Lord. He would move to save a peasant's son who could tend a herd, build and fight for God, but not one of their sluttish daughters.'

'The man was wrong to say that,' said Jehan.

'It cost him his life,' said Raven. His voice had lost all its earlier weakness. Now it was strong, certain, deepened by anger.

Jehan couldn't reply. His head was spinning. The odour of that stuff was in his nostrils again. The rage was growing inside him. He fought to hold on to it, to remember his purpose of finding out why this thing sought out the Lady Aelis, to understand it so he might defeat it.

'I went to her side and I knew that she was dying. My mother had called in a woman from the hills, one who kept to the older faith, who had burned her face for her art. She told me that this place, this valley, is a special place. The church was built on a spring sacred to the old god – the dead god, the god of the hanged, the keeper of the screaming runes. The Romans said there was a temple of their god Mercury here when they arrived. I know him by a different name: Odin. Others call him Wotan, Wodanaz, Godan, Christ.'

'Christ has nothing to do with idols, only in that he casts them down.' Jehan was focusing hard on the Raven now, trying to keep his mind away from ... from what?

'Your god is as hungry for blood as any men have bowed to since the world began,' said Hugin. 'Tell me, when the first stone struck the first martyr, when Stephen spilled his blood for Christ, did your god smile?'

From blood. The sensations of his torture at Saerda's hands came back – the taste of the flesh in his mouth, the coursing energy that had filled his body as the warm blood had trickled down his throat. It had been horrible then but now the memory seemed not horrible at all, dear to him even.

'The god needed a death. The valley wanted a death. She

showed me the triple knot.' The Raven's hands made a lazy pattern in the air. 'Three in one, the dead lord's necklace that slips until it sticks and then slips no more. I went to the abbot in his cell. He had drunk a bellyful and it was easy to do what the god asked.'

Jehan's throat was dry. The eyes of the child seemed to bore into him. He felt he desperately needed water, desperately needed to eat. He licked his lips. The taste of the stuff he had found beneath the snow was on them, but it did not fulfil him, only fired his will to seek more.

'By the morning my sister was well. The wild woman said that the price of my sister's life was her service. I followed them into the hills.'

The whole church seemed to Jehan to rock.

'Do you say the idol you seek to appease wants death now?'

'I have given him that. I don't know what he wants.'

Jehan could think no more about the Raven's words. The blood inside him was turning the veins and cavities of his body to sea caves, smashed by surf. He could only think of one thing.

'What is that?' said Jehan. He struggled to get the words out.

'What is what?'

'You have something on you. Something wet.' Jehan could scent it. He longed to lap it, to suck at the cloth of the Raven's cloak, to drink in the smell and the taste of the black ichor that covered the Raven's head, his shoulder and his hands.

'The same as you, monk. It is tough work that I do.'

'What is it?'

The Raven smiled. His face, thought Jehan, was familiar. It was a symptom of the sickness that had come upon him since he had come to the monastery, he was sure. He had seen the Raven's face somewhere before. It was torn, swollen, pockmarked and disfigured, but he knew it.

'What is it?'

'It is blood.' The child dropped back and the shadows

covered her. She was a face retreating into a mire of darkness. Then she was gone.

Blood. Jehan fell forward onto the flagstones. He had known what the smell was but he had blocked it from his mind. Blood, as he had tasted in the clearing, blood, as he had lapped it from the snow. The church seemed to spin about him. He felt his throat constricting and his skin clammy, sweaty and cold. His body seemed to bubble with the need for action.

Prayers and snatches of songs, articles of the Church, seemed to split apart and run through his mind, looking to coalesce into something intelligible, looking to bring him back to who he was. *One who vomits the host because his stomach is overloaded with food, if he casts it into the fire, shall do penance twenty days ... God from God, light from light, true God from true God, begotten, not made ... If those little beasts are found in the flour whatever is around their bodies shall be cast out ... We look for the resurrection of the dead, and the life of the world to come ... He would not defile himself with the king's food, nor with the wine which he drank ... If a dog should eat it, a hundred days ...*

The rage inside him felt as though it would split his skin. His throat was burning now with a thirst that demanded immediate satisfaction.

'You are ill, traveller,' said the Raven. He looked around him. 'This is your god's house but he is not here for you. My fellow, yes, my fellow, he waits in the dark where he has always waited. Here, quench your thirst.'

He passed the confessor a cup. The water in it smelled familiar, though Jehan's thoughts were too disordered to recognise it. He swallowed it down.

His thirst was not quenched. He wanted only one thing. Blood. He looked at the Raven and knew what he needed to do. He stood. He had the sword in his hand. The Raven stood. Jehan tried to lift his hand to strike but the sword wouldn't move. His arm would not obey his command.

'This place wants death,' said the Raven, 'and it seems it

wants yours.' He pushed Jehan in the middle of the chest and the monk fell back. Jehan was lying on the floor, the smell of blood filling his mind. He was coughing. He put his hand to his mouth. A black ooze was at his lips. The cup had been poisoned. He had known the taste if only his mind had been functioning well enough to recognise it. And yet the feeling had begun long before he'd drunk the poison.

'You have killed me.'

'Not yet,' said the Raven, 'not yet.'

Jehan looked up at the scarred mess of the sorcerer's face and finally recognised it. He had not looked in a mirror since he was seven years old, but there in front of him, thinner, eaten and torn by ritual and privation, scarred and misshapen, was his own face looking back at him.

Jehan collapsed and the Raven took him by the arms and dragged him to the crypt.

38   The Wolfstone

Prince Helgi the Prophet lay sweating in his bed. The *khagan* had a problem. He needed to be a bulwark for his people, a rock on which they could depend, so by day he presented a front, was bluff and cheerful, indulged in the drinking games and allowed his warriors to let him win the contests of strength and speed. But at night, in sleep, he had no such control over himself. He cried out in the dark, and his cries were cries of panic. The Norsemen were not a private people: they slept in their longhouses side by side, children, men and women all packed in together. Soon his night terrors were the stuff of marketplace gossip; they undermined him in his dealings with his *druzhina*, and he heard it whispered that Ingvar's party were using them to foment trouble against him.

It was as if his fear of the god's prophecy – that Ingvar would rule – was itself making that prophecy come true.

The rabble of soothsayers and magicians was still around him, living off his coin, but Helgi put no faith in any of them. He went again to the temple of Svarog, into its dark lodge, breathed in the burning herbs, endured the darkness and the waiting, but nothing came, just visions of Sváva, watching him, always watching him. He needed more.

He found himself unreasonably irritated with the normal night-time sounds of his hall – a child crying, a mother soothing it, a couple kissing and caressing, an old man snoring and farting – and went outside to look up at the deep stars. He would conquer everything under them, he thought, if only that awful prophecy didn't hang over his head like an enemy's axe.

'You need to take the girl from Paris.'

A voice. Helgi looked around him. There was no one, just the shadows under the lee of the hall roof.

'Who is this?'

'A friend.'

It was as if the shadows unwrapped, and the wolfman stepped forward, tall, dark, his face drawn but his limbs strong, the great wolf's pelt about him, its jaws over his head as if devouring it.

'I can bring her here. I can convince her. My destiny is entwined with hers. It has been revealed to me.'

'Who are you?'

'Sindre, called Myrkyrulf.'

'You are a sorcerer?'

'Of a sort.'

'How much are you looking for?'

'I don't want silver; I need something greater than treasures from you.'

'What?'

'Your promise. The one-eyed god is coming to earth and we must prevent it.'

Helgi swallowed. The man seemed to know about Loki's prophecy, but the god had revealed it no one, and no magician had even come close to guessing it so far.

'What promise?'

'You must keep her safe. You must find a place of safety for her.'

'That is my wish, but I cannot get to her.'

'I can.'

'So why do you need me?'

'Because it is my destiny to die at the hands of my brother. I can bring the girl here, I am sure, but her ongoing protection must be someone else's responsibility.'

'Who is your brother?'

'The sorcerer called the Raven. This has been revealed to me.'

'By who?'

'By my mother.'

'Who is your mother?'

'A slave from the north. Her name is Saitada and she is a wide-seeing woman and an enemy of the hanged god.'

'What do you know of the one-eyed god. Of Odin?'

'I am his enemy.'

'Is he coming to earth?'

'We can prevent him.'

'How?'

The wolfman touched his own neck. A pebble hung there, a common grey stone with the crude etching of a wolf's head upon it.

'This is a gift of Loki, the enemy of the gods. It stops magic, silences runes. To come here she will need her magic to defend herself. Once she is here, she must wear this, the Wolfstone. The wolf will not find her while she wears it. You will be able to get her to a place of safety.'

'Why will she not go to a place of safety without it? Does she seek death?'

'She doesn't, but the runes do. And she is pursued. There is another woman who carries the runes. She seeks the lady's death and is very capable of causing it. She and her brother – Hugin and Munin, strong sorcerers as I know to my cost – are servants of Odin.'

'I have heard of them.'

'I have fought them, but I cannot risk too much. It is my brother's destiny to kill me. This stone has been my protection.'

'Keep your stone. I have had enough of charms,' said Helgi.

'My mother is skilled in Seid magic and used this stone for many years to protect herself from witches. Put this on her, and you and she will be safe from the runes. The god cannot come together on earth. Ask yourself why I should lie about this when I have spoken so much truth about everything else.'

Helgi looked at the man and believed him. He knew so much; he wanted no reward; he had come unseen past the town's guards. All this was reason to accept what he said, but there was more: Helgi wanted the wolfman to be speaking the truth, so he decided that he was. 'The destiny will be prevented?' Helgi thought of Ingvar marching at the head of his army.

'This is my hope.'

'What do you need to get to Paris?'

'Only a guide,' said the wolfman.

'I will give you my strongest men.'

'Let me travel quietly,' said the wolfman. 'To conquer Paris and take the girl you would need ten thousand warriors. Better to send none at all than too few. We are to take the girl by stealth. I need only a guide, a little man who can go to an inn and buy food for me without sparking comment.'

It was then that Helgi had thought of the merchant who had come to him petitioning for a loan to help buy a cargo that he was certain could earn the prince ten times his outlay. Helgi had sent him from his hall. The man had been unlucky in business and the *khagan* thought it might be catching. But Leshii the silk man would do, he thought, for men came scarcely any littler than he.

Helgi had a question before granting the wolfman even a dog to guide him: 'If you are certain of death, then why do you try to save the girl? You will not be here for her.'

'Because I have died for her before. It is my destiny to do so. It is the nature of my bond to her. And if the god fails to come to earth, perhaps his spell will be broken and when we live again ...' he seemed briefly lost for words '... we can live unremarkable lives.'

'It is a blessing to be a hero,' said Helgi.

'I have not found it so,' said the wolfman.

Helgi held out his hand. 'The stone. I will need it if it is as you say, and the magic inside this girl can work independently of her will.'

'No,' said the wolfman. 'I will need it to fight the forces that are against me.'

'So how will it come to me?'

'We have a powerful god working for us in Loki. This is his

gift. If he wants you to have it, as I believe he will, then the stone will make its way to you.'

Helgi did not know what to believe but he was certain of one thing. The wolfman seemed confident he could recover the lady from Paris, and the prince would only have to risk the life of one failing merchant to let him try.

39 Song Everlasting

Water and darkness. Cold and noise. A voice singing. Singing? Jehan could see nothing. He was pinioned to something, tied with his hands behind his back, up to his chest in cold water. Someone next to him was singing. Plainsong. The words seemed curiously muted, a tight little echo that spoke of a low roof.

> 'You will not fear the terror of the night,
> Nor the arrow that flies by day,
> Nor the plague that prowls in the darkness,
> Nor the scourge that lays waste at noon.'

The voice was tremulous, the notes uneven, but Jehan could tell it had been trained in the monkish practice. The song was a psalm. He felt so strange he couldn't tell if he was dreaming or awake.

'Who is here?' said Jehan.

The sensation of hunger was no duller in him. He spat. The taste in his mouth was vile. Poison. Yes, he had been poisoned. He recalled the Vikings in the warming house. *The poison on their lips had not killed them – they had been asphyxiated by the smoke*. The thought came and went like a footprint in the sand, washed away by the cold tide of hunger.

One voice stopped singing and said, 'Brothers Paul and Simon. Who are you?'

'Brother Jehan, of Saint-Germain.' It was as if he was shouting his name over a high wind. He felt tormented, almost unable to think.

'The confessor of Paris?'

'Yes.'

'Have you come to save us?'

'I cannot save you.'

The song of the man on his right continued:

> 'A thousand may fall at your side,
> Ten thousand fall at your right,
> You, it will never approach,
> His faithfulness is buckler and shield.'

'Are you strong enough to sing, brother? We must keep the song going. This abomination has befallen us because we allowed it to stop.'

Jehan couldn't reply. He moved his leg. Something bobbed against it.

'We are to die,' said the monk. 'Thank God for the gift of our martyrdom.' His words were brave but his voice was quaking. Jehan could tell the man was cold. Jehan was cold too, very cold.

'Where are we?'

'In the lower cave, at Christ's well.'

The song went on:

> 'See how the wicked are repaid,
> You who have said, "Lord, my refuge!"'

'Where is that?'

'There is a tunnel from the crypt. It drops to here, a holy well beneath the earth. The Norsemen slaughtered us without pity. It is polluted now.'

Something else bobbed against the confessor's arm. Something else too, tickling his hands. Weed? No, there was a solid form behind it. Jehan grasped it and felt around with his fingers. He ran them across something hard and smooth, a semicircle of ridges and bumps. Then he let go. What he had in his hand was hair, he realised, and they were teeth he felt with his fingers.

'Can you move?' said Jehan.

'No. Are you not tied?'

'I am tied.'

'Then it is useless. He will be waiting for us. He means us to die here.'

Jehan swallowed. He was trembling too. The song to his right faltered.

He strained forward and coughed. Something was at his neck. A noose. He tried to work it free by twisting his head but that only made things worse. It was tight now, not crushing his windpipe, not even cutting off his blood, but he knew that any more struggling could kill him.

And then he saw it – a light coming towards him. It was a candle. Surely some of the monks had survived; surely some of the Vikings would become sick of waiting and break in. He saw where he was – a pool in a natural cavern, its ceiling an arm's reach above his head. Three big pillars of limestone sank from the roof into the water, and it was to these that the men had been bound. To his right was the singing monk, spluttering out the words of the psalm. To his left another, fatter monk. Both men were chattering and shaking with the cold.

All around them, the bodies floated or hung in the water, pale as dead fish in a pond, their human juices, blood, shit and piss, voided from the body by death, turning the pool to a stinking soup. The monks had been murdered, no doubt – some by the sword, some by the nooses tied with three close-fitting knots.

The Raven put down the candle by the edge of the pool. 'I'm sorry,' he said. 'This terror is ... required.'

'Unclean thing,' said Jehan, 'abomination, sorcerer—' The rope dug into his neck, choking him. 'I am not afraid of you.'

The Raven smiled at him but there was no humour in his eyes.

'It is not your terror the god wants. He looks for mine. These...' he searched for a word but could not find one, so he used the confessor's '... these abominations are not my inclination.

266

Do not mistake me for the Roman who gloried in torture.'

Jehan tried to speak but could only cough.

The Raven continued: 'We will both have what we want, monk. I will have my vision and you will be a martyr. When they find you they'll make some rare art to commemorate this death. The pilgrims will wear medallions for you, no doubt.'

'I—'

Jehan couldn't speak.

The Raven sat down at the water's edge. He rocked backwards and forwards intoning a chant quite different to the plainsong of the monks. This was low, guttural, and its metre pattered and stuttered, raced and paused in a dizzying tumble of Norse words.

'Fenrisulfr,
Pinioned and bound,
Wolf, ravenous and tortured,
Great eater,
Godbane and blight,
I will suffer as you suffer.
For my agony
Insight,
For my terror
A vision ...

The chant went on and on, the plainsong rising above it. The monk to his right failed and the other took up the recitation. The psalms had been sung every day in that place for hundreds of years. *For what?* thought Jehan. *To keep this horror at ba*y. Had this abomination lain unfed for so long because the monks had kept to their vigil?

The cold numbed him, the chants made his head feel like a ripe fig, straining to split its skin. *Do you know what they did to me? Do you know what they did?* There was a voice in his ear full of rage and hatred. He was in a different place. Or rather it was the same place but changed. There was no pool at all.

The room was dry, in fact parched. His nostrils stung and his tongue seemed cased in sand. Around the pillar to his right wound a great serpent, gold, red and green, dripping venom from its lips. It stretched up over his head, curled about the pillar that secured him and down the pillar to his left. On that, pinioned like him, was an extraordinary sight.

A tall pale man with a shock of red hair was screaming as the serpent dripped venom into his eyes. His skin was red raw where the venom burned it, his hair singed to patches, his eyes dark as liver, his lips black and charred. Acrid steam issued from the flesh as the venom trickled and seared.

'Can you not free me, my son?' The voice was imploring, between a sob and a scream.

'I am tied myself.' Suddenly Jehan's thinking was clear.

'They tied you like they tied me, the gods of darkness and slaughter.'

'Can we get out?'

'We will get out. It is foreseen.'

'Where is the Raven? Where is that creature?' Jehan shouted.

'Gone.'

'He deserves death.'

'He is death's servant. He serves the god in the noose.'

For the first time in his life Jehan felt afraid. This thing in front of him was in torment but it had a presence that seemed to make the air heavy around it. An awful thought came to him: *This is hell*. His pride had undone him and he had been sent to the lake of fire. 'You are a devil,' he said, 'and this is hell.'

'Hell fears you, Fenrisulfr. Its halls tremble to hear your voice.'

'Why do you call me that?' The name seemed to resonate in his head like the bell of hours.

'It is your name.'

'Release me from this place, devil.'

'Would you be free?'

'I would be free.'

'Then run free.'

Suddenly Jehan was choking again, drowning, back in the pool. Something was beside him in the dark, its great head lolling against him, its breath hot on his skin, the monstrous note of complaint and agony that issued from its throat threatening to burst his ears. The wolf was next to him, held down with bonds cruel and thin. Its agony consumed him, and he was no longer himself; he was the wolf, trying to stand, trying to breathe even, beneath the awful constriction of the vicious threads that held and cut him. He broke his bonds behind him and ripped at the noose around his neck with his fingers, tearing the rope to nothing.

Something at his side was in its death throes. The seductive beat of a failing heart, constricting veins and muscles, the shallow, frozen breath filled his mind. His body responded to it and he forced his way through the water to drink in the delicious rhythm of death, to take it in and express it like a dancer expresses music.

There was a great cry. It was so near that at first he thought it had come from himself. But it had not. It had come from the man lashed to the column of rock, the man dying under Jehan's fingers and teeth. More noise, more howling. The other monk was screaming for him to stop. Jehan went to him and made him quiet.

When he was done, Jehan lay a while in the water, like a corpse among corpses. He thought nothing, felt nothing. He did not question, did not think, as the pale child took his hand and led him from the pool.

40 A Commercial Decision

Leshii was dreadfully tired. The fire was warm and hypnotic and he allowed himself an old man's fancy of picking faces in it as he thought about his options.

The only hope he had was that the lady would arrange some sort of compensation for him when they returned to Paris. But how certain was that? The whole town was surrounded by a seething mass of Danes, like so many ants around the discarded core of a pear. There would be a fight to get in and Leshii wasn't up to that.

Even if he did get in, how would he get out, this time with no warriors to help him? *Accept it, you fool. You're a poor man now. All your labours have come to nothing.* He said the words to himself and felt very bitter.

Warriors – Franks or Danes – might think it noble to have striven and lost but he couldn't see it that way. He had planned an old age in a courtyard garden warmed by the sun. He had thought he might have a fountain in the Roman style, a woman to cook and clean for him, perhaps even a bed slave if he could afford one. All that was gone, just the memory of a dream.

He fell towards a miserable sort of sleep but his anxiety brought him jolting back to consciousness.

How long could he go on trading for? He could make a living, of course, scratch together enough for food and some mean lodgings, but he knew what faced him when his eyes failed, his back seized up or his knees – already painful – became unbearable. He would starve or have to cast himself on the mercy of the temple of Perun. It was no way to end your life.

The warmth of the fire lulled him and he started drifting away once more. A noise broke his dozing. It was the call of a bird. He looked around him. Two ravens were perched on the sleeping Frank. All the feelings he had been suppressing inside him seemed to come bursting out – anger, disappointment fear – and he picked up a stick to hurl it at the birds. Then he stopped himself. The Frank was Renier, the one who had implied Aelis was a whore for cutting her hair. Leshii had had a thought.

He put the stick back down and looked around him. There was no raven coming for him. He went across to the horse and the mule they had brought with them. Both animals were hobbled – a forefoot and a back leg tied together to make it impossible for them to wander too far. He removed the hobbles and tied the beasts loosely to a tree. He wanted to saddle up the horse but feared too much stamping and blowing would wake the Franks. Then he took his knife and went to Aelis's tent. As he passed the Frank, he saw in the moonlight that the bird had taken a peck at his cheek.

It hadn't woken the warrior, though the man was mumbling in his sleep: 'She is not of my party. She will counsel against me for my angry words. She will produce sons to frustrate the claims of my line. Eudes is not the man to lead the Franks. She is not of my party. She will counsel against me for my angry words. She will produce sons to frustrate the claims of my line. Eudes is not the man to lead the Franks.' He repeated the words again and again.

The raven flew from the man's shoulder up into a tree, fading to invisibility against the dark mass of the branches.

Leshii knelt by the flap of the tent. 'Lady, lady!'

There was no answer.

'Lady, lady. Quickly, before it's too late. The Frank is enchanted.'

'Who is there?'

'Shhhh! Do not attract his attention. You must come away with me now. The Frank is enchanted and who knows how many more of them. You are not safe with these men, lady.'

'What do you want, Leshii?'

'Quick, pull on your boots. You are in danger. Hurry.'

Aelis came to herself and did as Leshii asked. She looked out of the tent across the glade. The Frank sat, his sword drawn, looking down at it and mumbling to himself as if he didn't quite know what it was.

Aelis crawled out of her tent. 'Alert the others,' she said.

'No, I think they may be enchanted too, we have no way of knowing.' Leshii's voice was an urgent whisper.

'So what do we do?'

'Come away, now. You are not safe. The ravens will find you everywhere. Ladoga is your only course. Helgi can save you if we can keep the enchantment away until then. I have a plan how we might do it.'

She looked at the merchant. Aelis, who heard people as music and sensed them as colours, could tell he was lying, or rather that he was motivated by self-interest and was not telling her the whole truth. He seemed to hum with threat, like the buzz of a hornet across a summer's day. But when she looked at the mumbling Frank she sensed something of a different magnitude altogether. There was tumult there, disturbance, like a mighty flood driving a screaming waterwheel.

'We need to go,' said Leshii.

Aelis knew he was right, and they began to make their way across the camp. As they passed him, the Frank stood. 'Look at your hair. That is the mark of an enchantress. You are no princess but a peasant slut!'

'Get on the horse! Go back to where we met,' shouted Leshii, who had given up hope of not waking the other Franks. He formed his hands into an improvised stirrup and Aelis jumped up onto the horse with a gasp. Her ribs were terribly painful. She forced herself to forget that, pulling up a spear from where it was stuck butt first in the mud.

The Frank leaped towards her, and she flicked the hindquarters of the animal out of the way with the pressure of her leg. Leshii kicked at the Frank's legs and knocked him to the ground, but the man was up in a second. Other knights were pouring from the tents.

'He's enchanted; he's trying to kill the lady!' shouted Leshii.

Aelis put her legs to the horse, and it sprang forward into the night, away down a track. Renier went plunging after her, screaming and shouting.

'You see!' shouted Leshii. 'You see!'

'What has happened? Slowly!' It was Moselle, buckling on his sword.

'The lady is pursued by enchanters. They have possessed your bondsman. He means to kill her.'

'Crap,' said Moselle. 'Get me my horse. Never mind the saddle; just get my horse.'

A young knight unhobbled Moselle's mount while the others set to, freeing their animals. Moselle jumped up onto his horse and was gone through the trees after Renier and Aelis, the others charging after him.

Leshii looked around the camp. The last of the knights had disappeared. He was sorely tempted to look for any coins they might have left, but he knew that if Aelis was found and the Franks returned they would soon notice any missing money and only one person would get the blame.

Leshii wasn't about to let Aelis get away from him, so he threw a saddle over the horse that had carried Sindre, tacked it up as quickly as he could and tied his mule behind. The knights couldn't punish him for taking a horse that was rightfully his, and at that moment the horse and the mule were all Leshii possessed in the world.

As he worked, he glanced down at Sindre. The wolfman was flat unconscious.

'Ah, Chakhlyk,' he said, 'why did I bring you here? There has to be an easier way to earn a living.'

He squatted beside him and put his hand on his brow. The wolfman was cold, not long for life clearly. Leshii wanted something to remember him by and was about to take the wolfskin when he paused for a second. It was valuable but so dear to the wolfman that Leshii could not bear to steal it. The thought struck him as odd. The man was going to die; why not take his valuables? But the merchant could not.

'You'll need that for your magic in the afterlife,' he said.

But then he saw the stone at Sindre's neck, the pebble. He looked at it. So that was what the design was – the crude head of a wolf. It made sense, Leshii guessed. He studied the complicated knot that tied the stone to the thong. The pendant was worth nothing but it was something to remember the wolfman by. Leshii cut it from his neck. Then he got up onto the horse and looked down at him.

'Good luck,' he said, making his lightning bolt sign, then kicked his horse into a trot.

It wasn't difficult to discover where the Franks had gone. There was a terrible hullaballoo coming from within the trees. As Leshii got closer, he could hear the Franks were arguing with each other.

'You will not strike my brother!'

'You need to hold him.'

'Renier, put down your sword, man. What's wrong with you?'

There was a scream, some more shouting and then the unmistakable sound of swords clashing.

'Don't hurt him. The merchant was right – he's enchanted.'

'He got my arm! Christ, Renier, you'll pay for that.'

'Stand where you are!' It was Moselle's voice above the uproar. 'No one harm him. Get behind him. We'll mob him and tie him up.'

Leshii drove his horse forward to see the Franks circling Renier, who slashed out with his sword, his breath heavy and his eyes wild.

'Now!'

The knights leaped forward almost as one. In a few seconds they had him on the ground, disarmed but struggling.

'What is this, merchant?' Moselle stood and approached Leshii.

'I don't know. Witchcraft.'

'There's no such thing; the priests are firm on that.'

'What do you call it then?'

The knight shrugged. 'I don't know. How can we shake him from this?'

'The last time I saw it, we ran a sword through the victim. That cured him.'

'I'll run one through you in a moment,' said Moselle. 'You think this will pass?'

'It did before, but, as I said, the man was dying. Now, if you'll excuse me, I'm going to look for your count's sister.'

'Tie him,' said Moselle to the Franks; 'I'm going to get Lady Aelis.'

One of the knights ran back for some rope while the others held Renier down. Moselle jumped onto his horse. He said nothing to Leshii, but the merchant followed him. Behind them a cry went up.

'Get him!'

'He's over there!'

Renier had escaped and the Franks were hunting him through the trees. Leshii didn't look back, he just kicked the mule on, determined to be away from the enchanted knight.

Moselle was a considerably better rider than the easterner, and Leshii struggled to keep up. Eventually he gave up and just followed the path of the Frank's horse through the trees. He was confident he was on the right track as there was only one negotiable path. It was nearly dawn when he came upon them. Aelis was standing in front of Moselle and next to a stream. She'd had to pause to rest her horse, thought Leshii, and that was how she had been caught. Moselle was attempting to reason with her.

'Lady, the danger is over. We've restrained Renier. He is not himself. I cannot explain it but I can deal with it. He will proceed tied and under guard until we reach the city. It's only a day's good ride away. Please come with us.'

'My mind is made up,' said Aelis. 'I'm not coming back to

Paris. It's too dangerous. At any moment my kinsmen could be turned against me. I need to go to the root of the problem and end it there.'

'That is impossible. You are a woman,' said Moselle. 'Let me go. I am a warrior and veteran of many battles. Whatever it is that afflicts you, my men and I can put an end to it.'

'No, you can't,' said Aelis, 'though I wish you could. If you came with me, one of you would turn against me, then one more. I can't be near people, least of all warriors. Give me the sword.'

'Lady?'

'The sword. By my family's right of command, give me the sword that I gave to you — the Viking blade.' Moselle had clearly decided Sigfrid's sword was superior to his own and had taken to carrying it.

'What for? I am not enchanted; I'm not going to attack you.'

Aelis shook her head. She went to where Moselle's horse was standing. It was a fine grey, almost glowing in the pre-dawn light. Aelis stroked its nose and nuzzled her head into its neck. Then she turned to Moselle.

'Give me the sword.'

Moselle shrugged and untied the sword. Aelis took it and put it on.

'Another disguise?' said Moselle.

'No. I need it to defend myself. Do you have any money?'

'A few denier.'

'Give me those too.'

Moselle took a purse out of his tunic and passed it to her. Aelis was relieved to find it was relatively heavy.

'What do you plan to do, lady?'

'To go to the east, where I shall solve this problem or die.'

'This is unnatural. Only men should say such things,' said Moselle.'You are enchanted too.'

'The northerners have battle maidens,' said Leshii. 'I've seen one in Kiev. She did look unnatural — too tall for a woman and

276

not at all demure. Someone should have beaten her and put her in her place, but they were all too scared, I think.'

'Give me your knife and your axe,' said Aelis to Leshii.

'How many weapons do you need?'

'Just all the ones that are near me. You are coming with me, merchant; you're going to show me the way.'

For the first time in a long while Leshii smiled. 'I'd be delighted.'

'You'd trust a foreigner?' said Moselle.

'I don't trust him at all,' said Aelis, 'so at least we know where we stand. Besides, if he becomes enchanted he is old and unarmed so I can kill him.'

'A thousand advantages!' said Leshii.

'I will not allow it,' said Moselle. 'Your brother would not allow it, and I feel I am acting on his behalf. You will come with me willingly or, I regret to say, you will come unwillingly, but one way or another you are coming to Paris, lady.'

Aelis shook her head and whistled to her horse. The animal came to her, and she stepped onto a fallen tree trunk and mounted. Moselle wasn't slow to do the same.

'Lady, you cannot outride me. Do not make me carry you back to Paris.'

'I can outride you,' said Aelis. She turned her horse and trotted it down the path towards the rising sun. Leshii kicked his horse after her, the mule trailing behind.

'This is stupid,' said Moselle and squeezed his legs on his horse's flanks as a signal to advance. The animal didn't move. Moselle kicked again. The horse didn't budge. He kicked again and again, but still the animal stayed where it was. Then he got off and tried to lead it by the reins. It had never disobeyed him before, been alert to his every command as they'd cut their way through the press of Danes outside Paris, but now it simply would not go on. When he smacked its rump all it did was turn on the spot. When he led it in a circle it was happy to go back the way they had come but would take no more than a few paces to the east. Moselle knew it was insanity to follow her on foot without his men – there were legions of bandits, Slavs, Magyars, Norsemen and, who knew, even Saracens on the road to the east. A Frankish knight would be as vulnerable as – he tried to think – an old man and woman travelling alone.

Moselle had no choice, though: he would have to follow her, and for that he'd need another horse. He mounted and urged his horse forward one last time. The animal would not budge. He wheeled the horse around and kicked into its sides. It immediately trotted back down the path towards the camp where Sindre lay with the raven on his chest.

41 A Changed Man

'Monk? Monk?'

It was daylight, a weak dawn. Jehan was in the main court-yard of the monastery. The snow had stopped falling but the day was grey and the light flat. Ofaeti was in front of him. The fat berserker was wearing three cloaks and a pair of fine boots, and the bag at his side clunked and clanked with sacred vessels. There was bread on his lips and he was munching on a communion wafer.

'Hrafn?' said Jehan. It felt more natural to him now to use Norse than Latin.

'Gone,' said Ofaeti, 'thank Tyr. Came past us like the wolf after the moon. Left the door open too, which was nice of him. What have you been doing? You're soaked. Get some dry clothes off the bodies or you'll be dead before we've left this place.'

Jehan didn't feel cold. Next to him was the girl, the one who waited and hated at his side.

Ofaeti spoke. 'Come on, get some clothes, I don't want you dying on us. And sniff the wine before you drink it. Some of it's poisoned, by the look of what happened to Grettir's men.'

Jehan looked around him, trying to work out what had happened to him.

Ofaeti shook him. 'Monk, come on, hurry up. We need you more than ever now. The cover is that we're transferring this stuff on behalf of your Church. Getting it out of the way of those naughty Norsemen.'

The pale girl put her hand into Jehan's. It felt tiny to him, her fingers so delicate and fragile. His own hand seemed swollen and puffy, painful almost. His whole body felt the same, like a shirt he had outgrown. His skin was tight on him and he flexed and strained his muscles against it. He felt as if his actions were not his own, or rather that he was remote from his body – it a puppet, he a distracted and drunken puppet master.

'Do you not see her?' said Jehan.

'The whore you promised me?'

'The girl. Here. The girl.'

Ofaeti looked about him. 'Is this one of your stories? Fine, but wait until we're gone from here. This place seeps death and I don't want to give it mine.'

'The girl.'

'If we get back to Hordaland, I'll buy you a girl, shortly before I sell you. Come on! There are cloaks and boots by the cartload on Grettir's men. Get some, and take a spear too if you're wise. Come on, monk, Wc'll make a Viking of you yet.'

The girl turned to face Jehan. She hated him, he could tell, but he couldn't bring himself to tell her to go. He recalled the pond, the bodies – men and boys – and the Raven. His thoughts were returning to him, just there at the edge of his understanding, like a voice echoing from far down a valley.

Ofaeti shoved him towards the warming house. The door was open and bodies spilled out of it like a hideous tongue from a black mouth. Some were naked, some half dressed. The berserkers were still stripping them. Each living man had bags and sacks with him laden with as much gold as he could carry. The reliquary seat had been smashed, all its gilt panels and gems ripped from it. Astarth wore the fine silk robes of a priest, while Egil held the golden shepherd's crook used in the mass.

Jehan felt something inside him, the cold shadow of an anger he would once have known. Now he was a stranger to himself. The energy that had coursed through him on the journey to Saint-Maurice was gone, replaced by a torpor, a slowness of mind. He felt that unless he focused very hard on what was in front of him and around him – the courtyard beneath his feet, the voices of the Vikings – then another reality just behind it was ready to break through and devour it.

'Some quality stuff even for you, Christ's man,' said Egil.

'Hey, I'm a man of Christ too,' said Ofaeti. 'Half a day worshipping him and we get all this stuff. Take my advice: offer him a prayer. You won't be disappointed.'

Ofaeti threw Jehan a good cloak lined with fur. He sniffed it. Fox. The fur smelled to him as though it had never been washed. He sensed stress seeping from it, felt the animals' terror as they were caught and killed, told male from female, young from old. He put the fur about him.

'Here. What's wrong with you?' It was Ofaeti. 'You have to get dry.'

'The Raven's been at him, I reckon,' said Egil. 'Look at his teeth.'

Ofaeti peered into the confessor's mouth. 'He's bleeding,' he said.

'Strikes me that when a man gets cut in the mouth like that with no other mark on him then there's some funny stuff going on,' said Egil. 'And who's the king of funny stuff? The Raven.'

'Are you all right?' Ofaeti put his hand on the monk's shoulder and looked into his eyes. Then he shook his head. 'Reckon you're right, Egil. Some sort of sorcery. But he saved my life so I'll save his. Here, help me dress him.'

Ofaeti and Egil stripped Jehan, who made no effort to resist. Then they dressed him in clothes from Grettir's men – two tunics, two pairs of trousers, a pair of fine boots and a couple of cloaks. As they did, Jehan had a glimpse of himself as he used to be – infirm, crippled, twisted. The monks had dressed him; the monks had washed him. Since he was young he had relied on others to care for him. A strange feeling of comfort came to him, of familiar things in familiar surroundings.

Ofaeti tied a beaverskin hat about Jehan head and in his hand he put the staff with the cross on it. Jehan dropped it, watching it fall without interest or concern.

'Looks like I'll take that then. We'll need it until we reach our homelands,' said Ofaeti. 'You're a cunning man, monk, to come up with this idea.' He stared into Jehan's face and saw no response. 'Or at least you were. Shivering. Good sign. Often happens when you warm up.'

The Vikings had almost loaded up the horses they had found. Many wore three or four cloaks, fur hats and even gloves.

'I'll say this for Grettir,' said Astarth, 'he was a good king, a giver of rings. Look at this fine stuff.'

'He hit a trader coming down from the north just as he came to join the siege,' said Ofaeti. 'A good haul too, thank Tyr and Christ and Jesus for us.'

'Christ is Jesus, like Odin's Grimnir. It's a guise of his,' said Fastarr.

'All gods like a disguise,' said Ofaeti, 'the better to keep an eye on their followers.'

The kitchen had been raided but the food in the warming house had been left. The berserkers had seen the froth at the mouths of the dead and guessed they had been poisoned, so any bread, smoked meat or dried fruit was subjected to a lot of sniffing and poking. Egil was still doing this as he loaded it.

'Here's an idea,' said Astarth, 'we get the monk to eat it first.'

'Good plan,' said Varn. 'Shall we give him some now?'

'He's not having any from my share,' said Egil.

'Your share of poisoned meat?' said Astarth.

'Still my share,' said Egil.

'I'd say by the look of him he's eaten some. The man doesn't look well.'

Jehan looked around him. There was something strange about the light. It seemed more intense, the colours more vivid. The snow was no longer an even white. A sheen lay upon it, subtle, barely perceptible, with splashes of greens, reds and browns and around them an iridescence as the weak light split the water crystals to rainbows. And the walls of the monastery were slick and wet with colour. The colours brought smells:

plants that he recognised as belonging to the woods of Paris on the skin of the Vikings, the piss and shit of animals and humans, frozen mosses and moulds, the iron of the rust that streaked down from a horse ring sunk in the stone, the wet wood of the trough that stood next to it, the sweetness and corruption on the breath of the men, the death stink on the corpses that hung on their stolen clothes, where it mingled in with the living sweat and grime of the berserkers. It was intriguing to him, and lovely. The world seemed gloriously stained. Only the pale girl at his side had no odour, no sweat, no signature.

'You should soak us, monk. That way we'd get a haul like this every day,' said Varn.

'No one's pouring water on me in this weather,' said Egil

'How do you go about it if it's cold?' said Varn. 'They soak babies, you know. In their freezing churches in the middle of winter. I'm surprised it doesn't kill half of them.'

'It's a way of sorting out the tough ones,' said Astarth. 'If the kid cries they leave it out on the hills, and that's true because my uncle told me.'

They were talking about God, Jehan realised. God. The words from the Bible did not come easily to him now. He tried to think of a line, a prayer, a song, to clear his simmering head.

'Father, why have you forsaken me?'

'What?' said Ofaeti.

'He's raving,' said Egil. 'Leave him here.'

Ofaeti shook his head. 'There are twenty kinds of enemy between here and the north coast, and he may be able to help us with half of them. Tie him to a horse and stick another cloak on him. He'll freeze if he doesn't move. Come on. We'll scout a river out from the high ground and take it north. If we can buy or pinch a boat, we'll get through. We'll be face down in our ale in the halls of the Horda before the month's out.'

Jehan felt himself lifted, as he'd been lifted many times

before. This time it took two berserkers to get him into the saddle.

'What's he been eating?' said Varn.

'Stone, by the weight of him.'

'You're a hardy man, monk,' said Ofaeti. 'Even if you have eaten poison I'll bet you'll be right as rain in a couple of days.'

Jehan's hands were loosely tied to the pommel, his feet bound to the stirrups, and then the berserkers were on their way, heading back down the pass. Jehan glanced to his left. The girl with hate in her eyes walked beside him. He had the sense that she was happy with the direction they were travelling.

'What is your name?' he said. She did not reply, but for some reason a name came into his head, a name that seemed to trail a hundred others behind it. *Sváva*. It meant nothing to Jehan. He could tell hardly anything about the girl, form no impression of her. He only knew that she hated him and he felt bound to follow her wherever she chose to go.

42　The Shattered Lands

Aelis had to be wary as she headed north. She needed to get a boat downriver to the coast and from there go east. Her only hope was that the wolfman had been speaking the truth. She had to believe he had. He had nearly given his life for her twice, may in fact have given it already. And she sensed no dishonesty in him at all, unlike in the little man who rode beside her.

Of course she was careful. She refused to let Leshii sleep near her at night, leaving him to guard the horses while she found a place to hide. If he couldn't find her then he couldn't kill her no matter how many ravens came to warp his mind. A bigger problem would be getting hold of a boat. They needed to buy one outright and travel alone. She could not explain her odd behaviour to others and could not camp with any party of traders or pilgrims she encountered.

As it was, Leshii came up with the solution. He did a deal with a river family to take their boat down to the sea. There was no room for the horses so Leshii sold them at what, he kept repeating, was a scandalously low price. The problem was that there was only one buyer. He came from a day's travel away and had only a few deniers. It was a question of take it or leave it. The man didn't want the mule and Leshii was not about to leave the animal for whoever found it. He took it aboard and it settled down well enough after some initial coaxing. A boy and his two uncles followed in another vessel, to bring their boat back when they reached the sea. The men were fishermen not farmers, so there was no substantial spring planting to be done and they were glad to take the payment.

Leshii explained that Aelis was a young monk travelling east and preparing for the life of a hermit so would need to be alone to pray at night. The fishermen were not curious sorts and asked no more questions, though their gaze did linger on the sword at Aelis's side.

The weather broke as they travelled north, iron-black clouds igniting with halos of sunlight before blowing away to leave a clear and cold blue sky. The meltwater had gone and the river's flow was slower but still enough to take them on at a good pace.

Aelis sat in the boat huddled under her cloak. The enormous change her life had undergone since leaving Paris had come home to her and she found herself shivering and rocking, not just with the cold.

The river narrowed and broadened, bent and straightened; they passed through small settlements and larger ones where curious villagers stood on the banks to see them pass. Many of the people looked very poor, their clothes tattered and torn, a number with limbs missing or leaning for support on their fellows. The houses too were mean things, flimsy-looking, many of them burned shells. Norsemen had been there and the land was shattered. *Why did King Charles buy the Vikings off?* she wondered. He should have driven them out.

Leshii was puzzled. 'They have enough traders on this river. I don't know why they look at us as if we had the many heads of Triglav.'

'Who is Triglav?'

'A horse god of my people. Four heads. His worship has fallen into disuse. Helgi holds the horse in contempt and prefers to fight on foot. He won't have the animals worshipped in his lands.'

'What do you know of Helgi?'

'He's a Viking, but not from the same place as the lot besieging your brother.'

'How many did he slaughter to win his crown?'

'None. His ancestors conquered Ladoga, then we overthrew them and set up our own king, or rather kings. We are a fractious people, lady, many loyalties of tribe and family. We could agree nothing. So we invited the Norsemen back to rule us.'

'You asked them to make you slaves?'

'Not slaves, subjects. There are no ancient grudges against the Norsemen. When the Norseman makes a decision he does it on the facts, not to spite one tribe or favour another. It was for the best, and we have prospered under his rule. Helgi attacked the lands to the south and established Novgorod, which is to be the new capital when it's completed, and Kiev, which suffered badly under the rule of two wild Varangians, Askold and Dir.'

Aelis shook her head. 'You are not a proud people to invite another race to rule you.'

'We are too proud. That was the problem. We'd take a thousand indignities from a foreigner before we took one from a neighbour.'

Aelis looked out. The forest of the Arrouaise was tight about them, its big oaks in bud, the river gentle and pleasant.

'Do you think he can help me?'

Aelis knew what the answer would be – Leshii was never going to say 'no'. But she wanted some reassurance, even the sort the merchant had to offer – which was not much different to the patter he used to sell his wares.

'If Chakhlyk thinks so, then I think so. He has laid down his life for you, so I think you can trust him.'

'He said he was doing this for love. Do you know what he meant?'

'Love of money, very likely.' Leshii saw the joke had gone down badly. 'Who knows, lady? These men are full of riddles. He is a sorcerer, a shapeshifter. His words can have a thousand meanings and none. I do not look too deeply.'

Aelis leaned back in the boat. The mule had gone down onto its haunches. Leshii was steering – the current was strong enough that they didn't often need to row – and Aelis tried to sleep. It was cold but she was tired. The movement of the boat lulled her. She felt herself sinking and couldn't tell if she was awake or dreaming.

'You did it before; you can do it again.' A voice, a woman's voice.

She suddenly sat upright, reaching for her sword. She was on the boat still but it was night, the river cloaked in a strange dark in which moonlight turned the water to a shimmering veil of silver, the leaves of the trees to pewter, the sky to a forge-blackened steel. She had known that darkness before. At Loches, when she had walked in the night.

There was someone with her on the boat, but she couldn't make her head turn to look. Where was Leshii? Nowhere. Where was the mule? Nowhere.

'You did it before. Do it again.'

'What did I do before?'

'What you needed to. What you will do again. Do it.'

It seemed to Aelis that the river was flowing through a very strange place indeed. It was underground, and there were no stars, just the glimmer of strange shining pebbles in the dark; no trees, just great trunks of rock dropping from the ceiling of a huge tunnel.

The boat came to shore by a small black beach. A tunnel stretched away in front of her. She got out and followed it down into the earth. From somewhere far off she could hear a monstrous grinding sound, the like of which she had never heard. It was like a great stone moving over rock. In the streets of Paris she'd once seen a pair of horses harnessed to a cart spooked by a dancing bear. The cart had hit another, smashing a wheel and breaking a horse's leg. The uninjured animal had panicked and tried to bolt, the cart scraping behind, the lame horse screaming and staggering. This sound was also of something stricken, broken, and brought with it a sensation of deep agony, something wrong in the order of nature. But Aelis felt compelled to seek it out.

She walked down the tunnel, and though it was dark, she could see. A light seemed to shine from within her, and she realised that another of those strange symbols had lit up inside her. This was nothing like the horse symbol: it did not breathe, it did not sweat, and though it shone, it was not with the lustre of a horse's coat but with an intense flame. It was a much smaller presence than the horse symbol, not at all expansive but dense and bright with a light that seemed to illuminate not only her vision but her mind so that she became aware of the teeming darkness pricked by lights that spread out across the earth. There were so many living things around her shining from the vast night, she felt like a bright cold star in the twinkling field of the heavens.

'You did it before. Do it again.'

'What?'

'Your lover is dead but he will live again. Without you if your courage fails.'

Aelis looked around her. Just the tunnels, just the rock. She couldn't see where the voice was coming from. Then the tunnel dipped and turned, grew narrow. A gap was to her right, no more than a fissure in the rock. Something glistened and shone on the wall next to it. She put out her hand and touched it. She looked at her fingers. They were wet and shiny. She couldn't see the red of the blood, the whole cave was bathed in a lead light that turned everything to shades of grey but she sensed red. Aelis went through the crack in the rock, edging herself sideways to get in. She was not a big woman but still it was a breath-crushing push, the fissure so narrow that at points she had to wriggle to get through. But she did get through. She was in a room, a small chamber just high enough to stand in, though after ten paces it began to taper to nothing, the jagged ceiling coming down to a sharp and stony floor like the jaws of a great animal.

It was a scene of carnage. On the floor lay a huge wolf, its eyes vacant, its tongue lolling, its throat cut, a pool of blood about it. It was dying, and the noise it made was a wet rasp that seemed to fill up her mind, leaving her incapable of thinking of anything else. The wolf's breathing quickened when it saw

289

her and it tried to get up, though it seemed fatally wounded and could not stand. She did not feel afraid and went forward to put her hand on its great head. Its eyes turned to hers and they seemed almost human, full of longing.

Next to it lay three bodies, or the remains of bodies. One was a man with long silver hair, his hand still clasped around the handle of a strange curved sword. She had seen that before. It was the Raven's sword. The second hardly existed. It was no more than a ripped spinal cord hanging from a skull like a bloody plait. It was female, that was all she could say. The other body she knew. Its face was instantly familiar.

The man wore a dark wolfskin about him, and his muscles were strong and taut, but a gout of flesh had been ripped from his side. She thought of Sindre, who had struggled to rescue her from that thing with the torn face, but this was not Sindre. Though the face was much stronger, more vigorous, not drawn or wasted like that of the monk, still she recognised him. It was Jehan, the confessor. Aelis felt her throat tighten, tears come to her eyes. She heard her own voice speaking: 'I loved you but the gods did not love us.'

Someone was watching her but she could not see who.

She knelt at the confessor's side and pulled back the wolf-skin from his face. He was dead. She lifted him. His body felt light in her arms. She dragged him through the fissure in the rock, pulling him through until she was back in the larger passageway.

Aelis felt a breeze on her right side and looked to see where it was coming from. An archway of light was there. She walked towards it.

Lady! Lady! Another voice. She recognised it. It was the merchant.

She stepped into the arch and found herself looking out over a broad and beautiful land of mountains and rivers. To her right she saw the ocean, to her left a wide and fertile valley. She was very high up indeed; wisps of cloud hung beneath her. When she looked down, the ground seemed to rush and swim, and she knew that if she stepped forward, she would fall to her death.

'You did it before; you can do it again.'

Lady, put down the sword. Lady, you will hurt yourself.

'Do it. For your lover.'

She looked over her shoulder. Behind her was the creature with the defiled and torn face, the woman whose head looked like a gall apple on an oak rather than anything human.

But then she felt a light burning inside her. She felt something manifesting in her mind – a shape, two lines at an angle, like a K but without the vertical line, an arrowhead. It flamed and burned, crackled and shone, and when it shone it threw out a light that illuminated everything before it in a way far beyond sight.

The man in her arms had the confessor's face, but it was not the confessor.

'He is not dead,' she said.

'He is on the brink. If you go, he will know and he will follow you.'

'He is not dead. I know who he is and so do you.'

Lady, lady, put it down, for the sake of the lord of the holy lightning. What do you mean to do? Does not your religion forbid it? A Christian must not take his own life. You must not take your own life.

Leshii was gesturing at her with his hands raised as if trying to coax a valuable vase from the hands of a two-year-old. To Aelis he was an insubstantial figure. The reality of the caves seemed stronger.

'See my lover. Your pretence is undone,' Aelis said.

She turned and showed the face of the man in her arms to the woman behind her. The creature fell back and clasped the side of the cave, then fell to the floor and screamed, a piercing frightful noise that had within it the tortured cries of foxes in traps that Aelis had heard in the night at Loches, the screams of relatives of thieves hanging on the gallows, the cries of children in the burning buildings of Paris. It was the sound of the collapse of reason and sanity.

She looked down at the face of the man in her arms and now she screamed too. It was the Raven.

Aelis let the sword fall from her hands, and Leshii sprang forward to wipe away the blood where she had been pressing it into her neck beneath her chin.

'It was the witch. You were enchanted.'

'Yes.'

'What is to be done? What is to be done?' The merchant was talking as much to himself as to her.

Aelis sat back against the prow of the little boat. She was cold beyond measure.

'Get me to a fire, Leshii.'

'The night is falling, lady. We cannot risk the birds.'

'The birds will not come tonight.'

'How can you be sure?'

'She is scared, Leshii, I felt it. That woman who pursues us, she is terrified. She is acting out of fear.'

The face of the Raven seemed to hover before her. How had she not seen it? His skin was ripped and torn by the beaks of the birds; he was stronger, better fed, healthier than the confessor, but they were like brothers. It was as if they were the same man, his image reflected in some imperfect and distorting mirror.

'It is wiser to keep moving.'

'Let me have a fire, Leshii. I am so very cold.'

The merchant nodded and steered the boat into the bank. The mule gave a great sigh of relief and hopped ashore, and the fishermen beached their boat beside them.

'Problem?' said one, nodding to the bloody cloth Aelis held beneath her chin. His hair was grey and his face raw with years of wind and sun.

'No problem,' said Leshii. 'The lad is an ascetic.'

'A what?'

292

'A mystic. He seeks pain to put him nearer to God. They have them in every religion; I'm sure they have them in yours – what is it, brother?'

'We are Christians of the holy Catholic Church,' said the fisherman.

'As am I,' said Leshii. 'Come on, we'll have a fire. The lad will join us tonight.'

'Honoured indeed,' said the younger fisherman, a man with the slightly surprised look of one of his catches.

They sat together in the night, cooked river trout on the fire and ate it with samphire from the waterside. Aelis was hungry and gobbled it down.

The younger man bit a piece of samphire in two and waved the remaining half towards Leshii and Aelis. 'Getting near the sea now, as Saint Peter's plant shows.'

'We need to go east, brother. Will we pick up a ship there?'

'Who knows? Tomorrow we'll see what the Norsemen have left of the land. There's nothing out towards the coast; all the villagers have come inland. Those bastards were beaten here in the summer but people know they'll be back. You might find yourself on a boat to the west and north as a slave if you're not careful. I'm not sure ships go east any more.'

The fisherman's words stirred something in Aelis's memory. She felt she had been a prisoner before – taken north on a ship. The memory was so vivid to her. She saw great dark mountains rising out of a cold black sea, felt the bitter north wind, smelled the greasy wool of a sea cloak, heard the creak of the rigging.

Huddling into the fire, she touched her neck. It was sore from where she had pressed in the tip of the sword. She looked at the faces of the fishermen in the firelight. They seemed like spirits of the underworld to her.

At Loches there had been a little chapel. Her uncle had commissioned a man to paint some biblical scenes for it. She had sat and watched as he mixed his pigment and egg and made the faces of the apostles appear on sheets of wood. Every day Aelis watched him, and eventually he asked her if she would like to be the model for a picture of the child saint Agnes of Rome. He had painted her outside in the clear summer light, on a panel he had used before for an unsuccessful attempt at a depiction of Saint Catherine. She'd been fascinated to watch herself appear from the mess of colours he kept in his little pots and to hear the story of how Agnes had refused to marry the prefect's son, so the prefect had her put to death. Roman law didn't allow him to kill a virgin, so he had her dragged naked through the streets to a brothel to be raped. But she prayed, and hair grew all over her body to cover her nakedness, and each man who tried to rape her was struck blind. A pyre was made for her, but the wood would not burn, so a soldier stabbed her through the throat.

When the picture was done Aelis had gone with the artist to the kitchen to eat and flirt with him. When they returned, a shower of rain had blown into the clear blue day, washing part of his painting away. Through the face of the child, the eyes of the woman Catherine peered out. This image had come back to her because the same thing was happening to her now. Memory, or something like memory, was becoming so powerful that the world she walked through seemed no more than an impression, a shimmering of sun on water, a shadow on fog.

And then there was that face, not the woman but the man she had held in her arms. She had looked down at him and known him – the Raven, the thing that stalked her. She had once felt close to him. But when? The wolfman had said she had lived before, which was a belief contrary to holy law but one for which Aelis had a distinct sympathy.

A preacher from the east had been put to death at Loches for saying that Sophia of God's Left Hand was equal in divinity to Christ. She had heard him speak before he was arrested. Only one thing he had said remained in her mind: 'And the disciples said, "Tell us clearly how they came down from the invisibilities, from the immortal to the world that dies."'

His execution had enraged many of the servants, who said rightly that worse heresies were spoken at the table of the count. Aelis had not gone to see the hanging – she was too young and never had the stomach for that sort of thing anyway. The servants had said that he had shown no fear and declared that the world, his flesh, was only related to divine reality in the way a painting is related to the thing it represents. He no more feared to lose it than to see a child's doll broken.

These recollections chilled Aelis. Her mind seemed like a plundered house, its contents smashed and disordered, but at the same time a new clarity was upon her. She could connect things she had never connected before and sense a truth deeper than anything she had ever known. The preacher had been right, she felt it in her heart. The world was a painting and now the pigments were being washed away. But what was underneath? The caves, that figure in her arms and those terrible symbols that fizzed and spat, shone and chimed inside her mind, and most of all the figure of the man with the wolf's head who watched her in her dreams and whispered words of love in her ear?

Her heart beat fast and she was sweating despite the cold. She was terrified, though not of the things that stalked her nor the empty night and the strange men who surrounded her. Then of what? She tried to give it a name. Fate? Destiny? Or just time, like a weight that hampered her every movement? She felt a sense of the vast darkness before her birth, something that had been a blank to her but in which ghostly faces now seemed to loom. Everything she had known was wrong, or rather more complicated and dangerous than she had guessed.

And what of the man she had held in her arms in that vision? What of the Raven? There, by the riverbank, with the fire in front of her, the damp of the spring night cold on the back of her head, the discomforts of twigs and stones beneath her, the fishermen in front of her and the merchant nervously scanning the sky for birds, she was terrified of him. But she had had a vision, a vision that had seemed more real than the boat, the river, Leshii or his mule. She felt so strongly she was linked to that man she had seen in her arms by something that went beyond concerns of property, family or social position, the same thing that had made Judith run away with Iron Arm, the same thing the little merchant, the one who sat before her like a spirit of the fire in his turban, wide trousers and tapering beard, had wanted but never felt, the thing that the fishermen had never even contemplated, tied to the facts of net and boat, famine and plenty.

Aelis had felt it in her heart since she was a child. She was incomplete. Now she knew why she had gone wandering in the night at Loches, why her dreams were full of searching and never finding. She had been looking for him. To what purpose? So she might die? No. Then what? She had no idea, or couldn't name it to herself. Still she couldn't shake the feeling that it was for him she had walked barefoot by the dark River Indre at night, for him she had run through the corridors and caves of her dreams. That felt more terrible to her than anything she could imagine, and tears ran down her face as she watched the fire.

In the hills a wolf was calling. Somehow Aelis seemed to understand what it was saying. She spoke the words as she watched the fire: 'I am here. Where are you?'

43 View of a Monster

The Raven's hands had shaken as he'd nocked the arrow to kill the monk at the door. But he had let fly regardless, and the shaft had gone straight through the man's throat where the neck meets the chest. His hands had shaken too as he'd led Grettir's men in to cut down the monks singing at the altar and ended the song of ages with the hacks and slashes of his terrible curved sword. He'd trembled as he'd taken the monks to the pool. Nine of them were to die that way – one for each day Odin hung on the tree at the well of wisdom. He had beaten them, stamped on them, kicked and subdued them until he could tie them to the columns, each one secured at the neck with the tricky, sticky triple knot, the dead lord's necklace, the knot that slips and sticks, then slips no more.

Nine to die that way, the rest butchered and burned, bludgeoned and stabbed by the war band. He knew the old man, of course he knew him. He had sought him out, told the Vikings that none of the older men were to be killed. They'd found the monk on his knees in the little chapel. Hugin had not wanted to look into his eyes but he had done so anyway. The not wanting to was the point of the magic.

'Father Michael.'

'How do you know my name, abomination?'

'It's me, Louis.'

'I know no Louis.'

'You were my instructor. I killed the abbot and ran away.'

The old man shook his head. 'Louis? Is it you? What has happened to you, child?'

'I am a servant of the old gods now. I am your death.'

The monk looked up at him. 'You will show me kindness. I always showed you kindness. Intercede for me here, boy.'

The Raven had seized him and dragged him to the pool. The old man had taken some time to die, though not as long as the fat cook or the master of scrolls or the boys or the two who were still living when Hugin brought Jehan to the dark waters. Nine to die. The Raven had only killed eight by evening; the war band had got the rest. The traveller, Jehan, made nine – provided, Hugin had no doubt, by the hanged god himself to make up the magical number.

The old man's death had been very hard on Hugin. Father Michael had taken him under his wing as a boy, turned a blind eye if he slipped back down the valley to see his family. But it being hard was the point. Hugin knew that terror, humiliation, horror and shame were gateways through which magic might step. So he had borne the deaths, the thrashing and the choking, the pleading and the desperate psalms sung through throats tormented by rope. And the god had not granted him a vision.

But then, as Hugin sat on the verge of weeping in the dark of the church, the traveller had come, and the Raven had drugged him and taken him to the waters.

Show me my enemy, the sorcerer had thought. And as the bloated faces of the hanged and the drowned stared back at him, as the choked psalm had grated on his ears, the god had granted his wish. The traveller had torn the rope from around his neck as if it was the poorest thread and set upon the monks beside him.

Hugin had heard him speak a name: 'Fenrisulfr.'

The Raven had known then that it was under way – the twilight of the gods. Ragnarok was playing out on earth again, an event so cataclysmic that its echoes went backwards in time, its conflicts and terrors leaking into the world of men as history spun towards the terrible day when it would happen for real.

The god in his earthly form was to die, Hugin and his sister with him. There, rending the flesh of the fettered monks, was the thing that was to do it. He had thought the wolf would be just that – a wolf – but now he saw its spirit had come to earth as a man. He'd asked Odin to show him his enemy; he'd sacrificed the monks, the war band, his own human feelings to the hanged god and thought he had been shown nothing. Not so. The god had sat the wolf beside him in the church, put him at his mercy, and Hugin had failed to act, failed to save his god, himself and, most importantly, his sister. He knew he could not kill it – that was not his destiny and as much had been revealed to him – but he should have imprisoned the thing when he had the chance, dragged it unconscious through the waters of the pool to the caves beyond and sealed it in there for all time.

The prophecy his sister had given her eyes to see was clear. The girl would lead the wolf to the god then the god would die. The wolf had torn, the monks had screamed and their screams had rippled onto the waters of the pool sacred to Christ, sacred to Odin, Mercury, Wodanaz and whatever other names those who sensed the god's power had attributed to it down the centuries.

Munin had heard the screams, sitting in front of her fire of oak and ash in the forest outside Paris, and she had allowed her mind to travel through the wide darkness to settle inside her brother's thoughts, for the two to be one person.

'Sister?' Hugin sensed her presence, a fleeting idea of that torn and bloody face in his mind but, stronger than that, of things that lived inside her, the runes. Her runes were there. He felt a prickle on his skin. His movements seemed hampered and painful; his head ached and the image of Christ on the cross came to him, the crown of thorns about his head.

A sensation of distress swept over him and he knew his sister had failed to kill the girl.

'Sister?'

It was her. He felt warm and comforted by her presence. He saw a picture in his mind, a wagon with a bright star above it. He knew this was Odin's Wagon, the name of the pattern of stars next to which the Lodestar shone, the one that indicated the way north. An image of Aelis and of a city on a promontory at the junction of two rivers came to him. He had been there before, he was sure, or passed through. Yes, he recognised it; how could he not? It was the settlement at Aldeigjuborg in Gardarike, the realm of towns, to the east. He had been there once, at the invitation of the ruler Helgi, to try to help him interpret his dreams. His sister had refused to go with him and Hugin had not thought that strange at the time.

Nothing had come of the meeting but he couldn't forget the town, with its huge earth ramparts and walls of wood. He re-called the massive burial mounds behind it, which were both the graves of its kings and defensive works, and the people, who had greeted him as a friend and an ally, and not run from him or shrank away. So the girl had gone there? In which case there was a chance of killing her. Since Helgi had once sought the advice of Hugin, and through him of his sister, he might be persuaded to hand the Parisian woman over.

The Raven thought of Helgi. He sought the lady. He was known as the prophet. Could he be the god come to earth? Hugin thought he would have recognised him when he met him but what if the god hadn't discovered his own identity yet. If Odin's true nature was hidden from himself, how could a mortal be expected to discover it? Helgi might be the one. And he had made efforts to bring her to him, hadn't he, sent envoys to Eudes? If the lady went to Ladoga disaster could ensue. The wolf would surely follow. He needed to intercept her somehow.

He looked into the waters. The wolf was feeding. A rhyme from an ancient prophecy came into his head:

> I saw there wading in black waters
> Oath breakers, murderers and workers of ill,
> There the dread biter sucked the blood of the slain
> And the wolf tore men, would you know yet more?

It was coming true, the prophecy that had been told to him

by the woman who had led him and his sister to the hills, awakened what was within them and led them to the dead god. The wolf was free. He had missed his chance with him, maybe even failed to recognise Odin himself. That meant there was very little time now. It had occurred to him to put an arrow into the thing that guzzled, snuffled and sucked at the flesh of the bound monks. He knew it would be useless, though. The wolf was to kill a god, and the Raven and his sister, as that god's servants, would die with him. Arrows couldn't harm it. To protect his sister, to keep her from dying with the god, he needed to kill the lady as quickly as he could. He had horses; he knew where the lady was going; there was no reason to delay.

All he could have hoped for at Saint-Maurice was to see the wolf, to know his enemy. He had achieved that, and not in any vision, as he had anticipated. He ran from the crypt without looking back.

44 A Defensive Action

'We should go to Miklagard. We could exchange this lot for coin there. We'd get the best deal by far.'

It was dreadfully cold and the horses had laboured for a day into a stiff north wind, sharp with sleet. Now they had found some shelter in a turn of the valley and had decided to camp. They made a fire from the wood they had split from the monastery benches, piled on the clothes they had stolen and sat eating some fowl they had decided were free of poison.

'At Miklagard the merchants wouldn't even bother to barter. We'd be up to our nuts in dihrams,' said Egil.

'No,' said Ofaeti. 'If the men of the church there discover these treasures in our hands, they will just kill us. The whole thing is fraught with peril. Home, I say, then to Haithabu with enough men to make any pirates or churchmen think twice. Shit!'

'Shit what?'

'Franks! Someone must have escaped the abbey and got word to them.'

Two hundred paces away, where the valley twisted to resume its main course, seven horsemen were approaching at the trot.

'Shield wall?'

'With ten of us? We'd be skittled. Bollocks to that. Get up the slope – they can't ride up there.'

'What about the stuff?'

The Norsemen had their minds made up for them by the charge of the knights.

To Jehan the whole action happened as if in a dream. He saw the Norsemen flailing and cursing, trying to drag the gold-laden packhorses up the side of the valley; he heard the hooves of the charge thumping through the ground, the cries of the riders, the whistling wind. Then the horses were upon them, upon him.

Jehan was the only one who hadn't moved. He just stood there transfixed. Stupid thoughts came into his head. *These are rich men. They have fine mail coats. Their shields carry the red and white thorny cross of Richard the Justiciar. These are not Franks but Burgundians.* Small details seemed more important than the fact that a fully mailed warrior was charging towards him with a sharp spear levelled at his head. Jehan had a sword at his belt but he didn't draw it. At the last second the knight thought better of risking breaking his spear on an unarmed opponent and raised it. An enormous thump drove all the wind from Jehan's body, snapped back his head and smashed him to the ground. The man had spurred his horse on at a flat-out gallop and ridden Jehan down. Two other horses followed the first and both struck him, one with a hoof to the ribs and the other on his head.

For a second Jehan was convinced he was dead. He felt torpid and slow, as if he'd eaten and drunk too much at a monastery lunch. He was sated, full to bursting with food. And yet he couldn't remember eating. He had a headache and felt drowsy, although he was sure these weren't the effects of being knocked down and trampled. The cold didn't mean anything to him – the spikes of ice in the biting rain, the stinging wind, all meant nothing. He was sleepy. He had eaten, he was sure, and now he needed to rest.

Jehan fought off his torpor as five more riders appeared over the crest of the valley, screaming at the Vikings in their thick Burgundian dialect, 'Lay down your weapons! Lay down your weapons!'

The first party of Burgundians were urging their horses up the hill, but Ofaeti and his men had achieved a good defensive position. Astarth had his bow free and was loosing arrows at the horsemen, causing them to back off behind their shields. The fresh riders came by at a gallop, narrowly missing trampling Jehan. Now there were Burgundians blocking both exits from the valley.

The Vikings had only the slope behind them, which very quickly became so steep that it was impassable, particularly if they wanted to keep hold of their packhorses and plunder.

Jehan felt himself lifted to his feet. Two of the Burgundians had dismounted and seized him and another had a knife in his hand.

'I am not one of them,' said Jehan.

Jehan had only a smattering of the Burgundian language, but, faced by death, suddenly found words that might have eluded him sitting around a fire chatting to merchants.

'I am a monk and servant of the Roman emperor.'

There was a babble of talk among the warriors, too quick for Jehan, though he could understand that they were debating killing him. One voice pointed out that Jehan alone had not tried to run; another said that his clothes were soaked in blood – what more proof was needed that he had had a hand in the atrocity at the abbey?

'What is the emperor's name?'

'Charles, called Fat, who is ally to your great lord, Richard.'

The men glanced at each other. The mounted horsemen were still harrying the Norsemen, making abortive charges up the steep slope.

The man with the knife spoke: 'I'll kill him anyway. He's with the Varangians, that's as good as being one of them.'

'I am an honest pilgrim. My monastery will pay for my return.'

Jehan would normally have scorned to have bargained for his life, but there next to him was the girl, pale and ragged. Her eyes looked north and he knew that she was there to guide him to Aelis. This didn't seem at all strange; it felt natural that he should follow her, natural that she knew what he was thinking and would know where to take him. He had to save Aelis; that was why he had been freed from the fetters of his infirmity.

'You don't look like a monk to me. Which monastery?'

'Saint-Germain at Paris. I have travelled a long road and endured many hardships.'

Again the knights glanced at each other. A rock came whizzing past Jehan's head. Ofaeti and his men had found some stones and were beginning to rain them down on the Burgundians.

'Bring him back to the monastery,' said a tall knight, 'and we'll scale this valley and take those bastards on foot.'

'No,' said Jehan.

'Why not?'

'They are rich men in their own country – they too can be ransomed. I can broker it.'

'They killed our brothers.'

'You are monks?'

'As good as and as good as not. Richard is the abbot. We are his men. You can come before him at the abbey.'

So Richard the Justiciar was now abbot. That had happened recently, thought Jehan, or was it just that the drowsiness that had come down on him was robbing him of his memory? Richard's presence meant one thing for certain: all the Vikings were dead. He had fought a bitter and successful war against his elder brother Boso and proved himself an efficient and merciless opponent. Richard was a monk only in name and doubtless would soon be moving his retinue of whores, hawks and hunting dogs into the abbey.

'Those men are not your enemies,' said Jehan. 'We are pilgrims and happened upon the slaughter at the abbey. I instructed them to take your treasures to Saint-Germain. I did not know your lord would return and thought the abbey was at the mercy of brigands and thieves.'

The man with the knife laughed. 'Good of you to be so tender-hearted. I suppose we'd just have had to ask for it back and Saint-Germain would have coughed it up straight away.'

'I am not a thief,' said Jehan.

More rocks showered down.

'Tell them to lay down their arms then, and you can see the justiciar. He will see the truth, believe me.'

Jehan shouted up the hill in Norse. His head was still swimming. 'Ofaeti, you have one chance. The treasure is lost. You have the choice: if you want you can die for it.'

'I'll do that then!' shouted Ofaeti.

'Give it up. I'll lead you to greater fortune than this, I swear it. I led you here, didn't I? I'll bargain for your lives and lead you to ten times this gold.'

'It may seem hard for you to understand, Christ man, but dying in a damn good scrap up to my knees in gold has been an ambition of mine for years. Bring your Frankish cowards up here, and we'll make a nice pile of them for you.'

The pale girl at his side looked at Jehan and words came into his mouth: 'I can take you to the girl. Aelis, the count's daughter. I can take you to her.'

'How?'

'I know where she has gone.' Jehan didn't know where the words came from or what they meant, but he heard them spilling from his mouth. 'You will—'

He never finished his sentence. The Vikings had decided to take advantage of the distraction caused by his attempt at persuasion to mount an attack. Ofaeti leaped down the mountainside with his sword swinging, Astarth and Egil behind him.

The Burgundian with the knife thrust it at Jehan.

The monk's torpor seared away like silk under a flame, and Jehan's thoughts shrivelled in his head, burned to nothing in the fire of his temper. He dashed the blade from the knight's hand and the wolf ran free through the forest of his mind.

When it was done, when the bodies of men and animals lay broken, dead and dying on the frozen ground, when the snow was red with blood, and the fog fell on the valley as if the mountains could no longer bear to look at the slaughter, Jehan felt a small cold hand in his and recovered his calm.

In front of him nine men knelt, their heads bowed, their

swords held forward like crosses. The damp rattle of a dying horse's breath filled up his mind and made thinking all but impossible.

'We are Christ's men.'

Jehan looked around him. The Burgundians had been shattered as if a giant fist had descended from the heavens. A few had been cut down – fingers hacked to bloody stumps, a plume of scarlet spreading out from an eye – but most had not been so lucky. Limbs were twisted to impossible angles, heads wrenched to look almost backwards, ribcages dented like so much metal. The bodies had been stripped already and he noticed the men in front of him were wearing fine mail coats. Loose horses were collecting down the valley, seeking each other's warmth.

'We are Christ's men.' The fat one was on his knees.

There was a taste in Jehan's mouth. Blood, rich and salty.

'Lord, we must move or the rest of them will be upon us.'

Lord?

Again, Jehan felt dazed and dizzy. The young girl held his hand. He managed, 'Would you be baptised?'

'For a warrior such as you are we will undergo any trial,' said Fastarr.

'It is not a trial; it is to wash away your sins.'

'Let that be done, but first let us be gone. We can't stay here, lord.'

'Why do you call me lord?'

'You are a great man. A warrior, a berserker as they saw in my father's day.'

'I am not a warrior.'

'If you're not then I've never met one,' said Ofaeti. 'This is your work. No sooner do I think about following your god than riches beyond measure are deposited in my lap and my enemies are dashed to pieces in front of my eyes. Lord Tyr never brought such bounty. Christ has driven him out, as you said he would. We are for your Jesus and him only from now on. He is a warlike god indeed!'

Jehan looked around him, at the broken lances, the wide-eyed corpses. He now remembered how he had broken the knife man's arm and taken his throat. He remembered the screams of the warriors who had leaped upon him with sword and axe. He had cast them down and they had not stood again.

His attack had taken the attention of the Burgundians, distracting them for just a breath, enough for Ofaeti's charge to be upon them. And then Jehan had gone to work, dashing spears from men's hands, tearing, biting and killing.

He trembled. He had killed Christian men and now his soul was in peril.

He looked at the Vikings in front of him. They seemed almost fragile to him now, their bones too slender to hold together, too brittle for the men to move without them cracking. An image came back to him. A man tied to a pillar, his legs submerged in water, his face contorted in agony as cruel fingers pared away his flesh.

Blood. There was the taste again. He was full of it, and the person he had been, Jehan the Confessor, was revolted by what he had done. He had fallen on Christian warriors like a lion upon martyrs in the Colosseum. Something else though, a part of him that was waking and edging out the thoughts of the monk of Saint-Germain, could not find it wrong. His shame rose and grew and then fell away. How did he feel? Exultant. Scripture came back to him. Leviticus: *And you shall eat the flesh of your sons, and the flesh of your daughters you shall eat.* And John, the gospel that bore Jehan's name: *Therefore Jesus saith to them, Truly, truly, I say to you, but ye eat the flesh of man's Son, and drink his blood, ye shall not have life in you.* He was aware that his mind was warping, that he was misinterpreting the word of God, but it seemed not to matter any more. At the siege of Samaria, in extremis the people had eaten their children, and the Lord had not punished them.

'I cannot baptise you. Cannot save you.'

'Convert us to your faith.'

The girl by his side looked up at him. Jehan shook his head. 'Choose someone else for that.'

He walked down the valley towards the horses. The Vikings followed him. Nine now. Two had died in the snow. They were carried to spare horses and put over their saddles. The Norsemen wanted to take their dead with them, to honour them in their own way. Jehan thought of the bones of his brother monk, now discarded in favour of much greater riches. He wanted to care about what happened to them but couldn't. It was all he could do to concentrate on putting one foot in front of the other.

Jehan mounted. The sweat of battle was beginning to freeze on him. The pale girl sat in front of him on the saddle.

'Leave the monk. We have riches enough. Leave him.' It was Egil, fear in his eyes.

Ofaeti shook his head. 'He is a great warrior. This man brings luck. Let's stick with him.'

Jehan just shook his head and turned the horse down the valley. The bodies of their comrades secured on the horses, the Norsemen came after him at a trot.

Five days later they paused at a stream to water the horses.

'Here, monk, great monk, wash us for your god,' said Ofaeti.

'I will not.' Jehan hadn't eaten in days.

'Why not? You were keen enough to do it on the way here.'

Jehan knew that he would not baptise these men. He had tried to leave but they had followed him. Although the girl at his side guided him, he didn't know where he was going or how long it would take. Francia and Flanders were to the north, Christian lands.

How long had it been since the abomination in the pool? A week nearly, and he still didn't feel hungry. But Jehan knew that one day he would, that the hunger would descend upon him in a way that would not be denied. There would be no kitchen, no table that could satisfy him. The scent of blood was in him, and he knew that he would need the taste of human flesh again. He thought of suicide, but when he prayed received no guidance from God. Augustine, that learned father, said, 'He who knows it is unlawful to kill himself may nevertheless do so if he is ordered by God.' Aquinas had shown it to be the gravest of sins 'because it cannot be repented of'. Theology was clear. Cannibalism was the lesser sin. Was his thinking clear though? It seemed so but his head buzzed with a new energy, leaving him sleepless though not tired, unfed but not hungry. His thoughts were a jumble. Only one thing seemed clear. He had been hungry before. He would be hungry again.

He followed the child. Why? Because she had a direction. If he could not damp down the bloodlust that had grown inside him then he could at least ameliorate its effects. As he travelled north he would kill no Christian men. That, he realised, was why he had refused to baptise the Vikings.

Jehan tended the fire, shaking with fear at the thought of the hunger he knew was inside him.

45 Blood on the Sand

The estuary was enormous, mile after mile of slick flat mud, the morning turning the sky to mother-of-pearl, the water to a deep green. The fisherman had taken back their boat and told Aelis and Leshii that there was an abbey and village they could walk to at the mouth of the river – Saint-Valery. They were true to their word. The abbey was an impressive group of buildings of pale stone. It stood on a long promontory to the west, looking out over the wide sweep of ocean.

It was well positioned to see any attack coming, but the vantage point had clearly done it very little good. Three dragon ships had been pulled up onto the mud. Low, sleek and slim, they really did look like dragons, lain out asleep on the shining flats.

'We'll find no traders here,' said Aelis. They were crouched behind some bushes on the bank.

'No,' said Leshii, 'but we are luckier than you think. Come on.'

'I am afraid.'

Leshii shrugged. 'We have seen no birds for two weeks now.'

'There are three longboats full of Danes,' said Aelis, 'our sworn enemies. Even if you can persuade them to take us, I can't conceal my womanhood for weeks on the sea. Will I be the only man on the boat who doesn't piss over the side? What will happen to me – to us – when they realise?'

'They are not Danes,' said Leshii. 'I can tell by the ships.'

'What are they then?'

'They call themselves the sons of Freyr, who is their god. Ynglings, Scylfings, pirates and merchants of Birka.'

'And what is their purpose at the monastery?'

'Death and destruction most likely, but I doubt they dealt out any.'

'Why not?'

'The monks watch for them, and when they see them coming, take their treasures and run away. They'll have been lucky to find a goat to butcher.'

'That will put them in a good temper.'

'We'll see. Look at the ships. What's unusual about them?'

'I see nothing unusual.'

'Well there isn't much, but when we get closer you'll see that the prows aren't dragons, as they might seem from here. They are snakes.'

Aelis shook her head. 'I'm going no closer to those people.'

Leshii smiled. 'I know the ships,' he said. 'I know their king. This is our best way to Ladoga, and it's a rare piece of luck, believe me. This man trades out of Birka and Ladoga. I have met him. I have sold him silks.'

'But what are you going to tell him?'

'Something like the truth,' said Leshii, and he stood up and strode across the mud towards the ships, pulling the mule behind him.

Aelis watched him for a second. And then she offered a prayer and followed him.

Leshii was calling out as he went forward: 'Great Scylfings, lords of the ocean, descendants of Vanheim, greetings, friends, greetings. I bring you enormous fortune.'

Nine warriors, three to each boat, stood up, spears ready, swords drawn, axes across their shoulders.

'No need for weapons, friends. Only me, Leshii of Aldeigjuborg, and a boy servant here. We are unarmed.'

'Your servant carries a fine sword, friend.'

'Oh, that. That is mine. I am a trader not a warrior, and I don't choose to carry it or strap it to a mule where pilfering Franks can steal it. Where is Giuki? Where is your king? He will bless you that found me on this beach.'

'How do you know our lord's name?'

'He wears a shirt of red silk? I sold it to him.'

'That tore the first time a Frank grabbed it. You owe him his money back, merchant.'

'The famous Scylfing sense of humour!' said Leshii. 'Where is the king? Lead me to him.'

'I want that sword,' said a tall, rough man with a face as brown and mottled as a toad's back. He had a great axe across his shoulders and his voice was slow and low, stupid-sounding. He pointed to the weapon at Aelis's side.

'Give it to him and I'll ask Giuki to make him give it back.'

Aelis drew the sword. 'It's here,' she said, 'for anyone who will take it.'

'What's he say, merchant?'

'The sword is but poor quality. It looks fine but it would let you down in battle.'

'That is not what he said,' said the axeman.

'He is young, friends, and seeks to protect me.'

'Is he a Frank?'

'No, good lord, no! He is of my people.'

'I'll still take the sword.'

The axeman got down from the ship and Aelis pointed the sword towards him.

'You shouldn't have something you have no idea how to use, boy,' said the axeman. 'Give it to me now, or I'll kill you where you stand.'

Aelis couldn't understand his words but she sensed the animosity coming off him, sharp and cold as the winter wind. He took a pace forward, swinging his axe.

'Don't, Brodir,' said one of the men on the nearest boat. 'If this is a friend of Giuki, he'll make you pay compensation.'

'Thought of that,' said the axeman. 'How many dihrams for a slave? Seventy? That sword's worth 150.'

'You stupid bastard, he won't let you keep the sword.'

'Why not? It's mine, taken in battle.'

Another laughed. 'Easier to deal with learned men, eh, merchant?'

'Get the king and I will see you are rewarded,' said Leshii to the man as Brodir made his way across the sand towards Aelis.

'I would, my friend, but he's up in the monastery seeing if the monks have left us anything beyond dead mice. Your boy'll be dead by the time I get there.'

'Last chance,' said Brodir. 'Sword or death, boy.'

Aelis knew what these people respected and that, were she to give in, other indignities would come close behind. She'd acted as a servant for Leshii once, felt the kicks and prods of Saerda, the scorn of the berserkers, and she would not suffer that again, even if it meant death.

Brodir screamed and raised his axe. Aelis stumbled back, falling over and dropping the sword. Brodir laughed and stepped forward to pick it up. As she hit the sand, Aelis felt a lump in her back. She reached behind her, grasped the *francisca* and threw it hard at the Viking. The axe came at him quick and from below. Brodir turned his head, but it was too late. The axe took him in the throat under the jaw, splitting his windpipe and severing his neck arteries. He put his hand up to the axe, blood bubbling and spurting from the wound, his breath a sharp whistle, and tried to raise his own axe, but fell forward into the sand, turning it scarlet where he lay. There was a sound in Aelis's ears – the chiming and chuckling and clucking of one of those symbols that seemed to live and grow inside her mind.

'Ooh, that's a shot and no mistake!' said one Viking.

'O Freyr, help us now!' said another.

Aelis scrabbled for the sword, expecting the others to attack. But they just stood there looking at her and shaking their heads.

'You've got yourself a scrap now, merchant,' said a dark-haired Viking.

'Surely not,' said Leshii. 'He was defending himself. There's no recompense due for that!'

'I hated that bastard, but there's a monastery full of his brothers up there,' said another.

'He attacked the boy; the lad's entitled to defend himself,' said the first.

Leshii rolled his eyes and said to Aelis, 'I think you've started a blood feud.'

'I am of the line of Robert the Strong,' said Aelis, 'and I will no longer bow to these heathens.'

'I really wish you would,' said Leshii. 'It would make life immeasurably easier. I do. Look, it's easy.' He gave the Vikings an extravagant, deep bow.

Aelis stood, shaking the sand from herself. 'You do what you like, but I keep this sword. They may rape me, they may kill me, but one, maybe more, will die before they do.'

'Lady,' said Leshii, 'when you are Helgi's bride and sit in splendour in the prince's hall in Ladoga, surrounded by the fruits of many lands, the silks, the gold, the wine and the pearls, you remember how I worked for you here, how I rescued you and cared for you.'

'So you mean to sell me as his wife?'

The merchant smiled. 'That is your destiny, your safety. Is that not what your wolfman said?'

Aelis resheathed the sword. 'I'll come with you to the Viking king. We will tell him the truth. I am valuable for ransom, and if he has sense he will offer me his protection. You will translate for me. I've had enough of being in your care.'

'I think that's a very bad idea,' said Leshii.

Aelis stared at him. 'You are a merchant. You buy and sell. Leave the thinking to your betters.'

Leshii could see there was no arguing with her so just waved his hand and cursed his luck. He wondered if he'd get a dihram for her when they finally got to Ladoga. Still, he was going to have to make the best of what he had.

He turned towards the dark-haired Viking. 'Will you take us to Giuki?'

'If you like. Gets me off this freezing beach, anyhow.'

They walked up off the beach to a sandy path and followed it to the monastery. The smell of cooking was on the air. Aelis almost felt like crying. It reminded her of her childhood, coming home from days on the river or in the fields, catching the aroma of baking drifting from the walls of the fortress. More and more she seemed drawn to the past, her mind slipping back into memories, strange sensations coursing through her, strange knowledge coming to her. How did she know that the brown seaweed at her feet could be boiled and its juice used to treat stiff joints? How was it that the face of that monster the Raven haunted her, but not as she had seen it, torn and pocked, but whole and handsome? Aelis' own mother was still alive. But she thought of another woman, saw her outside a strange low house with a turf roof, drying herbs in the sun, and when she tried to speak her name, she said, 'Mother.'

The sand path turned to stone and soon they were at the monastery. There was a large pile of books at the door. The Danes — she thought of them as Danes — had stripped the leather and thrown them to the elements.

There were no great signs of attack or slaughter, no bodies or burned roofs. It was a pleasant day.

'Friend,' said Leshii, 'you will allow me to tell Giuki that one of his warriors is dead?'

'Can't do that,' said the Viking. 'If I do, his brothers might think I've been concealing the information.' He looked at Aelis. 'If I was you, I'd run for it now.'

'He thinks we should run,' said Leshii.

'Where to?' said Aelis. 'I'll face my destiny here, good or bad.'

'You sound like a Varangian,' said Leshii.

'I am to become one if you have your way,' she said.

'Yes, but a lady of the court, not a warrior. You kill like a Varangian; let's hope you don't grow a beard like one.'

They passed through the open door of the monastery, along a short passage and into the cloister, a tight square of buildings with a covered walkway around a courtyard. The kitchen roof vent was trailing a finger of smoke into the cold blue sky. Four mail hauberks lay on the ground along with padded jackets, shields and helmets. Spears and bows were leaning against walls, and a couple of Vikings sat in the sun sharpening their axes. At the centre of the square, deep in discussion with ten or so warriors, was an lean figure in a golden-yellow tunic and blue silk shirt. From the way the men all gave him their attention, Aelis guessed this was Giuki.

The men with the axes put down their whetstones and the conversation around the king died as Aelis and Leshii stepped out of the shade.

'Slaves, warrior?' said the man Aelis took to be Giuki.

'I don't know, lord. This one says he knows you.'

Giuki peered at Leshii. 'I don't think so,' he said. 'How do you know me, easterner?'

'At Aldeigjuborg, sir. Leshii, merchant of that place, servant of Helgi. Thank the gods that it is my blessing to be charged with fulfilling his wishes.'

Giuki glanced from Leshii to Aelis. 'And who's that?'

'Don't know, lord, but he just left Brodir dead on the beach.'

There was a great cry from one of the men near Giuki and he leaped at Aelis, drawing a long knife. Aelis pulled her sword from its scabbard and faced him.

'Hold,' said Giuki. 'Kylfa, as you are my kinsman and my retainer, I'm telling you to stop.'

The man with the knife rocked back and forth as if straining against some invisible leash.

'It's my right to take his life,' he said.

'No. It's your right to take his life if the law allows. Otherwise you can ask for weregild, which avoids a feud. You are servants of Helgi, merchant?'

'Yes, lord. It's me, Leshii the silk man. I sold you your shirts.'

Giuki nodded. 'You Slavs all look the same to me. How much did I pay?'

'Only three dihrams a shirt, my best price.'

The warlord laughed. 'Have you come to ask for more or to give me my money back?'

'Neither, lord. May we speak confidentially?'

'No. These are my kinsmen, and whatever you have to say to me you can say to them.'

'Lord.'

'Am I to kill this murderer or not?' said Kylfa.

'We're trying to work that out.'

'I am Lady Aelis, daughter of Robert the Strong, sister of Eudes of Paris, beloved of Helgi of Ladoga,' said Aelis. 'Tell him this, merchant.'

'Lady, I will not. You can't let all his men hear that – you'll be raped on the spot. Let me do the talking.'

'Is that your bodyguard, merchant?' said Giuki. 'He looks about ten years old. No wonder he's so full of fight, he's hardly ever been in one.'

'He killed my brother and so must die,' said Kylfa.

'Lord, I am on a mission to Helgi. This boy is a eunuch monk of the west and very dear to Helgi. He will pay well for his return. I am here to ask safe passage to Aldeigjuborg.'

Giuki nodded. 'I give my fealty to Prince Helgi. He is a great man and has secured us a great deal of work and plunder in the east. It would please me to please him and make a bit of coin into the bargain. We're returning to Birka now and it's only three weeks further journey. We'll take you.'

Leshii prostrated himself on the floor. 'Lord, you will have many rewards for this.'

'What about my vengeance?' said Kylfa. 'Will you not give me my right? Do not unman me, lord.'

'I can't sanction the killing of one of Helgi's men.'

'The warrior attacked the boy, lord. He was going to rob him,' said Leshii from the floor.

'My brother was an honourable man, merchant,' said Kylfa, 'and I'll cut your throat to prove it if you want me to.'

'I'd rather you didn't, on balance,' said Leshii.

'Our law provides us with an easy way to resolve this

and one with which Helgi can hardly quarrel if he discovers it. You'll have your right before the law, Kylfa – *hölmgang* – though tomorrow just before we leave. I won't have you injured while we're still at risk of attack.'

'What is *hölmgang*?' said Aelis. The emphasis Giuki placed upon it had caught her attention

Leshii beat his fists on the floor and then got up waving his arms in protest. 'If this boy is killed, where will be your reward from Helgi? Where will be your honour?'

'Relax,' said Giuki. 'Monks are ten a dihram around here. If he's killed, we'll just pick up a few others on the way back. It'll take a little trip inland maybe, but we need the plunder.'

'He needs this monk. This is the monk he needs. No other will do.'

'They're all alike,' said Giuki. 'I couldn't tell one from the other and you won't tell me that Helgi's a better man than me. A monk's a monk. He'll write for him, nag him and eventually Helgi will tire of him and kill him. The king couldn't care less what monk he gets; he just wants someone to write laws and record his dealings. That's the way it is with monks – old, young and everything in between. We'll give him a monk, and you can say it's the one he sent for, as I know you will. You are not a stupid man.'

'What is *hölmgang*?' said Aelis.

'A ritual duel to determine the rights of a situation,' said Leshii. 'You are a lucky woman, lady, but you are going to need to be to get through this one.'

'Now,' said Giuki, 'let us all sit around a fire, eat some seagulls and fish, and the merchant can tell us tales of the east. It'll be a good night for all.' He turned to Aelis. 'I'd enjoy it while you can, boy. Kylfa has killed five men this way, and I tell you, all of them would have done for you without breaking a sweat.'

Kylfa pointed at Aelis.

'You'll have me for a companion tonight. I shall be sitting

beside you, and when I sleep my brother will watch you. The monks here ran away. You won't.'

'I am to die somewhere,' said Aelis to Leshii. 'It may as well be here.'

Leshii bowed his head. For a moment the mad thought that he could take Aelis's body to Helgi occurred to him. But brides were not like the Christians' saints: no one would pay for them dead. He looked to the sky, wondering which god he had offended to make this girl the only chance of a comfortable life he had in the world. Somehow he would have to contrive to save her – again.

46 A Wolf's Treat

The horses allowed them to make the river quickly. The Vikings did not know this route north but Jehan guided them, guided himself by the pale girl at his side. He took up the cross again, hoping its contemplation would help quiet his teeming thoughts. It did not, though the simple act of walking gave some respite. In a high bowl valley in the mountains they saw a large town below them.

'We have horses,' said Astarth. 'We could trade them for a boat and take the river.'

Ofaeti shook his head. 'This is the enemy's country. Monk – lord – do you know who owns that town?'

Jehan had no idea what town it was but knew that the area, nominally at least, was under the rule of Charles the Fat and therefore allied to Paris and its ruler Count Eudes. But none of that seemed to matter now. His efforts were concentrated on fighting down the strange thoughts inside him and on prayer. The girl simplified things. She would take him to Aelis, to defend her from the hellish forces that were stalking her.

'The river's like a stream of goat's piss up here anyway,' said Ofaeti. 'We won't get a boat down it. Let's make our way downstream for a couple of days and see if there's anything we can make into a raft or steal if the flow gets bigger.'

Ofaeti had now taken up an ostentatious form of Christianity, cutting himself a cross and carrying it before him. The men were Danes – this was clear by their dress, their hair, the axes they carried – but not every Viking in that country had come to pillage. The Frankish lords had recruited plenty of mercenaries willing to fight their fellow Norsemen for silver, so the sight of Danes travelling through the country under the Christian cross aroused plenty of suspicion but no outright aggression.

The river valley fell through mountains which rose in great sweeps of rock and disappeared into cloud, tiny settlements visible on their slopes. At a roaring waterfall they encountered some bandits – ragged men appearing from the mists. They clearly wanted to attack but were nervous of the mail and the weapons of the Vikings. Ofaeti dismounted, drew his sword and made a stuttering charge towards them. It sent them running. The forts proved harder to negotiate. Men came to challenge them. But the gold was now hidden beneath Burgundian cloaks, and Jehan managed to control his voice and mind enough to explain that the Varangians were his guards and they were on a journey from Saint-Maurice to the pagan Vikings of the east, to convert them and turn them against the raiders who pillaged the north.

Was this a lie? It was not the whole truth, that was for sure, but Jehan was distant from himself, his war with what was inside him taking all his energy. Still, the words went round in his head: *These six things doth the Lord hate: yea, seven are an abomination unto him. A proud look, a lying tongue, and hands that shed innocent blood, a heart that deviseth wicked imaginations, feet that be swift in running to mischief, a false witness that speaketh lies, and he that soweth discord among brethren.*

He knew what he was – a sinner. They had called him a saint but they were wrong. Jehan felt as sure as he had felt when he had said Rouen would burn that he was going to hell. He was under an enchantment, he was sure. But even belief in such things was heresy. So then what had caused this rage in his veins, this excitement? His nights were turmoil. He saw her, the Virgin, there for him in the fields, but they were no fields he had ever known. He was on the side of a mountain, overlooking a body of water, and she was next to him, flowers in her hair. She was wearing a robe of black, not blue and white, and when she let it fall from her shoulders she was naked beneath.

Who are you?

Do you not know me by my robe?

You are the lady of sorrows.

And then he took her in his arms and kissed her, touched her naked body and lay with her. When he awoke he was sweating and his belly was slick with sperm.

The awakening of sexual feelings was very difficult for Jehan to deal with. Eudes had told him, 'It's easy to be pure when those natural urges are withered in you.' He was not so pure now. He thought of the touch of Lady Aelis in the Viking camp. It was almost as if that had sparked the energy inside him that had raised him up from his infirmity, enabled him to walk and damned him to hell. He thought of her voice, and when he dreamed of the Virgin now that was how she spoke as they lay on the riverbank, the sun on the water, cornflowers in her hair.

They continued north, scared away bandits, paid tolls and went on again as the river wound its way through a plunging valley, hour after hour of terraced vineyards. At a small town they finally traded the horses for a boat. It was a river craft, flat-bottomed, but the Vikings were pleased.

'Now we'll be at the sea before four days have gone,' said Ofaeti.

'You don't even know where we are,' said Fastarr.

'Not too far inland,' said Ofaeti. 'Look.'

Above them were gulls, big ones.

'It's the end of winter – they could be miles from the sea.'

'Not too far,' said Ofaeti. 'Believe me, I can smell it.'

Jehan did almost believe him. He had stepped through a gateway of sin into the earthly world, and it seemed so fresh and beautiful to him. The land was bursting into life all around him, spring coming to the land. The wet grass held a deep cold scent that transfixed him for hours; the smell of horse on his clothes smelled unlike any horse he had ever smelled before. Beneath the deep, pungent odour of its sweat was something else, a spicy succulence. The men too, the rancid stinking Vikings, had a subtlety to their aroma. It set his saliva running and he found himself frequently having to spit.

He breathed in. He could smell the ozone of the sea, smell

beach tar and the rot of seaweed, but he could smell a million things in between, pick them out, identify them, even take a guess at how far the nearest forge or cesspit, flock of sheep or market was. And with the smells came memories.

He was travelling north on a boat, and the boat was full of people, all of whom were looking at him. There was something strange about the people in the boat, and he tried to work out what it was. They were cold-eyed, pale and motionless. They were corpses. This wasn't a vision, he knew; this was a memory. He had travelled before as he travelled now, enchanted, in search of something, in search of her. But when? Were the Gnostics right? Was there a ladder of souls which we climb lifetime after lifetime towards heaven, reborn, striving towards perfection, touching a greater holiness and being reborn to do the same thing again? But he had not moved nearer to perfection in his lifetime. He had taken a step down the ladder. He knew the Gnostic heresy: the misdeeds of one life were punished in the next. He had been a cripple, hadn't he, unable to move? And now he was strong and his limbs loose, what had he done with his freedom? He had moved away from heaven, feasted on flesh and been filled by lust.

Cling then, cling to faith. Lord, hear me. I have been a vile and troublesome man, undeserving of the release you have given me. Strike me down, Lord, let me suffer again. Make me as I was and vanquish this demon that grows inside me.

'We're not taking this thing out to sea?' said Astarth.

'Do I look stupid?' said Ofaeti.

'Yes,' said the warriors as one, but Jehan couldn't join in their humour; he could only think of the north, the pale girl who sat beside him, her cold hand in his, drawing him on to an unknown destiny.

As they went on, they attracted less attention. The Vikings had been defeated there two years before, their king had become a Christian and some had settled. Though youths taunted them and called them ice munchers and whale fuckers, they suffered no attack. At one village they even received a welcome of a sort. A girl of around eight thrust a garland of snowdrops into Ofaeti's hand.

'For the blessing of the crowman,' she said, 'the wizard of your people.'

'We thought you all barbarians, but he saved my son from the fever,' said a woman.

Jehan could scarcely take in what they meant. He couldn't eat the food he was offered, though he tried to force it down. Chewing the bread was like eating a bandage, the meat of a cooked chicken like wet leather to his palate. He was not hungry, not yet, and he gave thanks to God for that.

They went on, into the flat lands, the river widening, the sky immense with a hollow blue light. When dusk came down, deep shadows fell across the river, but the water reflected the dying sun, and the faces and hands of the warriors seemed to glow in the copper light.

'We'll have to pick up a ship,' said Fastarr.

'All in the plan,' said Ofaeti.

'We have a plan?' said Egil.

'Oh yes,' said Ofaeti.

'Marvellous. Don't tell me what it is – I don't think I can bear the disappointment.'

'Don't worry,' said Ofaeti, tapping his nose. 'The plan will remain secret to you even after you've executed it.'

'As normal,' said Egil.

'As normal,' said Ofaeti. 'Can you sail, lord?'

Jehan said nothing.

'I'll take that as a no,' said Ofaeti. 'Is there a monastery near here, a nice juicy one?'

'I will not lead you to slaughter,' said Jehan.

'Not what I'm looking for. Smell the air. It's warmer, isn't it? What's that smell like to you, boys?'

'Raiding season!' they said as a man.

'Right. The winter storms are past. Horda, Roga, Scylfing and every other seafaring man of the northern lands'll be thinking the same. Anyone who's not tied up in Paris or the

Islands to the West will be down here, or some of them will. So where there's a monastery, there will be a ship.'

'I will not lead you to slaughter.'

'Calm yourself. The pirates won't be doing any slaughtering at the monasteries because the monks moved out years ago. The land's barren for miles around and the people have come together into large villages that are well defended. The days of easy plunder are over, let me tell you that, my friend. The pirates will have a look, though, to check the locals haven't moved back and that's when we'll approach them and ask them for their boat.'

'But will they give it?' said Astarth.

'Willingly,' said Ofaeti. 'No one's as willing as a dead man.'

At that each of the Vikings smirked and nodded. This, Jehan could see, was the sort of wit that impressed them, though it made the confessor feel ill.

The river was now wide and calm, opening into a large lake and then winding through low islands and marshes. There were few people about, just occasional fishermen who kept their distance. Then they saw, on a promontory of land, tall buildings, black against the oystershell sky.

'What is that place, lord?'

'A monastery. I do not know it,' said Jehan. He was speaking the truth. His head was now heavy, his thoughts jumbled. It was as if he was watching himself without any conscious knowledge that he was controlling what he did or said.

They moored the boat and walked across the salt marshes to the buildings. Ofaeti was right. There was no one there. The place had been burned within the past year or so. The roofs were gone and no attempt had been made to replace them. Graves had been dug in the cemetery and the grass had not yet grown over them. There were signs that the monastery had been used for shelter over the winter, but whoever had been there had left, not wanting to fall victim to the raiders.

'So what do we do now?' said Astarth.

'Wait,' said Ofaeti. 'We've got food for a few weeks, a nice sea full of fish. There'll be vegetables and mussels along the coast. We just wait for our boat home.'

'Ofaeti,' said Fastarr, 'when we go raiding we take five ships. That could be three hundred men.'

'Well let's hope it's not,' said Ofaeti. 'Look, the siege at Paris is going badly and a few of the lads will be coming back empty-handed. I think they'll have a look down the coast before they head home. It'll probably be Scylfings because this is on their way home. They stop to have a look at the church; we walk about outside without our weapons, looking like monks; they run up from the ship; we come down the back of these dunes and steal their ship.'

'With nine of us against a force of – how many? One, two, three hundred?'

'We distract them,' said Ofaeti. 'Wander about with our hands together like monks. They see us, they'll charge up like dogs after a hare.'

The pale girl at his side squeezed Jehan's hand and he spoke. He didn't know where the words came from but they seemed true to him. 'You have to wait for the right ship.'

'Lord, I'm not going to say no because it's got a bear on the prow and I'd prefer a dragon,' said Ofaeti.

'You have to wait for the right ship.'

'We'll take the first ship we see,' said Ofaeti.

'You want the lady?' said Jehan.

'Which lady.'

'The one you took at Paris.'

'If we could find her. She'd be a rare gift for Helgi, wouldn't she? It's well known he covets her.'

'Well, then you will wait for the right ship. Have I brought you fortune?'

'You have, lord.'

'Would you be Christ's men?'

'We would.'

'Then heed my word and wait for the right ship.'

The Vikings looked at him strangely but Jehan wasn't worried about them. He was certain of only two things. The first was that Aelis was near. The second was that he was becoming hungry.

The first boat to check the monastery was a battered Danish karvi, a tiny vessel with only sixteen oars. It was ideal, and Ofaeti had to work hard to restrain the Vikings. But then Jehan told them to leave it, and leave it they did. They had seen what he had done to the Burgundians and now his word was good enough for them.

The next raiders who came, a week later, were in seven big longships, two of them fast, sleek drakkar, out-and-out fighting vessels. The berserkers needed no encouragement to leave them alone and withdrew while the raiders searched the monastery. They spent the night ashore and sailed away the next day.

Two weeks went by, and there was no sign of further ships. Jehan sat in the ruined church, looking up at the bare altar. He was hungry and no mistake, and he prayed for strength to hold on to his appetites. Prayer took him deep within himself, searching for God, searching for instructions to which he might offer his obedience. He found only her, the Virgin – on the shore with the sun in her hair, by the hearth cocooned in the light of a low fire in a house that seemed at once strange and familiar. And then he saw her differently, lying broken on rocks in a narrow cavern. He knew it for a sign of what his thoughts were doing to her immaculate heart. He wanted her, body and soul. The spiritual desire was noble but the physical was not. He struggled against the blasphemy of his thoughts, against using his mind to defile the Lady of Grace.

The pale girl sat close by him, clinging to him, unwilling to be parted from him for a second. He prayed that he might be freed from her presence. She was a demon, a tender, comforting, attentive demon. The devil was a subtle fellow. Had Jehan expected him to come with smoke and flame? No, he came as the child who sat by him as he slept and watched him when he woke.

The girl motioned to him to follow her out of the church. A moon like a dihram hung in the sky stretching a silver path across the void of the ocean. She stood by a mound of earth and he understood that beneath it was the wolf, the thing that gurgled and growled in his mind, drowning out thought, drowning out personality.

He heard a voice, a hacking, coughing voice with a scrape to it like the fall of earth on a coffin lid. 'With my nails I'll dig for him.' Whose voice was it? His own but changed. He felt thicker in the limb and the body but not at all slow or torpid. His muscles rippled with a new power, and the world of the dark was lovely, the heavy moon, the road of light on the ocean, the pallor of the girl next to him and all the night scents of the awakening spring.

'In there? The wolf, in there?'

The pale girl said nothing.

'Yes, in there. They have bound him deeply but I'll scratch him out.'

He tore at the earth, pulling it out in wet clumps, his hands filthy, muddying his clothes on the soft damp soil.

'Lord, sails. Sails!' It was Ofaeti's voice. 'They're red! It's Grettir, who was at the siege. Three ships only. This could be our chance!'

Jehan could hear a low growling from beneath the earth accompanied by a terrible note of protest, the awful cry of an animal in distress. He dug and dug until his hands bled, but they had not buried the corpse deep. The raw snarl of the wolf was in his mind, the hunger eddying through his belly, his arms, his legs, hunger like a whirlpool sucking him down. His heart beat in flurries like rain on a tent. His mouth was wet, his senses keen. He needed to eat, so he ate.

'Lord, sails! This is our chance ... What are you doing. By Freyr's holy poke pole, what are you doing? Are you eating that? What are you doing? Egil, Fastarr, the monk's gone mad! He's dug up a corpse!' In the graveyard of the church, Ofaeti, a man who had fought in many battles and seen ten men die on the point of his sword, retched as he watched the monk crouching, spitting and howling above the ruined, rotten body at his feet.

Jehan tried to swallow the snarl that was inside him but remembered why he had refused to baptise the Vikings. But he would not do it, would not tear the man down. Ofaeti had been good to Jehan, in his way, and the confessor looked inside himself, to God who dwelled within him, to resist his body's impulse to murder. There were others to kill, righteous enemies.

He stood and looked over the bay. There was the ship, one of three. The boats under the moon seemed tiny and fragile as they put out their oars and pulled towards the beach. He threw down what he had in his hands, and as he looked towards the ships something seemed to flare in the darkness, a light like a second moon on the water, a symbol that seemed to rattle like hail, to chill like ice. Something was on that ship that meant him no good.

Jehan remembered the girl, the water, the sunlight, and then the shadow, the shadow of the wolf that blotted it all out, the shadow that he threw himself. He heard no howls; he heard only his own voice, crying out into the night, calling for Aelis, for whoever that girl was he saw in his memory: 'I am here. Where are you?'

47 Shadow of the Wolf

Kylfa sat glowering at Aelis in the light of the fire. There were too many to fit in the warming house so Aelis had opted to spend the night under the covered walkway at the corner of the cloister.

Leshii was inside, amusing the Vikings with a story. She heard some words in Latin – camel, gonads – and guessed that he was telling his usual tale of how a Saracen had lost his balls to a kick from a camel he was trying to castrate. She heard the nervousness in his voice, though the Vikings seemed not to notice it, and she could tell that he was at the limit of his endurance. He sounded old. He wanted his fire and his mug, his friends about him and his dog at his feet, not the company of strangers. She had watched him in the mornings, getting up from his place in front of the embers of the fire, creaking to his feet, crouching, resting again, stretching a leg, moving up to almost stand, his legs not quite straight and his back bent. Once he had relit the fire and sat in the morning sun, he was fine, able to continue the trip. But he was a man tired of moving, she could see.

What of herself? That sensitivity she'd had since a girl, the one that allowed her to hear people like music, to sense them as colours and textures, had rarely been used to look inward. She looked at Kylfa brooding in the corner, his axe across his knees. His brother was by him, huge and stupid with upper arms the girth of her thighs. Was she afraid of death? Yes. She heard a voice whispering inside her: *It happened before.*

Whose voice was that? A child's or a woman's, she couldn't tell. It was cracked and hoarse, full of suffering.

Aelis too was tired of moving, tired of the sensation of shadows watching her, of terrors lurking just beyond her everyday senses, of sleep being a kingdom of monsters that sweated and slavered in the dark.

Tomorrow she would die, she knew. But her maid at Loches had told her that before you die your whole life flashes before your eyes. Hers had not. What had she been? A woman to be married off, a token that a state might offer to another, her beauty just a way of making an advantageous trade, allying a count to a duke or even a king, something to make armies move one way or another. Important then. But she didn't feel important. She felt like a scrap of cloth blown on the wind.

Her memories came to her not as stories or even pictures but as colours, sounds and sensations. The green and gold of the summers at Loches, the metalled leaves of moon-dipped trees, the feel of river water and the smell of damp earth, the song of the skylark and the voice of the owl. From her window she had been able to hear the wolves calling to each other in the hills, and their voices had chilled her. A shadow now lay on her, the shadow of a wolf. She saw it, picked out by the swollen moon in front of her on the flagstones of the monastery, there on the eve of her death.

It happened before. That voice again.

She stood.

'Hey, you. Don't think you're sneaking off. If you want to piss or shit you do it where I can see you.' It was Kylfa, his axe in his hand. A squall of laughter came from the warming house. Leshii was saying something.

The shadow of the wolf. She wondered if it was another trick of those terrible things that lived inside her, those symbols that seemed to live off her like magic leeches, like mistletoe on the oak.

'Is this a vision?'

'It's an axe, my friend, as you'll find out tomorrow.'

The shadow moved. It was tracking behind Kylfa.

She looked up and, without thinking, said a name: 'Sindre!'

Something dropped to meet the shadow and Kylfa turned.

The wolfman brushed him aside and went for Aelis's throat. Her hands flew up to defend herself, to push him away, but he had her. His fingers crushed her neck. She tried to peel them off but it was no good. Seven heartbeats and she was no longer in the cloister.

She looked about her. That place again, the cave of blood. The wolf, the presence of her lover, death, death everywhere, her muscles tight on her head, as if the skull beneath was trying to break through to burst grinning from her skin.

'No,' she said, and the arrowhead rune, which shone like the moon shines when it is small and sharp in the sky, burst into fire.

She was back in the cloister, gasping on the floor. The wolfman had dropped her. The first thing she saw was a raven, looking down at her from the roof of the covered walkway, its cold glassy eye fixed on her. There was screaming and shouting. Three Vikings were grappling with Sindre, more pouring from the warming house. A big Norseman lay puking on the ground, his great axe, its haft smashed in two, beside him.

Four Vikings, five, were on Sindre but still he stood. A man's neck was broken, then the staggering mass fell into a wall, Sindre driving a Norseman's head into it as he went. Another had his feet swept from under him and sprawled on the stones. Sindre came back towards Aelis, dragging two men behind him. Vikings were everywhere – some laughing, some angry, all drunk. One aimed a kick at Sindre but only succeeded in thumping his foot into the side of one of his kinsmen.

The arrowhead of light still fizzed and spat inside Aelis. What did it mean? Illumination. Clarity.

He kept coming. Two steps more and he had one of the Vikings' knives from his belt. A breath later the man fell. Aelis looked up at the raven on the roof. She felt strange, dizzy, full of light. Four more came at Sindre, but he tore off the one clinging to him and threw the man at them. They all collapsed in a heap. She watched the raven on the roof. It watched her. And then she allowed the light inside her to travel to meet it. It was like learning to ride a horse, that moment when the beginner begins to feel how it should be done, when the stiff legs, back and arms give way to the rhythm of the animal and the rider becomes one with the gallop. It felt so easy.

Sindre was on her. There was a flutter. The raven had flown away. Aelis was down, Sindre on top of her, but the fury had left him.

'See,' she said to him. 'See who you are.'

And the light that was in her went to him as the Vikings hit him from every side. A lesser fighter than Sindre would have died where he was, but the wolfman needed no second of reflection, no fatal breath to assess where he was and who his enemies were. The trance snapped away from him and he blocked a sword cut at his attacker's hand, breaking the wrist and sending the sword spinning. He stood, driving the heel of his hand into an axeman's chin, putting him unconscious to the floor. Then he had Aelis up and was pushing her towards the doorway. The Danes leaped at him with sword and spear but he dodged and ducked, rolled and blocked. Then Aelis was at the the entrance to the cloister.

'Open the door!' he shouted. 'I was bewitched but I will save you. Go! I am destined to be with you – I cannot die here.'

Aelis slipped up the bar that held the door closed and stepped out. She didn't know where to go. The beach was bright with the light of the moon and she could see the men who guarded the ships running across it towards the monastery. The path led down to the ships or away across the marshes. A scruff of trees was just visible on the horizon. She'd have to run across the salt marshes in the dark with a bunch of wild Vikings behind her.

The light of the strange symbol that lived inside Aelis seemed to shine into every nook of her mind, bringing understanding and clarity. She could not run. She turned and went back into the monastery.

Sindre was very near the door, at the centre of a group of

Vikings, snarling and spitting, tearing spears out of hands, dodging attacks at his back, smashing men to the floor. His eyes turned to her for a heartbeat and Giuki ran him through with his sword.

He sank to his knees and tried to speak. Aelis read his eyes at the moment of his death. He wanted to say that it was impossible for him to die there, that his fate was woven in with hers, that a greater destiny, a more important death, awaited him. He coughed and lashed out, driving the Vikings back.

'I will meet you again,' he said to Aelis and fell forward. Then the Vikings were upon him like wolves themselves, spears, axes, swords, kicks and punches cutting his flesh and breaking his bones.

The wolfman was face down on the flagstones, blood pouring from countless wounds on his body, his head unrecognisable after the cuts and blows it had sustained. She bent to his corpse and put his hand upon it. She spoke but did not know what she said, the words just tumbling from her: 'It was not you, Sindre. It was not you. You died for me, and I thank you for that, but you have been misled. The rune is calling but not for you.'

The rune? She had given the symbol inside her a name, one she had no memory of hearing before but that seemed familiar to her.

She put her hand on the wolfman's head and stroked it. A tall Viking sank a kick into his body. Anger came over her, hot and sudden. 'You have killed him,' she said. 'Are you looking to kill him again?'

'If I can,' said the Viking and stamped on the wolfman's belly.

Aelis looked at him. 'You face him one-on-one now he's dead. You came more slowly to the fight when he had breath in his body.'

The Viking levelled his spear at her but Giuki tapped it away with his sword. He bent to her side. 'You're more interesting than you look, boy. Since when did you speak Norse?'

'I ...' Aelis could make no more words come out. She tried again, but when she spoke it was in Roman. 'I ...' She looked at Leshii. 'Tell him I need to speak to him. Alone.'

'*Domina*, that is not a good idea,' said Leshii.

'*Domina?*' said Giuki. 'I know only two words in Roman, one is "fuck" and the other who you do it to.'

Leshii threw up his hands.

'All pretence is gone,' said Leshii. 'By your duty as Helgi's vassal we really do need to speak to you alone.'

48 The Word of God

By the graves on the headland Jehan prayed: 'Deliver me, deliver me.'

A voice from the dark: 'Three ships, Ofaeti. It's too many!'

'It'd be a rare death, though, wouldn't it, Fastarr? They'd sing songs of us, wouldn't they? Grettir's people give credit to brave enemies – we'd live eternally in the songs of the skalds.'

'Are you sure we want to do this?'

'Sure.'

'Come on then. We'll lure them up to the monastery. Get some lights visible up here!'

Jehan couldn't see. Again, he couldn't see. A soft blackness had taken his vision. And then the raiders on the beach, the sweet stink of their aggression, the enticement of their excitement and fear cleared his mind like a whiff of Hammonicus salt, and he could see everything. The moon was like a cold sun to him, picking out the men on the broad wet expanse of sand.

His hearing was sharper than it had ever been, bursting on his mind in subtle shades of sound, his ears almost revealing as much as his eyes. He could hear the Vikings next to him breathe and rustle, the quick gulping inhalations of the young boy Astarth, Ofaeti more measured, forcing calm on his body by long slow breaths. He could hear the water slapping on the longships, the suck of the raiders' feet through the wet sand. He could hear the breath of the invaders, tight and fast. More than just sound, he could sense weakness, strength, doubt and resolve in the whistle of air in a man's chest.

The dark. Jehan had sought the dark. That howling, the noise from the boat, had set his skin tingling, his muscles seemed to creep on his bones like caterpillars on branches as he slunk tight to the shadows. He spat the meat from his mouth, its dead taste suddenly unpleasant to him. He was hungry, still, but now for something else, for the meat that is warm on the teeth, for the flesh marinated in the seepings and secretions of stress, for the tremble of the body as the soul looks down at the valley of death.

The shadows were strange to him, hardly shadows at all. He could see quite clearly within them but he knew their use on instinct. He clung to them, pressing his body to the walls of the courtyard, slipping down the alley between the scriptorium and the penitence cell. The moonlight caught him and for a second he stopped. He held up his hand. The palm was long and strong, the nails thick and the fingers muscular, like the claws on the gargoyle of a devil on the church at Saint-Denis. He stroked his jaw and clacked his tongue against the roof of his mouth, moistening his lips. His tongue felt almost too big and was cut and blistered where he had accidentally bitten it when feeding. Jehan breathed in. His lips too felt raw, his skin tight over his bones. The men, the raiders with their fast-beating hearts and miasma of tension that accompanied them, were coming. He spat and spat again, saliva filling his mouth.

Elation filled him and he heard himself giggle, though he could not think why. The shallowness of his laughter struck him.

Smell burst in on him in a million registers. It was as if all his life he had suffered from a heavy cold and had suddenly found himself free of it in a summer meadow. Rot was on the breath of the Vikings – from their teeth, from the meat between their teeth. Their sweat was sour but in a fascinating rainbow of shades. He breathed in the smell of the furs they wore, sensed the stress of the animals' deaths, smelled the wool of their cloaks, damp with dew, the odour of the farmyard clinging to it. And from down the beach, just detectable in the light breeze, he smelled something else. A woman. Not all of the raiders were men.

'We'll make it quick,' said Ofaeti. 'Double back around the dunes smartish. Slash the rudders on two of the boats then away.'

'They'll leave guards.'

'Like I say, we'll have to be quick.'

'What about the monk?'

'Leave him to his graveyard feast,' said Egil. 'The man is bewitched.'

'He led us to great gold,' said Ofaeti.

'I won't have a corpse-muncher on my ship,' said Fastarr.

'It's not your ship.'

'And it won't be yours if you don't hurry up.'

'We should leave him, Ofaeti. You know the Christians are cannibals. They freely admit that as their rite and ritual.'

'I ...' Ofaeti was going to say he had no time to argue, but the monk had gone. 'Right, lads, this is it. Death or glory. Maybe death and glory. Death anyway. Are you ready?'

'Let's have them,' said Fastarr.

The Vikings ran out of the back of the monastery and around the dunes to its side, crouching low.

Jehan heard them go. He crawled down the alley, drinking in its rich smells of mould and piss. They were as enticing to him as any posy he had smelled in his life. He came to the scriptorium, where the scrolls and books were made. The door was half open and the tang of the vellum drew him inside. He knew what he needed to do: he needed to read, to anchor his mind to the word of God. The bitterest thing about his blindness had been his inability to read, the necessity of listening to the Bible read by monks who had no feel for the words. He had memorised large sections, said them back to himself in the quiet of his cell, purging the snivelling syllables of Brother Frotlaicus, the leaden delivery of Brother Ragenard from his mind and recalling the words as he thought they should be said.

The roof was damaged, a hole an armspan wide allowing the moonlight in. There had been a fire in there, the previous raiders unable to resist the lure of the inflammable books and scrolls. Scraps of burned vellum were all over the floor, the smell of charred animal skin and damp thick in the room. The Vikings destroyed these works because they did not value them and their enemies did. They had marked their territory, imposed their values. The residue of the sweat of the raiders still clung to the room. He could smell the delight. It had been fun to burn and wreck.

Jehan sat down on the floor and picked up a sheet of vellum.

'And the angels who did not keep their positions of authority but abandoned their own home – these he has kept in darkness, bound with everlasting chains for judgement on the great day.' He said the words aloud, tried to will himself back into what he had been – the learned man of Saint-Germain, the man God had cursed in the body but lifted up in the soul and intellect. 'Clouds they are without water, carried about of winds; trees whose fruit withereth, without fruit, twice dead, plucked up by the roots; raging waves of the sea, foaming out their own shame; wandering stars, to whom is reserved the blackness of darkness for ever.'

The words meant nothing to him now, but their sounds, the collision of their consonants and the gong notes of their vowels in his ears, linked him to what he had been.

'I am man,' he said, 'in the image of a god.' *No, that was wrong.* 'I am a man, in the image of God.' He read out more: 'To the chosen lady and her children, whom I love in the truth – and not I only, but also all who know the truth – because of the truth, which lives in us and will be with us for ever—'

There was a sound in the courtyard. The feeling was on him again. He put the vellum to his mouth and bit, tasting skin and ashes. The hunger would not relent. He lay on the floor of the scriptorium trying to ignore it, trying to sate it, shoving pieces of script into his mouth, tasting ink, goat, the blood tang of the unborn kid used to make the uterine vellum. The hunger grew sharper still. He writhed on the floor, trying to banish it from his mind. He caught glimpses of fragments of script as he stuffed the vellum into his mouth – only a few words but enough to trigger the memory of the whole passage.

And about the ninth hour Jesus cried with a loud voice, saying, Eli, Eli, lama sabachthani? That is to say, My God, my God, why hast thou forsaken me?

Jehan shoved more into his mouth. He felt he was little more than a hunger trapped in flesh.

And, behold, the veil of the temple was rent in twain from the top to the bottom; and the earth did quake, and the rocks rent; and the graves were opened; and many bodies of the saints which slept arose, and came out of the graves after his resurrection, and went into the holy city, and appeared unto many.

'I am a man,' said Jehan.

There was shouting now: 'Look in there! Try in there! There is something here for us. The sorceress wouldn't lie.'

Boots outside the door. The door pushed open. A flood of moonlight rushing to meet the cascade that fell from the hole in the ceiling.

'Lads, lads, in here.' A big Viking was in the doorway, a flash of silver at his knees as he turned the haft of his axe around in his hands.

'In the image of a god,' said Jehan in Norse.

'What's that, matey. Where's your gold, you cringing coward? Lead us to your gold.'

'In the image of a god.'

'In the what? Lads, get in here. I've got one of them. Are you a monk, matey? Are you a monk?'

'I am a wolf,' said Jehan and leaped at the Viking's throat.

The kill was quick, the Viking's neck broken with one twist. Flat against a wall in the shadows, Jehan waited for the next. The corpse lay in the moonlight, its eyes wide, like a drowned man lying beneath a waterfall.

'There's someone in there.'

'Erik went in, didn't he?'

'He hasn't come out.'

'Don't be stupid. Hey, Erik, are you all right?'

Men were rushing all over the monastery. They seemed to be looking for something. He crouched, leaning forward on his hands, stretched out his back, turned his head. He felt powerful and strong, a deep energy welling inside him. When he had first been afflicted he had not come to terms with his condition easily and would find himself weeping in frustration on his bed, the smells of the summer outside enticing him to run in the fields, his body a fetter holding his spirit down. The feeling was similar – a desire for movement – but now it was exaltation that he felt inside. He could move. He would move. It was just a matter of biding his time.

'Erik! Erik!'

A man was in the doorway. He came inside, peering in with little pecking motions of the head, as if he feared the dark would bite him. It did. He was dragged into the room in a breath, dead before he could scream.

More voices: 'Erik! Oh no, Thengil! Thengil's in here. He's down.'

A Viking came in and crouched in the moonlight to look at his friend. 'By Freyr's fat cock, look at his neck! Look at his neck!' He put his hands to the fallen man's throat. Two more entered complaining about the dark. Their eyes were on the corpse, their movements slow and clumsy.

A new sense seemed to have opened in the confessor. He could tell very precisely where the Vikings were focusing their gaze, understand very clearly that he had not been seen. It wasn't just the movements of the warriors that seemed slow; their attention seemed to shift sluggishly. One of the men had a seax drawn – a cheaper alternative to a sword, a kind of very big knife. He was scanning the darkness of the room but his gaze seemed to take an age to move from one point to another.

'Can you hear something?' said one of the Vikings.

'What?'

'Breathing.'

'He's dead. His head's half off.'

'Not his breathing, you fool. Something else.'

Jehan heard. In the dark his senses were wide and deep. He heard the insects all around him – in the thatch of the remains of the roof, on the walls, in the woods outside. He heard them as never before. It was as if the night seethed with seduction songs and battle cries, tiny couplings for procreation or for slaughter all around him as the moths entwined, as the gall wasp fought the spider, a birthing aphid fell to a beetle and a bat swooped to carry off them both. He felt creation in all its slaughter and sex. Nautre's song eternal, sung since God breathed life into Eden.

The men stopped talking and seemed to freeze. Jehan struck.

The Viking with the seax went directly back into the wall, his head smashing into the stone in a wet crunch. The man nearest to Jehan was crouching with his back to him. Before the Viking could react, Jehan had grabbed him by the tunic and hair and rammed his head into the face of the man who knelt at his side. Both men were knocked cold. The entire attack had taken three heartbeats.

Jehan listened. No one was coming. The Vikings were creatures of habit and had gone to the church looking for gold. Some had lights now, brands that raced across the opening of the doorway in bright streaks.

Jehan's mind was almost gone. The confessor was just a distant voice inside him, as if heard through wind, his words just whispers, his thoughts unreachable. He crawled to an unconscious Viking and put his hands about his throat. Jehan crushed his neck and his teeth sank into the man's skin. Flesh and beard were in his mouth. He swallowed them down. The sniggering inside him became a snuffling sound that panted and slavered and howled in his head. He killed the second Viking as he had the first. The taste of the flesh seemed to fill him with strength. He sat in the moonlight, not caring if he was seen. To him the moonbeams were like showers of silver pennies, like something from the fairy tales that the monks had whispered to each other at Saint-Germain when he was a boy and was willing to listen to such things.

He stood. His body was liquid, the ease of movement intoxicating. He breathed in the scent of the salt and weed of the sea, the wet spring grass, the men who sweated and searched all around him.

Jehan crept out of the scriptorium, his body seeming to flow rather than to crawl. In the alley a Viking was taking a piss. He died with his trousers around his thighs, his neck broken with another quick twist. Jehan looked around, his personality drowned under the sensual tide that swept over him. Everything was more intense – the sounds of the raid, the feel of the cobbles beneath his feet, the black daubs of the thin clouds, the brightness of the moon that raced beneath them, and the taste, above all the taste, of blood in his mouth. He crouched low to the floor. The lattice of shadows was a forest, and he was a wolf hunting within it. Jehan let the corpse drop then doubled back towards the church. He was killing to kill now. The hunger was there but a more insistent sense had taken over – survival.

Voices behind him: 'There's someone dead here. One of us. There are defenders here!'

Footsteps running. 'In this room too. It's a slaughterhouse.'

The shadow was a blanket to him, cosy and safe. Some men came down the alley. The last was very young, no more than fifteen. Jehan took him at the throat, his sinuous fingers encircling his neck, denying him even a scream to mark his own death. He lowered the body quietly and stepped back into the darkness, sliding along the wall of the alley and out into the courtyard. Torches, men searching. The burning brands cut bright lines in the dark. Jehan felt his heart pounding but not with fear – with excitement, the excitement of the fox as he approaches the hen house. He clung to the wall knowing he was unseen. The blunt senses of the men around him were very clear to him. By a pillar he stood almost next to one

Viking while the man cursed and shouted, 'Show yourselves, you cowards, unmanly you are, like maids cowering in the dark!'

Jehan took him, ripping back his head by the hair and tearing out his throat with his nails. He shoved the man away and the Viking staggered forward into the main square, his hand at his neck. Torches lit up the stricken man. It was as if the Viking had taken the floor at a country dance and his companions were crowding in on him to the cue of the music. The man fell.

'What? What was it?'

'A monster. A troll and a wolf of the night!'

'Fetch Munin. She'll flush it out. Fetch Munin!'

Jehan watched again from the shadows as the Vikings vainly tried to help their comrade.

A huge man stood up and banged his shield. 'Let's find this fen dweller!' he screamed. And then it was as if they all went mad, as if they were rats and the corpse of their comrade a cat. They rushed from him, each man going in a different direction weapon out and swinging. They hacked into the shadows as if they thought they could kill the dark itself. Men were everywhere, tearing through the darkness, hacking, stabbing, screaming and slashing.

'Wolf, wolf, we'll have you, wolf!'

'Odin is here for you, troll witch. Your end is upon you!'

'Fen dweller, monster, show yourself.'

When an axe hacked into a shadow, Jehan was gone. When it moved on he was where it had been.

He slipped away from the courtyard and found himself in a tight alley between the church and the monastery wall. He slunk forward, low to the ground.

'There's no one here.' The voice was virtually on top of him. He had come across a group of four raiders. One of them held up a burning torch and was looking directly towards him, twenty paces away.

'What's that down there?'

'It's a monk.'

The words were the last the Viking ever spoke. Jehan's movements now seemed beyond his control. Faces loomed at him in the dark, eyes bursting with terror; limbs were on him and then gone, torn or snapped. Things were under his nails – hair, necks, eyes and arms. Jehan was squatting on the chest of a man – he thought it was a man. The Viking's face had been torn away, his scalp ripped clean off. He resembled a wax figure left to melt in the sun.

Something was coming slowly towards Jehan. It shone in the moonlight, twinkled like some precious rock. Jehan put out his hand and took it, studied it. It was attached to something long. He knew what it was, this thing. His mind fought for the language to describe it. *It was a harmer. A harming thing*. It was on the tip of his tongue. Something had thrown the harming thing towards him. Something living. He stepped forward and broke the living thing, the creature, that had thrown this object. *What was it called?*

The name came to his lips: 'Spear.' *Yes, a spear*. He dropped it and stepped over the body of the creature who had hurled it.

Words came into his mind: *Bless us, O Lord, and these thy gifts*.

Saliva was in his mouth. The prayer meant something to him. Torches flared in the darkness. *What was that prayer? It was grace*. He sat down on the floor to eat, fingers and teeth working the meat from the bone. He savoured the many tastes – the iron of the muscle, the sweetness of the liver, the farmyard pungency as he tore open the bowels and inspected their contents.

Voices. The war jabber.

'Grettir! Grettir, he is here. The prophecy is yours to fulfil. The wolf is here for you.'

The words meant nothing to Jehan as he guzzled at the meat. He had eaten too much of it, so he vomited and ate again.

Vikings were at both ends of the alley, sealing it. Jehan

didn't care. He was lost to his feeding. There were so many of them, thirty each way at least.

'Grettir!'

The throng at the end of the alley towards the sea parted. A huge man came through, shield and sword in his hand. He was wearing a mail hauberk and a coif covering his neck and head topped by a conical helmet. He was wary, stepping forward with the sword in front of him, prodding at the darkness.

'Wolf?' called the man. 'Wolf?'

There was a stir at the other end. A woman, her flesh hanging in delicious ribbons that smelled of iron and salt.

'Wolf?' called the big warrior.

'Fen dweller. Yes, fen dweller,' said the woman.

Jehan glanced up from the meat. Something about this woman was different. Her attention was focused into a narrow stream, like an animal prowling around him, sniffing him out, focused on nothing and no one but him. And she was scared. There was an acrid smell of fear about her.

The warrior walked down the alley towards Jehan. 'I am Odin!' he shouted.

Then the moon tumbled into the cloud and the alley went even darker, the torchlight weakly pushing at the blackness.

Jehan stood, reeling from the taste of the flesh, from the sensations crowding in him. He had a thin patina of hair on his arms, he noticed. It had an iridescence in the torchlight.

'I am Odin!' shouted the warrior again and rushed to close with Jehan, his body filling the alley, his sword like something only half there, catching the light of the moon and then disappearing into darkness as it moved. Jehan looked up and felt his muscles loosen, ready to strike, preparing for the snap into tension that would propel him towards his opponent.

But as the big man charged a scream split the darkness. The woman's scream seemed more than a sound to Jehan; it was a rush of icy wind, sharp with the bite of hail, a blast strong enough to drain all the power from his limbs. His legs gave way and he sank to his knees. He still had enough strength to ward aside the sword, but the huge Viking crashed into him, sending him sprawling. Jehan struck out, snapping the warrior's head sideways with a terrible blow, breaking his neck. The corpse of the Viking fell on him, its dead weight pinning him to the ground. The woman screamed again, and all the strength seemed to go from his body, but then he was in a very strange place indeed.

The Vikings were gone and so was the monastery. He stood on a high cliff overlooking a land of fjords and mountains. In front of him was the woman, her face torn and ripped, her eyes ragged holes. It was as if the full moon itself had floated down from the sky and settled on her shoulders in place of her head. She was two things: this being in front of him and something else – something that stood behind itself, a fleeting manifestation of something old and permanent, something around which the rest of the world revolved in all its chaos, tumult and beauty.

Then the Vikings were on him, all of them in a mass. He bit and he kicked and he struggled, but the scream seemed to have weakened him, drained the power of his limbs. He was pinioned and roped, his feet bound and his arms wrenched behind his back, lashed and lashed again. They were kicking him and spitting at him. They tied a rope around him and then another. His arms were crushed to his chest, his neck constricted so it was difficult to breathe. When they saw he was helpless the Vikings really laid into him. Fists, boots, the butts of spears came down on him.

'Hold.' The assault stopped. It was the woman's voice again.

He looked up. In front of him was the pale child. She turned and walked away from him and he knew that he had arrived at where she had been leading him. He was where she wanted him to be.

Suddenly Jehan began to weep. His mouth was full of the foul taste of flesh; his lips and his chin ran with blood. 'Father forgive me. Father forgive me.' He lay trembling on the cold stones. 'I have sinned, and have committed iniquity, and have done wickedness, and have rebelled, even by departing from thy precepts and from thy judgements.' Scripture came to his lips, and he remembered the taste of the vellum, his defilement of the holy word, his defilement of the human body.

The woman felt her way forward down the alley to kneel at his side.

'You have not found your teeth yet, Fenrisulfr. We will meet again when you do.' He recognised the voice – the woman who had held him and sung to him during his tortures at the hands of the Raven.

'Find the penitential cell and put him inside it.'

'Shall we not kill him now?'

Jehan sensed uncertainty coming from the woman. It was as if her thoughts buzzed with frustration like a fly against a cathedral window.

'No,' she said. 'The gods will see their doom played out in the realm of men. His fate is not to die at your spears.'

'What is it then?'

'He will kill his brother,' said Munin, 'and after that . . .' she seemed to search for the right words '. . . the dead god will go to his destiny. This is the eternal way and the end to which our powers are bent.'

49 A Parting

Giuki took three candles into a small chapel, a bare room with an image of Jesus on the cross painted on the wall behind a simple altar. The room was relatively untouched because there was nothing to steal.

The pirate chief stared at Aelis then stepped forward and suddenly thrust out his hand to her tunic, feeling the breast beneath. Aelis pulled back, but he made no attempt to follow her, just stood there shaking his head.

'*Domina*,' he said. 'A lady. I have been a long time in a boat, girl, as have all my men. You're welcome here tonight, indeed.'

Aelis returned his stare and spoke in Roman: 'I am Aelis of the line of Robert the Strong, betrothed to Helgi, harried by enemies, pursued and alone save for this servant. Congratulations, Giuki, you have won a great prize. If you return me to Helgi unharmed and still a virgin then you are a rich man. Tell him, Leshii.'

'You overheard me incorrectly, sir. This girl is my servant, no more,' said Leshii.

Aelis spoke again, but in halting Norse: 'You misrepresent me, merchant.'

Leshii's eyes widened. 'I thought I dreamed it in the courtyard,' he said. 'You can speak the language of the Normans.'

'Yes.'

'And you concealed it from me.'

Aelis turned to Giuki and spoke in Norse: 'I am a Frankish noblewoman, betrothed to Helgi the Prophet. Take me to him and win great gold.'

Giuki said nothing for a while, just looked at her in the candlelight. At last he said, 'Tell me, *domina*, why are you travelling with your hair cut like a country clot, in a man's clothes with a sword at your waist? Why do sorcerers drop from the roofs to try to free you? You are Christian. Why do the men of our gods seek to help you?'

'He is Helgi's man,' said Aelis, 'and came to take me to him. We have been chased from one end of the land to another. My protectors are gone. This is why I wear this disguise. As a woman alone I am helpless. As a warrior, I have a chance.'

'Are you a warrior?' said Giuki. 'I've heard of battle maidens but I've never seen one.'

'I killed the king who owned this sword,' she said. 'Sigfrid the Dane died at my hand.'

'That was a mighty king,' said Giuki, looking very troubled. 'I should call you a liar. No woman can kill a strong warrior. It is impossible. And yet on the beach you did for Brodir. That is odd, very odd.'

He stood quietly for a while.

Then he put his hand on the wall on the picture of Christ crucified and spoke to it: 'Odin,' he said, 'god of the hanged, god of kings, god of madness and magic, give me insight. Tell me what to do. You who hung on the tree for nine days and nights, chilled by the moon and pricked by starlight, stabbed by the spear and strangled by the noose, guide me now and I will seek battle at the earliest opportunity. I will kill nine men for you.'

Giuki held his hand against the wall for some time. The candle was burning low by the time he turned.

'It pleases me to fuck you now and throw you in the water. You're bad luck, lady. You draw wolves to you. A woman cannot kill a king, not one like Sigfrid. And yet I don't think you're lying. How far have you travelled with this little ape for company, unmolested, unrobbed, alive?'

'From Paris.'

'Then you must have had mighty protectors. That sorcerer killed five of my men.'

'He would have killed more but he was wounded when he arrived.'

'If you encounter the Raven you will lose many more,' said Leshii.

'Who?'

'The Raven. He is a sorcerer of your people. Sigfrid had use for him before he died.'

'I have heard of him,' said Giuki. 'He has a sister, does he not?'

'He does. She is watching you now, very likely.'

'How?'

Leshii swallowed.

'It was she who sent the wolfman. She is in league with Helgi and has placed her protection on this lady. Whoever moves against her, the Raven will move against.'

'Then we had better stop messing about and chuck her in the sea straight away,' said Giuki.

'They serve Odin,' said Leshii, gesturing towards the Christ figure. 'Tell me, is he a forgiving god? Do his enemies prosper?'

Giuki tapped his tongue against the roof of his mouth.

'Whatever you do,' said Leshii, 'they will come. But there is one way to save yourselves.'

'What is it?'

'Give me your oath not to harm me or the lady.'

'How about you tell me right now, or I cut out your tongue, nail it to my mast and see if it wags any truths in the wind?'

'You know I'm speaking the truth. You know they are coming. Look at the thing in the courtyard. How many men did it take to kill it? Do you want Helgi to thank the Raven and his sister in gold for returning this girl? They will just scatter it to the wind and return to some filthy nest in the woods. Cut out my tongue and my ghost will watch as the Raven does the same to you.'

'I'm not afraid to die,' said Giuki.

'But don't you want to go back to your people with gold and glory? Would you return empty-handed rather than face down your enemies?'

Giuki stood tall. 'You speak some sense,' he said. 'Tell me what we can do against this Raven.'

'Do you swear not to harm us?'

'I swear it,' he said, touching the picture, 'in front of Odin, who hung on the tree for lore.'

'He will not travel by water if he can help it,' said Leshii. 'Set sail. It's as simple as that.'

'Good,' said Giuki. 'It will be dawn very shortly. We'll leave then.'

There was a knock at the door of the chapel. It was Kylfa. He carried a candle, his face long in its light. 'I lost another brother,' he said. 'Hrodingr just died from the wounds he suffered at the wolfman's hand. I want to know what this boy is saying. He will not deny me my *hölmgang*.'

Giuki's mouth was halfway between a grin and a grimace. 'Let your brothers lie in peace, Kylfa,' he said.

'No man has the right to deny me under the law.'

'No,' said Giuki. 'But know this: no man killed him.'

'That is a man of fifteen summers at least.'

'No,' said Giuki, 'it is a woman.'

Kylfa's eyes widened.

'So,' said Giuki, 'you are welcome to your *hölmgang*, but when she dies it will become apparent that she is no man. And it will be known your brother died at the hands of a woman. This is a princess, of a sort. She is bound for Helgi in Aldeigjuborg. Better to let her claim her marriage bed and take weregild from the king than seek humiliation for your family in combat.'

Kylfa seemed to tremble. 'A woman could not have killed my brother. That is no woman.'

'Kylfa, I've had my hand up her tunic and felt the proof,' said Giuki, 'and she is protected by great forces. A woman did not kill your brother. The gods, working through her, did. How else could a Frankish virgin kill a warrior like Brodir?'

'We should rape her and kill her,' he said.

'Which would also reveal that Brodir died at the hands of a

353

woman. As I said, weregild restores your honour and preserves your pride.'

Kylfa nodded. 'It will have to be a good reward.'

'It will be,' said Giuki. 'Do not mention to the others that we have a woman on the ship. There's less chance of trouble that way.'

Kylfa grunted and walked out of the chapel.

Giuki turned to Aelis. 'Well, lady, you have your passage.'

'You will be rewarded for it,' said Aelis.

It was a cold dawn with a good offshore breeze.

The longships were stacked with plunder – several horses, some reasonable chairs and weaving, and many large sacks of wool. Leshii sat on the wool at the stern and smiled to himself. The lady was beside him. The longship was narrow and didn't have much room for cargo. The mule was browsing in the scrub at the top of the beach. He hated to lose the animal – not for any sentimental reason but because it had been his only possession other than Aelis, who was proving not at all easy to hold on to. He'd tried to bring the wolfman's pelt, but the Vikings had declared it *nithing* – a word in their language that meant something close to 'cursed'. Still, the ships would stop at Birka to trade and take on provisions. He knew merchants there and felt sure he could spirit the lady onto a ship and away before the Vikings knew she was gone. There were pilots who would start the crossing to the lands of the Rus at night, given the right moon. The promise of reward from Helgi would be enough to entice them.

Vikings were ready at the oars and in the water, pushing the boats off the beach. The boiled rabbit the lady had bought from the Norsemen was in Leshii's stomach, a cloak she'd purchased about his shoulders, and he was set for home, two good drakkar alongside the ship he sat in. They'd make any pirate think twice. He pulled his cloak about him and fell into a daydream of drinking wine in the sun of Ladoga, the temple girls and the spiced meats of the market stalls.

There was shouting and clattering. The Norsemen on the beach had shoved the boat free and were climbing on board. It was then that Leshii saw the warriors making their way towards him – two of them, big ones.

'Off,' said Kylfa.

'What?' said Leshii.

'Off. Now.'

Giuki was behind them, looking at Leshii with a smile on his face.

'You promised not to hurt me,' said Leshii. 'On oath you promised.'

'And I'll keep my oath. The water here's no more than a man's height deep. You can swim, can't you?'

'Yes, but—'

'That's all I needed to hear!' said Giuki. 'Get this eastern louse off my ship.'

Leshii struggled but it was useless. The two men picked him up and hurled him over the side, just beyond the last oar, which he was lucky not to hit.

The water was shallow and did little to break his fall. He smacked into the sand and all the breath went from him.

'Here, merchant!' Aelis threw something onto the beach. It was his silk-cutting knife. 'For your protection,' she called.

The merchant picked up the blade and stood up, soaked. 'You'll never get to Helgi without me!' he shouted after Giuki.

The Viking chief laughed. 'I fought with Helgi at Miklagard. He's like a brother and will welcome me well enough!'

Leshii fell forward onto his hands and knees and beat at the water. 'This is not fair,' he shouted. 'I have struggled. I have endured. What must I go through, Perun, to get your favour?'

No one heard. The sleek ships had already put twenty lengths between themselves and the beach.

Leshii collapsed sobbing in the water, wanting it to drown him, to carry him away to somewhere where the living was easy and profit fell from the trees. He rolled onto his back. 'I have nothing. I am the heir of nothing. I am the father of nothing. I have no friend, no ally and no country. I am nothing. Nothing. Nothing.' He splashed and thrashed like a grounded fish, and then he remembered. The mule. 'Cut the self-pity, boy,' he told himself, and got up and ran as fast as he could back towards the monastery.

Aelis watched him go, a silly little figure still doubtless chasing after his profit on an alien shore. She felt sorry for him but curiously relieved. She had depended on others to help her so far, but now she was on her own. She turned away from the shore. The light swam around her, grey on grey, the line between sea and air invisible, as if the ship cut through clouds not water. The sensation came to her again. She had travelled that way before. She saw herself on another boat, at another time, the same grey glow all about her.

Once, she thought, she had given up on life, slipped from the side of such a ship and prayed to die. She remembered the rush of the cold, her disobedient limbs fighting to swim, defying her will to drown. Now it was as if she was playing out a story, like a mummer at a fair, her actions echoes of other actions she had performed before. The immediate threats had been so great – the Raven, the wolfman, the Vikings and even the local people – that she hadn't had time to think of what was happening to her. She could now speak Norse. She had never understood more than a few words before. If she tried to think in it, almost nothing came, just fragments: *I shall live again, Vali. A bright magic entered me when the god died.*

She thought of the confessor. What had happened to him? She felt sure he was dead and she felt she had caused it. *As you caused it before.* The voice was not her own, more like that of a girl.

Days went by and the ship moved on in a sea mist. When the mist blew away it left a bright sky streaked with clouds like longships themselves on an ocean of deep blue. Then dusk

356

came, the sun turning the ocean to cloth of gold. When night fell the wind was good and the moon rose full and bright, the water glittering beneath it like the ridged back of a dragon. The ships didn't stop; just kept on as if flying on a moonbeam over a void of darkness.

There was a hushed call from one of the other ships.

'What?' said Giuki.

'Longboats. Against the headland. There's a monastery.'

Giuki shook his head. 'That carcass was picked clean years ago. Let them waste their time there. We'll sail on.'

'We could take their boats.'

'Or hit a sandbank and get beached ourselves. We've got our plunder and our guest, and we can't carry much else. Let's head for Birka and forget these pirates.'

'That's Grettir's ship. I'd know it anywhere.'

'Aaaah, now I am tempted. I hate that bastard,' said Giuki.

There was a noise from the beach, a terrible piercing howl. Another answered it, coming from further back, up towards the monastery.

Aelis looked over the water. A light seemed to emanate from one of the boats on the beach. She had a sensation of cold, of sharp prickles on her skin. She recognised the feeling. Hail. The symbols inside her, the ones that spoke to her and whispered their names – horse, torch, reindeer – stirred, fretted, guttered and brayed. Aelis spoke a single word in Norse: '*Kin.*' Whatever was awakening within her had recognised its counterpart across the water.

She glanced at the Vikings. They peered towards the shore but no one mentioned the shining, shifting thing above the black line of the beached longships. Was she the only one who could see it, that silver cloud, that thing that moved and shone in the hollow light like a fall of petals from the flower of the moon? She said its name: 'Hagaz.' It was a rune, she knew, manifesting on the beach. She was not the only one who carried those symbols inside her.

The howl fractured the darkness again. Aelis looked at the

faces of the Norsemen. They registered nothing – no one else on the ship seemed to hear it.

Giuki pondered for a second. 'If we get in close,' he said, 'we can snatch their boats while they're ashore and run them out to sea before they can stop us. And even if we don't we'll get a good scrap out of it. A drakkar and a fat couple of knarr, boys!' He turned to Aelis. 'You've brought us luck. Let's hope that continues at Ladoga. Come on. Crack open the sea barrels and let's have our weapons.'

50   An Encounter with Death

Leshii was relieved to find the mule still grazing where he'd left it. He quickly caught it and headed back to the monastery. He felt vulnerable, alone and very cold. He was soaked to the skin; there was a fresh sea breeze, and the clouds were a low and rolling grey that kept away any hope of the sun.

He would go east. He had an animal to carry him, which the mule would do once it got used to him. That was good. But it was the only positive. Against it he had huge forests full of brigands between him and home, no food, only a small knife and a very uncertain welcome once he got back. In fact, even if he did return his fate might be to be flogged or to starve.

Still, he had no choice. He couldn't sit in the monastery; he had to move. He was tempted to smash up some of the wood out of the little the Vikings had left and make a fire. Then he reminded himself that he had no way of making one. The flint had gone east with the lady. He'd seen people make fire with a firebow, of course, but he had never learned the knack. It was considered rather primitive in Ladoga. A man of standing, even a merchant of standing, used a flint.

There had to be something, he thought, in the monastery that would make his journey more comfortable. There was only the wolf pelt, which still lay encrusted with dirt where it had been stamped into the earth beside Chakhlyk's body. The Vikings had not buried the wolfman, just left him where they'd killed him.

Leshii examined the body. It was mutilated, the face swollen and blackened where it had been kicked and kicked again by the Vikings. The hands, though, were intact. He took one in both his and held it. The nails seemed unnaturally thick and sharp, the fingers stained with a kind of dark ink. He wondered if that was what caused the nails to grow like that. He turned the hand over in his. He looked at the scars on the fingers, the creases at the joints, the lines on the palm. He wondered if the fortune-tellers were right. Was this death, here on a strange shore, written in the wolfman's hand? But the hand had no future, just a past, revealed in the blood beneath the nails, the stain of the strange substance, the darkness of the skin showing a life outdoors.

Leshii looked at his own hand. The lines were supposed to tell him his wealth, the length of his life, the loves he would have. On two out of three counts Leshii was surprised he had any lines at all.

He studied the little whorls on the wolfman's fingers, some rubbed away or calloused into insignificance. He had not been so intimate with anyone for years. He had an impression of his long-dead mother, no more than a pink face and a shock of black hair. Beyond that, there had been whores, many as a young man, fewer in recent years.

But he had never sat and looked at the lines on someone's skin, the scars and marks, the wrinkles and veins that only they bore. His great family, his great love, the caravans that travelled south and east to Miklagard and Serkland admitted no such tenderness. He couldn't say that he felt it as a want in him, even then. He was just curious what it might have been like. Closeness to family or friends had always come second to his business. It was a door he had never opened. He wondered what might have happened if he'd walked through it.

Would he have been sitting in the monastery, holding a dead man's hand?

He would go to Helgi, he thought, though not because he expected reward. He knew princes too well to expect that. He would be flogged, probably, if he was lucky. Leshii's view of Helgi's likely greeting had darkened with his fortunes. But he would go anyway because he needed a place to fit in, however low that might be, not to be as an animal wandering the wilderness.

Leshii put down the wolfman's hand. Now he felt guilty for taking the man's charm. He took it from where he had stuffed it into the cloth wound at his waist and examined it. It was a curious thing, roughly triangular but with rounded edges. On it, conforming to the shape of the triangle, was scratched a rough wolf's head in the Varangian style.

'Would you like it back, Chakhlyk?' he said.

No, he thought, he would not give it back; he would wear it in the man's honour. He unwound his silk neckerchief and tied the thong about his own neck, replacing the scarf over it. Even though he wanted the memento, he was superstitious and didn't want the Norse god looking down at him and bestowing the same sort of luck as he had on the wolfman. The stone felt like a bond to Chakhlyk, something that made Leshii feel slightly less lonely, even though it was a connection to a man he had hardly known. He picked up the pelt and shook it.

'Goodbye, Chakhlyk,' he said. 'I am sorry for what has happened to you. Your story may earn me a cup of wine at a fireside and I thank you for that.'

He managed to mount the mule and set off, heading east into the woods that lay like an ocean between him and his home. The animal took to being ridden well, and Leshii fell to talking to it, reassuring it when he was really reassuring himself. There were wild men in those woods who respected only a large caravan and plenty of guards. 'There will be no bandits here, my mule, it is not the season, The grass is thick, is it not? Another short while and I'll let you eat.' Leshii shivered as he made his way through the forest. It was less cold in the trees than it had been on the coast but it still wasn't warm. He put the wolf pelt on, pulling the animal's head up over his own for warmth.

The track east was good, too good. It could attract bandits. He took it anyway, too old to hack through the denser forest. It was clearly a well-used trail, wet and too deep in mud for a man to pass through easily but no problem for the mule. Leshii would make good progress, he knew. After a day or two he would be far from the monastery and the villages of the coast.

It was a miracle he had come so far with the wolfman. On their journey from Ladoga they had travelled mainly by boat, and when they had been forced into the woods the wolfman's ears and tracking skills had kept them out of most trouble. Twice he had faced attack, green men of the woods, filthy and bedraggled, barring his path. They hadn't even bothered to ambush him by stealth, a lone merchant travelling the woods. They'd just come up to his animals and started unloading the packs. That was when Chakhlyk had struck. The first time three were laid motionless on the ground in the first breath of his assault, two more screaming for the trees holding broken arms in the next instant. Within ten breaths the wild men had disappeared. They were tree dwellers, outlaws hiding from normal men, and their traditions and ideas were strange. Chakhlyk's attacks seemed to them like visitations from a myth, and they had run from him as the Christian men who had come against them had run, as if he was the devil.

But there was no Chakhlyk now; only fear of the trees, the many darks of the forest, the mottled and uneven light bringing a terror of imagined things, things half glimpsed that were almost worse than the terrors of the night and of things unseen. It was spring and the woods were blooming, but Leshii couldn't enjoy their loveliness.

At least the mule ate well.

Leshii had rescued a waterskin from the monastery and could refill it in the streams, but as rain cast the wood in a slick green shine he felt miserable, old and vulnerable. He had no way to start a fire so just went on as far as he could into the evenings, found what shelter he could, which was not much, and hoped his exhaustion would overcome the cold and take him down to sleep. Most nights the cold won. He began to hallucinate with hunger and tiredness, became no more than cargo on his mule, allowing it to make its own way down the track. The animal seemed to know where to go, keeping straight on when paths split off, making good time in the wet woods. It was happy. The leaves were fresh from the bud and sweet, the pace easy and the old man its only burden.

After a week going east in the forest, Leshii ceased to care if he lived or died, so when he met Death he was ready to welcome him. Death was on his pale horse, his black cloak around him. Leshii saw him at a distance, down the track through a long avenue of trees. He was too tired to run.

Death shouted to him: 'I thought you were him.' He spoke in rough Roman, jabbing out the words as if they were dagger thrusts.

Leshii couldn't speak. He just looked at the figure barring his path and nodded. Why he nodded he didn't know.

There was something strange about the cloak. It had things thrust into it, things jutting out at many angles. *What were they?* Feathers, the merchant realised. It was Hrafn. Perhaps if he treated him as a normal man he would act as a normal man.

The merchant found his voice. 'I have a fine mule to sell here, brother, a splendid Frankish animal. I need to sell him but my companions won't let him go for less than a hundred dinars. I say he can go to the right man for eighty. Quick, they are coming in great numbers. If you buy him now even the mightiest of their warriors will not say anything against a deal done.'

Death spoke again: 'I caught a sniff of the wolfman in my dreams and came this way to find him. Where he is, the lady is not far away. That skin you wear on your back, you took it from him. Is he still alive? Is the lady with him?'

'He is dead but not by my hand.'

The Raven nodded.

'Did he die protecting her?'

'Does it matter how he died?'

'How did he die?' The voice of the rider was not emotional but Leshii could tell he was burning for an answer.

'He was bewitched and came to kill her. But he broke the

enchantment and tried to take her from the Varangians. They killed him, though he killed many of them.'

This news seemed to affect the rider deeply. 'That enchantment sprang from the rune that lives inside my sister. No man's magic could break it. Only a woman could do that, and a woman that held a rune, at that.'

'He died defending her.'

'He was not who he thought himself to be. We saw little about him but we saw that.'

'Who did he suppose he was?'

'The wolf's victim.'

Leshii shrugged. 'He was someone's victim anyway. Are you here to kill me? You are a servant of death. I know you by the name Hrafn.'

'Where is the lady?'

'Taken. Gone east to Ladoga.'

'On this road?'

'By the sea. Your Whale Road.'

'Then we have very little time. My sister has set a trap for her. If she is not successful in drawing her in, then we must take her at Ladoga. The end is near.'

'What end?'

'The wolf is coming and he is coming to kill. The lady, your King Helgi, me, my sister, you, very likely, and everyone that stands in his way. Ladoga will fall and who knows what else. The lady must die for it is she who brings him to the god.'

'I have no idea what you're talking about,' said Leshii.

'Odin is coming. The dead god, here on earth, seeking to die. We must frustrate his will. The god must live.'

'I thought you were his servant.'

'Sometimes we serve him best by opposing him. The god's will is a complex thing. It seems possible Helgi is the incarnation of the god, though he may not yet know it himself. My sister's visions are not clear. If he is Odin we must protect him from the lady who calls the wolf, even though he seeks her. The fact that he seeks her may be indication enough that he is the incarnation of the All Father. The god will come and the god will find his doom if we let him.'

Leshii didn't really follow. 'I wish my god would come,' he said, 'preferably with a nice pot of money.'

The Raven looked around him. He seemed nervous, thought the merchant.

'I may need your help at Ladoga if the lady makes it there,' said Hugin.

'Can you get me to Ladoga? It's a long way to walk.'

'I can escort you there but I need your help getting access to the prince. You are his servant, are you not – along with the wolfman?'

'I am his servant but it's a trading town; you can walk in there yourself. You don't look like a man who will be kept out of somewhere he wants to go.'

'The prince seeks to protect her and will be looking for attackers. That much has my sister foreseen. But neither he nor she will not suspect you. You can find her. You can tell me where she is.'

'Your magic seems weak. Do your prophecies fail you?'

'We are moving in the realms of the gods. Knowledge is not easily won.' He gestured to his face.

'Why should I risk my life for you?'

'I could kill you here.'

'And then how shall I serve you? You need to sweeten the deal, Raven.' Leshii was surprised by his own boldness but his merchant's instinct told him his was the stronger bargaining position.

'Here,' said the Raven. From his pack he took a necklace of twisted gold, hanging with rubies. 'This is yours. I have a hundred further dihrams in my pack.'

Leshii took the necklace. It was a beautiful thing. He had never seen its like, a twist of golden cables with deep red stones dangling beneath. It had to be worth two thousand dihrams, easily.

'Keep it,' said the Raven.

'Aren't you afraid I might not honour my bargain?'

'You will honour it,' said the Raven, and Leshii knew that if he valued his life he would.

Leshii did a quick sum in his head. That money was enough to see him through ten years of retirement or even twenty if he went easy on the dancing girls and fine wines, something he had no intention of doing. And the good luck did not stop there. This weird creature was certainly no servant of Mithras, as the Romans would have had it. He clearly hadn't a clue about money. There might be more to be had out of him. He would have to keep out of Helgi's way – maybe even travel down to Byzantium, but a rich retirement in the greatest city on earth was nothing to be afraid of.

Leshii offered a word of thanks to Perun and puckered up his lips as if in thought.

'Well,' he said, 'let me see what I can do.'

51   Friends and Enemies

Aelis went to the stern of the longship. There was no talk at all as the men put on their war gear, only small scrapes and clangs as mail coats, axes, swords and daggers were unpacked from barrels, spears unstrapped, helmets tied on and shields put into place on the side of the boat.

The purpose in the men's actions frightened Aelis. There were no faint hearts, she could tell. These men were used to battle and ready for what was ahead of them. There was excitement, slight nervousness, even mild glee. It reminded her of how the ladies at Loches had reacted when a marriage was arranged for one of them. But there was a darker current here. It was almost as if the men were conjuring something between themselves, something that smelled of iron and blood, something that waited behind their eyes like a wolf in a byre, ready to spring out.

'Best if we can keep the element of surprise.' Giuki's voice was low.

'They haven't heard us yet and it's dark enough that we won't be seen until we're almost upon them. They're up at the monastery. We can kill the guards and be out to sea by the time they react,' said a man by his side.

'We've got a couple of bows. Get them forward as soon as you can. There's a lot of ground between the monastery and boats. We'll make them pay for every step. Regin, are you ready?'

From forty feet away across the water came a strong low voice: 'As we'll ever be, lord.'

'Signal to the other boat to follow me in carefully. We don't know the waters and don't want to tear our hulls out. Let's go. Quietly. And let's make quick work of it.'

The boats turned towards the shore. Aelis gripped her sword, still in its scabbard. Her disguise put her at more risk now than if she was wearing a gown and wimple.

Giuki came to her. 'Stay here in the stern. There won't be too many guarding their boats. It will be done very quickly.'

Aelis nodded. The longboats streaked towards the shore. She couldn't believe the men on the beached boats couldn't hear the straining of the oars.

Then they did. 'Raiders!' She recognised the Norse word.

Now all attempt at quiet left the men on the attacking ships; all caution was abandoned.

The drakkar had seemed narrow and cramped, even badly designed, while they were making their way down the coast. It had been quick but unsteady. Now she saw its true function. As a sailing boat it worked about as well as a sword works for cutting cheese. That is, it can do it, but it's not the job it's intended for. Under oar, sprinting for the shore, the craft was transformed, singing through the waves like an arrow through the air. She saw the reason for the shields on the sides. They increased the freeboard. At speed the ship created more of a wake, and might even be swamped and sink if it ran too fast. The shields added half a cubit's height to the sides. Aelis had a sensation of great speed, the bulk of the land looming closer, the great moon behind her, the monastery low on the horizon of the headland as if crouching. The beach was white in the moonlight.

A tumult of shouts erupted from the attacking boats. She heard the names she'd heard screamed from the walls of Paris: 'Tyr is with me! Thor guides my hand! The wolf and the crow will feed tonight! Odin, death-maker, is our king and battle mate! Your ancestors are waiting for you, Danes, and I will send you to meet them!'

One man from the beached longboats went tearing across the sand towards the monastery. The others seemed to panic. They had been left there to guard the boats from land attack; they had not anticipated an assault from the sea. There was no time to launch the craft and they couldn't outrun or outmanoeuvre three quick ships. They knew that if they ran for reinforcements their ships would be taken. So they leaped out of the boats to meet the onrushing drakkar, knowing they would die and calling out to say that they knew.

'My father will have a welcome for me in the halls of the All Father tonight. You can serve my drinks, foreigner, because I'm going to take you with me.'

Aelis's ship crunched into the beach, throwing her forward. She jumped up but already most of the crew were over the side, screaming and hacking. There were perhaps ten of the enemy and they had marshalled themselves well, fighting in close formation, shields locked together, spears forward, trying to kill their opponents as they stepped from the ship.

Some men were leaping onto the empty boats while a scrum of nine or ten struggled to shove one off into the sea. The landing had been chaotic. The moon was not reliable, scudding in and out of the clouds, and the ships had beached some way from each other. No cordon of archers had been set despite Giuki's orders. In short order the raiders overwhelmed the last of the guards and ran to push a big snekke out to sea. It wouldn't budge and men were now streaming down the beach from the monastery. Aelis thought there were at least a hundred of them, all armed, though many had not had time to even grab their shields, armour or boots and were sprinting across the hard wet sand barefoot.

Giuki's men shoving the boats turned to meet the onrushing warriors. Those who had already got into the longships jumped out again onto the beach.

There was no order to attack or defence, just warrior against warrior with the moon turning the wide wet beach into a bridge of light on which men fought to decide who stayed on the earthly side and who passed over into the afterlife.

Aelis was terrified and shrank down in her longship.

A face popped up over the side. She recognised it. It was the big Viking, the fat one she had seen at Leshii's camp and who had led her to the confessor's torture. He peered at her in disbelief. Aelis didn't hesitate. She jumped down from the ship into the sea on the side away from the Viking, falling into waist-high water.

She ran. The berserkers she'd seen at Paris were shoving the drakkar out into the waves. She had to warn Giuki that his boat was being stolen or she would never get to Helgi. She grabbed at the back of the nearest Viking she saw. 'Your ship is—'

She never finished the sentence. The man spun round and smashed his fist into her face. White light splintered her vision and she went spinning to the sand. It was Kylfa, whose brother she had killed.

'There's my weregild, whore.'

He drew his knife and jumped on top of her. She regained her vision, though it was a blur, the beach was cold on her back, the moon danced behind the man's shoulder. The man raised his knife and stabbed it down, but then something happened that Aelis did not understand. The man's arm disappeared, there was a flood of red, a scream and he fell away from her.

A big arm was round her, bundling her towards the drakkar.

'You should choose your friends more carefully, lady,' said Ofaeti. She looked back at the sand. The arm of the man who had attacked her was lying five paces from his body and the top of his skull was caved in at the front from a second axe blow.

'They are stealing your ship! They are stealing you ship!' screamed Aelis as she was bundled down the beach.

A couple of Giuki's warriors heard her and came sprinting.

Ofaeti heaved her over the low side of the longship, where Fastarr took charge of her. Then he turned to face the men rushing towards him. The first ran into his shield as if into a wall and bounced back into the man behind. Ofaeti sunk his axe into the first man's head, released it and drew his knife to stab the second through the belly.

Aelis got to her feet, her senses scrambled. She stared up at the monastery. A light was there but not like any light she had ever seen. It was as if the moon had plunged into the body of the building and was now shining from within it. Again she heard that howl. Where was it coming from? She found herself answering it.

'I am here,' she said, 'and I am coming to you.'

Ofaeti had retrieved his axe and was in the boat as it slipped free of the sand, but four of Giuki's Vikings had followed him in. One ran towards Aelis, his axe high, and she cringed, but he went straight past her, smashing the axe into the ropes that tied the rudder to the back of the ship. In a couple of blows he'd cut them and made the boat unsailable at anything above a crawl. Then he turned to face the berserkers.

Aelis curled up into a ball in the bottom of the ship. There was screaming, shouting, a smack next to her. The fat Viking had fallen and crashed to the boards beside her. The other berserkers were fighting fiercely but they were being overwhelmed. She saw Varn lose his axe and four of his fingers to a seax blow, but the berserker grabbed at his man and leaped over the rail of the ship into the sea with him, pushing his head under the water to drown him.

The battle on the beach was still raging, though Giuki's men were outnumbered and giving ground towards the sea. Everywhere along the wide strand men lay, knelt or sat dying, some quietly rocking, nursing wounds to the stomach or the chest, others with no sign of damage unmoving on the sand. All around them the living fought, seax against spear, spear against sword against axe. Men staggered, screamed, hacked and were hacked. Shields were split, weapons broken, helmets were struck from heads to lie battered in the sand. Warriors were swinging at each other like drunks, some pausing to catch their breath halfway through an encounter; fighters on both sides wheezing and panting until they were strong enough to renew the fight or until someone cut them down from behind.

Giuki had two swords, parrying with one and attacking with the other in the Frankish style. Three men lay dead at his feet, though he was fighting a wearying encounter with a spearman – unable to get close enough to strike at him, always having to look to defence first, never getting the chance to attack. The battle's rhythm had changed. Where it had been a frenzy, now it was a sporadic and fitful thing, each man thinking more of his own security than his enemy's harm.

On the longship, though, the fight was still fierce. Two men crashed past Aelis down the length of the boat. Both had lost their weapons and were wrestling, kicking and biting. A spear stabbed into the deck by her thigh. A berserker ran through a man right in front of her, and she watched him fall and die at her feet, the berserker cursing as he struggled to free his sword from the corpse.

There was a judder and the boat tipped sideways. Aelis realised it was almost free of the beach. She forced herself to her feet – she needed to get to Giuki. She leaped for the side of the drakkar but a berserker caught her in one hand despite panting like a dog coming in from the hunt. The berserkers on the boat had finished off Giuki's men but they had paid a high price. Only four of them were left. The fat Viking had got up from where he'd fallen but he was bent double. At first she thought he was hurt but she saw he was only panting with exhaustion, fighting to regain his breath.

How long had the fight been going on? It seemed for ever. The beach was strewn with the wounded and the dying. The sides had now parted and stood facing each other, almost too weary to even insult each other. One warrior actually sat down, eyes on his enemy twenty paces away but catching his breath while he had the chance. Then the fight was renewed as if the men were fresh to it. Aelis saw terrible sights: a man impaled by a spear, his legs pumping like a bug on a pin, a man crawling for his weapon despite his hand being cut off.

Then a voice: 'Hold! I ask for peace!' It was Giuki.

The sides were glad of the rest and backed away from each

other. Giuki moved between the warriors. His shield had only one plank remaining on its boss and his remaining sword was bent almost into an L. Other warriors were in the same condition, trying to straighten their weapons with their feet but finding no purchase on the sand.

'Brothers, we have fought a good scrap, but now it seems that the profit in it is over. There'll be none of us left by morning. Surely this is the time to call a truce. Make peace even. You're good foes, lads; you could become good friends. Freyr knows we could do with your numbers now.'

A man from the other side put up his hand, panting and shaking his head. 'There is too much blood here to forget.'

'On both sides. We have served each other amply.'

Ofaeti touched Aelis's arm. 'We are too few now to sail this boat. Come away. I offer you safety and a guarantee you will not be raped.' His voice was low but insistent.

Aelis shook free of him. 'I will not be sold by pirates,' she said. 'I will stay here in the ship.'

'You will be sold, lady, one way or the other, as all women are, high-born or low. You are unusual, however, because you get to choose your seller.'

Giuki was addressing the warriors on the beach again: 'We were many men when this battle began. Now we have a hundred men, sixty between us truly able. It's time to act together brothers, though the blood we have spilled makes that difficult.'

Aelis spoke to Ofaeti: 'You are in my grip. Each side thinks you belong to the other. While they do, you live. As soon as they discover you are interlopers you will die.'

Ofaeti smiled. 'You would have been a power behind the Frankish throne, lady.'

'I still intend to be,' said Aelis.

'You have been in my care once and come to no harm. Be in it again.'

'I am going to Helgi.'

Ofaeti laughed. 'As are we. Let us guard you. I promise you

can choose the king I sell you to. We can even try to ransom you to your brother. Come on. These are wild men and will slit each other's throats by morning. We can walk off this beach while they are busy with other things.'

Aelis saw the sense in what Ofaeti said. She looked at the men Giuki was negotiating with. Could he control them as he controlled he own? And Ofaeti had acted with decency in the past – and when he had no profit in so doing. He had thought her a slave and treated her kindly. How much more care would he take of her now her true identity was known to him?

She let Ofaeti take her hand. Creeping to the side of the boat furthest from the carnage on the beach, they climbed down, Fastarr, Egil and Astarth following, their eyes flicking back to their dead fellows on the boat.

All the time the two groups of warriors were talking.'We must think on this,' said a tall Viking. 'You are the aggressors here and owe us compensation. There can be no deal without it, for the sake of our honour.'

Giuki nodded. 'We have a girl with us, a Frankish princess. She is worth many pounds of silver in ransom.'

'Where is she?'

Giuki looked around. 'Aelis, lady, show yourself.'

'Aelis?'

'Yes, of the line of that bastard Robert the Strong.'

'We've been looking for her the length of this coast. Hand her over and you are our brothers. Our seeress will bless you. We travel with Munin, that wide-seeing lady.'

'I have heard of her. It's painful to part with this girl because Helgi of the Rus wants her for his bride. But ours is the offence and you must have her.'

Aelis was amazed at the sudden courtesy with which the Vikings addressed each other, though she noticed they still kept a wary distance of thirty or so paces between the bands.

All this time Ofaeti, Aelis and the other berserkers kept moving. They were fifty paces away from the two sides when Giuki called after them: 'Do I know you, brothers? You are no

Danes and yet you're not with us, either. Where are you going with the lady?'

All faces turned to Ofaeti. He drew his sword.

'I am Thiörek, called Ofaeti, son of Thetmar, war chief of the Horda. I have lived well and in many battles, but now, I think, my time is over. Come on, lads, step forward. Let's take each other to the All Father's hall.'

'Thiörek? What are you doing here?'

Aelis could almost touch the dismay in Giuki's voice. She guessed the fat man had a reputation as a great warrior.

'Ship-stealing, same as you,' said Ofaeti.

'And making off with our hostage,' said another voice.

'That girl is promised as weregild,' said Giuki. 'She is not yours to take.'

'And yet I'm taking her,' said Ofaeti, 'unless you are so jealous of your dead friends here on the beach that you would follow them to the halls of the slain. Step forward. The All Father has a place at his mead bench for you.'

Ofaeti had three men with him. Those still standing on the beach numbered nearer sixty. They were exhausted from the fighting, a rabble with bent swords, broken spears and shattered shields, but were too many for so few to stand against.

'We will come on,' said Giuki. 'What did I tell you, Danes? We are brothers. No sooner do we discuss it than the gods give us a reason to fight together.'

The Vikings did not charge. The battle had seen them spread across the wide beach and some had sat to listen to their leaders talking. But all now stood, all picked up their weapons, or the remains of their weapons, and came towards Ofaeti and Aelis with purpose in their movement.

'You belong to the *vala*, girl, to the seeress. There's nowhere to run,' said a voice.

For a second Aelis considered running, but it would have been futile. The beach was too long. The Vikings might be tired but they would catch her sooner or later. The nearest cover was the monastery five hundred paces away or a treeline four times that distance on the headland. The route to the monastery was blocked and she didn't even know if there was a way off the flats if she ran for the trees. Behind Giuki were some dunes maybe two hundred paces away, but she couldn't run through the Vikings.

There was a noise from along the beach, faint, almost like a breath of wind, though there was none. It was like the tug of the wind at an ill-set sail or distant thunder. The Vikings didn't notice it but Aelis recognised the sound instantly. It was the cry of a horse, but not just any horse. She knew its voice, even from so far away.

'Kill the thieves!' said a Dane.

'Those are the bastards who've been skulking about killing our men in the monastery,' said another.

'Not me,' said Ofaeti, 'but come forward. I'll kill you without the skulking. You might want to get another sword, though; yours looks like it's taken a clout too many, son.' Ofaeti and the three berserkers at his side brandished their weapons. 'Come on, boys. You can serve me my first drink in the afterlife, because we're all going there tonight.'

Aelis' eyes were drawn to the dark dunes two hundred paces away. At first she thought it was just an effect of the moonlight. The dunes seemed to ripple. Then the horse cried again and there was a sound like thunder, like the beating of many drums. She said a word under her breath – 'Moselle' – and the Franks came on at the charge across the hard slick sand.

52   The Charge

Men panicked, didn't think straight. The obvious thing to do was to dive for the water or the boats, that was the best shelter from the charge. But they were spread out along the beach, exhausted from fighting, their minds not quite accepting they had another battle on their hands.

Some did run for the boats; some ran for the dunes, up towards the monastery; some turned and faced the enemy.

'Together. Shields together! Hold, hold!' screamed Giuki, but it was no good. The knights were too quick, streaming across the hard sand at a flat gallop, their lances before them. The cavalry crashed into the Vikings like a pulverising wave. Some tried to fight and were taken by the lances, some ran and were smashed down by the flying horses.

Aelis had the impression of men broken, shattered and pulped.

The noise of the first impact was awful, like the smack of a hammer tenderising a steak but magnified many times. This was a work of demolition, not war. The knights worked together. Even after the mass charge, they rode in twos and threes. Any warrior who faced them had two lances to deal with, the hooves of two horses even if he was lucky enough to avoid the spears. Few chose to stand. Most ran hard for anything that might afford them protection and they were scattered like field mice before a scythe.

And then the horses were on Aelis. She was paralysed by fear. She felt the vibration of the hooves through the sand, a deep drumming that seemed capable of casting her to the ground on its own. She saw the crazed faces of the horses, lips pulled back, teeth bared and eyes wide, heard the insane whoops of the riders, and then she was down, rolling in the water.

'Get to the boat! Run!' screamed Ofaeti.

He had torn her away at the last second and pulled her sprawling into a deep pool in the sand. She stood.

The Franks wheeled and charged again. Ofaeti had her by the back of her tunic, driving her towards the shelter of the longship. He lost his grip and she fell headlong into the water. She looked up and saw Moselle lose his lance in the chest of a Viking, its crosspiece breaking with the impact and failing to prevent the weapon going clean through its target. Moselle dropped it, drew his sword and beheaded a fleeing man. Then he turned his horse and, cackling with delight, he spurred it into another confrontation.

No more than ten paces from her, a horseman had come to a halt, three Vikings around him. One was on his left-hand side, away from the horseman's sword arm, and leaped on him with his knife, but suddenly he wasn't there. A horseman had come past at the gallop taking the Viking's head with the point of his lance as easily as he'd spear a target in the practice yard. In a blink the other two were dead, similarly dispatched by racing horsemen.

Some Vikings did get away: ten made a longboat and got it out to sea; five climbed the dunes towards the monastery.

'These are your people?' said Ofaeti. They were crouching in the beached longboat.

'Yes.'

She read his face. He was going to threaten her, force an oath from her, tell her that if she didn't promise to save them he would cut her throat there and then. But she saw him dismiss the idea. It was useless, he could see. 'Can you save us?' he said.

'No.'

'I got you here. You might have died under their lances too if it had not been for me.'

'I cannot save you.'

Ofaeti nodded. 'Then let's go to them, lads,' he said. 'Best die on the attack than cringing here like shrews from a hawk.'

Aelis looked up at the monastery. A sensation of icy air, the glimmer of hail under the moon that she had seen from across the water, came to her. She said a name: 'Munin.' Nothing had changed. She was still pursued by terrible forces, still in the grip of unseen and dangerous enemies. She still needed to get to Helgi. The wolfman had died for her striving to take her there.

She looked at Ofaeti. 'Will you take me to Helgi?'

'If he'll pay the ransom, love, he's as good as the next king.'

'Is that a yes?'

'Yes. On my oath, if you save us.'

She nodded. The battle was over. There was laughter. Two Frankish knights were chasing a Viking up and down the beach. The man had no weapon, and the riders kept cutting him off, slapping him with the flats of their swords, making him turn and turn again.

A rider came alongside the boat and looked in.

'Moselle! It's me, Lady Aelis. It's me. Put down your sword.'

'Lady! You're hard to find! We lost word of you halfway down the Somme. It's only by the grace of God we came up here. We heard downriver there were Normans at the monastery and thought we might as well take a look. We've been watching them here for days looking for our chance and then God gave it to us on a golden plate. It's good to have seen such a day!'

His face was flecked with sand and blood, his horse sweating up a lather, but he was grinning like an imbecile on the steps of a monastery.

'Well, you caught them.'

'You've seen your error, I take it. Shall I free you from these barbarians? You can die easy or hard, Norman. Touch the lady and you'll suffer for a month, I vouch that.'

'He doesn't understand you, Moselle,' said Aelis, 'but he won't harm me. These men are my paid protectors.'

'You have a preference for foreigners over your own men, lady. A Frank would die before he took money to fight against his kin.'

'A wonder then that we find so many of our fine swords sold to the enemy, and that the Norsemen have any spies at all. Let's thank God for the help these Danes have offered me. They are good men. Look, this one carries the cross chalked on his shield. He is of Christ.'

'Then I can have even fewer qualms about killing him if his soul is sure of heavenly reward.'

'You will not kill him because, by the right of my family, I command you not to. Do you have any food?'

Moselle nodded and glanced behind him. As a man of the aristocracy he did not find it at all odd that Aelis, from a better family, should demand his unquestioning deference. He would have found it odd if she did not, and would certainly have expected any one baser born than him to obey his orders without question.

'The monastery's as good a place as any to spend the night. My God, when I think what these heathens have done to this land I should rather crucify the lot of them – make that abbey a new Golgotha – than share my fire with them.' Moselle's attention had shifted to shelter and a meal.

'I ask again,' she said, 'do you have food?'

'Plenty. Let's go up to the monastery. They'll have a warming room, and it'll be good to sit by a fire and tell the deeds of the day. Not a man of us dead.' He smiled and pointed his sword at Ofaeti. 'All my life I've dreamed of catching these bastards in open order, and tonight that dream came true. If we could fight all our battles on sand like this there'd be no Norman threat. I'll allow myself a cup of wine, I think.'

'Good,' said Aelis. 'Lead the way. And tell your men not to harm my Danes.'

Moselle nodded. 'I'll tell them, though the northerners don't eat with us or share our fire. They can sit apart in their own stink.'

'Very good,' said Aelis.

'End your game!' he shouted to the men chasing the Viking along the beach. One of the horsemen drew his sword and tried to behead the tormented man with a stroke. The Viking raised his arms and blocked the blow but at a terrible cost. His right hand was severed at the wrist. He sank to his knees, and the second horseman trotted in behind him, impaling him with his sword by hanging off his saddle and stabbing it through him with a scooping motion. The knight leaped into a dismount to bow to Aelis, then he and his companion joined their fellows looting the dead.

Ofaeti watched them. Aelis could see he was longing to rifle a few bodies himself but knew it would anger the Frankish knights.

'Keep ready,' said Aelis in Norse to the big man. 'We'll leave tonight.'

Ofaeti nodded. 'Might as well be warm before we go then,' he said and turned towards the monastery. Aelis sensed Ofaeti's desire for a good fire – more than a fire, for the hearth, for home. He was sick of travelling, this Viking, and wanted to be among his people. That was why he would take her to Helgi and the Rus, the Normans of the east, to sit down in safety for a while among people he understood.

She looked up at the monastery. That sensation was gone: no more of that cold and silver rain that she had seen from the ship, no longer even the call of the wolf. But they would be back. The monsters were still hunting her, and she knew something had taken root in her mind, was growing there, sustaining her and being sustained – those symbols that seemed to burn and fizz, to chime and howl inside her. Their presence disturbed her. How had she controlled Moselle's horse? How had she survived on that beach while around her Death feasted? How had Moselle found her? Had she called to him without knowing it? Was she a witch, unknown to herself, claimed by the devil? The thought nauseated her.

Aelis followed Ofaeti across the sand and up towards the monastery. She still needed his protection, no matter how uncomfortable that made her feel.

53 A Fireside Tale

There were large advantages to travelling with the Raven. The first was that the man had a fire steel and flint, so it was possible to get warm and to cook. The second was that he was an experienced trapper and fisherman, so they actually had something to cook. The third, of course, was protection from bandits.

The wolfman had been able to sense most ambushes miles ahead and the Raven was no different. The similarity between the two ended there, though. Chakhlyk would put up his hand, motion for silence and then turn off the main track and find a way around the bandits to avoid confrontation. Hugin employed a more direct approach. They were three days into the forest when he put up his hand and motioned for Leshii to stay where he was. Then he dismounted and passed him the reins of his horse.

It was noon when he left and an hour before dusk when he returned and mounted again. They followed the trail down. Six men lay in the bushes. One still had a piece of bread in his hand and was sitting upright, a black-plumed arrow through his eye. Two others had fallen directly back off the log they had been sitting on. Only the legs of one were visible but the other had a big wound at the neck. The others had clearly had time to get their weapons – two staves and a spear. It had done them no good. They lay butchered on the trail.

'Are there others?' said Leshii.

'No.'

'How do you know?'

Hugin gestured to one of the corpses, the one with only his legs visible. Leshii steered his mule over and looked down. The man had been mutilated, great gouges taken from his face, his eyes sucking pits of scarlet.

Leshii glanced at Hugin. 'I guess he gave you his assurance.'

The Raven said nothing, just pressed on.

Leshii, of course, had asked to see the silver dihrams, and the Raven had shown them to him one evening as they camped. To Leshii silver had a beauty that was deeper than gold's. He let the money run through his fingers, listened to the satisfying rain of coins that had come to end his drought, felt the delicious tickle as they fell back into the bag like bright little fishes into water.

What, thought Leshii, was to stop him cutting the Raven's throat in his sleep and taking everything he had? He looked at the man, the torn ruin of his face, the slim sword that lay at his side, the cruel bow he carried on his back. He thought of the desperation with which the wolfman – Chakhlyk, the man who had slaughtered five men before they got him to the ground – had fought him on the riverbank.

'You're laughing, merchant, why?'

'Occasionally,' said Leshii, 'I amuse myself with my own stupidity.'

They sat for a while in silence while Leshii munched on a duck the Raven had caught in a dead fall trap. The fire they'd used to roast it was a risk as it could attract attention, but Leshii thought it was worth it to feel warm and dry for once.

'You haven't asked for a story,' said Leshii. Merchants, with their travels, were noted as story-tellers, and people commonly pressed them for tales of faraway lands.

The Raven said nothing.

'Then tell me one,' said Leshii. 'Come on. I am always telling my tales. I bore myself with them.'

The Raven picked at the wing of the duck he had in his fingers. 'I have no talent for them,' he said.

'You need no talent. Just tell me about yourself. How did you come to be such a mighty man?'

The Raven threw the remains of the wing into the fire. It was almost as if the merchant had read his mind. He was thinking of the mountains, of how he had stolen away from the monastery and his home in the valley to go with his sister and the strange woman with the burned face to the heights where no one ever went.

The paths were steep, the boulder fields draining. They climbed small cliffs, trudged over swampy ground, crossed perilous slopes where they were just a slip from falling into nothing, moved on across snow fields, up and up into the mists. It was dawn when they came to the cave, the light frogspawn grey. They approached it along a perilous path by a great waterfall. She had fed them there, bread, salt beef and strange pale mushrooms, almost translucent, that reminded him of the pale skin of the abbot as he'd lain on his bed, the dead god's necklace at his throat.

He had looked out at the land beneath him. No one ever climbed the mountains – the danger of falling and the presence of the hill spirits would have put them off even if there had been any good pasture up there. Looking out he had a sense of the vastness of creation and his tiny place within it. His valley home had been all he knew, but here he could see the great lake that stretched like a sea to the north; he could look down on the massive chain of mountains that stretched west, see hints of other places, other valleys. And there was the forest, the vast forest.

'Here,' said the woman, 'the gods will talk to you.'

'I cannot understand. You say our words wrongly.'

The woman spoke slowly: 'The gods are here.'

'I am scared,' said his sister. She'd used his name. What was it? Louis. Every second boy in the valley was called that. She usually called him Wolf, for his hunting skill and for his black hair.

'You will have your brother to cling to,' said the woman. 'Now go inside the cave. You will come to no harm. This is the first step on your path to service.'

'To serve what?' he'd said. He'd been the bold one in those days.

'You will see,' said the woman. 'He will speak to you. The darkness is a soil. You are seeds within it.'

They were just children and they'd trusted her so they'd entered the cave. And then she had piled up the stones, to seal them in. The woman had said they would cling to each other and they did, terrified by the darkness and the cold, by noises from the earth, which seemed to groan and wail about them, to creak like a house in a storm, and by the flashes and glimmers that danced at the corners of their eyes but which gave them no light to see by. They sobbed, desperate for food, desperate for water, licking the rocks for moisture, weeping but without tears.

It had been quiet for a long time when his sister broke the silence.

'Wolf.'

'Yes.' His voice was hoarse.

'Who is in here with us?'

'We are alone.'

'No. There is someone else in here. Feel.'

She took his hand and put it out, but he felt only a rock, smooth and cold.

'It is nothing.'

'It is a corpse. Can't you feel the rope at his neck? Touch his cold eyes. Here. Can't you feel? There is a dead thing in here with us.'

'There is only stone and darkness, Ysabella.'

He heard his sister swallow, felt her hand trembling in his.

'He is here.'

'Who is here?'

'The dead god. The lord of the hanged.'

'There is nothing.'

'He's singing. Listen.' She chanted a strange off-key melody.

'Three times deceived, I was,
Those treacherous knots,
One thing inside another,
Inside another held tight.
Unseen,
Unheard,
The dead god's necklace
Closes to open the way to magic.'

He heard her scrabbling in the dark, her hands pulling at
something. Only when he heard her begin to choke did he
know what it was. The rope. He reached for her in desperation,
hands tearing at the three knots at her neck, trying to loosen or
untie them, but his fingers were raw and numbed by the cold.
He tore and he ripped and he screamed and still she kept on
choking. He felt around him with desperate hands, trying to
find a stone sharp enough to cut the rope, but it was useless.
Tug and tear as he might, there was no way to get it off her.

Desperation, starvation and tiredness overwhelmed his
mind. He coughed and retched with the thirst in his throat.
And then she stood before him bathed in the light of strange
symbols that shone and spoke. He heard their voices, sounds
like the wind over water, thunder and rain, the rattle of hail
against the roof of a house – he heard the growing of the plants
and the decay of the autumn, felt summer sun and winter ice.

Ysabella stretched up her arms to the symbols. She took one,
picking it like a fruit from a branch. It disappeared within
her, its light undimmed. Other runes – he had seen the wise
woman carve them for the spell that had cured the fever, the
spell that he had completed by providing the final ingredient
of the abbot's death – were glowing and writhing on her skin.
Her face was inconstant, one moment bathed in a golden light,
ecstatic, the next blue and bloated, the ligature tight around
her neck, her tongue protruding, her eyes bulging, like a gargoyle leering at him as if through a mist.

She reached her hand to him and he took it. She guided his

hand to the rope, to the knots. As he touched them, he saw the truth. There was only her for him. They had been together before and they would be together again. They were two threads entwined in eternity, their fates linked in lifetimes past and in lives to come. Music sounded in the cave. He and she danced to it, had always danced, would always dance to it – their flesh and bone expressions of the eternal melody.

'I am here for you,' he told her, 'always.'

'Something comes to part us.'

'The rope is so tight on your neck. Let me loosen it.'

'It is my strength and I must return to it. We have a fierce enemy.'

She opened her hand and on it writhed another strange symbol but not quite like the others. It was a jagged black line with a slash through it, as if someone had carved it but then thought better of it and crossed it out. It was a half-thing, he thought, not one shape or another. The strangeness of that thought struck him and he couldn't shake it from his head. A sound came from it, a note of agony and distress.

He heard himself speak: 'That is the rune that will draw the killer to us.'

The symbol seemed to leap from her hand across his face, blinding him but sending him falling through the darkness. He saw bright lights streaming past him, heard voices calling for him. Then he was somewhere else, by a river in a summer night, the metal light of the moon turning the leaves on the trees to pewter.

Someone was walking towards him. It was a woman, or rather a girl, young and blonde, her face indistinct. She was looking for him, he knew. Hunting him? Not quite. Something followed her. The killer. His head felt as though it would burst. His thoughts were smashed to shards, but he knew that this woman was terribly significant to him and would be his undoing. Something was stalking her, and when it found her ... what? Harm. He felt it as real as the thirst, as real as the starvation and cold.

The moon above him was growing, its light swamping all vision. He fell to the ground, gasping, fighting to see in the harshness of its light. And then he realised it wasn't the moon and there was no garden. He was in the cave, face down on the floor, too weak to stand.

He felt cold air and wind, saw the woman with the burned face. In her hand was a short knife. She went to his sister and cut the rope. Then she put her hand on his head to comfort him.

'The road to safety is a hard one,' she said, 'and you have taken just a step.'

He heard himself ask a question, his throat dry and rough. It was a question that had never even occurred to him before. 'Who am I?'

'You are his servant,' she said, 'a raven flying on the wind.'

'I wish we had some wine.' Leshii was looking at the Raven over the fire. 'Perhaps then you'd relax a little and I'd get a tale.'

Hugin looked into the fire. 'Perhaps,' he said, 'and perhaps not.'

Leshii smiled and stretched out his hands. He was warm and the night was dry at least. 'Do you think it's safe to dry my clothes?' he said.

The Raven remained silent, which Leshii took for a yes. He was sure of one thing: none of the Norse animal priests seemed to let their religion improve their manners.

He drove some sticks into the ground, took off his trousers and shoes, and arranged them on top of the sticks. Then he unwound his turban and laid it out on the dry grass by the fire. Finally he took off his scarf and set that out to dry too, sitting in front of the fire in only his long shirt.

He was relaxed, or as relaxed as he'd been since he set off on this journey among wild men and sword-wielding women. He began to doze.

A thump to his shoulder woke him. He came back to himself to see the Raven's ravaged face staring directly into his.

'What?' said Leshii. Hugin's long fingers were at his throat.

'Not for you,' said Hugin, and lifted the wolfman's cord and pebble over Leshii's head.

54 Dark Magic

True to his word, Moselle did not allow Ofaeti and his men inside the warming house. His hospitality extended to letting the Norsemen live, no further. The remaining berserks built a fire outside, and though they went hungry were at least warm and safe. And, more importantly, the treasure they had buried lay undisturbed in the woods.

Moselle had searched the abbey for skulking Vikings but found nothing. Only the door to the penitential cell remained unopened and locked, but, looking through the hatch, the Franks saw nothing but straw and elected not to kick it down.

In the warming house, Aelis was shaking with the violence of the day and with what she had heard on the beach. All that war band had been searching for her, and that thing, the faceless hag, was near. She told Moselle in terms she thought he would understand what she feared. A sorceress was at large, she said, and his men must be alert and, above all, beware of birds. The witch could use them as a vessel for her magic, thought Aelis. She had won a battle against her but she sensed her enemy was far from defeated. She looked into Moselle's eyes for his reaction to what she told him. It was a risk to even introduce the idea of sorcery, but she needed clarity now; the time for even tiny deceit was over.

'Have you traded with devils, lady?'

'No, but devils have tried to trade with me. They beset me and I ask for your protection as a warrior and a knight. You are a champion of Christ, Moselle, a Michael to Lucifer. My life, and the life of my soul, is in your care.'

Moselle took her seriously and set a watch, telling his men to keep their bows near for any ravens that might appear, and made her as comfortable as he could in the warming house, giving her blankets to lie on. A table was turned on its side to screen her from the eyes of the men who slept around her.

As she lay awake the events of the day played out in her mind. At one instant she was rocking as if on the longship, but then she'd start as the awful moment that the ship hit the beach replayed itself, or the thunder of the cavalry charge came back to her. She wished she was with the little merchant again. He would take her to Helgi, her only hope. She trusted the wolfman who had died for her and had believed him when he said Helgi could help her. She pictured Leshii on his mule, imagined the horse symbol moving on the animal's skin, calling it to her.

There is a moment between waking and sleeping and between sleeping and waking when the mind seems to be in many places at once, when memories mingle with dreams, when what has been and what is yet to be exist side by side, and when the mind slips free of time and personality to wander in strange halls where the familiar and the strange become indistinguishable and ghosts and visions walk hand in hand. Aelis tumbled towards sleep and fell into this place, to the mind's borderlands, where magic is.

It seemed to her that she woke up. The warming house was empty and the fire was just embers, though the room seemed intolerably hot. She went to the door and opened it, drinking in the cold light of the silver moon above her. Aelis was not alone, she could sense. Her memories seemed to stalk her, and she knew she had walked like this before, entranced in the cool night air of the garden at Loches.

The cloister of the monastery was still. Her eye was drawn to a corner of the cloister and a door that opened the opposite way to all the others. The scriptorium, the warming house she had just emerged from, the kitchen and the chapels all had doors that opened into the cloister – so that they didn't take up interior space, she supposed. Only one door opened inwards. Why was that door different?

She walked to it. There was an open hatch in the door. She was drawn to it. She moved her hand towards the opening and caught a glimpse of something within. A puff of mist? Her breath was freezing on the air, coming out in white plumes in the moonlight. She shivered. The temperature had dropped and her hand was shaking.

Something inside her seemed to light up, almost in answer to the cold that had come over her. It was one of the symbols, a jagged S, which seemed to shine with the light of the sun, warming her and driving the cold away. Another symbol, like a fierce diamond, lit up in her. She felt the deep earth under her feet, currents passing through the land as they might pass through the sea, lapping around the roots of mountains, falling in torrents into deep, dark voids.

A feeling like a million little needles swept her skin; a smell like ocean rain filled the air. It was as if the symbols inside her had called out and the freezing sensation that had come over her was their answer. A memory arose in her mind. She was in the garden at Loches under a big moon and she had in her hand a rose as big as a baby's head, its scent heavy and intoxicating. There was a sharp sensation and she realised she had pricked her finger on a thorn. The blood ran down her finger in a great gout and she put it into her mouth. That heavy rose scent was in her nostrils now, sweet and menacing, mingling with the taste of blood and the memory of pain.

She turned and looked across the cloister. In the lattice of shadows stood two figures. The first was a woman in a pale white shift, her face no more than a pitted pumice stone like you might find on the beach. In her hand was a knife, long and thin. She was trembling and worried at the outside of her leg with it, so the shift was torn and stained at the thigh. Around her neck was a thin rope tied in an elaborate knot that made Aelis shiver. The figure next to her was a boy of around twelve years old – from the Danish war band, by the look of him. His eyes were dead and his face marked with blood from two puncture wounds at his cheek. He held the hand of the sorceress and guided her to where Aelis could see her clearly.

'My men are here. They will take you, witch,'said Aelis.

Another symbol flashed into Aelis's mind, two upright lines with an X between them. She felt a different kind of cold, saw a different light. It was a symbol of the new day, revelation, clarity. Aelis knew it was inside the sorceress. It washed like a sunrise over the darkness and then disappeared again, leaving the cloister to the moonlight.

Aelis screamed. All around her were the bodies of Franks, lying at grotesque angles, some with their faces to the floor, some with their eyes to the heavens, arms wide as if pleading with the stars to spare them. The symbols inside her seemed to increase her sensitivities, and the colours that attended the warriors, the night music that seeped from them, was not that of death but of sleep. They were enchanted, she knew, but alive.

'What are you?' Aelis heard herself speak.

The woman bowed her head. 'You,' she said. 'I am you.'

'You make no sense to me, witch.'

'We are pieces of a broken urn. But the urn can be mended.'

'You are my enemy.'

'Yes. I have struck at you. But it was no good. I cannot harm you, and you cannot harm me.'

'Then why do you tremble?'

'Because of the certainty of death.'

'Whose death?'

'Yours and mine.'

'I will not die. Not by your hand or the hand of any of your disciples.'

'No, you will not. But the runes will come together. He will be here on earth again, erasing you, erasing me. This is the truth of it.' The woman touched the knot at her neck. 'The dead lord's necklace, the triple knot that was untied, shall be made anew when he is here again, present in the runes.'

'When who is here again?'

'The god of the runes. The god who is the runes. I know what is in you. It is more than just the howling rune.'

Aelis swallowed. The howling rune. That was as good a name for it as any, the rune that stood apart from the eight others, the one that cried out with the lonely voice of a wolf in the hills. Calling to what? To the thing that had seemed to stalk her in her midnight walks at Loches. The wolf.

'That is why you and your hideous brother pursue me?'

'It is why I pursue you. My brother would not understand those motivations. He cannot understand the true nature of the runes, what it means that they are in me, the unshakeable destiny they decree.'

Aelis felt a strong sensation come from the woman, not unlike the one she had felt coming from the merchant with the taste of vinegar and pitch. Deceit. The witch had lied to her brother. But about what?

The woman continued: 'When the runes are united by death the god will be here, the wolf will kill his brother and fight with the corpse lord. My destiny will be complete as I die under the teeth of the wolf.'

Aelis couldn't make sense of what she said but the symbols inside her were now in tumult. They jabbered and clanged, moaned and shook. Images came to her – the sheen on a horse's coat, the flow of water over a slick black rock, the spray making rainbows a waterfall, the sun firing the tops of the clouds, the glowing fields of the Indre Valley, the glimmer of light on a scythe's edge as it reaps the golden wheat, the bright bushels of corn loaded onto a wagon and the great light of joy in the windows of Saint-Etienne, casting blue pools on the flagstones below, where she knelt asking for salvation and grace. The runes gleamed and shone and she knew it was with the light of God. But what had awakened them?

Something was calling to them, winter to their summer. The same light lit them up in towering columns of shining ice, gleamed off frosted leaves thick with thorns, turned a fall of hail to a silver veil, gleamed on the steaming skin of a white wild ox. These visions too were caused by symbols but not those that lived inside Aelis. These, she knew, belonged to the witch. The discomfort Aelis felt told her very clearly that the runes inside her were screaming to join the ones the witch carried.

Somehow, the witch must die.

It was as if Munin caught her thought. She threw the knife towards Aelis. It clattered at her feet and Aelis picked it up. The knife was a wicked gleaming splinter of steel under the moon. The witch said nothing, the vacant pits of her eyes staring into nothing. Aelis walked towards her and went to drive the knife into her belly. But she hesitated. It was as if her arm was no longer hers to command.

The witch spoke: 'If it was that easy you would have been dead years ago.'

Aelis summoned up her strength, took the knife in both her hands and tried to stab it into the witch's neck. But she couldn't do it. She could sense what was stopping her: the runes, the ones the witch carried. They wouldn't let her act and yet they wanted to be together. Each set of eight runes, it appeared, wanted the other's host to die and defended its own.

Aelis threw down the knife in frustration.

'There may yet be a way,' said the witch.

At a sound Aelis turned. Moselle and Ofaeti were coming into the cloister, Astarth, Egil and Fastarr behind them. Ofaeti and Moselle carried a long rope between them. Instantly Aelis noticed what was odd about them. They were both unarmed. Neither man would ever forget his weapon in this company, she thought. Where was Moselle's sword? Where was Ofaeti's axe?

She ran towards them. 'This woman is my enemy. Strike her down,' she said.

Neither man spoke; they just stared at the witch.

Aelis shook Moselle, but he didn't react. She withdrew her hands. The knight, for some reason, was soaking wet.

55 The Tides

The tide was out but they didn't sink the stake near the waves. Moselle and Ofaeti drove it in further up the beach though still on the flats, before the sand became lighter and drier. They tied her to the stake in a sitting position. Aelis felt the cold water seeping into her trousers, glanced at the pools by her side and knew she was within the reach of the tide. They intended her to drown – but slowly.

Of course she had struggled, but Ofaeti was terribly strong and he and Moselle had bound her easily. They were enchanted, she could see. Neither spoke nor seemed to focus on what they were doing, and Moselle kept licking his lips, clacking his teeth together and even belching in a way he would never allow himself to do if he had been in possession of his mind.

She remembered Sigfrid and how the rune had manifested inside her to cause his horse to bolt, and she looked inside her now, to try to find something that might break the spell they were under. Nothing came. She could not make the runes hear her. They were occupied with something else – the presence of their sisters in the mind of Munin.

'I know what you are trying to do,' said Munin, who stood beside her, 'but such control comes at a high price.' She gestured to her face. 'They move in their own way unless you force them, in agony and denial, to move to yours. You will suffer and you will give up what you have to me.'

Aelis looked up at the bright half-moon and called out to the witch, asking why she didn't just have her slaves kill her there and then, as she had tried to do with her enchantments before. The witch said nothing, but Aelis guessed that had failed. The words of the wolfman came back to her. When she had asked him why Hrafn, as she thought of the male sorcerer, had tried to kill her, he had said, *He is afraid of you*. So Aelis and the witch were not able to harm each other directly. That was why she would be left for the sea.

The boy led the witch in front of Aelis and she sat down on the wet sand. She was scarcely human to Aelis now, more a shifting vision, something that was there and then gone. The woman's presence was like a blizzard wind full of grit that forced Aelis to turn her head away.

They waited on the beach. It was a cloudy dawn, the sun only visible as a smudge of lighter sky. Aelis was frozen and her body convulsed in shivers. The witch sang a song about the beginnings of things, and about how they would end. One verse she repeated again and again in her strange, high, piping voice, the notes in no key Aelis had ever heard but strangely beautiful.

> I know that I hung on the wind-torn tree,
> Hung there for nights full nine;
> With the spear I was wounded, and offered I was
> To Odin, myself to myself.
> On the tree that none may ever know
> What root beneath it runs,
> None gave me comfort with loaf or drink.
> Down I looked
> And took up the runes. Shrieking I took them.
> From there I fell back.

That day the tide did not reach her and no one tried to move her. She was so cold but her mind was clear. She knew what they intended. She looked up at the moon, the queen of the tides as it was called, still sharp in the blue sky. Her fate was linked to it. She had not been raised near the sea but she knew the water could come higher in some seasons than others. How long would that take? A day, a week?

The kept singing her song and one phrase seemed to stick in Aelis's mind. *Nights full nine*.

Aelis prayed to God to save her or to take her to him quickly. Night fell and she fainted away with the cold and was woken by the dawn, the clouds seeming to boil into great white columns and then disperse under the rising sun. Now the sun was strong and, though at first its warmth was welcome, soon Aelis felt sick as her skin crisped under its heat. Her lips were dry and she longed for a drink. Someone brought her a rag soaked in water. *They were keeping her alive!* Against herself, she sucked at it. Then she fell unconscious, and when she woke it was to a deep field of stars.

The water was lapping at her legs. She looked around her and the whole beach seemed to sway. The song continued, though she could not see the witch. Straining to look behind her, she saw some boots. Ofaeti was still standing there.

She called out to God and, when that brought no release, to the runes she nurtured inside her. She could hear the symbols and feel their presence, the rush of sensations of light, water, earth and hooves, but they were not there for her. The runes were stretching out, away from her, towards their sisters in the witch. The water covered her legs. Her body convulsed. Then the water was at her waist. She prayed to God, prayed and prayed. But it wasn't God that sprang to her mind. One rune was not searching for the others; one rune stood apart, that jagged S that lay on its side, a cross-bar through it like a spear through a corpse.

She saw a wolf and a man, and a man who was a wolf, she saw thunderclouds bubbling on the horizon, and she heard a dreadful keening, a terrible note of anguish with the quality of a funeral lamentation, the grief of those whose loved ones had gone too soon. The names of the rune came to her: *storm, wolf trap*. There was another name, she knew, just on the tip of her tongue. The rune had three names but she could name only two : *storm, wolf trap, storm, wolf trap, storm, wolf trap.* Then the third name came to her as she thought of the man, the man who was a wolf – *werewolf.*

A scream came from inside her, more of a howl than any

woman's cry. It was the rune expressing itself in sound, singing out through the human apparatus of lungs, throat and mouth but resonating in another way too, speaking to the mind that neither wakes nor sleeps, speaking to the dark corners of the memory, unearthing childish fears, stirring the wolves that snuffle through dreams and crouch waiting for the midnight waker who dares to move in their bed.

On the beach there was a thump as Ofaeti sat down heavily. The witch stopped her singing.

The water was at Aelis's chest, the ropes beginning to swell, cutting off the blood to her hands and restricting her breathing. She struggled against the bonds but knew it was no good.

Another howl, this time from the monastery, an answering call to the one that had come from Aelis. The water was at her chin. She tried to push back her head but the stake wouldn't allow it.

Terror swept over her, blanking her mind. But the runes were within her, lighting the darkness of fear that had fallen upon her, warming her and sustaining her in the cold sea. And then she was somewhere else.

She was high on a bare mountainside overlooking a green land of hills and rivers. Beside her were two men – identical, dark-haired and their skin tanned by the sun. One was a wolf, she knew. Or both were wolves. They didn't look like wolves but she knew them to be one. The thought struck her as strange. How can two people be one thing?

'Vali, help me!' The words spilled from her. 'Feileg, I am dying.'

'I will not abandon you.' The two men spoke together.

'Help me now!'

'I will come to you.' They both spoke again. 'But do not trust him, not after what he did. He is a killer to his bones.'

She knew the men were referring to each other.

'Who are you?'

She stared hard at one of them and thought that she recognised him. His face was so familiar. A name came into her mind: *Jehan?* No, this man stood straight and strong; he was no cripple.

Then she heard the rhyme in her head again but this time it was not sung by the witch. The voice was a child's. *Nine days and nights I hung on that wind-racked tree.*

She was falling, down into blackness. The tide at her neck receded, came again but not so far, fell away and away and then over days it crept to return. The sun chased the moon across the sky, rose and fell in a blur. Rhymes split her mind about a wolf called Hate who chased the moon, about a wolf called Treachery who hunted the sun.

> *Axe age, sword age*
> *Shields will be split*
> *Wind age, wolf age*
> *Before the world's ruin.*

She was screaming, really screaming. The water had gone, come back, gone again, and now it was back about her chest and she felt sure she would drown. The song of the witch was in her ears again. She craned her head to the left. She could see the witch on the beach. She stood bolt upright, as if entranced. Aelis felt tearing and ripping inside her. The runes were trying to get free, trying to go to the witch. She was dying. The song went on and on: *Nine days and nights I hung on that wind-racked tree.*

The howl came again, like the voice of the night. A sound of splintering. The witch's song faltered but resumed. Now the howl was stronger, not muted. She strained to see what was happening on the beach. She heard a voice she recognised: 'Not the lady, not the lady!'

Someone was splashing towards her through the water. 'I am coming, lady. I am here!'

She took in great mouthfuls of salt water. The runes were going from her, being pulled towards the witch on the beach. She saw them, eight of them, straining towards eight others that surrounded and inhabited the witch.

'I am dying,' she said.

But a knife was at her bonds, slicing them away. She didn't know who pulled her from the water. She had a vision of him as a thing of parts rather than a whole, a shaped beard, a turban, that dark and foreign face. He dragged her from the sea and laid her down on the beach.

Aelis was cold beyond shivering. She looked up. Walking towards her behind the witch was that monster, Hrafn. His wicked crescent sword was drawn and he was coming across the sand at a determined pace.

She felt the exultation of the witch. Aelis, in the certainty of her death, saw deeply. The witch would take her runes; the runes would unite, and the god would be on earth. The wolf – Aelis could hear his keyless howl – would kill his brother, and the god's chosen destiny of death would be at hand. The wolf whose jaws were red with his brother's blood would tear down the god and offer him the gift and the knowledge of earthly death. Hrafn, the Raven, was the brother of the wolf and was coming forward to die.

Something was coming towards them, something that ran like an animal, loping and grunting across the sand.

Aelis tried to stand but couldn't. She had no strength. She lay ready for death, ready for the cut of the sword and whatever came after. The witch, led by the boy, was bending over her; Hrafn was above her, his sword raised. The howl, very close, very loud. It was almost as if she could understand it.

'Flee me! Flee me!'

Hrafn's sword descended. For a second there was nothing but then something bumped against Aelis's arm. She opened her eyes to see the severed head of the witch lying like a gift of the sea in front of her. Hrafn was staring down at her, the silver edge of his sword red with blood, his ruined face trembling as he spoke: 'My love,' he said, 'I have come for you.'

And then the runes came shrieking upon her, the wolf crashed in, and the world went wild.

56 Werewolf

In the penitential cell Jehan's chest was wet with drool. The odours of the battles on the beach were all he smelled – iron on the breeze, a salt that didn't come from the sea but from blood. Horses were there, the deep smell of their sweat seeming so strong that it clung to his skin.

He broke free of his bonds, tearing them with his nails, biting them, gulping down mouthfuls of rope, unable to stop the instinct to swallow what he bit. Jehan scrabbled on the floor, rolled and stretched, turning his head round and round as if that might clear his thoughts. He stood but that felt wrong. Instead he crawled on all fours around the cell. Something was happening to his legs. His knees felt very odd, too flexible, as if they could bend the wrong way; the whole geometry of his body seemed unfamiliar and strange. He couldn't stop stretching his back, which felt too long for his body. His shoulders too seemed wrong, restricted, though large and powerful.

He stroked the thick hair on his arms. His teeth were large, and he ran his tongue back and forth in his mouth, picking out the shape of the canines. It was as if he had a mouth full of boat nails. Jehan put his hand to his brow and ran his fingers through his hair. When he brought his hand down he could smell blood on it. He examined his fingers. They had become long and muscular, the nails talons. He had cut himself just by touching his head.

Jehan was unaccountably hot. He panted and slavered, writhing on the flagstones trying to take their coolness in. His skin crawled on his skull; his cock was hard and he seethed with lust, though he fought to force it from his mind. And he was thirsty, terribly thirsty. When had he last drunk? He couldn't remember. Days before.

The confessor breathed deeply, trying to find himself in the thought storm. There was a screaming inside him, a sound like that of an animal caught in a trap, of something scraped and scratched, like metal on stone. An aggression he had never known was in him. He laughed.

'I am such a thing that will tear the enemies of God.'

No, he told himself. He fought for clarity. The truth, when it came to him, was terrible. He had been cursed. Some pagan, perhaps the one who had forced that vile and bloody mass on him, had cursed him, and he was powerless to resist. And God had let this happen to him. *Why?* Because he had not been holy enough, not tried hard enough, not sacrificed enough of his mind to Jesus.

He came up to a crouch, feeling the strength in his limbs. He could break the door, he knew, splinter it to nothing, but he would not. How long had he been in that cell? The question came into his head and vanished again, meaning nothing to him any more.

The power in him was from the devil and he would not use it. It was a test. His senses sang. His teeth were spikes, sharp and ready and his nails were blades, itching to tear and kill. He stretched and clenched his fingers – they were tense with the desire for murder.

But he would not.

'I will not be this thing,' he said out loud, his voice rasping like a rain-swollen door on the flagstones. He prayed: 'Jesus, hear me now. Jesus, strike me down. Afflict me again, Lord. Blind me and wither my limbs. These hands turn only to evil, these eyes profit me nothing. Return me to the piety of darkness.'

From down on the beach he could hear someone calling.

'Vali, help me! Feileg, I am dying.'

He recognised the voice. It was the Lady Aelis. He remembered the Viking camp, her touch on his shoulder.

'Help me now!'

She was calling him, he knew. And then something seemed

to break open his consciousness like it was a walnut. The scream, the animal howl, shaking his thoughts to nothing.

'Vali!' He saw himself as the fit young man he had never been, walking on a hillside hand in hand with a girl. She was blonde but he couldn't see her face. The sun was on the meadows, and the buzz of bees was in the air. He heard voices.

'Prince, prince!' A man was next to him – a big old Norseman with a battle-scarred face – but he didn't recognise him. 'Where is your spear? Where is your bow?'

The man looked angry but Jehan was not afraid. Was this a vision sent by the devil? It felt so real.

The mountain seemed to fade away and he was by a waterfront, a small landing stage. Out to sea three Viking ships sped towards the shore. She was in front of him again, the blonde girl, holding his hands, looking into his eyes.

'Kill a hundred of them for me,' she said.

'I have known you before.'

'I have always known you.'

'I will find you.'

'That is your destiny,' she said.

Jehan came back to himself. The corner of the cell was rank with shit and piss; vomited blood lay all over the floor. How long had he been there? A long time, he sensed. He heard the woman's voice: 'I am dying.' He felt tormented and hot as if he had a head full of flies. 'I am dying.'

It was time to leave. The door cracked under his first blow. He hit it again and the wood gave some more. The effort of smashing the door bored and frustrated him, and he looked up at the broken roof. It had not occurred to him to climb before. The walls were smooth so Jehan jumped, his strong, long fingers forcing their way through the thatch. He pulled himself up and through it.

The fat moon hung above him, the sky swarmed with stars and he felt as if all of creation had turned out to watch him, as if the night was a city and he was its champion going out to battle under its anxious eyes. The thick beat of his heart was in his ears, the scent of blood in his nostrils and the thatch cool beneath him.

He looked out over the silver sand. Something was happening. Figures were on the beach. His eyes were sharp and he saw clearly in the dark. A man struggled with a large burden. Jehan's ears picked up the man's exertion, the coughs and retches of the woman in his arms. Next to him stood six figures, upright but their presences dull. It was the sense that had awoken in him in the cloister, the ability to feel the quality and the direction of attention of all those around him, to feel the focus of their thoughts without even looking at them. In some strange way, he knew, the men down there were different to normal humans. If he closed his eyes he could feel how focused the man who was pulling the woman from the water was, feel the desperation of the woman in his arms, almost as if she was fighting to regain her senses and bring her mind back to the beach and sanity. The men who waited by the water, though, the six who watched impassively as the figures struggled in front of them, were not there. In some sense, the werewolf knew, they were both present and not.

Across the sand strode a man, a curved sword flashing in the light of the moon. And there was a woman, her body reeking with blood and filth, her hands stretched to the couple who staggered from the water.

Jehan leaped from the roof into the dunes and made his way down to the beach under the burning moon, Slinking low to the sand, he moved forward as swiftly as the shadow of a bird in flight.

57   Alone

Aelis fell back under the collision of images. She seemed to tumble through a thicket of thorns, her skin lighting up in agony. Fear was now a sensation she could touch, cold and hard. She saw a brilliant blue sky above her, felt the pull of the tide as it sucked at the sand beneath her feet, saw visions of a man sacrificed, hanging from a tree whose branches were the darkness of night and whose leaves were the stars. She felt his expiring heart beating as her heart and a need, stronger than hunger, stronger than thirst, a compulsion, to become what she could be. There were faces on the beach, and she knew that she knew them, but she couldn't remember who they were under the runes that fell on her like a torrent. Eight found eight to become sixteen – purring, singing, shouting and rejoicing inside her.

On the River Indre there had been a sort of rapids in the river a morning's walk from her hall. In the summer the children loved to swim in them, to shoot down the river in the rush of white water, shoving off from the rocks with arms and feet, the world flashing by in glimpses of sunlight. They were terrified and ecstatic all at once. One summer, though, after heavy rain, she had gone there with her cousin Matilde. Matilde wasn't brave enough to swim in such a flow but Aelis had gone in. She'd quickly realised that swimming was impossible as she was forced forwards through the raging water, throwing up her arms to protect her head, hoping to live. She had the same feeling there on the beach but magnified many many times – that of being caught in a terrible flood that tore and pulled at her, driving all thought away other than the bursting need to survive. Here, though, it was not one flow that battered and tormented her but many, sixteen flows, surging to meet each other in the pool of her mind. The runes inside her were calling to the runes that had lived in the witch and a rush of bright symbols poured towards her through the dark. She could not distinguish, in that frenzied moment, the visions from the real, the past from the present, nor recall exactly what had happened on the beach.

The wolf, the thing, had killed Moselle, she thought. The knight had slumped to the sand at the moment Hugin had decapitated his own sister. Moselle had then tried to stand, to fling himself at Hugin. Aelis felt sure he had thought the sorcerer was going to attack her and, brave Moselle, he had tried to throw his drained and starving body between her and the Raven's sword. Something else took him, though, dragging him into the sea in an explosion of flailing limbs, water and blood. The wolf. The wolf seemed crazed by the kill, tearing into the knight's body, oblivious of everything around it.

A figure came into Aelis's view. It was Ofaeti, his eyes vacant, the big man staggering about like a hungover drunk awaking in an unrecognised place. There were shouts from up the beach. The Franks who had been bewitched had woken up and were pouring onto the shore, swinging their swords as they came. There were Vikings too — the fat one's companions.

Aelis looked down at her feet. There was the head of the witch, like a worm-eaten nub of wood. Against herself she bent to touch it. Her body felt sore and broken, her mind overwhelmed by the cascade of sensations tumbling through it.

Hugin took off his sword belt and lay it on the sand. He had something around his neck — a pebble worn as a pendant. He undid it and used the cords that tied his scabbard to his sword belt to extend the length of the thong that held the pebble. The berserkers had recovered from their enchantment and were circling the great wolf, Astarth moving left in the water, Egil to the right, Fastarr facing it, while Ofaeti hunted through the bodies on the beach for a weapon.

'A fine time for weaving, crowman,' said Ofaeti.

'This is a wolf-fetter,' said Raven.

He finished his work then sprinted towards the wolf through the water. The creature was too concerned with feeding to see him coming. Hugin leaped on its back, trying to tie the pendant about its neck, but was flung off, flying clear of the water to land on the sand with a heavy thump.

'What a death this will be!' said Astarth, sidling towards the wolf. 'Come on, come on. My place in a thousand sagas beckons me!'

Now Aelis saw the werewolf properly, its night-black fur and green-disc eyes, like something made not born, standing on its back legs, its front limbs more like arms, its hands talons. It was tall, half as big again as even Ofaeti.

'Come on!' called Fastarr. 'This death will see me at Odin's right hand, to feast for ever.'

Fastarr talked of living for ever but the wolf's snarl brought out the mortal in him, sent the chill of oblivion shivering through his bones. He dropped the spear from his hand, his shaking fingers traitors to his will.

The wolf sprang.

Fastarr recovered himself enough to swing a punch at the animal's head but was too late. A blood geyser burst in the surf. Astarth died next, a rag of meat in the jaws of the snarling wolf, which shook the life from him as easily as a gull shakes water from seaweed. It threw him down to guzzle at his ravaged body, driving its muzzle into his chest, ripping away his flesh with its terrible teeth.

Now the Franks came howling in, their swords and spears at the ready, around fifteen on foot and a couple bareback on their horses. They smashed through the bloody waves towards the creature. It picked the first to arrive from the sand and flung him back towards the rest, knocking two men down. A horsemen hit it at the gallop, but the spear was torn from his hand, his horse sent crashing back down, its limbs broken.

The knights were brave and fell in to the attack, but the wolf was like a demon, thought Aelis. It was huge, twice her size, its twisted body like the unbaked clay figure of a man that had been stretched and pulled by a naughty child. She knew it from her dreams.

Egil had arrived. He stood at the water's edge, weighing his sword in his hand. He took a pace back and pointed at the werewolf.

'I know that I am to die but know this slaughter beast that seasons many have I ...' The fine words would not come. 'Bollocks,' he said, 'let's have it.' He leapt at the wolf but the creature rounded on him, biting away his head and the shoulder of his sword arm as its muzzle drove him down into the bloody water.

Ofaeti had picked up the Raven's sword and plunged towards the fight howling out the name of his father and grandfather, telling the wolf he was from a noble line of killers. 'This day, creature, you have met your match!'

Aelis felt a pull at her arm. It was the Raven. She tried to get away but he held her fast and pressed something into her hand. The pebble on the thong.

'Make him wear this amulet,' said Hugin. 'Make him put it on. It is hope to us.'

Aelis hardly registered his words.

'Get away from me, monster!'

'I have been your saviour. Look to the dead witch. Make him wear this amulet. Make him wear it!'

The werewolf levelled its great eyes at her. Something like recognition flashed within them. Men were all over it, clinging to it, stabbing at it. It tried to shake them from it as it walked towards her.

Aelis staggered back, gripping the pebble.

The creature spoke, its voice like stone on stone. 'You came to me before. In the shining green fields of unripe corn, under a bright sky when the sun turned the water to a field of diamonds. You came and you blessed me, Holy Mary.'

Aelis ran. Blind panic had taken her. Still, she couldn't help looking over her shoulder.

Ofaeti jumped at the wolf, swinging the Raven's sword. The creature was fast and threw its body aside, but the sword cut into the black fur on its flank. The animal leaped at Ofaeti, but the Raven threw his arms around the Viking to pull him down as the great beast's jaws brushed his neck. The were-wolf touched its flank and put its fingers to its lips to taste the blood.

'Kill it!' screamed the Raven as Ofaeti leaped at it again. This time the wolf was too quick. It seized Ofaeti, lifting him off the wet sand.

Aelis turned. 'Vali, no!' She didn't know where the words came from nor what they meant, but they seemed to have an effect on the creature.

It let Ofaeti fall from its fingers. The Viking hit the water and lay clutching his bloody sides, rasping for breath. Still men beset the wolf, and it turned to rip them down, losing itself in its fury as it bit and tore.

A rune arose inside Aelis, the first one she had ever known by name. Horse. Down the beach at a gallop came a grey mare, one of the Frankish mounts.

'Lady, you must stay with us. I offer you my protection!' It was the Raven. He had his own sword again but had not returned to the fight.

Aelis shook her head, backing away.

'Lady!'

She took a handful of mane and pulled herself up onto the mare's back.

'He will kill you! The wolf will be your end!' shouted Raven.

Go! she thought, and the animal kicked hard across the sand for the trees.

58 A Hunting Party

Aelis was gone, the wolf too. As soon as she had ridden away it had fought free of the Franks and run for the woods, dragging a knight's corpse behind it.

Raven wiped his sword on his cloak and sheathed it. 'Nastrond,' he said.

Ofaeti, still panting from where the wolf had seized him, nodded. 'The corpse shore.' He looked around at the bodies on the beach, recovered his breath and said,

> 'She saw there wading
> in tides of blood
> Oathsworn men
> and murderers too
> and betrayers of friends.
> There ravens fed on
> The corpses of the dead,
> and the wolf tore men.'

'That is the time-worn prophecy,' said Hugin, 'the beginning of the twilight of the gods.'

Ofaeti put his hands to his sides. They came away wet with blood but the wounds were superficial. The werewolf could not have wanted to kill him, he thought. It had left twenty or more men dead on that beach. He had never, in all his battles, seen men so ripped and broken. The gulls and crows were circling already. The Viking had been shocked by the appearance of the werewolf and the ferocity of its attack but not by its existence. Unlike the confessor, he had no difficulty accepting the reality of magic. He had been raised on a hill farm and grown up with the certainty that elves, dwarves, trolls and wolfmen were as real as the sheep he tended, the rain that soaked him and the frost that chilled him.

Leshii appeared from behind a dune.

'You were absent when the war work was done,' said Ofaeti.

'I brought the Raven here, showed him the nearest place to catch a ship, knowing this monastery would attract them.'

'You brought no one anywhere. These meetings are preordained,' said Hugin; 'they were destined to happen.'

'And is it preordained for you to get into Ladoga? Because if it is, you don't need my help.'

'You may have your part to play in what is to come,' said Hugin, 'but do not imagine that you can avoid your fate.'

'My wars are the wars of coin and exchange,' said the merchant. 'I would have got in your way fighting that thing. What was it?'

'An enemy of Death,' said Hugin.

Leshii looked around him.

'I wouldn't like to meet Death's friends then,' he said.

Ofaeti for once did not feel like joking. He wanted to honour his dead comrades with poetry in the traditional way of warriors.

'Empty the mead benches of Valhalla were,
So the dark god sent his wolf to fill them.
Now the sands run with the blood of the brave
And the warrior's hands itch to hold the weapons of
    revenge.'

Hugin listened carefully. He had not been raised among the northmen but was steeped in their traditions. He knew the honour that Ofaeti was giving his friends was as deep as that the Franks gave their dead with their prayers and tears, or the Moors with their wailing and lamentations.

'My kinsmen are dead,' said Ofaeti, 'and I have no way back to my homeland. I have three ships I can't sail and treasure I can't carry. Food and drink to me now are treasure. I have had smoke in my head for days and it will not clear but by cool water.'

Raven stood. 'Walk up to the monastery; there will be food and water there.'

'You wear a rich robe, warrior,' said Leshii. 'Did any other treasure come with it?'

'It's already in the ground,' said Ofaeti, 'so don't think to rob me of it.'

'The reverse,' said Leshii. 'I was thinking to secure you a good price.'

'I will follow the wolf,' said Raven.

'I'll come with you. That wolf has killed three of my friends and I would have the payment of its pelt for that,' said Ofaeti.

Hugin nodded. 'Yes,' he said. 'I have a use for you.'

'No one uses me,' said Ofaeti.

'The gods do, as they use us all,' said Hugin. 'There is a destiny in train here, a destiny of blood. It is up to me to stop it.'

'I thought you said destinies couldn't be avoided,' said Leshii.

'Not by you,' said Hugin, 'but with effort and determination heroes may stand against the gods.'

'So modest,' said Leshii.

'How will you avoid this destiny?' said Ofaeti.

'Find her.'

'She was going to Helgi, if that helps,' said Ofaeti.

'That was her intention when she left me with a wet arse in Francia,' said Leshii.

Raven thought for a moment. 'Then it's as I thought. Helgi must die,' he said.

'What good will that do?'

'The god is on earth. This I saw in visions, and I am sure it is true. My sister was a sincere defender of the god and she sought to protect him from his destiny by killing the lady and using me to help her. The wolf follows the lady. The lady goes to Helgi. There, then, is where the skein of fate ends – when the wolf fights the corpse god.'

'You think Helgi is your god?' said Ofaeti.

'I don't know.'

'What if he is?'

'Then I must try to kill him before the wolf does. I must stop the destiny unfolding.'

'And what good will that do?'

'It will end it.'

'What?'

'The cycle of blood – the god comes to earth, the wolf comes to earth and kills him.'

'Why do you care?'

'Because the lady draws the wolf on, the lady dies too.'

'I ask again,' said Leshii, 'why do you care?'

'Because when the enchantment broke,' said Hugin, 'I remembered.'

'What?'

'Before. When I swore to protect her.'

'Before when?' said Leshii. 'You've been trying to kill her all the way from Paris.'

The Raven ignored him and spoke to Ofaeti: 'I ask a service of you, fat man, for freeing you from the enchantment of the witch.'

'I do not know it was her enchantment but I do know it ended when you killed her, so I might believe it was so. What is the service?'

'A simple one. Find a woman, raise many good sons and tell the story I am to pass to you. Have them tell it to their sons as long as the world lasts. You will have a noble task.'

Ofaeti gestured at Leshii.'Why can't you or he have many sons and tell them these stories?'

'He is old, and my fate is to die.'

'How to die?'

'Opposing the wolf, as I have before and will again. It is my destiny.'

'How do you know this?'

'My sister, that thing that I took for my sister, showed it to me, but in a guise I could not recognise.'

'She was a wide-seeing woman,' said Ofaeti, 'skilled in Seid magic. You know your end, and yet you do not seem happy. A man goes smiling to his fate once he knows it.'

'Because, for all the witch's lies, there must be a way to break the curse. If not then I will live in the future as I have lived so far – ignorant of myself, beguiled. It may be too late for me in this flesh but not too late as I will be tomorrow. In our future incarnations one of us might recognise what is going on and be able to act to stop it before we are damned to misery and suffering again. We are going to send a message to eternity, fat man, and you are going to carry it.'

'I will come with you to Helgi,' said Ofaeti. 'Not to serve your purpose but because I swore an oath to the girl to protect her. She is in danger, so I will follow you, shapeshifter, not for fame, not for gold or for sons. I will follow because the girl asked me for protection and I offered it. The witch who lies dead on this shore enchanted me and made me harm the lady against my word. I need to repay that or it will be a hard welcome for me in the halls of the dead. And my kinsmen must be avenged. We will find this wolf and kill it. I struck it once and it bled well enough. No reason why I can't strike it again and see it bleed some more.'

'You will not be able to kill it,' said Hugin, 'until it has performed its part in the god's great ritual and sent the All Father to death.'

'We'll see,' said Ofaeti. 'I have met many men who claimed to be invulnerable, Eric Harm-Hard for one.'

'What happened to him?' said Leshii.

The fat man winked. 'He didn't live up to his name when he fought me.'

'This is different,' said Raven.

Ofaeti just grunted and turned towards the monastery.

Leshii looked up at the treeline. There was a lot of forest between them and Ladoga, and mountains too – haunts for all sorts of wild men. And what were they chasing? The thing that had loomed from the darkness to take the lady? That was the sort of creature that wise men ran away from, not towards. Still, he wanted to keep the necklace the Raven had given him, the one he now wore concealed beneath his kaftan. How much did he want it, though? Enough to stay with these madmen who set out to spite the gods. Probably not.

Leshii ran to catch up with Ofaeti. 'I told you you should have left me on the hill,' he said. 'The lady has brought you no luck.'

Ofaeti smiled, though tears were in his eyes. Leshii guessed he was thinking of his dead kinsmen. 'Too late for that now,' he said. 'The past is a wind at our backs. We cannot unblow it.'

Ofaeti walked away across the wet sand to the monastery and Leshii began collecting weapons and other valuables from the corpses. There were ten fine swords there at least, which would give him plenty to trade, should he stop at Birka. The necklace was hugely valuable, and there were also the hundred dirhams in the sorcerer's pack, but Leshii had had his fill of adventure. When they reached the first market town he would say his goodbyes.

59   The Lamps in the Garden

Aelis rode into the woods. The runes were all around her like a garland of bright stars. They whispered the wolf's names to her, one familiar, one strange and one that seemed to shimmer between the two: *He is Jehan, he is Fenrisulfr, and he is Vali that is, was and will be.*

She seemed to burst with memories – mushroom-hunting at dawn in the woods at Loches, the hawkmoths among the jasmine rising around her as she passed, the flutter of their wings close at her ear like the fear that dogged her. She had told herself it was fear of nothing at all, but she still went running from the dark of the trees to the sunlight of a clearing. Everything had seemed so intense: the inky stains on the cloth with which she lined her basket, the dark juice on her fingers, the rising sun pulling the mist from the dew-soaked grass, her face warm but her feet wet and cold.

She had been looking for something beyond mushrooms, she sensed, and was chased by something more than the rays of the sun. There was a menace to the birth of morning, she felt it in her core. She walked as the deer walks, in fear of the wolf.

Vali.

The name conjured something from her. She saw herself in a place she had never known, by some strange houses that were low and mean, turf roofs not waist-high, a bright river below her down a small hill. She heard the excited cries of children and looked down to see them bathing in the sunlight. Someone was at her side. When she turned to him his face was familiar but she couldn't place it. It was as if she had seen it before but only through an imperfect glass, its features distorted and blurred.

She looked at her hand. It was the same hand she had always known. The runes had reunited but she had not become a god, nor had she died as the witch had predicted. She made herself calm down and saw the runes all around her in two spinning orbits of eight, the howling rune at their centre, twisting and slinking like a crawling wolf. That one seemed more important to her than all the others put together. But something was missing. A third orbit. While that was not in her she was human still.

She still had not let go of the stone the Raven had given her; in her panic she had hardly noticed it was in her hand. She held it up to examine it, and nearly dropped it. It was just a pebble tied within an elaborate knot on to a thong, but it was etched with the face of a wolf. A phrase came to her: *When the gods saw that the wolf was fully bound, they took a fetter and lashed it to a rock called Scream.* In her mind she saw a huge wolf, its jaws stretched wide by a cruel sword, tied to an enormous rock by a rope as fine as a ribbon. It thrashed and groaned and howled but could not get free. It was night and a man came to the rock. He was tall and pale with a shock of red hair and he tried to break the fetters. But the fetters would not break. So the man took up a pebble that lay at the bottom of the rock, of the same stone as that to which the wolf was bound. And then, as the day came up, he stole away to inscribe something on it – the head of a wolf.

The runes were showing her these things. The runes knew.

She drove the horse on through the trees. Eventually the animal tired and she stopped to let it forage and rest. The spring was lovely, the forest full of flowers, thick with full-leafed sycamore, birch and oak. The sun dappled through the leaves and turned the light to water; the bark of pale trees flashed from the deep green like the skins of silver fish; mustard lichen changed the carcass of a fallen oak to a chest of gold; flowers of yellow and white seemed to dance on the branches as if caught on unseen currents.

Suddenly the effects of her ordeal by water swept over her.

She was aching everywhere, her skin cut from the ropes, sore from the salt water. She was terribly thirsty too. Aelis looked around for water. There was no stream but the woods were damp and it had rained recently. She licked the moisture from leaves and when she found a muddy puddle put her head in and lapped like a dog. She was too exhausted to forage for anything to eat. Spectres of tiredness loomed at her from the trees. She thought she saw movement, heard noises. She was full of fear and remounted, walking the horse on through the forest.

The greens and the golds blurred and she slumped down on the horse's mane, jolting back to wakefulness for a moment before falling forward again. For a second she would think there was a threat, the runes would wake in her and all tiredness leave her. Then, as the horse plodded forward, she would feel more secure and start to doze. She drifted awake. The horse had stopped, she noticed. It was cold, though the low sun split the trees in blinding rays.

'It will devour me.' A voice terrible and guttural. Suddenly she was fully awake. The wolf was in front of her, its great jaws red with the blood of her countrymen.

She kicked the horse around and sent it leaping away from the creature, but it was no good. The dread wolf had her, springing forward to take her from the horse's back and drag her to the ground. As she hit the forest floor it was as if all the tiredness she had been holding at bay came back to her and she fainted into unconsciousness.

When she came to, her horse was nowhere to be seen and the creature was on all fours above her, its great muzzle thrust into her face.

'It will devour me,' it said again. Its voice was like a fall of hail, like the scrape of the keel of a boat on a beach.

Aelis could not speak. She looked for the runes. They were nowhere. It was as if they had run from the wolf.

She tried to back away but it held her by the leg with one great clawed hand.

'I have struggled,' it said. 'Do you not know me?'

'You are a monster.'

'I am Jehan, the confessor. I tried to help you, to save you from the thing that pursues you.'

'Then why did you not kill him on the beach?'

The beast bowed its head. 'I saw only you. You. I have tried to protect you, but I cannot be near you. The rage I feel will consume me.'

It stood upright and turned from her as if to walk away then dropped to all fours, snapping and spinning as if tormented by a fly. It crouched and snarled out through bared teeth, 'Leave me. Walk away because I have a wolf inside me that I cannot quiet.'

'Then why did you come?'

'To see you. To touch you.'

Aelis looked down at the pebble she held in her hand. The Raven had lengthened the leather thong so it would go around the wolf's neck. She did not believe it would work but had no other option. She edged towards the writhing wolf. It crouched, seething like a dog beneath a table who fears someone will take its bone. She reached forward to tie the stone around the creature's neck but it bared its huge yellow teeth. Aelis recoiled. The stink of death was on its breath.

It spoke in that growling voice that sounded like the crunching of cartilage, of a joint being torn apart. 'I will not wear it. "Thou shalt not make unto thee any graven image, or any likeness of any thing that is in heaven above, or that is in the earth beneath, or that is in the water under the earth. Thou shalt not bow down thyself to them, nor serve them: for I the lord thy God am a jealous God, visiting the iniquity of the fathers upon the children unto the third and fourth generation of them that hate me. And showing mercy unto thousands of them that love me, and keep my commandments." Show mercy on me now, God. Show mercy on me now!'

She put out her hand to comfort the great animal but it flinched away, rolled and snapped. Then it came for her with paralysing speed. It threw her to the earth, stood over her keening for a few moments and then bounded off into the trees. It was gone in a few strides. Aelis was alone in the deep forest with the night falling, starving and cold. But suddenly she wasn't alone, nor was she hungry, and an odd warmth sprang up in her. She saw a sunrise in her mind, filling the forest with a crisp, clear light; she saw the track of the wolf in the darkness bright and clear. A rune had lit up inside her.

Aelis followed the track through the trees. It was night, she knew, and yet it was not night. The light in her mind made everything as clear as full day but it didn't quite banish the reality of the dark forest. It was as if she was walking through two forests at the same time, one light and one dark, existing equally in both.

She walked on and on, the perfumes of the forest all about her – wet earth and grass, the resin that clung to her hands from the tree trunks she touched as she passed. Moths moved in the dark; things burrowed and sighed in the loam and the deeper earth beneath it. As the sky moved from pitch to silver there was birdsong, warmth and spears of light shot through the trees.

It was just after dawn when she came upon the sleeping wolf. It had wedged itself against a fallen tree and covered itself with earth. Asleep, the creature did not seem to terrify the runes in the same way that it did when awake. Her mind was alive with the crawling and glimmering symbols. Aelis looked down at the pendant. Like the night that she could see as day, like the wolf she had seen as a man, it seemed two things. One was a stone with a wolf's head on it; the other was a pocket of darkness, as if torn from the night sky, much bigger than the pebble she saw in the real world.

She knew it for magic and she knew it for a sin, but the runes filled her with exhilaration. She felt stronger than she ever had in her life, though the nightmare land she had fallen into in her dreams as a young girl was coming into being about her, the trees seeming more like carvings than living things, the sky metal, more a roof than a natural creation, the grass sticking up like shards of dark glass. She was not afraid. She felt safe in that place between reality and hallucination with the runes as her guides.

She peered into the darkness that was the pebble and saw that she could not tell how big it was. It seemed as if it would fit into her hand but it was as wide as the stars. The world was a strange and beautiful place. The wolf seemed an entrancing thing, not frightening at all. It lay in the dusk like another long shadow among the shadows of the ancient trees. She tied the pendant around the wolf's neck and then lay down to sleep against its side, putting her head onto its flank, feeling safe in its animal warmth.

The creature did not wake – not that morning, nor that afternoon, nor in the evening when the shadows of the trees stretched towards her and bars of light spread from the setting sun. Night did not wake it, not the buzz of insects by its ears, nor the damp mist that clung to its fur in the dawn. The morning sun was strong but the wolf did not stir.

Aelis stayed beside it. Her clothes were just rags, but she did not feel cold nor scarcely hungry. The runes kept her warm. She sank into them, searching for them in the dark of her mind, learning how to find them at the little drop where consciousness becomes sleep, and to allow them to emerge to consume her. She was a horse racing under the sun, a sunset stretching fingers of light to the dark hills, a hawthorn bristling with spikes, a hailstorm battering the land, a river feeding and shaping the terrain that fed and shaped it.

In the evenings she sat by the wolf, watching the colours of the forest die their long deaths, greens, reds, purples and lilacs falling to grey under the dusk. But when night came, new colours were born – the brilliant silver of the moonstruck leaves, the inky blue of the far distance, the soft mauve light of things near to her. She had never seen nights like them, though she had dreamed of them often. She slept by the wolf, seeing herself as a shield, keeping him from harm, and woke to walk the woods, sometimes as herself, sometimes as an expression of a rune, to stand before a birch and see the light of spring burning within it.

She could not say how long she was there nor what she ate. The days grew longer but the day of her mind seemed never to end. She was the day, a warming force calling the woods to song, a thing that looked up to the night moon and saw itself reflected in its bright surface. She felt renewed. Berries stained her fingers; she had the taste of mushrooms in her mouth. Only sometimes, when drinking from a stream, would the cold hit her. She would look up into the wood and see the world as if it had just been made, shining new, green and brilliant.

The first to come were two boys, curious and fearful. She saw them in so many ways: their sweat-slick skin shining with life, the colours they brought splitting in her mind like light through a glass bead. She heard them as music, fragile and wavering as might be made by a child on a pipe. It was if her sight was itself attuned in a musical way, able to see in many registers, and to Aelis it appeared that each boy had a light inside him like a candle glow illuminating the darkness of his mortal flesh.

They returned with men in numbers, and the echo of her former self, the Lady Aelis to whom they were peril, went through her mind. The inner voice of panic that told her to run was like a noise in the distance, faint and almost inaudible. There were about forty of them – a robber band. It was evening, she realised. The dusk was dying in tonight and it was cold.

'They've been robbed before. Look at them.' It was her language, just. The men were Franks but not her brother's nor any ruler's. They were outlaws, some dressed in rags, others wearing finer stuff, obviously stolen.

'That one would be pretty enough with a good meal inside her.'

'She'd be pretty enough with something else inside her.

What are we waiting for? There are two good slaves here. Let's fuck her for a bit and then get them sold.' It was a young man who spoke, small and hard with skin baked brown by the sun. He had broken teeth and a torn ear, and seemed to Aelis to sizzle with colours and sounds – the green stains of mosses at his knees, gold pollen on his sleeves, a sound like burning wood that seemed to express his personality. He was fascinating to her.

She spoke:

> 'Alone I sat when the Old One sought me,
> That terror of gods, who gazed in my eyes:
> "What hast thou to ask? Why comest thou hither?"
> "Odin," said he, "I know you are from yourself
>   hidden."'

'Is that the Normans' tongue? She's a Viking slut. Danes! We'll get a good price for them.'

'We're far from the sea.' Another voice.

Aelis could sense its disquiet like a cold wind. She looked for the wolf behind her. There was no wolf, only the confessor lying naked on the ground. *Jehan? Where was the wolf?* But Jehan was not as she had known him. He was no longer afflicted but whole and handsome. She spoke again:

> 'One did I see in the wet woods bound,
> A lover of ill, and to Loki like.'

'This is sorcery,' said another. 'Kill her before she bewitches us.'

'That is not sorcery, or if it is she doesn't prosper on it,' said yet another.

The rhyme spoke through Aelis again. The poem was like a wind and she was just a reed through which it sounded.

'The giantess old in Ironwood sat,
In the east, and bore the brood of Fenrir;
Among these one in monster's guise
Would soon steal the sun from the sky.
There feeds he full on the flesh of the dead,
And the home of the gods he reddens with blood;
Dark grows the sun, and in summer soon
Come mighty storms: would you know yet more?'

Night was falling. The trees were dark and a wind was in them. How long had the storm been coming? She couldn't tell. Fat drops of rain fell cold on her skin. The dying sun turned the stormclouds to gold and lead, and the forest seemed to glow around her.

'Let's just take them and go. It's going to be a filthy night.'

'I'll have my fun first – it'll warm me up.' The man with the broken teeth and a torn ear had a knife.

Her pulse raced and she felt the blood drain from her face. But he seemed so fragile, such a delicate bloom, like a wild flower she could pick at any minute to amuse herself for a moment before casting it away. She felt so strange, as if she existed in many places at once, her mind a wide and several thing.

He touched her.

Aelis was in the forest and not in the forest, in the caverns of her mind where the runes shone and sang and not in that place. *Where else?* she wondered. In the moon garden of her youth, where the scent of jasmine lay upon the dew and the night air warmed her as she wandered barefoot and dreaming. She saw a tiny candle in a recess in a wall. There were many lamps there, now she came to look. She reached out and extinguished the nearest one to her.

The man in front of her in the forest, the hard young man with the broken teeth, one hand on his knife, the other loosening his trousers, dropped dead.

She felt confusion run through the outlaws, a rustle of

thoughts that passed through their minds like the first wind of autumn through the woods of summer.

A couple of the outlaws dropped to their knees and touched the corpse's face. The man had been dead for only a moment but was already cold. Then weapons were drawn and a word was on their lips: 'Witch.' In the moonlit garden she moved her hand; a breeze blew and all the candles went out.

The rain came down hard, turning the leaves to little drums pattering out a rhythm so pleasing it made her want to dance. She went to Jehan, sat him up and lifted his face to the falling rain.

'Wake now,' she said. 'I have washed the wolf away.'

He opened his mouth to the clouds and blinked as the raindrops, each one as big as a berry, burst upon him.

He turned to her and put his hand to her hair. 'It is me,' he said, 'as I was, and as I am. I have travelled so far to find you.'

She knew. In that instant she knew they had lived before and had been lovers whose love had outlived death. What had been her name? What his? She could not recall. The words came to her unbidden: 'And I have waited so long for you to be here.'

Aelis kissed him and lay down with him among the corpses of the wild men and for the first time since she was a child she did not feel alone.

60 Thought and Memory

Hugin looked down at the body of his sister on the beach. He had taken her head from her shoulders with a single blow and it lay washed by the surf five paces away from where he squatted by her head. He did not go to it.

The enchantment she had laid upon him had broken when he put on the Wolfstone, he thought. But in truth it had been weakened even before that – when he had seen the lady's face at the river as she struggled and froze in the water. Why hadn't he killed Aelis then? He had thought it due to curiosity. He had wondered if she could drown, given her place in the schemes of the gods. They had set her a crueller fate than drowning, he'd thought, but would they relent and let her die of cold in those waters? Or would he, Odin's servant, take her?

There was another reason he hadn't killed Aelis as soon as he had the chance – he knew that now. He had sought her in his dreams, though the witch he called his sister had usurped her place. Had he sensed that deceit when he looked at Aelis struggling in the river?

Frozen and parched in the mountain cave, groping in the sightless dark, striving to hold on to sanity, to personality, he had dreamed such dreams. He had been a raven flying on the breeze, hunting the wide land for something he could sense but not name. And he had been in that strange avenue of trees, alongside the river and the wall where the ivy grew and where the small shrine of candles shone in the night. And he had searched for someone he could not name through the dead air of the constricting tunnels, above the mountainsides in the wind and the sun, and under the moon where the water was crumpled lead and the bark of the trees seemed shot with quartz. Always his sister had been there, under the ivy, by the shrine. She had made him believe he was bound to her eternally. She had entered the garden of his dreams and taken the place of Aelis.

Hugin felt very bitter. He had killed for his sister, abandoned his home among the monks, taken her to the mountains and lived as a wild animal, shivering through the winters, soaked in the storms, holding her hand in the dark as the first hallucinations came upon her, following her as the magic seemed to possess her, hearing strange voices in a language that was foreign to him but eventually became more familiar than his own. The gods of the Norsemen were speaking to them, and in ritual, privation and darkness he began to understand them. Still, he wanted to leave.

'Let us go back,' he had said, 'away from this wild woman and her sorceries. Let's go to some lord or farmer and offer ourselves as workers, profess ourselves displaced by war. Let us leave her. Let us leave this magic.'

But his sister had sat, stirring the pebbles in front of her with her feet, looking out from the mountain over the valleys. Then she had swallowed the mushrooms, gone back to the dark, and he, impelled by their bond, had gone with her, had joined her in her sufferings, given his mind to magic as her protector.

He had seen, crammed into the tiny space of the cave, sealed in by rocks that the wild woman piled over its mouth, he had seen. The god had come to him, lain next to him pale in the darkness – the one-eyed god of the shrieking runes, his face blank with madness, the strange hangman's knot at his neck. Louis – he had still been Louis then – had touched his skin and found it cold. And though the god was dead, his mind was a web into which Louis felt he might fall. He shrank from the corpse god in the tunnel, pressed himself into the wall, but when he opened his eyes, the rocks at the entrance of the cave had been moved away; the weak light of the misty mountain was coming in, and it was only his sister who lay next to him on the stony floor.

When he emerged from the cave he was weeping, but his sister came to him, told him that the path to magic was not easy.

'What was it in the darkness?' he'd asked, but his sister said nothing; she just sat holding his hand. Then she had gone back to the dark, and though he loved her, he could not follow her in.

The wild woman had come and sat by him. 'He is coming here –' she tapped the ground with her foot '– to die by the teeth of the wolf. The god you met in the darkness will take flesh on earth to fight and die against his eternal enemy. When he does, you die, your sister dies. Many people.'

He tried to ask why but he was raw-headed and tired. A feeling like grief was inside him.

The woman just looked into his eyes.

'How shall I prevent this?' he said.

'Serve him.'

'I don't understand.'

'At the centre of the universe sit the weavers of fate, the Norns, three women beneath the world tree Yggdrasil. All the nine worlds are beholden to them – gods and men. The god is doomed to die at the twilight of the gods. The Norns require it. So the god offers them many deaths in many ages, rehearsing the end to please those fateful women and forestall his own annihilation. You are caught in that grim cycle, part of a ritual the king of gods offers to the fates. Your sister too. You are destined to die.'

'How do you know this?'

She put her hand to the burn on her face, to her blood-red eye. 'I gave this and lifetimes of silence to see it. I too am caught in the schemes of the gods.'

'How can I prevent it?'

'Protect your sister. While she lives it will be harder for the god to come to earth.'

'Why?'

'Some things, Hugin, must be taken as a matter of faith.'

The name seemed resonant to him, to speak to his core. He turned from her and went hunting on the mountain. The thing in the tunnel had wakened something in him. His eyes were sharper, his hand surer, his step quieter. When he drew back his bow and let fly, he couldn't miss – hare, sheep, even wolves fell to his arrows. He was strong, and when men came, they learned to bring tribute and requests for healing, rather than axes and swords.

He would sit in the dawn watching the darkness drain into the valleys as the sunlight freed the gold in the gorse, and he sat in the evening as the tide of shadow rose from the rivers to submerge the hills once more.

In the winter they built a fire in the mouth of the cave and sheltered from the mountain winds, huddling together beneath furs and fleeces.

The wild woman had sung a song in her native tongue, of two brothers who the gods had destined to kill each other, and he had understood it. The god of the north had awakened the speech of the north in him, connected him to something he had been when he had lived before and that language had been his birthright. The brothers had to dance to a song the gods sang, a song that foretold the death of the gods. The boys' fate was to die as the gods would die on their final day, by the teeth of the wolf. Their mother hid the boys – one with the wolves in the woods of the east, one with a family in the Valley of Songs – hoping to keep them apart. But a woman, within whom lived an ancient rune feared by the gods, threatened to draw the boys together, so the mother had sent one of them to kill her. He had done this, and though it saddened the boy, his lands and his family prospered.

The darkness of the cave, the presence of the god, the starving and the freezing, had seemed to knock Louis's mind sideways. The song seemed almost as real as the mountain, the cold and the mist, real as his sister's affinity for that terrible cave. It was about him, he knew.

'He is waking in you,' said the woman, 'this . . .' she touched his arm '... and this ...' she touched his eyes to indicate his sight '... are him. In you. They are him. You are a raven, flying on the wind.'

'And Ysabella? What is happening to her?'

'She is learning what she carries inside her.'

'She's having a child?'

'No child. The runes.'

He had seen them, the strange symbols that glowed and twisted in the blackness of the cave, the runes that chimed and sang, brought light, rain and the smell of the harvest into the tiny space.

'I'll go to her.' He turned and made to go into the back of the cave, to the tunnel in the rock, to remove the pile of stones that he had used to block the passage when he had left.

'No.' The woman shook her head. 'The god walks beside her. She is beyond your help. She will be your guide now. When the weather lifts, I'll be gone.'

'Where?'

'Away. I have other work to do to prevent your death. I will leave you a gift.'

'What gift?'

'Something even the wolf fears. When the god is dead, it will kill the wolf. Treat it carefully – it is poisoned with the nightmares of witches.'

Then she had said nothing, just sat staring past the fire, into the mountain mists. He had slept, and in the morning the wild woman had gone. In her place was the sword, the slim curve of steel in its black scabbard. He had drawn it and watched it shine in the morning sun. An echo of his previous life came to him. He thought that from the sale of such a sword he could eat for years, live in comfort if he could find some town or village where he could spend his money without coming to the attention of the nobles. Perhaps he could become a merchant? He had seen the pack trains labouring up through Lombardy on their way to the Frankish kingdoms. They were free men, those merchants, not tied to any count or margrave.

But then his sister had emerged from the cave to sit filthy by the fire. He made her stew, fed her roots he had foraged and baked and tried to make her comfortable, but she had only stayed long enough to regain her strength. Then she had gone back.

He could not bear her to face what was in there alone, so he had gone with her and when he emerged was something different.

He had left Louis sleeping in the darkness. Now he was Hugin, sharp-eyed and strong, bound to the god who had come to him in the tomb dark of the cave. Ritual and self-denial became the basis of his life. He tended to his sister, found the mushrooms and roots she needed for her trances, hunted, fed and grew ever stronger. It was as if the plants of the mountain could speak to him. He knew which to pick to cure, which to send himself spiralling into trances of gods and monsters. Munin shared the magic she dug from the darkness, allowing the god to touch and bless her brother. In the sightless space, the air wet and the rock cold, Hugin felt the corpse god hold him and whisper his name: 'Odin.' Hugin knew what that meant. He had been claimed as a servant of death.

He saw things too. The cave seemed to grow and to flicker with the light of candles. He stood before a gigantic wolf, sheltering his sister from its teeth. He saw a huge warrior, one-eyed and fierce, thrusting a spear into the wolf on the final day. It was coming, he knew, the wolf to kill the god, drawn on by a terrible rune. He saw it writhing in the air in front of him and he knew that it lived inside a person, as the runes seemed to live inside his sister. It hissed with threat like the cobras which the merchants had brought to the monastery to delight the monks.

They had been on the mountain four summers when his sister emerged from the cave and gestured to the valley with her eyes. His bond to her was now so strong it was without words. He only had to touch her to feel what she felt and see what she saw.

'It is waking in her,' she said, 'the rune that draws on the god-killer.' He knew she was talking about the wolf and the girl who led him to his fate.

'Then she must die,' Hugin said, as much in his mind as with his voice.

'Yes.'

Munin had stood up, her body frail and her hair wild, and she had headed down towards the valley. Hugin had followed, wary. He had the sword, he had his bow and he had a spear he had cut and shaped in the fire, but he had not been off the mountain since he was a boy. They went down through the pine and the fir to a wood of birch and ash, where they stayed for a season, his sister calling the birds to her, using her agony as a gateway to insight. Hugin had feared every dusk, black wings falling out of the summer sky to tear and rip at her flesh. Norsemen were in the country, killing and burning, but when they discovered Hugin and his sister in the wood, they bowed down before them and asked for blessing. Then they stayed to protect them, to watch as the birds came down on the body of the sorceress.

Hugin had made a shield for her eyes with wood and twine, but she couldn't find the woman who held the howling rune, the rune that would draw the wolf. He begged her not to do what he knew she intended. He put himself in her place, suffering and screaming under the beaks of the birds, but it was no good. The dead god wanted more, so she had given her eyes, and Munin had found her. She would be in Paris when the town burned. They had travelled to tell Sigfrid his destiny lay at the little town on the Seine and the king had chosen to believe them.

Then the wolfman had begun to harry them. He seemed untouchable by Munin's magic, though it never occurred to the Raven or his sister that he had the Wolfstone, the fragment of the rock called Scream against which all magic was useless. He was not, however, untouchable by Hugin's sword. Twice

Raven thought he had killed the wolfman but twice he had returned to oppose him.

On the riverbank, where he had caught Aelis, he had fought the wolfman for the final time. Had he known it, he would face a tougher struggle — with himself as he had been and would wish to be. When he had found Aelis something had moved inside him, as if he — Hugin, servant of death — was a clay figure which the sight of the lady had cracked to reveal something else entirely. When he had put on the Wolfstone the Raven had fallen to dust and he, Louis, had stood in the dawn light of the forest with the little merchant at his side and known that his life had been a long deception. His memory was clear now. There had been no fever in his sister when they were young. She had killed her parents with magic and bound him to her will. He had not even been her brother; he was just a monastery boy the wild woman had used.

The wild woman who had demanded he kill the abbot for the cure had actually demanded no such thing. The girl, the little girl, had entered his mind, made him love her and do her will. The wild woman was her servant, not her teacher. The girl had known what was in her — death, suffering, terrible trials — and how to awaken it. And she had brought him with her on that journey. For what?

Ysabella — Munin — had come into his dreams and displaced Aelis of Paris and the women she had been in lives before. But the enchantment had crumbled and Hugin now understood clearly what he had seen during his travels with the dead god. Aelis was the woman he had died for when he had lived before. The thing that had called itself his sister had taken her place and stolen his love for her. And he had helped her, gone willingly into the darkness with her, lain at her side and journeyed in his mind to places where she might deepen her enchantment. All that had crumbled away.

He had lived before, he knew, and he had died before — for that girl he had pursued and harried, tortured and nearly killed. Under a witch's enchantment he had betrayed a bond that was stronger than death.

He sensed the true identity of his sister and who the wild woman had been. He felt that if only his thoughts would clear a little more he would know their names. But they did not clear. All he knew was that, as Munin's enchantment faded, hate had come into his heart where there had once been love. She had moved to a different agenda, unguessable motivations. Had she wanted to die? Well, now she had.

He guessed what had happened. Munin had set out to control the runes, believing that by suffering and devotion she could possess them without them destroying her, and could devise strategies that might let her live. He had no doubt she had not wanted to die at first. But the eight runes that she had taken from the dead god had lit up in her and called for their sisters, and their longing was not for life but for death. Munin had lost herself in those rituals and woken something else – the fragment of a god that sought to be whole and to die, sacrificing himself to himself, slaughtered in the realm of men so he might live in the realm of gods.

But why had she needed him, Louis? Why keep him so close? He knew that he would die violently; she had foreseen it. But was there a purpose to that death? She had wanted the god to come to earth in her and to die, to have the knowledge of death. What was his part in that? It didn't matter. She had wanted Aelis dead. So that meant he would strive to keep her alive.

Hugin knelt at the edge of the sea and watched Ofaeti return from the monastery with two horses laden with arms and armour. The Viking wore a long Norman cloak with the richer, shorter cloak of a Frankish nobleman over the top. The rest of his clothes too were Frankish – a blue silk tunic with a vest of ratskin around his shoulders. At his belt he wore a fine sword. Ofaeti might almost have been a Frank, but no Frank was ever that big or that red-haired. He looked like what he was – a pirate in stolen finery. The merchant was behind him, similarly dressed, leading a string of six horses.

Ofaeti waved to Raven and called, 'I am ready to fulfil my oath to the lady.'

Free of Munin's enchantment, the Raven's mind had fallen in on itself through the magical gateways that had opened in the cave at the corpse god's side. An image came to him. He was on a mountainside; he was holding a woman's hands, unable to look into her eyes for fear his love for her would show and prompt a rejection. He heard his own voice in his mind, an echo from a lifetime before: *I will always protect you.*

He nodded to the big Viking. 'And I am ready to fulfil mine,' he said.

'Let's go and bag us a wolf, then,' said Ofaeti. He took one last look at the beached ships, shook his head and followed the tracks of the monster across the wet sand and into the trees, the Raven and Leshii close behind.

61 The Devouring Now

Aelis sat next to Jehan in the long light of evening, her fair hair a halo in the low sun. All the colours of autumn were about them, though Jehan was not cold. He had a Lombard's thick cloak around his shoulders, a good woollen shirt on his body, fine trousers and good boots. They were not the first people the wild men had attacked, though they were the last.

A smudge of memory was in his mind – faint echoes of distant bells, the chanting of prayers, Brother Guillaume's incessant coughing during mass, the feeling of restriction, of limbs that wanted to move but couldn't. Other recollections seemed sharper: bright water, a green riverbank and a girl, her hair long, almost white beneath the sun, laughing and splashing. He had loved her for so long, he knew, missed her for so long. Yet none of it mattered. He was there, beside her, the past and the future swallowed by the ravenous present, the sensual instant, the thrill of her touch, her eyes blue against the scarlet autumn, the forest hanging in a million wet jewels of light.

He touched the stone at his neck and she moved her hand onto his to tell him to leave it where it was. A memory of himself came back to him and he had the strong urge to cast it away as an idolatrous image, but he did not. He felt the wolf he had been like a skin he had not quite shed. When he moved he sometimes seemed impelled by a raging force and he had the urge to run snarling through the trees. The stone, though, would save him. Some sense told him this was his lifeline to sanity, the key that had released him from the slaughterhouse of his thoughts.

They hunted together – Aelis taking one of the bandits' bows, Jehan using stealth and surprise to kill a deer with a spear. That night they cooked the meat and lay in a clearing under the forest stars.

Jehan had a sense of what he had been – a man who had loved a woman so strongly that he had come back from the dead to find her – but could not put it into words. His connection to Aelis was based on a feeling worse than hunger, closer to the fear of suffocation. She was the air to him, and he could not think that he would ever be apart from her.

They had watched the men look for them throughout the summer – the fat one like a giant, the crowman and the merchant – but they had not allowed themselves to be seen, just moved into the trees. The men had stayed a long time searching the woods but had not found them. The lady walked among them unseen, sitting by their fire, stroking their horses, even eating their food, before coming back to join Jehan. She did not want them to be discovered, so they would not be discovered.

Then one day when the air was cold Aelis had kissed him and taken his hand, leading him through the trees for miles. They came to a house, a low hut with a turf roof. No one was inside, though the remains of a life were there – a table overturned, a chair smashed and a straw bed. Someone had left quickly, and Jehan did not wonder why. The forest was a lawless place and the lives lived there were precarious. Aelis found a bow and made a fire for the hearth; Jehan laid down the pack he was carrying and opened it to find the meat and roots inside. Then they cooked their food and sat on the bed late into the evening, falling asleep in each other's arms.

In the hut Jehan slept and dreamed of nothing – not God, not the wolf, not the cripple he had been, the man he was nor the woman by his side. He was at peace.

He awoke, feeling the late autumn cold on his skin. She had been up before him and was out collecting mushrooms. He heard her at the door, coming down the low step, putting the basket she had found in the hut down on the table.

He stretched out on the bed and opened his eyes. At first he thought the sunlight had bleached his vision away. But there was no sunlight. He was inside.

'You are awake?' It was Aelis's voice.

Jehan blinked and blinked again.

'Jehan?'

Jehan swallowed. Then he put his hand to the stone at his neck.

'I cannot see,' he said.

62 An Impediment to the Journey

They'd searched the forest for far too long. The sorcerer and Ofaeti were relatively young men. Not so Leshii. He would have found the going hard even if he'd had any enthusiasm for the hunt, but with so much plunder in his bags, he was in a state of terror the whole time. The woods were full of bandits and worse. Who knew what monsters lurked in the deep wood? Ofaeti and the Raven had been puzzled and frustrated. They found the wolf's tracks, even its strange spoor, but never saw the beast itself.

For a couple of days they lay low, aware there were forest men in the area. Leshii had six horses with him, trailing behind his calm, reliable mule. Ofaeti had wanted to cut them free, saying they would draw any bandit with their mess and their noise. The Raven, though, had waved away his objections.

'Let the merchant keep his plunder,' he'd said. 'Our fates are tight woven; woodsmen will not bring us to death.'

So it seemed the next day, when they came upon the bodies.

Ofaeti had bent to examine the dead men, while Leshii checked their bags and pouches.

'These men did not die warriors' deaths,' said Ofaeti.

'Plague?' said Leshii, backing away from a corpse.

'In a circle, all at once?' said Ofaeti. 'A strange plague that does that. Is this Seid magic, sorcerer?'

The Raven shrugged. He crouched in front of the body of a bandit and touched his face.

'Not your magic?' said Ofaeti.

'My magic is of the body and the fight. Not this,' said Hugin.

'So what is this?'

The Raven tapped his tongue against his teeth. 'Women's magic, but I have never seen so many taken.'

'Your sister could do this?' said Leshii to the Raven.

Ofaeti laughed. 'I'd call it the rarest troll work if any woman could stick her head back on her shoulders and kill these men. We might have ended the siege of Paris and been drunk for a year on Frankish wine if she'd pulled that trick on the ramparts.'

'I have seen one man killed this way but never as many,' said Hugin. He sat on his haunches, staring out into the trees. After a while he said, 'The witch is dead – you saw me cut her head from her shoulders. This is troll work but it can't be hers.'

'Then what?' said Leshii.

'Something,' said Hugin. His face was pale.

'We should stay here and see if it returns,' said Ofaeti.

'Agreed,' said Hugin. 'Something capable of this might be able to find the lady.'

Leshii rubbed at his ears as if he couldn't believe they were working properly. 'We stay here to meet something that has killed forty men and left them cold on the ground?'

'We need to find the lady. If there is a witch here, we should talk to her,' said Hugin.

'And if she kills us?'

Ofaeti shook his head. 'Why are you afraid to die, little merchant?'

'Is that something that requires explanation? Why are you not?'

'I will live on in the halls of the All Father, to battle all day and feast all night. It's not right for a man to love his life too much because he must lose it one day. Fear of its loss poisons its living. Death is fun, looked at the right way.'

'I am not afraid to die,' said Leshii, 'but I am a merchant as you are a warrior, and I do not want to die before I have done great deeds, won caskets of gold and built great houses. I live as a little man, I would not die as one.'

'Well spoken,' said Ofaeti, 'but wrong. Even the greatest merchant, surrounded by money, women and cattle, is nothing to the man of war. Gold is superior to steel in all regards except one – when it is held in the hand. There the deeds of steel outvalue those of gold a hundred-fold.'

'You are learned in the ways of steel,' said Leshii, 'and for that reason I shall bow to your knowledge and call you the argument's master.'

Leshii knew the Norsemen and how they argued. Ofaeti's words had become elevated, even poetic, as all his kinsmen's did when they considered themselves in a contest of wits. It was as well to let the warrior win, he thought, and praise him for his skill with words.

'So you are happy to stay here?'

'Delighted,' said Leshii. 'May the lord of lightning forbid that I should be afraid of being murdered in a violent and unpleasant fashion.'

Ofaeti sat back on a log and scratched his head. 'You are a clever man, merchant. Anyone who can trade without the implied threat of violence to help his haggling has a fair tongue in his head.'

'My fair tongue has often been aided by bodyguards' fair swords,' said Leshii.

'They speak in a language all men can under—'

'Quiet!' The Raven held up his hand. 'Can you hear?'

'What?'

'Laughter,' said Hugin.

Leshii turned his head from side to side, trying to catch any sound. 'I hear nothing.'

'There is laughter here,' said the Raven, 'and it is her.'

'Who?'

'Aelis.'

'Is she with the wolf?' said Ofaeti.

'This is some tree spirit trying to ensnare you,' said Leshii. 'This is—'

And Leshii heard it. A breath, no more, but it was her, he knew it.

Ofaeti's sword was out and he was looking around.

'Enchantment?' said Leshii.

'Seid,' said Ofaeti. Leshii had never seen the big man nervous before and that made the merchant very scared indeed.

'What is Seid?'

'Magic. Women's magic.'

'Weak then?' Leshii said the words knowing the answer. The Norsemen held their female seers in great regard, he knew.

Ofaeti just gave him a look that seemed to question if the merchant had finally lost the little sense he believed him to have.

And then they saw her. She stepped out of the liquid air of the evening, shimmering into view and disappearing like a trick of the light. She was frightening in her beauty, something too perfect to be of the earth. Aelis, but changed and strange.

'Lady, we are your protectors,' said Leshii, Helgi's reward coming to mind. She had grown so beautiful that Helgi would set him up in his own palace if he brought her to him. The thought suddenly nauseated him. Could he not look on a woman like that without his thoughts immediately turning to selling her? He shook himself. What was happening to the practical man of profit and loss?

She vanished and his head was clear. There was a sound in the distance, the neigh of a horse.

Leshii glanced to his right. The mule was alone, browsing the grass next to Leshii's treasure of swords. 'Our horses,' he said, 'have gone.'

63 A Choice for Jehan

Aelis put her hand to Jehan's head. He was cold but sweating. His eyes toured the hut in circles as if they could make up in industry what they lacked in effectiveness.

'You have a fever.'

'Yes.'

'It will pass.'

But it didn't pass, and Aelis sat watching Jehan weaken on the straw bed. She was not alone. The runes were with her, breathing and singing inside, floating at the edge of her vision. She reached up towards one and allowed it to settle in her hands like a snowflake. It was shaped like a cup, and when she held it she thought it was deep enough to hold the sea. She peered into its depths and saw the cause of Jehan's fever. The stone. She parted her hands and the rune vanished. Then she took the stone from his neck and set it on the table.

She sat beside him, listening to the chiming, the low wind moan and the ocean crash of the runes. She slept. When she awoke Jehan was gone and it was night.

Aelis felt no alarm but followed him, his trail clear to her in the moonlight of the silver wood. She was no tracker, but the magic inside her told her the way to go, or, rather, made any other way to go seem ridiculous and awkward, like someone who had turned right out of her door to her flock every morning for thirty years might find it strange to have to suddenly turn left.

He was among the corpses, the rotting dead men. She guessed he had come to them by smell because she knew wolves find the dead an irresistible lure.

The confessor was sitting on the ground, his blind eyes moving in mad circles, as if searching for some elusive scrap of light. The head of one of the bandits was on his lap.

'Do not feed, Jehan. Let the wolf starve inside you.'

Jehan was mumbling to himself in Latin, making the sign of the cross over the head of the dead man.

Aelis recognised the Office for the Dead, translating the words in her mind, as she had been used to doing in church ever since she was a girl: *The fear of death confounds me. The cords of death entangled me, the anguish of the grave came upon me, I was overcome by trouble and sorrow, then I called on the name of the Lord. O Lord, save me!*

The confessor fell to weeping, holding the head of the corpse as he might have held the head of a lover, as he had held her head.

'Jehan, come away from this.'

'You are a sorceress. You have bewitched me!'

His voice was full of anguish rather than hatred.

'I have not bewitched you. My love, it has always been the same between us. We are here, flowers of the flesh to wax and then die. But we, like the flowers, only know a seeming death. We go on to bloom again for ever. I have seen it – the runes have shown me.'

'There is no future life, only the resurrection of the flesh through Christ,' said Jehan. He collapsed sideways on to the ground, coughing. 'I will not be this ... devourer.'

'Nor need you be. The fever will pass. Come back and be my love.'

'It will not pass. It is the stone or the monster. I will weaken or I will eat.'

Aelis looked inside herself. Who was she? Could she really recall? There was a memory of the girl who would have been repulsed by the sight in front of her but it was like the smoke of a campfire in the hills – distant, faint, then gone. Then she saw herself clearly. She was the thing that stood beside him. He made her what she was, like the sea makes the land the shore.

'God will not let you suffer like this. There is a prince in the east, a sorcerer. Let us go to him.'

'I will not consort with the worshippers of idols.' Jehan's religion had returned, it seemed, along with his infirmity.

'The magic of the stone saved you from being the wolf. Why cannot magic save you now?'

'God has made me weak and set this trial to punish me. I will wear no pagan stone, but the wolf will go unfed, muzzled by my will.'

A caul of sweat was about his head, his hands and voice shook.

'And yet here you are, among the corpses.'

Aelis looked for the runes to help her, to heal him, make him well. But in his presence they seemed to tremble and wither and the sound she heard in her head was of that of searing and burning. She went away from him, walking through the moon-lit forest, the trees shining white like a foretaste of winter. She wanted to help him, to comfort him, but she knew that Jehan would only ever find his own way, or rather God's way.

When she returned, Jehan was still kneeling among the corpses, drooling out his psalms. There was blood on his lips and the corpse in front of him was torn and ripped, its guts spilled.

'I cannot command it. I am a man, not an angel. I cannot command it. It is my love for you that has weakened me.'

'I would be your strength.'

'Our love has been a sin against my deepest vows. God has turned his face against me.'

'How can He hate you for loving?'

Jehan had tears in his eyes. 'I do not know, but He does.'

Still she felt his will, the strength of his soul.

'What will you do?'

'The choice is infirmity or abomination, the unholy and pro-scribed use of magic or to be the victim of magic. One way or another I am bound for hell. The choice that faces my mortal body is its pain or the world's. In imitation of Christ, I choose my own. I will be what I was. Tie on the stone.'

She put it about his neck. As she did so, the runes returned to her, shining, chiming, melodious. 'You can remove it when you become too weak.'

'I will not remove it.' He swallowed hard and stiffened his jaw.

'Then what of us?'

'It cannot be. It cannot be.' Tears were in his eyes and he was panting great reedy breaths like a man dying of consumption.

'Whatever you become, I will be by your side,' she said. 'I will take you to Helgi. He will make us both whole again, free us from the magic that holds us in its grip.'

She reached out with her mind to the horse rune, its golden lustre colouring her sight, turning the silver trees to a breathing bronze.

'We will need,' she said, 'an animal.'

64 A Seat at the Oar

It quickly became clear that there was no way through by land for Leshii, Ofaeti and Hugin. The road to the east was alive with hostile warriors – Franks and Norsemen hard at war with each other. If they went far enough someone from either side would decide to kill them for their possessions.

The rain poured down and the three struck for the coast under heavy skies, Ofaeti and Hugin trudging through the mud and Leshii riding the mule. There had been no sign of the horses. When the weather cleared the land seemed fresh and there was smoke on the breeze. This was pleasant to Hugin. On his high mountain he had often caught the scent of fires in the valleys below and wondered what it would be like to live his life around home and hearth.

The Raven knew that when Sigfrid had died a large contingent of the Vikings besieging Paris had decided to head off and try their luck in the lands of Arnulf, the East Frankish king, so that was where they headed, hoping to pick up a boat. There should be either local Frankish craft to be bought or stolen and the chance of Viking ships with room for passengers.

He had quit the woods in frustration, though his every instinct told him that was where she was. When all sign of her or the wolf had ceased he had given in and decided to try with Helgi, reasoning that she may still seek out the prince. And if she wasn't there? If he was right in his suspicions she had to be. Could he kill Helgi? Perhaps, if the god did not yet know himself. But should he? Perhaps it would be better to protect Helgi from the wolf. But the god had a way of finding his chosen death, he suspected. So what options did that leave him? Find Aelis and protect her from the wolf, from the god and whatever other perils lay in her path. Defy the will of fate.

Ofaeti followed, happy to let Hugin take the lead. Leshii was just glad to be out of the forest. Searching there had been a fool's errand, he thought. And whatever waited for him at Ladoga, he would be glad to see home again, out of the forest in the cold autumn.

A couple of weeks into their journey they crested a small hill and saw a wide marshy plain laid out before them with a town tucked into the crook of a river. The buildings were smouldering, a banner of smoke hanging over them in the windless air. Even at a distance Hugin could see that a terrible battle had taken place.

The town was large and circular with tall and grassy ramparts. Twenty longboats were moored in front of it, and people were just visible, working among them, wading or using small boats, dragging things out of the river onto the swampy ground that bordered it. Grey light, grey water, Hugin had difficulty seeing what it was they were moving. Then his eyes focused and he saw bodies.

'The Franks have held out,' he said.

'A cold welcome for Northmen here, I think,' said Ofaeti.

The Raven nodded.

'Arnulf of Carinthia's a different man to Charles the Fat,' said Leshii.

'I've heard of him,' said Ofaeti, 'a man with glory to his name. It's said that if he was the emperor in the west instead of fat Charles then we'd have slimmer pickings by far.'

'Only pickings here for crows,' said Hugin. He noticed Ofaeti giving him a funny look. 'There are plenty of boats down there. If we can steal or buy one then we can catch the fleet as it retreats.'

'If I had but eight of my beserkers we'd take one of those drakkar and be away as rich men,' said Ofaeti.

'A river barge would be better,' said Hugin. 'We'll go down tonight.'

'A good plan,' said Ofaeti.

When the night came little fires sprang up across the plain.

On an island in the river a feast seemed to be taking place. Torches were everywhere – on the island and on the boats that shuttled between the town and the celebration.

The three moved off the hill into a network of tiny hedged fields. Luckily there was a good path, and as they passed along they heard sounds of rejoicing from every little farm. It was late in the year; the Norsemen hadn't burned the fields and the harvest was in. People had reason to be happy. It was cold, but the three men moved quickly and didn't feel it. The path led to the raised riverbank.

'Merchant, you can do the talking,' said Hugin.

The Raven and Ofaeti watched from a distance until Leshii had struck his bargain, then approached, their heads cowled. The Franks who had sold Leshii the boat watched the odd figures climb aboard. Strangers should in theory have been reported to the lord, but the people had been hungry during the Viking siege and the money was welcome. The merchant had bought a good-sized river boat with oars and a mast that Ofaeti shook in a disapproving way. The Viking said nothing, though. The Franks were within earshot, and the Frankish clothes he had taken from the outlaws were a thin disguise.

A greasy moon put a smear of light onto the clouds and visibility, though not perfect, was good enough for them to set off immediately, so they got the mule on board.

Ofaeti took the oars, and they pushed off out into the current. The boat slipped forward through the water with the flow towards the sea. Progress was steady, although every once in a while an oar would snag on a floating corpse or the boat would bump something. Ofaeti smiled and said, 'A bit late for swimming, isn't it?'

Leshii kept his eyes on his feet and the Raven was silent. He knew what Munin had prophesied for him, and there, in the faces of the dead men looming like pale fish under the weak moon, he saw his future. Death by water. Given the choice he would never have gone by boat, but he had travelled that way before and intended to go east under sail if he could. He had a great destiny, Munin had said. But she had lied about so much. Perhaps he was destined to die in a stupid way – a fall from a boat, a spear from a villager. The fact of his death did not concern him, only that he would not be there to protect Aelis from her fate. He had died for her before. He saw the teeth of the wolf coming towards him, heard her screams in that tight little cavern where he had faced the creature. It wouldn't be like that this time, he knew. Death by water.

Dawn came up under a slate sky. There was a little wind and Ofaeti put up the sail. The current was with them and they made good progress. The river fed into another bigger one and they kept with its flow, heading for the sea. All around them the land was burned – houses and crops reduced to nothing.

They tried to buy food but the people were destitute. Their farms and houses had been smashed and those who remained were just haunting their old lives, not living them. So the three went hungry.

When it got too dark to see they pulled into the bank. The Raven lit a fire, Leshii let the mule stretch its legs, and they sat neither eating nor speaking until they slept. The next day was the same. The Vikings had not had it all their own way, even before their defeat at the upriver town. Norse heads adorned spikes at one farm, and Ofaeti had to be talked out of going ashore to avenge the injustice. It was one thing for a man to be left for the crows where he lay, another to flaunt his death in that way.

On they went, the sky grey, the air spotting with rain.

'I had not thought we had come this far inland,' said Leshii.

'The forest is difficult to read,' said Ofaeti.

The current was faster now so Ofaeti took down the sail but the boat did not feel steady 'This is not boatbuilding,' he said; 'this is throwing wood in a pile, nailing it together and hoping it floats. The Franks should stick to their horses.'

Finally a bay, broad and lovely, the iron clouds lighting up with the dusk.

'The sun forges a blade of clouds,
The oath wind fills our sails.'

'I didn't have you down as a poet,' said Leshii to Ofaeti.

'A warrior must be able to do the brave deed, but he must also be able to immortalise it, to have his sons sing it for ever.'

Hugin nodded. 'Such things allow our sons to honour us. I'm glad you have this talent, Ofaeti. You will sing a song of our adventures for me to hear in future lives.'

Leshii had more pressing concerns. 'Can this thing take us all the way?'

Ofaeti shook his head. 'It's not an ocean vessel; it's hardly even a river vessel. It'll be swamped by any decent-sized wave. But, trust me, there will be northern men here. After a battle like that, someone will have a damaged ship to repair; someone will need to replenish his crew with slaves or be waiting for stragglers. They will be here and not far.'

They disembarked and camped, and in the morning abandoned the boat and headed east. They'd walked half the morning when they found themselves above a little cove. There on the beach was a longship, men working on its steering oar at the stern. It was a big ship, long and low to the water, but its figurehead had been removed. There were only about twenty Vikings, three of them clearly wounded and laid out on the sand.

'This is our ship,' said Ofaeti and started to make his way down to the cove.

'Hold, Frankish man!' The Vikings had spotted him. 'Know that we are ready for death but still ready to charge dearly for our lives. No horse can you bring against us here and must fight on your feet like a man.' The man who spoke was tall and thin. He'd picked up an axe with one hand, though the other hung limp at his side and Hugin guessed it was broken.

'Brothers,' shouted Ofaeti, 'I am no mare-bound Frank but an honest scrapper like yourselves.'

'You're a Horda man! I know you by your speech.'

'To my bones,' shouted Ofaeti, 'which are cold enough. May I warm them by your fire?'

'You speak fine words, friend, and I can see you are a witty man. Come, you are welcome,' said another of the band.

They were given a good reception. The men had some fish stew, which they shared. They were Danes but had traded with the Horda and Roga peoples and so were well disposed towards the three. Hugin saw they were wary of him, recognising him as a sorcerer, but he did what he could for them, tending their wounds, splinting their arms and making poultices and bandages from what he could find. The Vikings agreed it was a lucky day that they had come upon such men.

As Hugin worked, Ofaeti came to his side. 'A word,' he said, slapping the Raven on the back as if telling him a joke.

Hugin stood and followed Ofaeti to the longship, where the big Viking pretended to be examining the steering oar, asking Hugin's opinion on how it might be replaced.

'I know these men, or one of them,' he said. 'This is Skakki the Long. He is an outlaw in our lands. It's not enough for him to trade; he has snatched slaves too – good Horda men. I will repay him with his death.'

'We need him and his crew,' said Hugin.

'I know. But know this: when we are nearly at land I will kill him and his men.'

'They are twenty.'

'Yes, and I will die. But they will be fifteen or less by the time I do.'

'We can't dock a ship with just you. I am no sailor.'

'I will do it near the shore. Very near. With luck his men will jump and swim for it. If they don't, you can swim in too. I expect no help in this.'

Hugin nodded but he couldn't allow this to happen. He had to kill Helgi, that now seemed like the best course to stop the prophecy that the god would die at the teeth of the wolf. He was becoming convinced that Helgi was the god made flesh. Helgi was a great warrior, a patron of poets and of sorcerers.

453

Odin was god of war, poetry and magic. And madness too. There could be no delay, so Hugin would have to kill Ofaeti. And yet he didn't want to. The Viking had brought him a sort of luck. Was he Odin's reward for all the warriors Hugin had sent to his halls? The fat man had shown him the wolf could be cut too. The Raven touched his sword. If he'd realised that in the monastery at Saint-Maurice, how different might things have been? When the wolf had still been in human form he might have been killable. *Now?* Hugin doubted it.

Could he call on Odin? Hadn't he betrayed the god? Wasn't he going to try to save the woman who would call the wolf? Who could he call on then? Loki? The words went through his mind before he could stop them: *Lord of lies, friend to man, help me to my purpose.*

The tall Viking joined them at the ship. 'We're trying to repair it but we can't work with green wood.' He tapped the broken steering oar. 'We've had no luck at all on this voyage. We hit the Franks here with over a hundred ships, but Arnulf is a mighty king and he knows his land. He brought his cavalry through the marshes to attack us. I had never seen so many horses. We were slaughtered and only just made our ships. The oar got torn off landing here. Sandbanks.'

'Don't you have anything to show for your troubles at all?' said Ofaeti.

'Nothing. Well, only them – slaves we picked up down the river.'

Hugin followed the man's nod to where two men sat tied back to back. He hadn't noticed them before. One was a farm boy, terribly beaten, scarcely conscious. The other was a very strange fellow indeed – tall and muscular, his skin looked almost as if it belonged to the sea, pallid like the belly of a shark. His hair was bright red and stood up in a shock.

'The boy's not likely to make it, but the big one'll fetch a bit at market.'

'Let me look at the oar,' said Ofaeti. 'I have some skill as a shipwright and it won't be too much bother to fix. I can borrow a bit from your deck and our little boat, if it's still where we left it.'

'I like you!' said Skakki, slapping Ofaeti's back. 'I'm glad you're aboard. Maybe now our luck has changed!'

65   The Ice

Jehan's heart felt like a cooling rock, his once strong body was now a useless weight as Aelis had pushed his baggage of limbs up onto the horse. The world was fading. His sight had gone, and now the night sounds, once so sharp and clear, seemed muted, far off. Smell, a sense that had been stronger than vision to him, seemed stifled and blunt. The flavours he had known – the laden breezes of the forest, the teeming airs of the meadows, the tarry stink of far-off oceans, the million rots of bog and fen – were gone. In their place was the thin palette of human perceptions.

Aelis had called the horse – a big brindled mare. The animal had come trotting out of the woods to wait beside her while she helped him up.

The two travelled north to the coast and then turned east. Aelis easily found the way through the vast forest, guided by a rune that shone like a beacon. The other horses she had taken from the Raven and his companions followed them at the beginning of their journey. Then she raised her hand to dismiss them and they turned into the deep woods.

Jehan was finding the going very hard physically, almost impossible. His body chafed with the movement of the horse, his joints ached and his muscles trembled. His mind came back to him and he often wept with the memory of the things he had done, the people he had killed.

Aelis was beside him. 'Do you want me to take off the stone for a moment?'

'I cannot give in to murder.'

She nodded. The girl she had been was just like a movement of the light inside her, a rainbow that appeared in a fleeting alignment of sun and cloud and then was gone, as the runes took her mind once more.

When she did return to herself she longed for him – his voice, his touch but the confessor's voice was weakening, his limbs no more use than dead branches to a tree.

Aelis knew they could not go on much further. She sensed people in the woods, watching from the darkness, and she reached out to them to send them away, to push them shuddering into madness or to blind their eyes to their presence. She sensed the Northmen on the coast before she saw them – a beaten and bedraggled band seeking shelter in an inlet, hiding from the Franks, who would kill them in a second. They had wounded with them and men who smelled of rot and decay. She watched their camp, their ship on its side providing scant shelter from the sheets of fine mizzle.

She told the horse to go. Then she took the confessor in her arms and walked down through the gorse to the little beach, calling a rune into her mind as she did so, the one that whispered of ocean depths, secrets and shadows. There on the sand she laid him down and ate with the northerners at their fire. None noticed her or the confessor because she did not choose to let them notice them.

When it came time to set sail, she climbed onto the boat with the confessor and sat at a vacant oar – there were many. The boat got under way in a good breeze and headed east. Aelis watched the land rolling by, the men around her. She asked one for some food. He gave it to her, his eyes blank, and she knew he did not know they were there.

She went to the man at the steering oar. He was a tall chieftain with a dirty yellow beard.

'Where are we headed, brother?'

'To Skania and home.'

'Try your luck at Ladoga,' she said. 'There are riches there.'

'Aldeigjuborg? You are a wise fellow, easterner,' said the

chieftain. 'I'll head there. Svan has been before and will tell us the way.'

Aelis looked down the ship. She saw the crew as themselves and as their magical selves, little candles in that wall in the garden. She went to each flame, warming her hands on it, sensing it, controlling it. The crew would go where she wanted.

It grew cold as she went east and ice began to appear on the shore and on the sea. The confessor shook and trembled at her feet, and she longed to remove that stone from around his neck, to see him stand again. But she would not. She just found a sea blanket for him and saw to it that he was clean and as warm as anyone could be on an open boat.

The sea narrowed to a channel and eventually to a river, where the men threw buckets over the side to draw in the fresh water. Here the way was tight, a ship's width of water remaining in the ice, and the crew regularly climbed out to smash their way through with axes and clubs. They came to a broad big lake, where the men caught and cooked fish. From there they headed into another river, wide at first and then clogged with ice. A haze was on the water, then a mist that reduced visibility to a few boat lengths. After a time the murk was impenetrable. The ship's prow was invisible from where Aelis sat at the stern. She could only see the crew nearest to her, gazing around her, their hands at the oars.

She kept them rowing, sending her will to them, keeping them working to speed her to Helgi, taking the rudder to guide the longship through the fog, lit by the rune of illumination, the one that glowed with the colour of the sharpest moons. They rowed on, the ice becoming thicker, but she always found a course.

Night came and she saw the confessor was freezing, so Aelis lay down beside him, hugging him to lend him her warmth. The crew stopped rowing. Lost in her concern for the confessor, she forgot the men at the oars. Enchanted, they just sat with the ice thick about them, their furs in the chests they sat on. No rower needs too much clothing, even in the coldest weather – a jerkin is enough – but in the frigid air of winter in the lands of the Rus, once the oars are still it is necessary to put on whatever insulation you have as quickly as you can. Aelis held the confessor to her. The runes would not warm him, but she kept him well covered and held him tight. The Vikings sat unmoving on the boat as the mist thickened and the frost formed on the sails and the rigging. The confessor's breath mingled with hers, clouding the air about their faces. She shivered and adjusted her furs.

Aelis lost track of time in the cold, concentrating only on the human warmth of the confessor and the uncommon love she felt towards him. She looked at her fingers. They were blue and she couldn't feel them. Her body was dying, but the symbols inside her were bright. Sometimes she was calm, accepting of her fate and certain that she would live on in the runes, but then a dread would take her, and a glimpse of her true self would come back to her – terrified to die, terrified not of oblivion but of loneliness. She had travelled so far to meet Jehan, she could not begin that journey again. She thought of the wolfman, of his promise: *Helgi will help you*. She sensed this was true. The king would help her, would keep her from her fate, from the runes reaching out to their sisters and annihilating her.

'Helgi,' she said to herself, 'we are here. Come and help us.'

A light was approaching across the ice. She needed to find out where she was, to find her way to the magician king.

'Row towards the light,' she told the men at the oars.

But the boat didn't move. It was locked in the ice. And the oarsmen couldn't row anyway because they were dead of the cold.

66   A Merchant's Tale

In Helgi's great hall the fire burned low. A fog was tight about the building, and it was as if the warriors and women in the hall felt its constriction, huddling together almost as if bound. The prince sat near to the fire, half dozing

There was a movement at the corner of his eye. For a minute he thought it was her, Sváva, creeping to his side once again. But it was only a cat – Huldre, the big pregnant mouser hunting for scraps. How old would Sváva have been now? Old enough that one of the cat's kittens might be given to her as a present for her new house, a traditional gift to set her on her way in her married life.

He has not yet come with the girl. He was thinking of the wolfman, entrusted to do a job that a band of *druzhina* could not. *Had he ever got to Paris? Had he managed to find the girl?* Helgi had no doubt a man who could slip past his guards into Aldeigjuborg could slip into Paris, so he must have had a chance. *Had he lost her on the way? Worse, had she been killed?* If she died then the runes would leave her and go to one of the others who nurtured their sisters in their minds. The god would be nearer to being on earth, Helgi's lands a step closer to waste and ruin. The severed knot might be whole once more.

In nightmares Helgi was pursued by the terrible Odin, his spear stabbing towards him, the eight legs of his horse carving a wake through the snow, the god's face contorted with anger and hate. Everything Helgi saw confirmed what the wolfman had told him – Odin was coming. But what of his bargain with that red-haired fellow? *Who had he been?* Loki, Helgi was now sure. The god's names told him all he needed to know: lie smith, prince of the burning air, deceiver, enemy of the gods.

'The god promised I should be a great king,' said Helgi under his breath, 'and yet we are beset.'

He thought back on the strange things that had happened to him since the birth of Aeringunnr, the worse things that had happened since her death. Kiev was rising as a mighty power under Ingvar, while Novgorod, the new capital he was building as a staging post to the east, had been wrecked by fire. His people were in a fret of apprehension and had been for ten years. The week after Sváva died they put Gillingr in his barrow, sealing him in with his spear and sword, his bed and his lyre surrounded by everything he would need for the afterlife – food, perfumes, clothes.

It had not been a good sign, he thought, that tunnels had been unearthed during the grave digging. They were deep and they were narrow, most likely Roman mines, according to those who had seen such things before. His people had no skill in mining and had covered the entrance to the tunnels when they sealed the barrow.

But the barrow collapsed shortly afterwards, falling in on itself, and when they dug it out to make it good they found the things missing from the tomb. The jewels were gone, though the lyre was all smashed and broken. The food was gone too and the blankets, the spear. No man had laid hands on any of these things because Gillingr's family and a good number of Helgi's *druzhina* had overseen the whole burial.

People said then that Gillingr's ghost was living in the tunnels, so he was reburied elsewhere. In the years that followed the townsfolk left tributes to the ghost at the tunnel entrance in his old barrow. Foxes might have taken the bread or the meat left there, but no animal took the pots of honey, the beer, the blankets and the boots that the people laid at the cave mouth. Something did, though.

Helgi seemed called to the spot. He would sit on the mud of the collapse at the mouth of the tunnel watching the pupil-dark entrance. Of course, he had gone inside to look. The entrance was very small and he'd had to force his shoulders through

461

into the tunnel beyond. He found nothing. The passages were too tight, too winding – his way was blocked by a collapse here, a flood there. Now the soil of the barrow excavation was overgrown with grass, but still sometimes he went to the tunnel mouth to sit and think.

Looking into the fire, his mind felt raw and vulnerable. He went outside. The fog that had engulfed the town for a week was still thick, only the guards' fires glowing like little cocoons of light giving any idea of direction.

'A ship! A ship!' The voice was coming from the loading tower.

Impossible. The river had been solid for a week, totally impassable to boats. And even if it wasn't, the fog made travel almost out of the question. You couldn't set out from one side of Lake Ladoga confident you would ever see the other.

He went to the tower, thinking it was just a fog spectre and that he would tell the guard to stop being stupid. He climbed up the ladders inside and went to the loading bay.

'What?'

'A ship, *khagan*, I swear it. It was there a moment ago.'

Helgi peered into the fog but saw nothing at all. From his vantage point, though, the fog was thinner. His guards weren't idiots, so he waited a while. And then, as the fog swirled away for a second, he saw it – a mast and the top of a sail, both heavy with ice, the ship listing to one side.

'Well let's see what the gods have served us up here.' In front of his men he still played the carefree and fearless monarch, the man of action. It was all they understood, and to share his gnawing fears would have been to lose his authority. The guard went to follow him down the ladder but Helgi told him to stay where he was. 'You'll need to guide me towards it,' he said.

'I won't see you, lord.'

'You will see me.'

Helgi ran to the hall to his great chest and pulled out his skates, stout leather shoes bottomed with a folded copper blade. Then he ran for the town gates, took a wall torch and went out to the river, his warriors streaming behind him through the fog. At the river he passed the torch to a *druzhina* and strapped his skates on. Then he took it back and set off across the ice, the torch a glow-worm in the white darkness.

He could scarcely see four paces and called up to the man on the tower, 'Can you see my light?'

'I can, *khagan*.' The voice was flat through the stillness of the fog.

'Then guide me to it.'

He skated forward slowly and the guard shouted for him to turn left. Already he had lost his bearings. On he went, falling twice but regaining the torch.

'Keep going, lord. Straight ahead.'

He went forward again until the fog seemed to lift slightly and he could see further. There on its side with its oars trapped in the ice like an insect stuck in pine gum lay the longship. The ship was entirely white, like an apparition thrown up by the cold, its sail torn by the weight of crystals, its rigging sagging with jagged icicles.

Helgi went round to the low side of the ship and started back. At each oar was a man, his hands still on the shaft, but frozen where he sat as if enchanted.

One of his *druzhina* had followed him, and Helgi steeled himself to play the bluff warrior, the jaunty, fearless king, although dread was bound fast to him like the ice was bound fast to the ship.

'A curious one, lord.'

'When the gods deliver us booty, let's not bother ourselves asking how it got here,' said Helgi. 'When we drink the wine we don't ask to see the feet of the man who pressed the grapes.'

The man laughed. 'Shall I go aboard?'

'Let us both.'

The man began to clamber up but stopped. On the longship something had moved. Both drew their swords.

'Who is there?' said Helgi. 'This is a trading town, and honest men have nothing to fear from me. I am Helgi, lord of the Eastern Lake, and you are under my protection.'

From the back of the ship a strange figure moved towards them. It was dressed in bulky furs and carried a sword at its waist, but was clearly either injured or bitten by the wolf of the cold. It staggered down the length of the skewed longship, leaning on oars and dead men for support. Five paces from them it bent to catch its breath.

'Say who you are, stranger,' said the *druzhina*. More men came skating in. 'Say who you are!' The guard repeated his command.

The figure breathed in and stumbled against the side of the boat.

'Who are you? I ask again,' Helgi said.

The figure looked up, gasping and shivering, and stammered, 'I am Lady Aelis, sister of Eudes of Paris. You are Helgi, prince of the Rus, and you are my salvation. I am travelling with an invalid monk who needs your help.'

Helgi could see that the cold had her in its grip. Panic rose up in him as he pointed the way back to the town and shouted, 'Get her to my hall! Get her there! This lady must not die! She must not die!'

67   A Reckoning at Sea

The Danes were intent on going home, not east for the convenience of Leshii, Hugin and Ofaeti. Still, the idea of a port appealed to Leshii – a place where there might be rest, good food, a bed, girls and, who knew, even a living. He had enough money now in the five looted swords he'd been able to take with him on the mule to set up wherever he liked, if he could buy permission from the lord of the town and other merchants. And if he could keep them from the prying eyes of the Vikings on the ship. He'd wrapped them in one of the Frankish cloaks he'd taken and tied cut staves into the bundle to make it look like a camping roll. He knew the disguise wouldn't stand much scrutiny but, so far, the sailors had kept their manners.

Leshii had intended to jump ship at Kaupanangan, but the Danes were heading back to Haithabu. All well and good. A hundred years before, the king there had kidnapped merchants from the east. His successor was bound to welcome one offering his services to the throne.

The Raven and Ofaeti had made the best of it. Winter was coming and they'd have a better chance of getting a boat at Haithabu than waiting on a freezing shore, they told the merchant, even if it meant going the wrong way for a while. Hugin hadn't liked it but he had no choice. He was no sailor and even going via Haithabu would get him to Ladoga quicker than walking.

They were five days into their journey, the going slow as they kept having to stop at coves or inlets to repair the steering oar. Ofaeti worked well with the little crafting axe Skakki had on his ship. Eventually he secured enough good wood – by dismantling a hut on a beach – to make the repair stick.

Ofaeti watched Skakki eyeing him and felt his sword hand

flex. The slaver had taken no one he knew well but some he knew enough. Kinsmen. When he chopped at the wood with the axe, he imagined it was Skakki's head. Skakki, however, was not a stupid man. He knew there were few Danes who matched his description and saw the iron in Ofaeti's eyes, no matter how much he tried to hide it.

'We are a day from Haithabu,' said Skakki as he sat beside Leshii. Ofaeti was tending to the sail, cajoling the men to better effort, for a moment consumed by the task of sailing. The Raven was tending an injured man, cleaning his wounds of pus.

'It will be good to wash the salt from my clothes,' said Leshii.

'And to be in a trading town.'

'I have nothing to trade, but if I can be of service to you, mention it and the task is done,' said Leshii. He didn't like this man, with the scar at the corner of his mouth that gave the impression of a lopsided smile.

'Do you think you can get us a good price for the slaves?'

'I was born a long time ago, chieftain, and I have traded since I was a boy. I can buy at half the price and sell at double compared to any merchant you have ever met.'

Skakki looked out to sea. 'I heard you say you are no longer welcome in Aldeigjuborg.'

'I'm only welcome if I can bring a gift I do not have.'

'What gift?'

'A woman.'

Skakki nodded. 'My trade is slaves,' he said, 'though I am a fighter not a bargainer. I lose half I have won in battle in the marketplace.'

'You are suggesting we work together? I am no fighting man.'

'I see that,' said Skakki, 'but you can win out in a deal all right, I think. You have the look about you.'

'That I can do.'

'So I will test you,' he said. 'The men you travel with are not kin to you?'

'I never saw them before the spring.'

'Good. I intend to take them as slaves. The healer will sell for a great price and the Horda man will sell to the prince himself, I think. He is too unruly for a farmer to keep.'

'It is late in the season,' said Leshii. 'You will not get a good price.'

'I will get a better one with you on my side.'

'The merchants there will not have me.'

'On my word, they will accept you. I've brought them riches in slaves and plunder. They will accept you all right.'

Leshii continued his objections, as much to hear them himself as to convince the Viking. 'And if there are Horda men in this port, what then? There will be a mighty fight if you bump into one of their ships. Those men are not slow to draw their swords.'

'The Horda are all in Britannia,' Skakki said, 'and the king of the west does not welcome them to his shores. I am a reckless man but not that reckless.'

'Then you have a deal. I warn you, neither is a weakling nor a coward. The fat one is a mighty warrior and the thin one mightier. They have killed many, many men and employed powerful sorceries.'

'Good,' said Skakki. 'It will win me more renown to have them as my captives. But I counsel *you*, if you attempt to warn them I will cut your throat.'

Leshii blanched. 'When do you intend to act?'

'Tomorrow.'

Leshii breathed out. At least he had time to think about what he would do. He went over to the mule and threw some of its shit over the side. The animal was a good lesson to him, he thought. It took what life threw at it and never complained. It just sat chewing on the hay they had taken from a deserted farm on the shore, looked out to sea and shat. Leshii almost laughed. It was like a motto for him:. 'Look out to sea and shit.' A good maxim by which to live your life – look forward but don't forget to take care of the practicalities. What was his choice here? Be a hero or a pragmatist?

'Friend!' Skakki had his arm around Ofaeti, or as far around him as he could get it.

'I am not your friend,' said Ofaeti, trying to control his temper. 'We are companions. Many years must pass, and you must give proof of brave deeds before I call you friend. I have only three I call friend in this world. That man by the prow, who though he is quiet at the fire is loud in battle, has proved himself to me. That merchant there, who lives in fear but acts bravely, and so is braver than many who were born bold, who is willing to crawl into an enemy nest at night to secure me a boat, who shares his food without question and, though he is old, complains but little.'

'And your third friend?'

'The sword at my side,' said Ofaeti and patted the sword.

As his hand went back to the tiller, Skakki had a fit of coughing and tapped his hand three times on the rail of the boat. Then he reached forward in a quick movement, drew Ofaeti's sword from his belt and took a swift step backwards.

The coughing had been a signal. As Skakki grabbed the sword six men fell upon the Raven, but Hugin wasn't so easily surprised. Though he too had his sword taken, he was quick, nimble and vigilant. He was on his feet and had thrown one man down before the others had realised he had moved. However, he was surrounded, the bulk of the men concentrating on him.

Skakki hadn't trusted Leshii either. A young Viking with a wispy beard and no front teeth drew a knife on him and smiled, an expression that made him look more fierce than if he'd scowled. *Tomorrow.* Of course Skakki wasn't going to risk Leshii telling Ofaeti and Hugin what he planned. In fact he had approached the merchant before he moved against them to put doubt into his mind, to remove him from the fight and to ensure he didn't endanger himself on impulse.

Ofaeti stepped towards Skakki, his hands out wide.

'Come on,' he said. 'I have lived long enough and I think you have too. Let us go to visit Ran, that lady of the waves, together. Let us see where she dwells on the ocean floor.'

'You will fight for the Danish king as part of his warrior elite.'

'Right now I am busy fighting for myself,' said Ofaeti, 'and I doubt the high lord of Haithabu is so soft as to want a man who has been so easily bested in battle by one as meek and girlish as you. Come, hit at me, or do you only face Horda women and children, keeping away as you do when their men are home from the sea?'

'I have killed plenty of your kinsmen,' said Skakki.

'Then make it one more. You are many. Can you be so womanly as to give way to one unarmed man?'

'We would rather not damage the goods,' said Skakki.

'My grandfather was a berserker, a man who raged his way across the world with spear and sword, never taking a backward step. My father was a milder man, yet still the wolves grew fat wherever his ship landed. I am Thiörek, son of Thetmar, son of Thetleif, and I will not yield to you. I have seen women bolder with sewing needles than you with your swords and spears.' He took his knife from his belt and threw it to the floor.

'Come, I have no weapon!' He was screaming at his enemies, banging at his chest.

Leshii marvelled at the big berserker's courage. These northerners had something inside them, values and ideals that shaped and ordered their lives and made them so much more than he was. *What would it be like to have a purpose beyond life, beyond pleasure, beyond having enough money for dancing girls and a fine house, to see further than an abacus, profit and loss?* Happiness was all very well but it passed in a moment. Always something came to take it away – bandit attack, a blight or famine in the east or, more mundanely, the little irritations of life: a bad stomach, an argument with a friend, a bad buy in a mule or a slave. He understood the Norsemen now. Their hunger for fame was not just a matter of pride; it was a spur to great things – to have lived magnificently and to be remembered for it. They wanted to do something that would endure. To them that was more important than happiness, than comfort, than anything at all.

Few people had ever really done anything for Leshii. This Norseman had protected him. The sorcerer too had helped him, offered to reward him out of all proportion to the service he required. Leshii knew that either would only need a moment's distraction to gain the upper hand in a fight, so he reached inside his kaftan, took off the necklace, held it up and shouted at the top of his voice, 'Leave them be, or I will drop this over the side. It belonged to a princess of Serkland. It broke her heart when she lost it, and she died of sadness.'

Skakki turned.

'I have rarely seen such a piece,' he said, 'but I think rather that you will give it than bargain for it.'

'You will have to kill me first.'

'Then I will. Such a necklace will beat the profit of ten years of trading. I can find another little merchant in that time, should I live so long.'

The merchant held the necklace over the side of the boat. 'If you do not release us you will never have this.'

'You can't sit with your hand over the side all the way to Haithabu. Are you offering that for your lives?'

Leshii suddenly saw the hopelessness of the situation. The Raven had been forced to a sitting position, eight men around him, one choking him, two on each arm and three sitting on his legs. He was doomed and Ofaeti was unarmed. Leshii could try to cut a deal, bargain for his life, accept the loss of the necklace and start again at Haithabu. But what was the point? Better to die in a beautiful moment than the slow degradation of old age. His hip felt bad, his feet were weary. His time was up.

'I'm saying that you will kill me anyway, for I will never give it to you. Ofaeti, give me one of your gods.'

'Loki is their god,' said the slave with the red hair.

'Not him,' said Ofaeti, 'he is a god of strife.'

'It seems to me you people love strife. And as for you, Skakki, I wish strife on you. For Loki then,' said Leshii and threw the necklace over the side.

Skakki went white with rage and leaped towards Leshii to cut him down. Leshii dodged his sword and ran down the ship but he stumbled into the back of his standing mule. Leshii rolled underneath the mule and out the other side as Skakki charged. Then they were running around the creature like a childhood game, Skakki suddenly changing direction to try to catch Leshii out, screaming and shouting that he would kill the fool who could waste such a treasure.

The men around Ofaeti looked away from the big Viking for a heartbeat, who seized his chance, felling one with a tooth-powdering punch and grabbing his spear. A breath later a second warrior had been knocked over the side of the ship and another's knee was shattered by the fat man's stamp.

The merchant was good for twice around the mule, no more. He was old and Skakki was quick. The third time around, the slaver caught him and lifted his sword to strike, grabbing Leshii's kaftan with his free hand. Leshii caught Skakki's sword arm, but the Viking drove a headbutt into his face, making him release his grip. Skakki swung again, putting his hand on the mule's rump for balance.

The animal, uncomplaining from Ladoga to Paris and halfway back again, suddenly decided it had had enough, launching a good kick, not into the Viking but into Leshii's leg. Leshii hit the floor like a discarded coat and Skakki's hack sliced the air.

Ofaeti didn't even bother to weigh the spear in his hand. He threw it half the length of the ship. It caught Skakki above the temple, sending him spinning to the deck. Then Ofaeti had an axe from one of the fallen men. A mob of crewmen were still occupied pinning down the Raven, a tricky task without killing him or injuring him beyond use as a slave. Three slavers lay dead on the boards or drowning overboard, then it was four as Ofaeti smashed the axe down into the skull of the writhing man he had maimed with his kick. The rest were free to face Ofaeti. But whereas before they had found it amusing to watch their chieftain chase the merchant and four of their kinsmen bait the unarmed fat man, there were no smiles on their faces now.

'Come on, brothers,' said Ofaeti. 'Four of your men lie dead who faced me unarmed. Who would like to try me now I have this skull-biter in my hand? Or will you cut your losses and join me? You know my fame! I am renowned for my fighting skill wherever warriors gather to talk.' He tapped the axe on his palm.

A squat man with a big blond beard spoke: 'Much would I like to join a warrior like you. Skakki was a harsh chief and I do not mourn his loss. And I think you would be a better leader, as it is clear you are a mighty man. But the Valkyries are swooping for our kinsmen now. And though I think it likely they will soon swoop for me, our dead must be avenged.'

The man was doing his best to use fine words, Leshii noted, as the Norsemen did when they thought death might be close.

'No kinsmen of mine,' said a voice.

'Nor mine, neither.'

Four warriors came to Ofaeti's side and stood to face their fellows.

'You are six,' said Ofaeti, 'and we are five. So it looks as though the weaving of my fate may not yet be done.'

'We are thirteen,' said the warrior, 'when my fellows have slit your man's throat.'

'Too late for that,' said one of the warriors on top of the Raven.

'Why?'

'He's already dead.'

Ofaeti pursed his lips and nodded. 'One of my kinsmen is dead, four of yours. Will the gods worry about the numbers?'

'It is some sort of recompense and enough, I think, for honour,' said the blond Viking. 'We will place ourselves under your command, fat warrior.'

Leshii went to the body of the Raven. It was losing heat already and there was no pulse. He spoke to him: 'So, your destiny was not as great as you thought. Still, my friend, I am sorry you have gone. You offered me friendship, not in word but in deed, and for that I am grateful.'

Leshii looked out to sea. *Now for Haithabu*, he thought, with a hundred dihrams and a fine stash of swords. He made the lightning-bolt sign and looked up at the sky. 'Good fortune at last,' he said. Then he remembered his dedication as he'd thrown the necklace into the sea. 'And thanks to Loki too,' he said. 'You are a generous god indeed.'

68 Prayers Unanswered

Jehan lay still. His limbs had an ice in them that was nothing to do with the winter. His bones had twisted, turned and set, and were no more use to him than the icicles hanging from the rigging. He had gone beyond shivering, felt drowsy and could hardly keep his eyes open. He knew that he could change things, knew that all he had to do was take off the stone at his neck and the wolf would come out inside him – the wolf would find a way. But he would not remove it. Death, and Jehan was sure he was dying, was preferable to the alternative.

He said psalms in his head, but they were nothing more than a jumble of words. He felt the world fading. Any sort of movement was beyond him now, even the rocking that had blighted him since he was a child.

Her face came to him. The Virgin in the fields, Aelis in the fields. 'Do not seek me,' she had told him. And yet he had. He had tracked her down, lain with her and been happy, the worst sin of all – luxuriating in his offence to God.

Jehan chose death, not as a way out but to welcome in the punishment the Almighty had in store for him. He had eaten of unclean meat, he had fornicated and laughed in the face of God. He deserved to suffer eternally.

Men were on the ship. People were moving things, the sea chests, weapons. Two stood over him.

'This is the monk?'

'A cripple, *khagan*.'

Jehan felt a hand touch his face.

'Let me see him. Is he alive?'

'Who knows?'

Jehan hoped the men would not help him. He needed to die. He was an abomination. If he could have moved, he would have attacked the men and made them kill him. But he couldn't move, couldn't give any sign of life. Jehan felt a hand at his chest checking for breathing. It rested on the Wolfstone, felt its shape through his tunic and pulled the cloth aside.

'What is that?'

'It's just a pebble, *khagan*, the man is as poor as a Pecheneg. No jewels here.'

'Let me see.'

Jehan felt someone else take the stone.

'Not a fit ornament for a king, *khagan*.'

'This is the necessary stone.'

'*Khagan?*'

'There is a prophecy. Great fortune was promised to me if I found this stone. This will fetter a god.' The voice was urgent, talking to no one in particular.

'I'm glad to hear it, sir.'

'This is safety,' said Helgi. 'This is the end of our enemies.'

Jehan felt a quick tension in the thong at his neck. There was a *snick* and it disappeared.

'You're going to wear that thing, lord?'

'It is a gift of the god. This is a blight to witches, a fetter to trolls and wolves. We are blessed, greatly blessed. I will wear it until we are back at the hall. There is one who needs it more than me.'

Jehan felt that a terrible burden had been lifted from him, a heaviness removed from his head. Was this the certainty of death coming to him? The lightness of the soul freeing itself from the shackles of the mortal body?

'We need to get back to the lady.'

'What of the monk, lord?'

'The fates have shown the death they require for him,' said Helgi. 'Take off his furs and leave him to the cold.'

Jehan felt rough hands stripping him, the cold biting at his body, the deck burning his naked skin. Then he heard the men climb off the ship, the sound of a horse breathing, its tack chinking and clinking and finally moving away.

So what now? The cold gripped him so hard. Jehan saw himself as if through a sheet of ice, heard himself speaking to Aelis and she replying.

I will be myself again.

But I will never be me. You are an enemy of the gods.

I will be myself again.

You are a killer, a slayer of your own kin.

His head turned. It felt full of ice shards. He was a killer, had killed, would always kill, he knew. He had to try to die.

This time, he said, *I will die for you.*

You will be my death. Last time you made it impossible for me to live. This time you will kill me.

No!

He closed his eyes and prayed for the cold to take him. But it didn't. The hunger did.

69   Helgi's Salvation

Aelis lay alone by the fire in Helgi's great hall. She had been put on a feather mattress and was beginning to feel properly warm for the first time since she had left the forest. At first the heat had been painful on her toes and fingers, but eventually they regained a delicious suppleness. As the cold melted from her blood the pliability felt new, as though her limbs had never been so free before. She stretched out her hands, relieved she had finally arrived somewhere she might find her former self again. Her intuition about Helgi was that he sought to protect her. The runes did not tell her he was her friend, or even that he was well disposed towards her, but she had the strong feeling that her safety was his first concern and was too happy that she had found refuge to wonder why.

She kept expecting Jehan to be brought in. The cold had been so intense that her thinking had slowed and she had become lost in her magical self, in the singing and the chiming of the runes. Now, as warmth returned, she began to wonder where the confessor was.

The hall was a large bare space in the Viking style, benches lining the walls with bedding stacked in one corner of the room. People were at the doorway, craning in to see her. She saw a priestess, smeared in white clay, her hair wild and woven with ribbons and trinkets; children were there and a couple of stern warriors, their faces tense and fearful. She sensed their disquiet like tuneless and dissonant music.

The faces parted and Helgi came in. He was a tall man with wide shoulders and long fair hair. He wore a rich tunic of blue wool laced high at the neck and baggy trousers in the eastern fashion.

Helgi squatted down by the mattress and Aelis looked

into his eyes. All her life she had been able to sense people's intentions, their underlying motivations – not as words or sentences but as colours and music – but with Helgi she felt nothing. There was no wider resonance to his spirit, and he seemed almost dead to her. The glow of life that was in the people at the doorway, the candlelight that seemed to burn within them, the light she could see shining from the nooks in the wall in the garden of her mind, was absent in him. In the boat she had sensed his overwhelming concern that she should live, his care so strong that it blotted out every other signature of his mind. But now, nothing.

'You are the Magician, the Prophet,' she said.

'So men call me.'

'Do you know who I am?'

'Aelis of Paris. I have sought you a long time, lady.'

'Well, now I have come to you. Can you help me? Can you help Confessor Jehan?'

Helgi guessed she was talking about the monk on the boat.

'The man you travelled with?'

'Yes.'

'We have cared for him,' he said; 'now let us care for you.'

'I am not myself,' said Aelis. 'There is a magic inside me, and I cannot shake it.'

'I can help you,' said Helgi, 'but you need to let me. The things inside you are powerful and will not leave you easily. Can you be their mistress for a second? If I try to vanquish them, can you give me the space of a breath to act?'

Aelis felt the runes stirring, shapes that were more than shapes – that were colours, sounds, perfumes and textures too – whirling through her head.

'I don't know,' she said, 'but I can try.'

'Try. But first sleep. You have come a long way and suffered many things.' He clapped his hands and a man came in. 'Get hot wine for the lady and some food. Do I need to give instruction in the smallest details of hospitality?'

'I will see to it, *khagan*.'

Aelis felt the warrior's fear like a blast of cold air.

Wine was brought and heated in a pot over the fire. Aelis drank in its sweet aroma. She was given roast goat's meat and flat bread, which tasted wonderful to her. The wine made her feel sleepy, and when the food was finished she lay back on the mattress.

Aelis drifted off to sleep and she dreamed. She was back in the forests of her youth, chasing hawkmoths that fluttered around her in the wet dawn. The moths sang and chimed with an odd music as she tried to catch them, some sounding high and melodious, some like the wind on the sea. She was lost to rapture in the morning light but then felt something uncomfortable at her neck. She looked down. It was the stone, the Wolfstone. She tried to take it off, but her hands wouldn't do her bidding. It was ridiculous that she couldn't do such a simple thing as remove a pendant from about her neck. She looked at the pebble and knew she had seen it before. It was a fragment like her, a shattered piece of a bigger thing. She knew its name – Gjöll in the language of the Norsemen – Scream. She looked around her. The woods had grown dark and the moths were all gone.

Helgi stepped back from her bed. 'Watch her,' he said, 'and do not let her take that pendant from around her neck.'

70 The Price of Lore

'What have I in my hand, my cold friend?'

To the Raven it seemed as if he was alone on the open deck. He couldn't tell where the voice was coming from. He stood up. The sky was clear and dark, the still ocean its perfect reflection, and it seemed as though the ship floated on a bubble of stars.

'I do not know.'

'It is your death.'

The slavers' captive with the moon-glow skin was standing at his side. No one else was on the ship. *Had they all been killed?* The man put out his fist and opened it. Inside was a tooth. Hugin recognised it as the tooth of a wolf.

'My death is by water.'

'What is Helgi's death?'

'By the creature of hoof and mane.'

'In a manner of speaking. And the girl?'

'By the teeth of the wolf.'

'How do you know?'

'All these things I have seen. Shown to me.'

'By who?'

'By Munin.'

'You know the truth of that lady's tongue,' said the god, as now the Raven was sure he must be.

'Who was she?'

The pale god moved his hands and a cord appeared in it. 'Tie it,' he said. 'The knot the wild woman showed you. His symbol, the dead god's necklace.'

Hugin tried to tie it but couldn't. Only two of the three knots would come. He just couldn't think how to tie the final one.

The god took the rope. 'She was here,' he said, pointing to one of the two knots. He pulled very hard on both ends of the rope. 'And now she is here.'

Hugin looked and the knots had been forced together, becoming indistinguishable from each other, becoming one.

'Why couldn't I tie the noose?'

'Because Odin is not here on earth. The three knots are not yet together.'

'How will the last knot be tied?'

'What does the knot do? What is its purpose?'

'Murder. Death.'

'You have your answer.'

'Aelis's death?'

'She carries the runes. One way or the other she will cease to exist.'

'She carries the one rune, the howling rune, the one that draws the wolf.'

'She does, but Munin found that she carried more. She sought the lady's death to speed the god to earth, not to slow him.'

'That is not true.'

'She deceived you in everything, and yet you think she told the truth in that. This rune was in her.'

He held out his hand again. A shape wriggled and turned on it, making it difficult to say exactly how it was composed. Sometimes its lines seemed horizontal, sometimes vertical, sometimes a mix. It was Ansuz. Odin's rune.

The Raven swallowed. He felt the blood drain from his face and a tightness came into his stomach. 'The god set his runes in Aelis too? Then everything I have done has been against myself. I sped her to this fate when in rage I killed Munin.'

'You are a warrior. That is what they do – indulge themselves at everyone else's cost.'

'I did not know.'

'What killer ever knows what skeins go unwoven because of his interceding knife?'

'If I had not killed her the god's day would be further off.'

'You would have needed to go further. The runes seek to unite. One rune carrier seeks to kill the others. You would have needed to protect Munin, even against her will.'

'It is what I was raised to do.'

'Well, I do try to be of service.'

'You were the wild woman who said she was my mother?'

'I am your mother and your father both. Like many gods I have many selves, eternal and temporary. Mine are lovely, seductive, wrong-headed and fecund.'

'You served Munin.'

'I am the hanged god's servant, if one who hates and frustrates his master.'

'I will atone for my errors.'

'Then make sure that this does not happen.'

The god took the cord from Hugin's fingers, twisted it, and the third knot was in place.

'How?'

'The knot's bond is death.'

Hugin saw what the god meant. He needed to keep Aelis and whoever bore the other runes alive. While they lived, the runes could not unite and the god could not come to earth.

'Is she at Aldeigjuborg?'

'There can be no revelation without compensation. What will you do for me?'

Hugin said nothing, his head heavy and his senses beginning to dull in the presence of the god. *Loki, lord of lies.* The name came to Hugin with a sound like frying meat.

The god continued: 'Would you live? Would you walk away? Will you be content to have played the wolf and never the shepherd? Will you join the ranks of those joyous and god-blessed murderers we call heroes?' He clicked his fingers near Hugin's ear and the Raven's senses cleared.

'I do not fear for my own life.'

'Good job, considering,' said the man, 'but are you not dead?'

'You know I only appear that way.'

'A spell.'

'A trick. I have lain by the side of the dead god in the darkness, and I have shared in his knowledge, no matter how fleetingly.'

'So what will you do?'

'What would you have me do?'

'I hate the gods.'

'You are the only god here.'

Loki waved his hand and the boat was full again, the whole crew asleep under the stars.

'The men of this boat would act as gods. Like the gods they snatch children from their mothers for their amusement and profit. Like the gods they are cowardly and corrupt, though people esteem them heroes. I hate the heroes, with their murders and their wars.'

'Then you must hate me for I have killed many men.'

'Are you a hero, Hugin? Hrafn, my fine bird? Do you seek fame and glory?'

'No.'

'What do you seek?'

'I have only ever sought ... safety,' said Hugin, surprising himself with the word.

'Then give me what I want.'

'A sacrifice?'

'Not a sacrifice. You do not care for these men.'

'We cannot sail a boat with three of us.'

'Then it is a sacrifice.'

'Kill them?'

'Yes.'

'And what do I get in return, god?'

'To see your lady.''

'Will I save her?'

'The future is a teeming city. How numberless its avenues.'

'I will die.'

'A horrible and excruciating death.'

'Will it save her?'

The god leaned forward and whispered in Hugin's ear, 'I have shown you enough. Now what will you do for me?'

The Raven woke up. The night was overcast and almost light-less, though his sharp eyes could see shapes in the darkness. It was enough. Behind him, against the faint, faint light of the sky, he could see a man at the steering oar, there more out of habit than for any useful purpose. Hugin guessed that the cloud had blown in quickly and the longship had had no time to make for shore before being caught in the pitch dark. When that happened it was better to sit tight and bargain with your gods than make for the land unsighted.

Hugin did not move, he just said his charm under his breath.

> 'I am a raven,
> A rag upon the breeze.
> I am a raven,
> The hungry mouth of death.
> I am a raven,
> The cracked voice of the night.'

He said the charm over and over, opening that part of his mind that had opened in the mountain tunnel, that part that ritual and suffering had allowed him to touch. His knife had been driven into the ship's rail. He pulled it from the wood, then he was just a shadow among shadows, a darkness with a blade.

The helmsman was taken below the ribcage with a stab to the heart and died before he had a chance to scream. Hugin lowered him to the deck. The next few died quickly and silently, throats cut in their sleep. He took five that way, and crawled forwards to reach the midship. There was the smell of the mule, the bulk of the creature just visible. Hugin put his hand out, felt a turbaned head and crawled forward with his knife. *No, the god had spoken of wanting murderers. Not him. Nor the fat Viking.* He crawled round the merchant and touched a fat belly.

'What's going on?' Ofaeti's voice.

Hugin had no time to lose. He sprang through the darkness, working his knife to deadly effect.

'Hey!'

'I'm cut!'

'A troll witch!'

'I'm cut. I'm cut!'

'Aaaah!'

'Stay calm!' It was Ofaeti's voice.

But the men went for their weapons and cut at the darkness, sightless and terrified.

Hugin ducked to the deck as axe and sword bit, as arms lashed out and panic swept the ship.

'I cannot see! I cannot see!'

'Then stop fighting!'

'Is this your work, Horda man?'

There was a splash. Someone had fallen overboard. Then more screaming and the sound of axe, sword and spear striking home.

It was quiet for a while. The first rays of dawn came from behind the horizon. Hugin sat at the prow. He had recovered his curved sword. It was in his hand, naked and gleaming in the new day's light. Only five other men still lived on the longship.

'You!' said a slaver.

The merchant was lying at the back of the boat with his hands over his head, while Ofaeti stood near him at the helm, a spear pointing forward to skewer anyone who came for him.

'He has come back from the grave for us!' The gap-toothed boy let his axe slip to the deck.

'I'll kill you again, ghost!' Another slaver was not so easily scared and leaped towards Hugin with a spear. But the boat was full of dead and the dying, and he tripped as he advanced.

Hugin grabbed the spear, stepped past its point and beheaded him. In a breath a second man had his leg cut off below the shield. He fell to the blood-wet deck and took a mortal blow from Hugin's sword to the side of the head. Only the youth remained. He was crying and cowering from Hugin.

'Why have you done this? Skakki's dead. Honour is satisfied!' Ofaeti threw up his hands in disbelief.

Hugin pointed at the youth. 'He must die too.'

'Your magic?'

'The gods.'

Ofaeti turned to the youth. 'Then there's nothing for it, son. You have to fight him.'

'He will kill me! He has killed us all!'

'Believe me, the doors of Valhalla will open wide for the man who dies fighting him. It's death one way or another, so stand up and face him. Don't die snivelling and go to Hell.' He pressed an axe into the youth's hand.

'Help me against him. He might kill you too.'

'I have travelled with him for many days and he has had plenty of opportunity to do that if he wanted to. And even if that weren't the case, he has offered me no harm, so why should I seek it from him? It's a choice between you fighting him and me fighting him. You'll excuse me if I choose you. Now go on, summon your courage.'

At first the youth was tentative, but then his courage bit and he swung an overhead blow at Hugin, who closed and blocked high with the curved sword, taking off both the youth's hands at the wrist. Hugin caught the axe and turned to strike the youth from the back, hacking deep into his neck and dropping him to the deck.

Hugin looked down at the corpse he had just made.

'Are you a ghost?' said Ofaeti.

'No. It was an enchantment.'

'Nice trick. Good job we kept your body on the boat, though.'

'Is it not bad weather luck to throw a witch into the sea, even a dead one?'

'It is that. And thank your gods they were men of that opinion. I see one slave survived.'

The pale red-haired man was by the mule, still tied to the farm boy, who had been speared straight through, the weapon still stuck in him. The red-haired man said nothing. Hugin looked at him but did not associate him with the visitation of the god.

'Well,' said Ofaeti, 'there can be no slaves now. Free him and let's see if we can sail this ship.'

Leshii was convinced his leg had been broken by the mule. He swallowed down the pain and held out his knife. Ofaeti took it and went to free the slave. The man stood, seemingly no worse for his long ordeal.

'Are you a sailor, friend?' said Ofaeti.

'I am a rare salt,' said the pale man.

'Then help me sort out the sail. Hugin, merchant, you help too. Then we can get the bodies overboard. That lot smelled enough when they were alive; death will not improve them.'

The pale man was no liar and seemed a skilled sailor. The sail was up quickly, though the merchant was no help. His leg was really broken and he could not stand.

'My people have a wind charm,' said the pale man. 'Which way do you want to go?'

'Aldeigjuborg!'

The man picked up a cord from the deck. There was a strange, complicated knot in it. He unpicked the knot and shook it at the sail. The wind filled its belly and the ship moved forward with a lurch.

'We should have released you earlier,' said Ofaeti, rushing to take the tiller. 'I see you and I will be friends!'

The pale man smiled. 'Any service I give,' he said, 'I am sure you will repay.'

71 The Table of Demons

This time it was happening faster. Before, the wolf had slunk out of him; now it came raging. The hunger was irresistible. Jehan groaned and screamed as his wasted muscles twitched into movement. His limbs seemed to crack and grate as he squirmed across the cold deck.

He knew what he was going to do, knew what he needed. He was weak, his human thoughts locked below ice. Only the hunger of the wolf, the same hunger that kept him from death, was in his mind now.

He writhed his way forwards until he bumped into something. He could tell it was not part of the structure of the boat, but something softer. He couldn't make his body roll, so, shivering and shaking, he turned himself round on the floor with his legs. The effort was enormous, and, despite the cold, he was sweating. Now his head was against something that felt like a man's coat. Groaning, he wriggled his way up the body. An arm. Again, he slithered along the icy deck in increments, his muscles impelling him on and then rebelling into spasms, his joints as solidly locked as the icebound ship. And then, an ungloved hand. The men who had come onto the ship had stripped the oarsmen looking for jewellery. Jehan was next to a half-naked Viking.

He worked his head around until he had a finger in his mouth. He had too much of it, the whole finger, and couldn't bite down. Jehan pushed back with his lips until only a fold of flesh was in his teeth. The first bite was agony. He could hardly puncture the flesh. His jaw was like an old gate long surrendered to decay and rust. But move it did, and the taste of blood, rich and deep, was in his mouth with the promise of more. He swallowed. Then he bit again.

A flash of his old life came to him: the chapel at evening, the smoke of beeswax candles in the air. And then the memory slipped away, flickering into darkness like a hare into the woods. His old life was gone.

While the monks of Saint-Germain went about their duties between vespers and compline he managed two bites. Between compline and nocturns he ate six. By lauds, as the sun turned the mist to a glowing grey, he had eaten the flesh of the whole hand, his neck freer, his jaw stronger. By prime he had removed most of the flesh of the arm. By terce he had the strength to tear open the belly and eat the lights, the liver and heart. By the time vespers came round again he was sitting up on the boat, the cold freezing the Viking's blood to his clothes. But the blood in his veins was now warm, the confessor's thoughts released from their shackles of cold.

Jehan stood up and put his hand to his neck. The stone was missing. He looked down at what he had done. He felt the wolf inside him almost smirk, content to rest a while before feeding some more. Already his teeth felt too big for his head, his mouth more central to his consciousness than his hands. The change he had known before was rushing upon him now. That feeling was in him – a mixture of dread and glee as the human recognised the animal.

Why had God put him through this again? He had regained himself only to lose himself. He had been content to die and to face the mercy of God. Now he was condemned to walk again, prey to the vilest lusts.

He recalled Corinthians: *You cannot drink the cup of the Lord and the cup of demons too; you cannot have a part in both the Lord's table and the table of demons*. He looked at the wreckage of the corpse. What was that if not the table of demons? The Lord had shut him out or he had shut himself out. Whatever had happened, there was no heaven after this. So what then? Embrace hell? Never.

The wolf, he realised, had done more than give him the appetites of a beast; it had reduced him spiritually to the status of an animal. His whole life had been shaped by the idea of future reward, of heaven. That idea had been devoured by the wolf, and now he was chained to the present, his past life destroyed, his future unguessable. The instant was all he had, an endless rush of moments. That and Aelis, with whom the present was enough. She had been taken. *Captured? Enslaved or murdered?* He would find out. *So seek her out.* The wolf could find her, it had found her before. The idea was a boulder on the edge of a precipice. He only had to touch it to send it irreversibly forward.

The smirking hunger rose in him again, the feeling that hoarded bones like a miser hoards gold.

'No!'

But he was what he was, and there was no way to fight the wolf. Even now the odour of the cold corpses drifted up at him, calling him to abomination. He felt his chin wet with saliva, his teeth begin to grind.

'God,' he said, looking to the sky. 'Jesus, the test you set me was too hard.'

And then he fell upon the corpses to cool his burning appetite.

The wolf inside him would not let Jehan leave the ship until its hunger was sated. The winter deepened around him, snow was on his back but he felt no cold. No one came to interrupt his feeding. Helgi had forbidden the ship to his people, fearing that he would lose it to firewood if they were allowed near it.

So Jehan remained, icebound, eating.

Still, he heard men out on the river, their hammers breaking the ice to fish, the thick scent of oily wool drifting in on the fog, the smell of the fish themselves.

The transformation was coming fast upon him and he could sense himself growing. He would stretch out his fingers and find that when he folded them again they lay strangely in his palm.

His tongue was a bloody mess where he kept catching it as

he chewed, while his back began to hunch and his shoulders' movement to feel restricted and cramped.

The frozen days burst with odours – it was almost as if he could smell the cold. The fires of Ladoga told their stories: – old wood burning, very dry and musty as from deep in a store, first the smell of roasting meat, later only fish.

The old human stinks drifted in on him – shit and piss, sweat and bad teeth, secretions that seemed to sparkle in his mind telling their own tales of too much drink, of the exertions of work, sex and fever. He ate.

The corpses smelled wonderful to him, fascinating in their trade-off between the odours of life and the tiny decay the cold would allow them. They smelled so different to live men: the fluids of the stomach and bowels stronger, the sweat weaker, the blood full of the scent of iron.

He turned the corpses over, noting the redness of the back and buttocks where the blood had settled after death, marvelling at the mortal detail. Then suddenly his moral self would return, and he would run to the stern of the ship, putting his fingers into his mouth, trying to make himself vomit. But eventually that faded, and he felt no more revulsion that he would have chewing on an apple. The change that worried him most was the delight he seemed to take in feeding. He tried to hold back, to retreat from the euphoria, but he could not. He lay on the deck laughing and grinning, stretching his back again and again. It felt so long and so lithe.

But the confessor was a man of great will. Though he knew he could not fight the wolf, he did his best to cling to himself. Prayers and psalms seemed no use – he was separate from God, a cursed thing that crawled in blood and slime – but he thought of her. He had seen her when he was seven and she had told him, 'Do not seek me.' Yet he had looked for her, not with his body but with his will. He had wanted her at his side. Even in his affliction he had called out to her, though he had tried to muffle his inner voice with prayer.

Now he called to her again: 'Aelis, please. Come to me.

Adisla. In my life before I said I would find you and I am here.'

The fog meant nothing to him. His sense of smell and his hearing guided him across the land at night when there was no light. In the day, when the light from the sun was no more than a brightening of the fog's grey, his eyes could pick out shapes – men fishing on the ice, animals moving across the frozen river – though they did not see him. He roamed, looking for her, but she had gone, it seemed. He couldn't smell her, couldn't hear her. On the barrows beyond the town walls he sat and watched for her. He called but she didn't answer. When he saw the stir his cries caused, the men running to the ramparts with torches; when he smelled their fear and heard their hearts beating quicker than their steps, he went back to the ship, back to the bodies and his feeding and his growing until the remains of the Vikings were all gone.

He awoke one morning when the air was the colour of cloudy steel and spoke.

'I am hungry,' he said.

He first took a fisherman at his hole in the ice. The next day he took a guard from the ramparts of the town, leaping up to drag him down to his death on the frozen river.

Then he was hunted, men moving through the fog with torches and dogs. The words on their lips were harsh and he knew they were meant for him: 'troll-witch, fen dweller, monster, wolf'.

He went deep into the fog and waited until they retreated. The boat was now closed to him, just a place where men waited, a brazier on the ice, spears and axes at their sides.

He watched them in silence, trying to make himself leave, trying to resist the urge to see them as prey.

But then, when the hint of a thaw was on the breeze, people came with a mule. His memory sparked and he saw himself in a river, pulling a fat man from the black waters, remembered Saint-Maurice, the blood, that terrible sorcerer watching him.

He remembered the merchant who had fretted and sweated in the forest where the Viking Saerda had pushed him down the path to abomination. He crept closer and could make them out quite clearly – the fat Viking, the little merchant with his mule and the Raven, the one who had killed the witch. He knew them, but not as he had known them before – by vision and voice – but by scent. But he would not go to them. His animal drives were stronger than his human thoughts. He tried to understand what he was feeling. A phrase came to him: *I am full of food and do not need to exert myself.*

He watched as the travellers greeted the men on the boat. Then a guard left along the frozen river with the merchant following on his plodding mule.

72 Unexpected Welcome

The fog did not lift and it seemed that winter would go on for ever. Helgi sat in his hall, Aelis silent and brooding nearby on a bench. Since he had put the stone on her she had hardly spoken a word. However, the girl's inability to remove the pendant told him he had been right to do so. *She was one of them that Loki had mentioned, for sure. The fragments of the god.* Helgi felt he had for the moment neutralised her.

Aelis looked at him with anger in her eyes. He knew she wanted to know what had happened to the monk. She had even tried to return to the ice herself, but he'd had his guards stop her. Her persistent questioning almost made him wish he had rescued the monk too. He couldn't understand her attachment to the cripple. She seemed convinced he was enchanted, which made Helgi nervous. Eventually, Helgi felt he had to come up with a story and told her he had sent the monk to a mountain witch for a cure.

'You cannot explain this to me as you would to a child whose dog has died,' she had said.

'I am a king,' said Helgi, 'and I owe you no explanation. You should thank me. You asked me to free you from the magic, and I did. We are all safer now.' She'd just looked at him with her even stare, shaken her head and said nothing.

The townsfolk were used to her now and the hall was thronged with the everyday crowd, a small market in operation, inside to shelter from the cold.

'Lord.'

It was one of the *druzhina*, the cold clinging to him as he entered the hall.

'What is it?'

'The merchant has returned. Leshii is back.'

Helgi stood. 'And the wolfman too? Myrkyrulf?'

'I don't know, *khagan*.'

'Don't know?'

'It's difficult to say. He has a companion, but he's a sorcerer and I never look too closely at those. They can bewitch you with their eyes. They have warnings for you, *khagan*.'

'What warnings?'

'They would not say.' The merchant had decided to leave all that to the Raven to explain.

Helgi glanced at Aelis. He knew that her power was contained and felt secure as long as the winter lasted, but also knew the runes would aim to reunite, that the other fragments of the god might come searching. He now had a more secure home for her. Despite the fog, work on it had continued, and it was finished.

She was looking at him. Helgi had used the Norse word *ulfhethinn* – wolfman – and had mentioned the name, Myrkyrulf.

'Sindre is dead,' she said. Her Norse was faltering and unclear since he had put the stone on her.

'What?'

She said it again in Roman. A spice seller – who had found little appetite for his wares since the fog descended – translated for the king: 'The wolfman you sent for me died in the north of my country.'

'And the merchant I sent with him?'

The spice seller translated: 'Without the wolfman's protection perhaps he lived, but I cannot see how.'

'You are sure this is the wolfman?' said Helgi to the guard.

'I'm sure it's the merchant, sir. He's thinner than he was but I'm sure it's him. The wolfman, no. I remember the fellow and he was a head above me. This man is the same size.'

'And yet he claims to be the same sorcerer who came here?'

'He said to tell the *khagan* that Sindre was here with the merchant and they had urgent business with him. They have a Viking with them – fat and tall. A great warrior, I should say.'

Helgi looked at the girl. Could this be the one that was prophesied? The half-god, looking to be complete? Odin, god of the hanged, of the spear, of magic and poetry, come to kill him and steal his crown.

'The merchant is outside?'

'Yes, sir.'

'Take the lady to the gate by the back door of this hall. Do not let him see you. Leave her there and come back.'

Aelis was led out. She wanted to protest, but with the stone about her neck she was torpid and dull-witted; her limbs were heavy and her head ached.

'Bring the merchant in.'

Leshii hobbled into the great hall feeling as if he might be sick. His leg was very painful despite the Raven's artful splints and herbs, and it was beginning to swell and blacken. It had been shattered, and had it not been for the Raven's medicines Leshii would have been unable to stand. The Raven had offered to remove the leg but Leshii had refused. He knew his time was up and saw no reason to spend what he had left in any more pain than he needed to.

Still, he could not quite bring himself to leave his swords and used the bundle in which they were tied as a sort of cumbersome crutch as he came before the king.

The murderous thing stalking the fog meant that no stranger would be allowed in to town. Leshii, however, had known the guards and been led to the king to bargain for his companion's entrance while they waited on the ice. He was not hopeful.

Only the certainty of his death had given him the courage to enter the town. He still had to find the lady for the Raven and Ofaeti if he could but he was glad he would not have to sell her. He would be protecting her, saving her from the teeth of the wolf. And if the Raven fulfilled his threat to kill Helgi? So what? Leshii knew he did not have long and Helgi, he felt sure, would punish him for returning empty-handed.

But he would die at home, after a life on the trail. No foreign sands would cover his bones; he would lie in no perilous forest or high mountain pass. He would die within a few paces of the market where he had traded for thirty years, within an apple-pip spit of the land upon which he had hoped to build his comfortable house and fuck his dancing girls.

Helgi was seated on his big chair, the one he used on market days to judge the people's disputes.

'Dread *khagan*,' said Leshii, attempting a bow.

'You have the girl?'

'No, lord.'

'Then you are a bold fellow, returning here. What is your purpose?'

'I seek news of her. She should be here by now – I sent her ahead.'

Helgi's face was a mask. 'You do not fear the wrath of your lord?'

'I do, *khagan*, but I am old and I tried very hard to bring her here. We were separated to the north of Francia and I have not seen her since. I was with her on a boat but was washed overboard in a high sea. Thankfully a whale delivered me to the shore and I was saved, but the lady was gone.'

Leshii did not want to admit he had been thrown off the ship by the Vikings because that would have made him look weak. Neither did he want to start mentioning werewolves as he knew there were those in the town who might think he had brought the fog monster with him.

'A whale?'

'Yes, lord.'

Helgi nodded. 'I have heard it said they will sometimes save a drowning man.'

'And so it proved for me, lord. But I set the lady on a ship with paid guards. I am surprised she is not here by now.'

'Did you not fear for a lady on a ship full of strangers?'

'She is a powerful sorcerer, lord. Men move against her and die like mayflies. She appears from the shimmering air; kings fall dead before her, and evil powers cannot touch her.'

Helgi nodded. 'These are the signs I expected. It was your doing that she came by boat to Aldeigjuborg?'

'Yes, *khagan*.'

'And the wolfman?'

'Dead in north Francia.'

Helgi turned to a *druzhina*. 'Bring the merchant a bench – can't you see he's wounded. And a cup of hot wine.'

Leshii had to resist the temptation to rub his ears. He couldn't quite believe what he had just heard.

The bench was provided and Leshii gulped the wine down. Then he knocked back another cup.

'A third,' said Helgi, and the merchant's cup was refreshed again. The prince was staring at Leshii like a money changer who suspects a coin to be false but can see no proof that it actually is.

'But who are the two who travel with you?'

Leshii thought he should stress the fine qualities of Ofaeti and Hugin in order that Helgi might find them some service if their mission to find Aelis failed. 'They helped me on my journey here. One is a mighty warrior of the north, a prince in his own realm. He is the most formidable warrior I have ever seen – next to yourself, *khagan*.'

'Bring him in and let's test that claim,' said one of the *druzhina*. Helgi waved his hand to silence him.

'On a ship here he was unarmed and yet went unflinching into a battle with five men and emerged the victor. He throws a spear well enough to pin a fly to the wall and is a mighty and formidable poet. His name is Ofaeti but he has many others that speak flatteringly of his battle prowess.'

'And the other, his companion?'

'A sorcerer and servant to your northern gods. He bears a message for you and would seek an audience.'

'What is his name?'

'Hugin, my lord.'

Helgi swallowed. 'Did he travel with another?'

'His sister, my lord. The witch Munin, though she is dead.'

498

Again Helgi swallowed and called for wine himself. Then he stood and spoke:

> 'Over the spacious earth each day
> Hugin and Munin set forth to fly.
> For Hugin I fear lest he not come home,
> But for Munin my care is more.'

He sipped at his cup. 'Do you know the rhyme, merchant?'

'I have heard it at the fire, *khagan*.'

'Do you know where it comes from?'

Leshii didn't want to belittle the northerners' religion by calling it a story, so he said, 'Is it not holy lore?'

'It is the sayings of the mad god Odin, god of kings, magic and the hanged. So Munin is dead.'

'The sorceress died in Flanders.'

Helgi nodded. 'I had never thought that verse could be a prophecy too.'

Leshii knew better than to question kings uninvited but he wondered to himself what exactly it might prophesy.

'The signs are all here,' said Helgi, 'all of them. This fog is not natural and a mighty warrior walks out of the ice in the company of ravens.'

'That is not as mysterious as it sounds,' said Leshii. 'We met another sorcerer on the boat, a man of great power. He guided us here, helped us on our way.'

'How?'

'He caused the wind to blow and the frost to melt away. We sailed past the lake and a good way up the river before he took the ship and turned back.'

Helgi went white. 'No man has power like that. Magic is a woman's art. Only the gods in man's form can perform such feats.'

'This was a man, sir, tall and pale. One of your people, by his hair.'

'What of his hair?'

'It was bright red. As red as the comb on a cock, all stood up in a shock. He steered us here himself and kept us from the shore, which was a good thing because the Franks and the Jomsvikings have the whole coast in flames between them.'

The prince threw his cup down. The god, the one who had wandered in from the blizzard – Loki, on a ship. Helgi recalled the prophecy:

> *A ship journeys from the east.*
> *The people of the land of fire are coming over the waves,*
> *And Loki steers.*
> *There are the monstrous brood with all the raveners.*

It was a prediction of what would happen in the end time, before Odin fought the wolf on the Gods' final day. *This ship came from the west, though. But what was west? It had come through the Eastern Lake.* Prophecies, he knew, were rarely clear.

The *khagan* regained his temper. 'See the merchant is rewarded,' he said. 'Give him fifty dinars and he may stay in our hall if he wishes. Or wherever he chooses. I expect he wants a bed slave, and these Slavs have a peculiar love of solitude in such matters.' He turned to a *druzhina*. 'It is time,' he said. 'Bring the girl to the gate.'

'And the foreigners on the ice, lord?'

'Kill them. Take sixty men.'

'Yes, *khagan*,' said the warrior, and ran from the hall.

73   Helgi's Destiny

The shaft had been very difficult to construct and had already cost the lives of three eastern slaves when it collapsed half dug. Now it was done, smooth-sided, the depth of three men, sunk down to where Gillingr's tomb had been.

Aelis was led forward, a spear at her back. The pebble was a dead weight and she stumbled forward through the fog. There was no need to bind her. Since the stone had been placed around her neck her mind had felt slow, her limbs heavy. She could not have run if she had tried. The runes were silent inside her. At the mouth of the shaft she stood and looked around. The fog had sucked all the colour out of the landscape; black rocks lay on a grey hillside.

A straggle of people followed – curious women and children glad to get out of the town under the protection of the *druzhina* after so long locked in by the fog. The merchant came along too, on his mule, though he had finally given up on his swords and left them in the hall. He had heard what was to happen to Aelis and had no appetite for profit.

At the mouth of the shaft he dismounted and hobbled over to Helgi. He seemed to be imploring the king or asking him something, but she didn't understand what. Her Norse had faded. However, she had lived before, she knew, and she remembered much of what had happened to her then, not as a story but as flashes of images, faces looming at her, visions of ships, of a burning village, of someone she cared for dead, butchered on a bed.

'What is to happen to me, merchant?' she asked in Roman.

Leshii was pale. 'You are to go down the ladder. I am sorry, lady. I took you from your home for profit. I thought you would be his bride. I did not think this fate awaited you.'

Aelis looked around her. She turned to Helgi. 'Is this the island?' She spoke in Roman.

Helgi replied in Norse and she did not understand him.

He saw by her blank look that she did not and tried again in rough Roman: 'What island?'

'The island where you buried me before.'

'You make no sense. Have you lost your Norse?' Helgi was more certain than ever that he was following the right course of action.

'He came for me then. He will come for me again.'

'What is she saying?' He turned to Leshii beside him.

'She says he came for her before and will come for her again.'

'Who?'

'The wolf.'

'You are the only wolf, lady.'

'You will not kill me.'

Helgi rattled off something in Norse to the merchant who repeated slowly, 'He does not intend to kill you. He intends you to live.'

'In there?'

'In there. For protection,' said Helgi.

'To the dark?'

'To the dark. Though you are ...' He couldn't think of the right Roman word so he gestured to some baskets containing blankets, food, flint and candles.

'How long must I stay there?'

'Until things are put right.'

'For ever?'

Helgi spoke to Leshii again, and the little merchant translated: 'Do you know who you are?'

'A little broken thing,' said Aelis.

'Three would become one,' said Helgi in ponderous Roman. 'Cannot happen. One conqueror, one lord. Odin must wait.'

'If I am so magical, how can you constrain me?'

Leshii translated and Helgi tapped the pebble at her neck. 'Loki, Odin. Great wolf. No magic,' he said.

Aelis had seen the stone's effect on Jehan and knew what he was trying to say. What had happened to the confessor without it? Was he dead or, worse, transformed, his jaws red with murder? She felt more connected to the gods Helgi had mentioned than she did to the faith in which she had been raised. Her faith had always been one of duty rather than passion — she spent dull Sundays in church more interested in catching up on the gossip than hearing the works of Jesus. When Helgi spoke of the wolf and of Odin, she felt the truth of it in her bones. *Look around at the world*, she thought, *and say it was made in the image of a gentle god.*

When the gods saw that the wolf was fully bound, they took a fetter and lashed it to a rock called Scream. Why were those words so deep in her mind, why did she recall them instead of a prayer or a psalm?

'The ladder,' said Helgi.

Aelis put her hands to her neck to remove the pendant but she found she still could not. Her fingers wouldn't do her bidding and she could not make them remove the thong.

'Good proof,' said Helgi. 'Lady, it is time. Go into the mine.'

Aelis looked at the northern barbarian, his ridiculous kaftan, his ballooning trousers. She was of the line of Robert the Strong, more noble by far than he. So she would not struggle, would not weep. Instead she smiled at him. 'When you war with gods, first be sure your grave is dug, barbarian. Your men who sweated to make this hole will sweat over their spades for you before long, I think.' She spat at him, and from somewhere words came back to her: '*I dag deyr thú.*'

'This will be my death day?' said Helgi. 'Perhaps, and perhaps not. Horse will kill me. Foreseen. Have no horse, so I am a safe man.'

'The gods do not like to hear such talk,' said Aelis. 'They may take that as a challenge.'

Helgi understood little of what she said but grasped its sentiment well enough. He pursed his lips. 'Fine woman, you,' he said. 'Sorry to do this. It is the only way.'

Aelis turned away from him to show that he was beneath her notice. Then she went to the ladder and climbed down. It was drawn up and the baskets were lowered after her. She looked up. There was a square of grey light. Helgi looked down at her.

'Tunnels are warm lower down,' said Helgi. 'You live, I promise. Here to live, not die.'

From down the river a wolf was howling.

'And you will die very soon,' said Aelis. 'My promise holds equally true.'

Helgi turned to his warriors. 'Who am I?'

'Helgi the Prophet!' they shouted as one.

'What is Helgi's destiny?'

'To be killed by his horse!'

'How many horses does Helgi own?'

'None?'

'Then who can oppose him?'

'No man!'

'Who can oppose him?'

'No man!'

From down on the river past the town came the sound of a great crash and then men shouting. Leshii looked around. Helgi's men had found his friends.

'Who can oppose him?' Helgi had his sword in the air, waving it above his head.

'No man!'

The *druzhina* cheered and howled, banging on their shields.

Leshii came up behind the *khagan*. He slipped the knife from his waistband, the silk cutter he had used on Aelis's hair, and drove it hard into Helgi's back.

'I am your mule, *khagan*, so men call me,' he said, 'though in reality I am a just a little man, unconsidered by kings and heroes.'

Helgi's hand went to his back and clawed at the knife, but it would not come out.

'Sváva,' said Helgi. He tried to say something more but couldn't. He took a pace, stumbled and fell into the shaft.

Then the *druzhina* cut Leshii down.

74 Brave Fatty

Ofaeti and Hugin sat by the brazier with the guards.

'This is a curious vessel,' said Ofaeti, 'a ship with no oars-men but a deal of blood here frozen on the boards.'

Hugin stared into the mist. The riverbanks were no more than shadows, but on the one furthest from the boat was an-other shadow – not a rock, he was sure. He sniffed hard. There was a smell to it. Wolf.

'There's something out there,' he said. 'A wolf.'

'Where?'

The Raven pointed. A howl came from the bank, eerily flat in the heavy air.

'Our friend the wolf?'

'I think so,' said Hugin.

'Then we are in good luck to have found him so soon. We can kill him and go home.'

There was movement on the ice – black shapes, fog spectres. But not spectres, men. Twenty paces from the ship the *druzhina* emerged. They were terrifying-looking warriors – gigantic in their furs, their breath steaming about them as if they were creatures of the mist. They faced the ship in a line, silently staring at the men by the brazier. The Raven's sword was free from its scabbard and the two guards soon lay dead.

'Too late to worry about what's out there, I think,' said Ofaeti, glancing down at the corpses. He looked at the fog; it was still reducing vision to less than the throw of a stone. He could run, he thought, lose himself in the murk. Maybe. But he would probably be cut down before he got away. Unlike the Raven, he wasn't quick on his feet. Besides, he hadn't been raised that way. Running was not for Thiörek, called Ofaeti, son of Thetmar of the berserker line of Thetleif. He vaulted into the ship and drew his sword.

The Raven gave him a questioning look.

'Go if you need to,' said Ofaeti, 'but tell my tale. Say how the brave fatty faced the many at Aldeigjuborg and made a few widows before he died.'

'Run. We'll make the shore before they do. *You* are to tell *my* tale.'

'And miss this glory? Find another skald to sing your songs, crow balls.' Ofaeti grinned and raised his shield. The warriors advanced at the walk. They had cords tied about the soles of their boots and had a good grip on the snow that lay on the river's ice.

'They're coming. Go on.' The Raven held out his hand across the rail of the ship. Ofaeti took it. 'Tell my tale,' he said. Hugin nodded and was gone, a scrap of black fading to grey in the fog.

Ofaeti addressed the *druzhina*: 'Now, my ice maidens, which one of you wants to face me in single combat here in the boat? What say you send forward your best man, and if I kill him you send me on my way with a pat on the back?'

Ofaeti forced his grip to relax on his sword. His mind went back to the victory they had won on the boat after the merchant had sacrificed the necklace.

The warriors kept coming, their pace increasing. 'Come on then! But I warn you – you are many and I am one but I have Loki's luck!'

The *druzhina* broke into a charge and Ofaeti prepared himself to die.

75 A Leap of Faith

The shaft had been cut down into a tunnel which was propped up with pillars of stone and baked brick and extended away from Aelis, ahead and behind. In the shaft she could stand and see, while the day lasted. To gain any shelter from rain or cold she would have to crawl into the darkness.

Aelis struck at her flint. The momentary flash revealed little. It was as if the tunnel ahead of her ate the light, sucking it down into two black pits. She struck again, got some tinder going and lit the little lamp that had been provided for her.

Aelis sat for a while. Her hands went again to the pendant at her neck but she could not remove it, couldn't make her fingers lift it or undo the knot. She looked up at the sky. The greyness was losing its glow. Soon it would be night. Rational thought seemed to evade her. *How to get out?* She just couldn't force her terrified mind to concentrate.

Slowly, some sort of calm returned. Being scared was not going to get her out of the pit. Helgi had called it a mine, and if it was a mine then there would be wood or something she could drive into the wall of the shaft to climb out. Yes, it would be easy to climb up the inside of the shaft if only she could find some wood. She put the flint and tinder away in its pouch, which she tucked inside her tunic. She couldn't afford to lose that.

There was a thump and something hit her hard across the face, knocking the lamp to the floor. She put out her hand and felt something. *An arm!* She could just make it out in the guttering flame of the lamp. Aelis drove herself back against the wall to get away from the dead man. She heard screams and shouts from above, some in Norse, some in Roman.

'Witch!'

'She bewitched the merchant!'

'Kill her!'

'He's dead, Helgi is dead!'

'Troll-witch, houserider!'

There was a dead body in front of her. It was him, Helgi. There was no time for horror or elation;, she had to save herself. She forced herself to crawl forwards. Protruding from the dead prince's back was the handle of a knife. She pulled it out, kneeling on the body's blood-wet furs. It came free. She looked at it and knew who had killed the *khagan*.

Aelis picked up the lamp and scrambled into the tunnel. She crawled, putting the lamp in front of her. But the tunnel quickly became very low and she was panicking. As she moved the lamp forward, she drove it into a rock. Its clay bulb burst. All she had was the oil on the wick. When that was gone she would be in darkness. She had gone no more than a body length when the flame guttered and died. Now she felt her way with her hands. The passage dropped steeply but she went on, scraping her knees and crying out when her head hit the low roof.

Men were coming down the ladder. Again the word she had heard so many times in Norse she needed no magic to translate it: 'Witch!'

Aelis put her hand to the floor in front of her and felt nothing. The ground had disappeared. She turned around and dangled her legs into the void. They touched nothing, not even when she stretched them forward.

'Get a torch!' The voice was one of the *khagan*'s wider army because it spoke in rough Greek.

So many voices now, she wondered the shaft could contain them all. She could hear five men at least behind her and other more distant voices, shouting and angry.

What to do? It wouldn't be long before her mind was made up for her. She felt for a ladder going down, a foothold, anything. There was nothing. A fluttering yellow light came from behind her. Her pursuers had their torch. They were coming, crawling down the tunnel. Something flashed in the dark. A spear tip.

'Witch!'

The man thrust with his spear but he wasn't near enough. He crawled forward and pulled back his arms to strike again.

She searched for something to pray to. God? He had gone from her life. The runes? Never. They had robbed her of herself. She could think of nothing to help her at all.

'Die, witch,' said the man.

Then a name came to her, a name at once familiar and strange, from the life she had lived before. Not a magical creation at all; now more a memory, like a bright flash of childhood alive for a second in the adult mind.

'Vali, help me!' she whispered and jumped into the darkness.

76 Down

Hugin followed the riverbank back into town. He would need to go in there alone. No matter; he had done that before. As he drew near to Ladoga's walls he could hear voices – screaming and shouting – women, children. What had happened? A name was on their lips: 'Helgi!'

He ran towards the shouting. When the voices were almost on top of him, he looked to his left and saw a large wooden tower looming above him from the fog. The gatehouse. He knew that entering the town was almost certain death. Helgi had clearly ordered him killed, along with his companions. He crossed the river on the ice. Women, children and old men were pushing in through the gate. Some were crying, others seemed panic-stricken.

Hugin grabbed a woman who was trying to encourage a young child to move faster. 'What's happened?' he said.

'You are the sorcerer they are looking for you. Get away from me!'

He drew his sword to show a thumb's width of steel.

'What has happened?'

'You should know, troll-witch. Our Helgi is dead. Our protector is dead.'

'How?'

'He put her in the earth and she struck at him. The Frankish witch cast a glamour on a man who Helgi had well rewarded. Our prince is dead. Dead, and we must look to our defences.'

Hugin turned away from the gate and ran back along the stream of people. The woman screamed after him that an enemy was among them, but the confusion was too great, the fog too thick. He was just a shape in the mist.

He was running up a hill now. Men's voices shouting,

'Witch, witch, kill the witch!' Hugin knew there was no time for reason, debate or argument. These men had found Aelis and were going to kill her.

Black shadows in front of him. Another four paces and they were men – *druzhina* with spears, not looking at him but peering down at their feet. He charged, beheading one with a left-to-right diagonal swipe and kicking the man next to him in the small of the back, hoping to put him out of the fight for long enough to deal with his two comrades. Hugin took off the hand of a *druzhina* who was trying to draw his sword and booted him into the man behind him, sending both warriors sprawling. He then killed the uninjured man with a blow to the head. The sword jammed in the skull. Hugin let it go. The handless man was in shock, staring at his bloody stump. Hugin drew his knife and gutted him then turned to face the *druzhina* he had kicked at the start of the attack. The man wasn't there.

Only then did Hugin realise there was a pit in front of him and the man had fallen in. The townswoman's words came back to him: *He put her in the earth.*

A face appeared over the lip of the hole and Hugin kicked it as hard as he could. The man fell back and Hugin heard shouting below. He looked down. A *druzhina* with a torch was looking up – eight or nine more of them in the tiny pit, fearful faces gazing at him. He tried to pull up the ladder but the men grabbed it, though none of them looked as though they wanted to climb it to their deaths.

Working quickly, Hugin shoved the nearest body to the edge of the pit and booted it in. More shouting from below. He could tell the pit was deep but not so deep he couldn't jump down. He rolled another body to the edge and hurled the corpse down. Then he freed his sword from the warrior's skull and rolled that man in to the pit too. He was about to leap down himself when he saw something from the corner of his eye. The body of the merchant. He could only really tell it was him from his silk turban because his corpse had been reduced to mere meat by the ferocity of the attack that had killed him.

'Come on,' said the Raven. 'You can join me in a last battle, merchant.'

He rolled the body to the edge of the pit with his foot and then booted it in, jumping in after it without a sound, his long knife drawn. He wanted the *druzhina* to think that he was just another body, harmless beyond its initial impact. For the first breath when he landed he would be just a corpse. Then he would start to make them.

Men broke his fall – dead and living, the torch hitting the floor and going out as he smashed into the warriors. Hugin went wild, slashing and stabbing as he had never done before. No one could see, but Hugin had eight targets, his opponents only one. Swords were too big, axes useless, but the *druzhina* used them anyway. Friend killed friend in the tiny space, Rus axe struck Rus flesh, Rus sword tore Rus guts. At last it was quiet and the Raven stood on his corpse mound, not knowing whether to hold his shoulder or his face. Both were cut and his tongue came out of the wound in his cheek all the way to his back teeth. Never mind, his sword arm was in good order.

Light came from a tunnel at his feet.

He hauled the bodies out of the way and crawled into the tiny space. It was about ten body lengths long and tight as a coffin. He wriggled forward, hoping there was no *druzhina* coming the other way. If there was one with a spear then Hugin was dead. There was no *druzhina*; only a torch burning weakly on the floor of the tunnel. Hugin shouldered his way forward. The torch was near the lip of a shaft that disappeared into darkness. He could see nothing down there.

Then he heard a voice: 'Witch! Where are you, witch?'

There was a woman's scream and a man's roar.

Hugin pulled himself forward. The ceiling was a little higher over the pit and he managed to sit upright. He sheathed his knife, checked the tie on his sword and jumped into the darkness, into the cold black water.

77 The Dread Wolf Fenrir

Black, freezing water, so cold and dark it numbed all sense of where the surface was. Aelis kicked up, breathed in and choked, kicked again in panic and finally took air into her lungs. Her limbs were dead, her heart pounding. She could see nothing and the water was deep. And then a tiny light, wavering in the darkness. She kicked towards it, taking in mouthfuls of icy water, flailing her arms.

Her hand hit something solid. A shelf of some sort. She blinked the water out of her eyes and looked around her. She seemed to be in a large cavern, the water ending at a ledge that had clearly been cut rather than formed by nature.

A man dropped into the pool behind her and panic took over. She couldn't lift herself out of the water. She had hit her head when she fell. Pain spread across her forehead and she feared she would pass out. She glanced over her shoulder. The man behind her was much taller than she was and had found the bottom with his feet. He was walking towards her, his head out of the water. She was trembling, her hands unable to grasp her knife.

A searing pain shot into her guts. She reached down to feel something hard and sharp protruding from her belly. The man had a spear and he had thrust it straight through her, she realised. She retched and and cried out, one hand reaching for the bank, the other grasping the spearhead.

And then from above her she felt hands reaching down about her neck.

'It is time,' said a childish voice. 'The stone has protected your deliverers. Its task is over.' The pendant was untied and the runes lit up all around her again.

The warrior leaped at her, pushing her head underwater.

The spear twisted as their bodies came together and the runes shrieked and sang as they spun in three orbits of eight around Aelis and around the figure on the side of the pool.

Aelis tried to go to the garden of her mind, to that place at Loches where the candles burned, but the runes were dancing, and she could not make them send her there. She gulped in freezing mouthfuls. Then it was quiet. She heard a girl's voice in her head: *I have waited so long in the dark for you. The runes showed me you would come here if I led the wolf to you.'*

Who are you?

My name is your name.

Who are you?

Odin.

I am not a god, said Aelis.

The runes are inside you. Sixteen strong. When they become twenty-four you and I will be the god.

How shall they become twenty-four?

In Odin's old way. Death, said the voice.

Do not give in to him.

He is you. This is our destiny. Three will become one, the knot will be retied and the dead lord will live to die in Middle Earth, to make his sacrifice to fate. We are three, made whole and new again in death, tied in the knot of death.

The god is in us but he is not us. Let him wait for death, let him not live to die. If I live then you can live too.

But you will not live.

I will live.

You will not live, said the voice.

The runes in Aelis were singing, answering voices in perfect counterpoint to the other ones in the chamber.

I am not what I was.

What were you? said the voice.

A woman in a garden.

And I am not what I was.

What were you?

A child beneath a bench.

What have we become?

Little broken things.

Parts of a whole, said Aelis.

The runes spun and danced, and Aelis felt herself returning – Aelis, the frightened girl who had run from Paris, she of the line of Robert the Strong who only wanted to go back to that garden at Loches and see the moths dancing in the torchlight. But the moths weren't dancing, she remembered; they were burning and dying.

She was underwater, Aelis realised, not breathing. The connection with her runes was weak. They were grouping together, eight, eight and eight, a triple knot forming in her mind, a knot older than the gods. Aelis felt behind her and put her fingers to the shaft of the spear that impaled her. She felt as if she had eaten too much, stuffed herself with an agonisingly enormous amount of food. She felt the runes' departure like a tugging on her skin. She heard a noise like tearing gristle, smelled burning and knew that the thing with the childish voice intended her to die.

But there was one rune the child-thing that spoke to her had not seen, did not want. In her agony Aelis felt something step from the shadows of her mind and watched the rune slink forward, like a hunting wolf, low and lithe. Aelis heard a howl rupture the dead air of the cavern – like a wolf's but wilder, more distressed. The rune snaked and pulsed in front of her, a dark slash in the fabric of reality. It was older than all the others, and it said so many things, but loudest of all it said, *Wolf trap*.

It spoke to Aelis, and she saw that it had been in her far longer than the other runes, stretching back many lives. And Aelis realised the voice was wrong: she did not have sixteen runes within her. She had seventeen. This rune did not dance in the orbits of eight, this rune did not chime or cheep or sing, but slunk and crept in the shadows of her mind. It was the rune that seemed like a rip in the daylight, the rune that howled.

'Vali! Help me! Jehan, as you have become, help me!'

The rune's darkness intensified inside her and a cold howl seemed to splinter her mind. All the fragments of what she had been rushed in on her. A girl by a hut by the water, a captive travelling north to be the instrument of sorcerers, a traveller rushing south in the snow, a girl in a garden by a river, a lady kneeling in the dark of a church, a fugitive, hunted and harried, a vessel, a cup to hold magical and perilous powers.

Breath! She was up from the water and in the air. Hands were around her waist, trying to push her out of the pool, but the spear that impaled her was too much of an encumbrance. The water was warmer, she noticed, and the warrior who had tried to drown her was gone.

'Who?'

'Hugin. Yours. I am he that protected you before, come for you. Feileg.'

The last word was a name, spoken uncertainly. It stirred memories in her, as the wind brings sound from the smoke vent of a house. She had been there before, in such a place underground, facing a terrible and murderous child. Words came back to her said in regret and misery, but words that she meant more than anything she had ever said in her life before.

'I will live again without you, Vali. You are hated by the dead god.'

In the garden at Loches, where the moon metalled the trees and the river lay like a bridge of light between the darkness it came from and the darkness into which it disappeared, something had chased her. Now she could turn to face it. She saw him standing there. The confessor, Jehan, the man who, when she looked again, was a wolf. Ahead of her on the path through the trees stood another man, almost identical, his face untorn by scars or welts, a man who beckoned her with love in his eyes. It was Hugin, the Raven – Feileg as she had known him in the life before. The truth was clear to anyone. The two men were brothers.

In the underground chamber there was a crash and the

ceiling shook, sending stalactites crashing into the water.

'He is coming.' The childish voice again. 'Kill her.' Suáva spoke to Hugin. But the runes were still locked in their embrace, not listening to what she said.

There was another enormous crash and part of the ceiling collapsed into the pool.

Suáva shouted,

'A ship sails from across the sea,
And Loki is steering.
There with the wolf
Comes the lord of lies.'

There was a shuddering blow stronger than that of a gale sea into a headland – Aelis felt it in her chest – and the ceiling collapsed. Grey daylight flooded in, and with it a terrible howl, a sound from the dungeons where the mind buries its fears.

The voice was nearly screaming now:

'Stone cliffs tumble
And troll-witches stumble.
Men tread the road to hell
And the sky is sundered.'

The wolf's head came drooling through the gap in the ceiling, snapping and biting at the air, dislodging a torrent of soil.

'Will it harm us?'

'It is here to kill us,' said the voice, 'but it needs a littler murder first.'

The wolf dropped into the pool with a huge splash and Aelis clung to Hugin as the water swept over her head. He had her and, despite the spear, pushed her up onto the lip of the pool. She thought she would black out with the agony. Her vision blurred and she vomited blood. When she regained her sight she looked up to see two figures beside her. One was Hugin. He'd dragged her from the water, away from those huge jaws, which opened to the height of a man. The other was the emaciated figure of a woman or a child, it was difficult to tell which. Her body was terribly thin and her face was the face of the drowned.

'Stop!' Aelis screamed at the wolf as it fixed the child with a stare, drawing its lips back from its dripping jaws.

It turned its great head. 'Aelis,' it said, 'I am here for you. I am here to protect you.'

'I am dying and you cannot.' Another piece of the ceiling fell into the pool. The rest was crumbling and looked ready to cave in.

'I am a healer. I can help you.'

'Do you know yourself, Confessor? You are a killer and a slayer of many.'

'I am lost, Aelis.'

The runes were humming around her like moths and butterflies, bees and sparrows. They were uniting, she could feel, and she knew for sure she was dying. 'This is our destiny,' she said. 'It has always been and will always be. You are the killer and I draw you to the kill.'

'We will oppose it,' said Hugin. In future lives perhaps we will know ourselves and avoid this fate.'

'Then we all must die,' said the wolf, 'so we all might live again.' It leaned out of the water, its head over the shelf of rock.

'This is the skein that is woven,' said Sváva, 'again and again and again. The slaughter-fond god will come and he will have his death.'

'Then let us die,' said Hugin.

'No!' Aelis cried out but Hugin came forward and struck the wolf across the muzzle with his sword, sheering away a great flap of flesh and exposing the teeth beneath.

The great wolf howled and shook. Jehan could no longer control the animal he was.

Hugin raised his blade for a second blow but the wolf was too quick. It drove its jaws into his body, seized him about the waist, tearing a handspan of flesh from his side, and threw him behind it into the water, the sword still gripped in his hand, slashing wildly. Hugin tried to get up, but there was a rumble and a great slab of ceiling fell away, crashing down on top of him.

Ofaeti, standing deep inside the hole the wolf had torn in the barrow, watched Hugin sink. He swung himself down on a tree root onto the pile of rock and earth that had fallen from the ceiling and groped in the water. He gripped something. A hand, still holding that curved sword. Ofaeti pulled and the Raven came free, gasping and choking into the air.

The wolf stared down at Aelis. 'I will not kill you.'

'There will be no need,' said Aelis.

'I have loved you.'

'And I have loved you, but this destiny is too terrible. If I live again, Jehan, you must never come near me.'

'I will find a way to come to you in safety.'

'There is none.'

'Our destiny is death, torture and suffering, again and again, into eternity,' said Sváva.

'No!' said the wolf and drove its teeth towards her. She threw out her girl's arms to fend off his jaws but he caught her by them, pulling her forward, tearing off both limbs and then snapping her body in two with a bite.

The runes came shrieking in, filling Aelis with delight. She saw fire and battle, smelled grave earth and rot, heard the creaking of hangmen's nooses, felt the cold skin of the dead on her fingers, tasted the ashes of funeral pyres in her mouth, and all these things seemed wonderful to her. She pulled the spear from her body and held it above her head. Magic filled her in waves of ecstasy. With her free hand, she tore out her right eye.

The chamber had gone. She stood on a burning plain full of the battle dead, surrounded by numberless flies. The spear was in her hand; she wore a hauberk and helmet and carried a shield. To her side lay an eight-legged horse, dead and torn. The runes were around her no more; they *were* her, who she was – she was just an expression of their unity.

'Brother has killed brother – the prophecy is fulfilled. Now I fare to fight with the wolf,' she said and advanced upon the creature.

The wolf fixed her with burning green eyes. 'I am Fenrir, devourer of the gods.'

'And I am Odin, one-eye, master of poetry and magic, who you exist to kill. This is our destiny – let us honour it.'

Aelis charged towards the animal, her spear forward. She ran the creature through its breast, but the wolf could not be stopped and was at her throat.

For an instant Aelis and Jehan saw each other differently – they were lovers on a mountainside; he was not a wolf and she was not a god.

'I will find you,' he said.

'Do not seek me,' she said.

And then Aelis was quiet, limp and broken in the jaws of the wolf.

Ofaeti had Hugin in his arms. The sorcerer was lying on a slope of rubble, his head just out of the water. The man was mortally wounded, his bowels exposed and much of one side torn away, though he still held his sword. Around them soil poured into the pool from the ceiling like a black waterfall.

'Let me die here,' said the Raven. 'Return me to the water so I might go quickly and not face a rotting death.' He pressed the sword into Ofaeti's fingers. 'The time is now. This will kill him. It is poisoned with the nightmares of witches, so the wild woman told me.'

'I can get you out.'

'No. This is my destiny. The prophecy must be fulfilled. I will go now to be surer of meeting her again next time. Kill me.'

Ofaeti let the Raven sink into the water, then leaned on his chest. The sorcerer gave an instinctive moment of struggle but then controlled himself and lay still. When Ofaeti felt the grip on his arm fade, he picked up the Moonsword and moved away. The Raven did not rise.

Ofaeti advanced on the wolf, only his head and his shoulders clear of the water. It was massive, twice as tall as a man, its teeth and snout red, its eyes wild and green. It was panting and shaking, its head low to the water.

The creature lifted its head and stared at Ofaeti.

The big Viking, wading through the freezing water, trembled for the first time in his life. 'Are you to kill me too, fen dweller?'

Jehan, the confessor, living saint and paragon of Christ, faced down the animal inside him and spoke: 'My senses are red and I am minded to murder, though I am enough of the man I was to resist it. I am Christ's. I am for Jesus. Though I go to suffer the damnation of hell, I would spare my brothers the bane that I am. I am ready to die.'

'I am ready to do you that service. You killed many of my kin.'

The wolf turned its great head away from him again. 'Strike hard and kill me,' it said, 'for you will not get a second blow. I am a slave to my temper and will kill you if you do not kill me.'

It lowered its head into the pool. Ofaeti steadied himself, lifted the sword high in two hands and struck hard. The creature was half beheaded and died almost as the blade fell, its blood drenching the Viking.

Ofaeti had no time to ponder what had happened. He looked up at the remains of the cavern roof. It seemed very unstable. He needed to see if Aelis, whom he had vowed to protect, was by some miracle alive. He pulled himself out of the pool and onto the rock shelf. Nothing was recognisable as Aelis – it was just meat and bones – but in the grey light he saw something on the floor – a stone, the pendant the Raven had given to Aelis on the corpse shore where the vala Munin had died. He picked it up and tied it around his own neck as a keepsake. Then he dropped back into the pool.

In later years he would say it was a good job he was a tall man. Standing on the rocks and earth that had fallen from the roof, he could just reach the root he had used to swing down. He pulled himself up into the hole the wolf had dug on its way down and, bit by bit, edged his way to the surface.

It was midday and the mist was clearing. The day was still and the snow of the land was sparkling under the new sun. He looked across at Aldeigjuborg, that marvel among towns, tucked into the elbow of the river. He had seen many marvels that day though, too many, and was sick of them. When he had stood to face the *druzhina* he had been sure he would die. But he had shouted to them that he had Loki's luck, and so it had proved. The ice, which had seemed so sturdy around the ship, had suddenly given way, a black fissure opening from bank to bank, sending men tumbling into the killing cold of the river. He hadn't stopped to see how they fared.

He was freezing in his wet furs and needed to find shelter and a fire. He couldn't go to the town, he knew – some of the *druzhina* might have survived and be looking for him. What did he have? Flint and tinder, soaking wet, the Raven's sword and some rings. He needed to get a ship to get back to Francia and liberate that gold he had buried. But how? He looked east. It was March and the rivers south would be thawing. He could pick up a boat and go to Kiev. There he would be just another northerner looking to make his fortune as a fighting man.

He felt a rumble through his feet and guessed the cavern roof had finally fallen in. He thought of his friends down there. They had died good deaths, deaths that would make them legends. He was sad for them, but no one could have hoped for more, he thought. He almost envied them. He would not die such a fine death.

So east then. He'd survive in the sun but by nightfall he'd need a fire. The trouble was that the forest, where he would be safe from any patrols of vengeful *druzhina*, was a day away.

523

He needed a horse. Ofaeti heard something behind him. The wolf had dug an enormous hole, scattering snow everywhere and leaving the grass exposed. Unseen and unheard, the mule had approached and was now munching on the grass.

'Come on,' said Ofaeti. 'Team up with me and I promise you adventure. The east, no snow, grass as high as your ears.'

The mule just looked at him. Ofaeti walked over and took its halter. He mounted.

'Part of the bargain is that you have to carry a heavier burden than before, but you look after me and I'll look after you. What do you say? I have a tale to tell to honour a great warrior and I'll practise on you. Here goes. The gods in their schemes ...'

He turned the animal east, past the barrows and towards the woods.

78 Byzantium

The winter moon hung low in the still evening, its light catching the spear tips of the army, turning them to little candles shining from the dark.

They were camped in fields three days' march from Miklagard. The boy they called Snake in the Eye for the odd dark shape that seemed to surround the pupil of his left eye was excited and had even learned to speak some of the language of the Rus. The camp was enormous, six thousand men plus women and children in tow, and Snake in the Eye, who had a facility for languages, had become the conduit between his family and the rest of the grand prince's force. They were all of northern stock, which is why Snake in the Eye and his kin had been greeted warmly, but the manners and dress of the Rus were alien to the boy. They fascinated him, though, these men of Kiev – tall, blond but dressed like easterners, their wide trousers bound at the ankle, their war gear decorated with silver and gold.

Snake in the Eye huddled into the fire. He loved the smell of the camp at night – all smoke and cooking – and the cold that nipped you if you left the fire but that made the heat when you returned all the more delicious.

He looked down at the pendant he wore at his neck. He had pestered his father for it for long enough and the old man had eventually given in. It was only a pebble – strange to make a pendant of a thing like that – but it held a fascination for him. There was a design scratched on it, a wolf's head in the northern style. The way it was held by the thong was curious too – a little harness made of three knots. His father had told him it was a luck charm and that the leather would eventually rot. So he had showed Snake in the Eye the knots until he could tie them with ease. That was part of the magic, or so his father said.

The men were in good spirits because they were finally going to be paid. Prince Vladimir was a stingy ruler and his bravest and strongest warriors – those descended from the northern lords – had threatened to quit unless paid better and more promptly. His solution was to send them to Miklagard – Byzantium, the world city – to help the emperor defend against the rebel Phokas. So, despite the cold by the rocky river, the men were happy. Those who went by boat were three days from the city, the walkers a little further. But everyone would arrive together, that was the plan. They wanted to put on a display, to show the emperor he would have value for his gold.

The whole family was huddled around the fire when the stranger approached. He was tall and pale with a shock of red hair. Over his shoulder he had a big black wolfskin but was otherwise lightly dressed – only pantaloons in the eastern style and a raw-silk shirt. He dropped the wolfskin onto the ground in front of Snake in the Eye and said, 'What am I bid?'

Snake in the Eye looked at the man not knowing what to say.

'The boy has nothing to offer,' said his father. 'Let me see it and I will tell you what it's worth.'

The man bent and picked up the skin. He passed it to the boy's father – a tall fat man with hair the colour of straw.

'It's still bloody, man. No great coin can be paid for that.' Snake in the Eye's father was careful to use formal language, to show the trader he was a man of substance.

'I do not ask for coin,' said the man; 'just to rest my traveller's bones by your fire and to hear a tale or two.'

'You should look to trade the skin for a cloak,' said Snake in the Eye's father. 'You will freeze those traveller's bones if you stay dressed like that.'

'The fire of poetry warms me,' said the man. 'Let me have a story and I will need no fur to drape me.'

Snake in the Eye's father shrugged. 'Very well. I will begin by telling of a man who was called Sigi. It was said he was the son of Odin. Now there is this to be told—'

The traveller held up his hand. 'I have heard this tale many times. I require a new one. Let the boy tell me a story.'

'Do you want the story of a child?'

'The story of a child or a child's story – either will suit my appetites.'

Snake in the Eye felt embarrassed, put on the spot. 'I know no stories.'

'Did your grandfather tell you none?'

The boy thought for a little and then said, 'It was years ago, before even the time of the great king Ingvar, who took the name of his mentor Helgi, called the Prophet, and, using it, conquered mightily so his renown echoed down the ages. In those days, as now, a mute slave was the most prized of possessions to those of royal blood, for all secrets do they keep. Just such a slave was in our lands, to the north. The slave had lived a long time, longer than her masters, but she grew neither old nor grey and was greatly valued for her diligence and honesty.

'One year she travelled east with a princess to care for her and comb her hair as she went to marry a Wendish prince. The slave was well prized because, on account of a burn she bore on her face, no man would look at her so she was unlikely to fall pregnant and put herself at risk of death. The journey was smooth and the sea as glass, but on arriving at a certain market port the princess encountered a rich traveller who coveted the mute slave and wanted her for his own.

'He offered the princess a great fortune for her – bars of gold and green emeralds – but the princess scorned him and told him she would rather die than part with such a treasured possession. The woman was blessed by the gods – or cursed – to never age so was an heirloom that would be passed to her sons and beyond.

'Then the princess set off down a certain river to the land of the Wendish king and a fever set in on her ship. One by one her crewmen died until only the princess and the slave were left alive. Then the princess herself began to boil and bake and eventually died. The slave sat on the boat wondering what to do but then noticed the rich traveller sitting next to her on the deck.

'"Who are you?" she said, because in this man's presence she found her voice.

'"I am a fever," he replied, "and I have lived inside your companions. Now I ask you — as you have no master to refer to — will you have me?"

'And the slave said she would. So she lay with the man on the boat of the dead and he reminded her that he had loved her many generations before and she had borne him two sons. She said she remembered but that her sons were dead.

'The traveller said they had died because he, their father, was an enemy of the king of gods, Odin, who had wrapped them in his schemes. The dead lord drew them on to fight him here on Middle Earth, to act out the battle on the gods' final day when the wolf will kill the All Father and then be killed himself. So the boys had grown and become men and then one became a wolf who ate the other, killed the All Father in his earthly guise as a witch and scattered the magic runes. Some fell near and some fell far, but all fell to be reborn in human flesh. So the boys were born once more.

'While they were apart they were safe, but when they came together their destiny pulled them down to face Odin, in the flesh here on earth, enacting a ritual that embraced death and rejected it in the same breath. She did not know what he meant. She knew only that she loved him and was afraid of him.

'So the mother fell pregnant again and put the children far apart. She raised another boy in the ways of magic, a wolfman, to try to fool the god, to let him be ensnared in the god's death ritual and let her own son go free. But the plan went wrong because Loki, who loved her and loved her sons too, knew that death in one lifetime did not matter. He wanted to free the boys from Odin's schemes but knew that it was the work of ages. Loki was bound, tied and pinioned on a great rock as his son the wolf was tied and pinioned. And though he could send his mind forth to travel the nine worlds, there was a limit to his powers because if his scheming came to the attention of the king of gods, his torments would double. So he could not approach the boys directly but needed to influence their fate by more subtle means.

'So he pretended to be on Odin's side and used a prideful and arrogant king who thought he could defy the gods to speed the dead god to earth. In looking to prevent Odin living in the world of men, Helgi drew the hanged god ever on.

'But the boys too tried to fight the will of the king of gods, to run from him and avoid their fate. The god had been crafty and hidden his runes well when last he died. Some had gone to a child in the mountains, some to a Varangian princess beyond the Eastern Lake. But the dying god's slyest and cruellest plot had been to send his runes to the girl who the brothers loved, a girl who had formerly borne only one rune – the howling rune that stood apart from all the others and drew the wolf to itself. Now Odin's runes stood alongside the rune that would call his killer and guarantee his death.'

'Why does this god seek to be born in the world of men, only to die?' asked the boy's father.

'I will come to that,' said the boy. He poked a stick into the fire and went on: 'The mountain child had guessed her divine identity. She tricked one of the brothers and kept him close, using him to track the other runes, to free them from their human carriers by death. She made him skilled in shapeshifting magic, strong and clever, so he might find the wolf and play his part by dying under its teeth. But this part of the god, who had by instinct sought the rituals to bring out and nurture the runes within her, thought the runes had been sundered only in two, when they had been split in three. Her enchantments failed her, and the brother she had deceived saw through her and killed her, placing her head before his true love's feet.

'Through many battles, which are too mighty in number to recount on a night so cold, the brothers fought to save the girl while one fell to his old ways and became a wolf. They came at last to a barrow, a hollow place for the dead, and they went inside. There brother slew brother and the god was made flesh in the girl.

'This has happened many times and will happen many times again in years to come. There are three women – the Norns – who sit spinning out destinies beneath the world tree and even the gods must bow to them. The women require Ragnarok, they require the death of the gods. So Odin – wise in magic – gives them their deaths, ever rehearsing the gods' final battle here on earth, played out by himself and the wolf made flesh. It is a ritual, but a ritual performed by the father of gods, an offering to destiny, to keep the end at bay. But when he fails in his ritual, as one day he will fail, then Ragnarok will happen for real. The twilight of the gods will be upon us and the old gods, those ancient savages, will die.

'Old Loki works to this end. He is an enemy of the gods. And, though he sped the brothers to death at Aldeigjuborg, he knew in that death were the seeds of life. The wise and kind god Vidar had taken flesh as a fat warrior and, with Loki's help, survived to kill the wolf. It is he from whom this story springs. He will carry the message to eternity, so that the humans who are the victims of Odin's great ritual can realise their role and resist it.

'It is said the telling of this story brings good luck, for if the brothers are reborn they may hear it and perhaps, in this lifetime or many to come, eventually avoid their fates. The god Loki, the lord of lies, prince of the darkened air, enemy of the gods of Asgard, blesses this story and smiles upon those who tell it.'

The boy finished his story and the traveller laid the wolf pelt before him. 'Loki does bring you luck, boy, for the tale has won you this fine pelt.'

'I thank you for it, sir.'

530

'I hope my gift will encourage you to tell this tale in Miklagard. For I tell you this: if you do, you and your family will prosper to the tenth generation. Tell it when you can on the steps of the church of wisdom and you will have a greater reward than just a wolf pelt.'

'Are you a seer?' said the boy's father.

'To make the future is to see it, so I suppose I am a seer,' said the traveller. He stood.

'Let us at least offer you a cup of ale for your generosity,' said the boy's father.

'It is you who are generous to share such a story,' said the man, 'but now I must leave. There are others I must visit before the night is over.'

'You will be a welcome guest if you bring such gifts,' said the boy's father.

'I am always well rewarded for my exertions,' said the man with a bow.

The next morning the bright winter sun woke the boy and he wondered if he had dreamed the night before. But the wolf pelt was beside him. His father was up and making some porridge. He smiled at the boy as he came out of the tent.

'I didn't know we had a famous storyteller among us, Snake in the Eye. Where did you get that tale from?'

The boy walked to his father's side. 'Didn't you tell it to me?'

'One like it,' he said. 'It was said your great-grandfather once fought a great wolf, though few believed him when he said he had.'

'He returned with a great treasure, didn't he?'

'He did, and tales of the east.'

The boy nodded. 'Perhaps one day they will tell tales of me.'

'Perhaps they will, Snake in the Eye, for you have a poet's heart and so will be sturdy in battle. The emperor will let you write your own story.'

'I will write it with my sword on the bodies of my enemies,' said the boy.

'You are a poet and a warrior,' said his father. 'I am proud to call you my son.'

'I will be a great slayer.'

The boy touched the stone at his neck for luck. In the clear morning the ocean was visible. In a day they would sail towards the dying sun, he thought, west for Miklagard, for hope and for a future of blood.

Acknowledgements

Thanks to Adam Roberts for reading the first draft of this book and for his supportive comments. Thanks to Claire my wife for taking more than her fair share of childcare to give me the chance to finish this. Apologies to Eddo Brandes for taking the biscuit.